CRYSTAL BOYS

CRYSTAL BOYS

a novel by
PAI HSIEN-YUNG

*translated from the Chinese
by Howard Goldblatt*

Gay Sunshine Press
San Francisco

Second Printing 1995

Cover photo © 1995 by Franco/Ram Studios, San Francisco.
Cover design by Rupert Kinnard.

ISBN 0-940567-10-5 (cloth edition)
      0-940567-11-3 (paperback)

This project is funded in part by the California Arts Council, a state agency.
Any findings, opinions, or conclusions contained herein are not necessarily
those of the California Arts Council.

Gay Sunshine Press
P.O. Box 410690
San Francisco, CA 94141

Complete catalogue of available books: $1 ppd.

CONTENTS

Translator's Note

In Taiwan, the gay community is known as the *buoliquan*, literally "glass community," while the individuals are referred to as "glass boys." The term "crystal boy" has been used in this translation. Owing to the strong Japanese influence in Taiwan, many Japanese terms have become standard, such as Obasan (old woman, nanny), *san* (Mister), and Hai (yes). Terms of address, a complex, hierarchical system in Chinese, have been simplified and made consistent, so that *Laoye* (master, elder, sometimes grandfather, depending upon context) has been rendered simply as Papa; "Old" and "Little" are terms of familiarity that have none of the "demeaning" connotations that may apply in English.

While the pinyin system of romanization has been adopted for the translation, such commonly accepted spellings as Sun Yat-sen, Nanking, Chungking, Taipei, and Kaohsiung have been retained.

The translator is indebted to the author for his enthusiastic support and assistance.

—H.G.

List of Principal Characters

A-FENG (PHOENIX BOY): Star-crossed lover of Dragon Prince

A-QING (LI QING, LITTLE HAWK): The narrator, one of the "boys of New Park"

A-XIONG: Chief Yang's dull-witted protégé

BUDDY: A-qing's deceased younger brother

CHEF LU (FATTY LU): Chef at the Cornucopia Restaurant

DEATH ANGEL ZHAO: Aging, sicky denizen of New Park

FU CHONGSHAN (PAPA FU): Aging benefactor of boys in trouble, a former general whose gay son committed suicide

FU WEI: Papa Fu's deceased son

GOLDEN TREASURE: Dragon Prince's protégé, a club-footed hustler

GRANDPA GUO: Gardener at New Park, owner of the Youth Photo Studio

HEAVENSENT FU: Handicapped child taken care of by Papa Fu

HUA GUOBAO (BUTCH QUEEN): Heart-throb of aging park denizens

HUANG LIXIA: A-qing's mother

LIN MAOXIONG: Little Jade's patron, an overseas Chinese from Japan

LIN ZHENGXIONG (NAKAJIMA): Little Jade's father

LITTLE FAIRY (XIAO QINKUAI): Mr. Zhang's latest lover

LITTLE JADE (LITTLE JADE WANG): A-qing's friend and room-mate, one of the "boys of New Park"

LORD SHENG: Chairman of the Board of Eternal Youth Film Studio, a former actor and patron of the "boys of New Park"

MOON BEAUTY: Little Jade's cousin, a bar girl

MOUSEY: A-qing's friend, known for his "sticky fingers," one of the "boys of New Park"

MR. ZHANG: Owner of an export company, Wu Min's sugar daddy

OLD DICK-HEAD: An aging "sex fiend"

OLD ZHOU: One of Little Jade's sugar daddies

PEACH BLOSSOM: Raven's mistress

RAVEN: Mousey's brother, a violent brothel bouncer

SONNY: Retarded boy taken in by A-qing

WANG KUILONG (DRAGON PRINCE): Disowned son of a high-ranking official, tragic lover of Phoenix Boy (A-feng)

WANG SHANGDE: Dragon Prince's father, a ranking government official

WU MIN: A-qing's suicidal friend, one of the "boys of New Park"

YANG FENG: One-time actor, Huo Guobao's patron

YANG JINHAI (CHIEF YANG, CHUBBY YANG): Leader of the "boys of New Park"

YU HAO: English teacher who befriends A-qing

BOOK ONE

BANISHMENT

1

Three months and ten days ago, on a spectacularly sunny afternoon, Father kicked me out of the house. The sun's rays lit up the area as I ran barefoot down the little lane as though my life depended on it. When I reached the end of the lane I turned around to take a look. Father was running after me, his large, husky frame swaying as he ran. He was brandishing the pistol he'd carried as a brigade commander back on the Mainland. His white hair was standing straight up, there was rage in his bloodshot eyes. He was screaming in a trembling, hoarse voice filled with anguish and fury:

YOU SCUM! YOU FILTHY SCUM!

2

NOTICE

On the night of 3 May, at approximately eleven o'clock, Li Qing, a night-school student in the final semester of his senior year, was caught in an immoral act with the lab supervisor, Zhao Wusheng, in the Chemistry Lab. Student Li, a bad influence, has damaged the reputation of the school with his unacceptable conduct. Having received three serious demerits, he is hereby expelled as a warning to others

Gao Yitian, Principal
Yude Provincial High School
5 May 1970

BOOK TWO

IN OUR KINGDOM

I

There are no days in our kingdom, only nights. As soon as the sun comes up, our kingdom goes into hiding, for it is an unlawful nation; we have no government and no constitution, we are neither recognized nor respected by anyone, our citizenry is little more than rabble. Sometimes we have a leader—a person who's been around for a while, someone who's good-looking, impressive, popular. But we have no qualms about dethroning him any time we feel like it, because we are a fickle, unruly people. The area between our borders is pitifully small, no more than two or three hundred meters long by a hundred meters wide—that narrow strip of land surrounding the oval lotus pond in Taipei's New Park, on Guanqian Street. The fringes of our territory are planted with all sorts of tropical trees: green coral, breadfruit, palms so old their drooping fronds nearly touch the ground, and, of course, the stand of old coconut trees alongside the road that wave their heads in exasperation the day long. It's as though our kingdom were surrounded and hidden by a tightly woven fence— cut off from the outside world, isolated for the time being. But we are always keenly aware of the constant threat to our existence by the boundless world on the other side of the fence. Loud-speakers from beyond the trees frequently broadcast sensational news from the outside world. The CBC broadcaster, a woman with a standard Peking accent, announces: An American astronaut has walked on the moon! International drug traffickers from Hong Kong and Taiwan arrested! The corruption trial in the Bureau of Human Waste Management begins tomorrow!

We prick up our ears like a herd of frightened antelope in a predator-infested forest, forever on guard against the slightest sign of danger. The wind gusts, the grasses stir; every sound carries a warning. We listen for the sound of the policemen's hobnailed boots as they march past the green barrier that separates us; the minute we hear that they are invading our territory we scatter and flee as if on command: some mix with the crowds in front of the bandstand; some rush into the public toilets, where they pretend to be standing at the urinals or squatting in the toilets; some run to the main gate of the park and hide behind the stone columns on the steps of the old tomb-like museum, whose shade and protection give them a chance to catch their breath. Our anarchical kingdom can offer us no protection; we must rely on our animal instincts as we grope in the dark for a path to survival.

The history of this kingdom is shrouded in mystery; no one knows who founded it, or when. But over the years this hidden, unlawful, tiny state of ours has been the scene of a history so tragic yet so hidden to the outside world that tears are inadequate to describe it. The few white-haired oldtimers among us tell stories of the motley past, traces of pride showing through their sentimentality:

"You guys are no match for what we were back in those days."

Years ago, we were told, the lotus pond in the middle of the park was planted with red water lilies; when summer came, they blossomed and spread out over the surface of the pond until they looked like a vast array of bright red lanterns. But later on, for reasons no one knew, the municipal government sent out workers to pull up the red water lilies and build an octagonal pavilion in the middle of the pond; small gazebos with red posts and green roof tiles were built around the pond. So what had once been a land of simple, primitive beauty became, through the unwarranted addition of artificial "relics," an unnatural setting. Whenever one of the oldtimers related this page from the past to us, he'd sigh as he looked back in time:

"Those bright red water lilies were more beautiful than words!"

Then they'd recall for us the names of people we'd never heard of and remind each other of heartbreaking incidents from years long past. The heroes of these stories had long since given up their citizenship in our kingdom to forge a life in the outside world. Of some there had been no news for years; others had died in their youth, and their graves were now covered by weeds. But there were some who, after an absence of five or ten or even fifteen or twenty years, would suddenly show up on a moonless night beside the lotus pond to pay a return visit to the dark kingdom of their youth. They would stroll anxiously around the pond, as though looking for the souls they'd left behind. The oldtimers would nod their heads and lower their eyelids slightly, looks of pity on their faces. Knowingly and in voices filled with emotion, they would put the scene in front of them into perspective:

"It always happens like this. You think there's a great big world out there, don't you? Well, someday, someday for sure, you'll all come flying back to the nest, like good little boys."

The thermometer climbed to a hundred and four in Taipei the day before. The newspapers said it was the hottest, driest summer in over twenty years. Not a drop of rain in the month of August. The trees in the park were so overheated they steamed. A blanket of steamy hot air hung over the stands of palm, green coral, and coconut trees. The concrete steps and handrails around the lotus pond were baked by the sun during the day, then gave off steam as they cooled down at night. The heat rising from the steps was so intense that people standing on them grew lightheaded and numb. The sky was black, the cloud cover seemed almost low enough to touch. Off in the corner of the sky a full moon hung above the coconut trees, the deep red color of a chunk of fetid, steamy raw meat. Not a breath of wind anywhere. The trees stood deathly still in the darkness. The air was thick, hot, clammy, like a gelatinous mass.

Since it was a weekend evening, we were all there, standing shoulder to shoulder on the steps of the lotus pond and leaning against the handrails. A sea of heads nodding and weaving in the darkness, making the pond appear to be in motion. In the ghostly darkness we could see a bobbing bald head over here, a graying head over there, and all around, the wide, desire-filled stares of countless pairs of eyes, like cats glaring in the darkness. Low, hushed, secretive voices began private, intimate conversations. Once in a while the stillness was broken by loud laughter cascading over the area, then dying out. Everyone knew that the laughter belonged to our leader, Chief Yang. He was wearing a crimson skin-tight pullover that accentuated his huge paunch, and a pair of shiny black orlon slacks that held his butt tightly in place, making him look like he was hiding a pair of inflated balloons, one in front and one in back. Chief Yang made his way through the crowd, busily greeting everyone. He carried a two-foot-long paper fan in his hand, and whenever he opened it, there were the words "Light Breezes Come Slowly" on one side and "Good Dreams Are Gentle" on the other in large ornate calligraphy. He walked around puffing and blowing and laughing loudly, and every time he moved, the fleshy bulges, front and rear, shook and undulated; there was no doubt who was in charge here. Chief Yang considered himself to be the absolute leader in the park. According to him, he had, at one time or another, counted every blade of grass in this nest of ours, and the number of his disciples and their disciples in turn was, conservatively speaking, half a hundred. He frequently waved his fan like a conductor's baton as he rushed up to us, shouting obscenities:

"You cunt-brats! I made my mark in this park when the lot of you were still squirming around in your mothers' wombs. Who the hell are you to show off in front of me? You bunch of shit-eating fairies!"

Little Jade once came over wearing a scarlet shirt with a turn-down collar and sapphire-blue bellbottoms. He pranced back and forth on the steps in a pair of three-quarter-length boots, handsome and fetching. For some reason this made the chief mad. He grabbed Little Jade by the wrist and twisted his arm behind his back.

"Who the hell are you swishing those fragile little bones of yours for?" he mocked him. "Trying to show off your charms for me? When I was your age I could play the role of Yang Zongbao! Let's see how much those bones of yours weigh."

He wrapped his arm around Little Jade's neck and began to squeeze, hard, until Little Jade shrieked in pain, shouting "uncle" at least twenty times.

This leader of ours, Chief Yang Jinhai, was the most experienced and valued denizen of the park. Not only was he one of the kingdom's most venerable citizens, but he knew every one of his fellow park dwellers, including what made them tick. A man of many tricks and considerable abilities, he had several clever and powerful backers, which was why his position in the park was secure. In the past, he'd worked as manager or maître d'hôtel at a number of taverns and restaurants out in the glitzy section of Sun Yat-sen North Road, where he'd dealt with all sorts of people, seen and heard more than most men, and learned the ropes. He still had contacts in plenty of those taverns and restaurants. Hallo, Hallo! He had quite a repertoire of pidgin English. Dō desu ka? A little Japanese as well. Everyone called him the wizard, since nothing seemed beyond his abilities.

People said he came from a respectable family. His father, a one-time local official in the Shandong city of Yantai, had fled to Taiwan with the Nationalists in 1949 and opened a small tavern and late-night cafe on Taoyuan Street in Taipei. It was called Taoyuan Spring. With Chief Yang running the place for his father, it had been the favorite nighttime gathering place for the denizens of the park. Business was great. But eventually, the ranks of the regulars were swelled by some hooligans who hung out in the park. Trouble soon broke out, the police were called in, and business slackened off as people stayed away to avoid trouble. It was only a matter of time before the "grand closing." Other taverns opened to fill the void, but it was never the same. Denizens of the park still talk of Chief Yang's Taoyuan Spring with nostalgia. On cold winter nights, they recall, everyone squeezed into Taoyuan Spring for a carafe of heated rice wine and some snacks to go with it. As the wine began to take effect, they'd set up a rhythm by tapping their glasses and plates and begin singing popular songs as they swayed together. A time of good feelings. Chief Yang always spoke of Taoyuan Spring with unconcealed pride:

"That Taoyuan Spring of mine was a real haven from the outside world! All the birds came there to take shelter from the wind and rain. They knew it was a place where they could be comfortable *and* safe. And me, I was the Buddha of a Thousand Arms, always ready to take a tormented soul under my wing!"

But one day Chief Yang and his father had a falling out and he left. It had happened when his father discovered that he'd withdrawn a large sum of money from his father's bank account, which, according to those in the know, he'd spent on his favorite protégé, the primitive A-xiong. A-xiong, an aborigine, was also an epileptic. On this particular occasion he'd had a seizure in the middle of the street and was run over by a car, badly mangling his leg. Chief Yang had footed the enormous hospital bills during his six months in a convalescent hospital. A-xiong was well over six feet tall, dark-skinned, and had muscles like tempered steel. His huge hands were as powerful as the paws of a bear. Sometimes he'd playfully wrap his powerful arms around you in a bear hug that would nearly choke the wind out of you and make you ache like you'd been drawn through a ringer. His favorite activity was eating, and our favorite activity around him was waving a popsicle under his nose and teasing him: "It's yours if you call me Older Brother!" He'd reach out for it, a foolish grin on his face as he chewed his tongue and pled: "Older Brudder!" This, even though he was at least ten years older than the rest of us, thirty if he was a day. We never saw him except in the company of Chief Yang, following along with an armload of food—dried plums, dried apricots, peanut brittle—which he stuffed into his mouth as he walked. He'd hold up whatever he had in his hand when he saw us and ask, "Want some?" Everyone always got a share. It was sometimes more than Chief Yang could take.

"Aren't you the big-hearted one!" he'd snap as he rapped him on the head with his fan. "When it's all gone I'll buy a dog's dick for you to gnaw on!"

"Well boys, what are you doing standing around here like a bunch of idiots?" Chief Yang walked up to us, pointing his fan at each of us in turn and shouting. "If you don't get a move on, all the fish out there are going to be caught by those hustlers from Three Rivers Street, and you'll wind up with soggy leftovers. Is that what you want?"

He flipped open his fan — "Light Breezes Come Slowly," "Good Dreams Are Gentle" — and began fanning himself hard. A-xiong stood behind him like a colossus, his big-top dancing bear. He was wearing a tight-fitting purple nylon jersey, obviously brand new, that showed off his muscular chest.

"Hey, A-xiong, that's quite a shirt you've got. A present from Old Dick-Head?"

Little Jade reached out and thumped A-xiong on the shoulder. This got a laugh out of us. Whenever we felt like getting our leader's goat we started in on A-xiong. Old Dick-Head was a sixty-year-old sex fiend whose neck was covered with scaly skin. None of the denizens of the park would have anything to do with him, and he was reduced to lurking in the shadows and grabbing us when we weren't looking. He'd tricked A-xiong into going with him once with a bag of peanuts, and when the chief found out about it he was fit to be tied. He beat Old Dick-Head half to death.

"You fucking bitch, you're the one who's wearing clothes given to him by Old Dick-Head!" Chief Yang hit Little Jade on the forehead with his fan. "A-xiong, you tell him who bought that shirt for you."

"Dada bought it for me," A-xiong answered with a foolish grin as he chewed on his tongue.

"You idiot, where was it bought?"

"The Today Department Store."

"How much?"

"A hundred . . ."

"God damn it, it was one-eighty!" He thumped A-xiong on his broad back and laughed loudly. "Aha! So that's where the little sneak thief's been hiding!"

Chief Yang spotted Mousey cowering behind Little Jade. He grabbed him by the ear and dragged him out, then held his wrists.

"Bring a knife over here," he shouted, "and hurry! I'm going to cut off these sticky-fingered hands! They're no good to anybody. All they know how to do is steal. Why don't you spend your time having fun instead of looking for trouble? I introduce you to people for a roll in the hay, not as a source for your ill-gotten gains! Thanks to you I've completely lost face around here. Instead of waiting for someone to report you, I'm going to drag you and your sticky fingers over to the police station myself. Then you'll get what's coming to you. Tomorrow I'm going to tell Raven to string you up and give you a good beating!"

"Chief ..." Mousey struggled to get free as he begged for mercy, a painfully distorted look on his pointy face.

"So," Chief Yang sneered, "you know what it means to be scared, after all. If it hadn't been for me that last time, Raven would've beaten you to a pulp. You haven't forgotten what that cat-o'-nine-tails tasted like, have you?"

Chief Yang gave Mousey a couple of slaps that made him see stars, then smacked him on the head with his fan before heading off, with A-xiong on his heels. His blubber swayed and shifted rhythmically as he walked.

"What'd you steal this time?" Little Jade asked him.

"All I took was his fountain pen. What's the big fucking deal?" Mousey screwed up his mouth and spat on the ground. "The bastard promised me three hundred but only gave me two."

"Oh? When did your price go up? Three hundred?" Little Jade asked in amazement.

Mousey fidgeted for a moment, an embarrassed smile on his face, before sputtering:

"He wanted to do you-know-what."

He stuck out his thin arm and rolled up his sleeve. We all gathered around him and, by the light of a nearby streetlamp, noticed the three welts on his upper arm.

"What the hell are those?" Little Jade reached out to touch them.

"Ouch!" Mousey jumped like he was struck by lightning. "Don't touch 'em, they hurt, they're blisters ... that bastard burned me with his cigarette."

"You worthless piece of shit, so you're up to that again," Little Jade pointed threateningly at Mousey. "One of these days you're gonna run into someone who'll chop you up into bite-size snacks!"

Mousey thought that was pretty funny; his stained teeth showed as he grinned.

"Little Jade," he said in a pleading voice, "go talk to the chief for me, tell him not to say anything to Raven, okay?"

"How will you thank me if I do? Take me to see *The Hanging Tree* at the New South Seas Theater?" He tugged Mousey's ear. "The next time you steal something, my precious little thief, don't forget to cut me in."

"No problem," Mousey said with a broad grin. He looked down at the blisters on his arm. He found it all very absorbing.

Little Jade returned in a few minutes.

"The chief says he's gonna spare your scrawny neck this time," he reported to Mousey, "but if you do it again you're really in for it. You should have seen yourself when Raven's name was mentioned—I thought you'd shit your pants. Why are you so afraid of him? Is that thing of his so big it drives the soul right out of you? Or what?"

We all laughed, Mousey included. Raven was Mousey's older brother. Mousey said he'd been left an orphan when he was very young and had grown up in Raven's home. Raven, a mean-tempered bouncer in a local brothel, was always beating up on Mousey like he was his slave. We asked him why he didn't run away. But he just shrugged his shoulders and couldn't give us any reason other than he'd gotten used to being around Raven. He once stole a watch from one of his customers, and the police came over to Raven's house. After they left, Raven strung Mousey up and beat him with a three-foot-long cat-o'-nine-tails so badly the poor guy couldn't stand up straight for days. When we bumped into him, all hunched up like that, he'd look up at us out of the corner of his eye and give us a strange smile.

"A-qing."

Little Jade whispered in my ear as he tugged on my sleeve. I followed him down the steps and into the grove of camphorwood trees.

"I need a favor," he begged me excitedly as he tugged on my shirt.

"Now what? You want me to lie for you again? What's in it for me?"

"I'll bring you a couple of mangos tomorrow," he said with a smile. "When Old Zhou comes looking for me in a little while, you tell him my mother's sick and I had to go back to Sanchong City to take care of her."

"No deal," I shook my head. "That's the same excuse you used last time. You think he'll believe it again?"

"Who cares if he believes it or not?" he sneered. "I'm not his private property, but I don't feel like arguing with him."

Old Zhou was Little Jade's sugar daddy. The two of them had been together off and on for a year or more. He ran a dye shop out in the suburbs, and was doing pretty well. He was always buying things for Little Jade. Just the week before he'd given him a new Seiko wristwatch, which Little Jade showed off everywhere he went. "This was a present from Old Zhou!" When I asked him if he and Old Zhou were going steady, he sighed and said, "Sure, he treats me pretty good, but he doesn't give me any breathing room. I can't take it any more!" The old guy was putting pressure on him to move in with him out in the suburbs, but Little Jade didn't want to. He compromised by promising to spend three or four nights a week with him. Little Jade was too wild to be tamed by Old Zhou, and this was the cause of frequent arguments.

"Got another date tonight?" I asked him.

"I'll tell you, but you have to keep it a secret. It's an overseas Chinese."

"So you're getting adopted by an overseas Chinese, are you!"

"The chief says he's a Taiwanese who lives in Tokyo. I'm told he's really something. I'm off to meet him at the Inn of the Sixth Happiness right now."

With that he sprang out of the grove of trees, turning back to remind me:

"That business with Old Zhou, please don't forget!"

The grove was swarming with mosquitoes, and in those few minutes I'd picked up several bites on my arms. As I walked out scratching the bites, a hand reached out and grabbed my shoulder.

"Who's that?"

Frightened, I spun around to see who it was. I could make out the face of Wu Min, looking like a sheet of white paper floating in the surrounding darkness.

"So it's you! When did you get out of the hospital?"

"This afternoon." His voice was weak and shaky.

"A good friend you are, not even telling us you're out."

"That's why I'm here. Mousey told me you and Little Jade walked over here together."

I looked over toward the lotus pond. Wu Min held my arm and pleaded with me:

"Let's not go over there, okay? Too many people."

I turned and headed toward the museum next to the main gate. Wu Min's face was illuminated by the fluorescent streetlamps on either side of the path, giving it a waxen sheen, pale and bloodless. His once glossy cheeks were drawn, his once sparkling eyes sunken and lifeless. As he reached up to mop his brow with his arm, I noticed the white bandage around his wrist. It reminded me of a colorless handcuff. I thought back to that day when he was lying in the emergency room at Taiwan University Hospital with a two-inch-long gash on his left wrist, so deep I could see his tendons amid the blood that seemed to nearly cover him. Since he was broke, he couldn't pay for a transfusion, and he was lucky that Little Jade, Mousey, and I arrived in time to donate five hundred cc's of blood each. That saved his life. He looked up at us with his lackluster eyes and blinked lethargically, his mouth hanging slack as he tried unsuccessfully to say something. Little Jade was fit to be tied.

"God damn you!" he railed. "You piece of shit, why didn't you jump out a window? That way you could've done a neat job, and I wouldn't have to be giving you my blood!"

The day before he slashed his wrist, Wu Min came to the park. When he saw us he said:

"A-qing, I don't want to go on living."

He was smiling when he said it, and we thought he was kidding. So Little Jade picked up on the joke:

"Okay, you go ahead and off yourself. You can count on me to burn some spirit money for you when you're gone."

No one would have dreamed that he'd actually slash his wrist with a razor blade.

"A-qing..." Wu Min called out hoarsely. We were sitting up against the stone columns on the steps of the museum.

"Hm?" I looked over at him.

"Can you lend me some money?" He didn't raise his head. "I haven't had any dinner."

I fished around in my pocket and came up with three crumpled, sweat-stained ten-yuan bills. I handed them to him.

"That's all I've got."

"I'll pay you back in a couple of days," he mumbled.

"Forget it," I said with a wave of my hand. "If you're broke why don't you ask the chief for some?"

"I'm ashamed to ask him for any more," he said with a hollow laugh. "He footed the entire hospital bill — more than ten thousand."

"Wow, that was generous of him," I exclaimed. "You're obviously his fair-haired boy!"

"I promised I'd find a way to pay him back."

"You couldn't pay back that much if you lived to be a hundred. If you're smart you'll go out and find yourself a sugar daddy. Let him pay back the money." I laughed.

Wu Min still hadn't looked up. He kept tracing words on the ground with his bandaged hand.

"A-qing," he said softly, "that day when you went over to Mr. Zhang's house, did you see him or not? What did he say to you?"

On the afternoon Wu Min slashed his wrists I went over to Guangwu Villa on Dunhua South Road to see Mr. Zhang. I'd been there once before, to see Wu Min when he was living there. He was on his hands and knees mopping the floor with a rag. Shirtless, barefoot, and covered with sweat, he was so happy to see me he went over to the refrigerator and got me a bottle of apple cider. Then he got back down on his hands and knees to continue mopping the floor as we chatted. Mr. Zhang lived in a classy apartment furnished with high-backed black leather sofas and chrome and glass tables. The front wall of the living room was nearly filled with a wet bar stocked with every imaginable type of Western liquor.

"This place is so nice I wouldn't mind living here for the rest of my life," Wu Min said as he looked up at me with a smile on his red, sweaty face.

When I went to see Mr. Zhang that day, he was sitting on one of the living-room sofas with his feet up, watching TV. The air conditioning made the room nice and cool. He was dressed only in a pair of steel-gray silk pajama bottoms and blue satin slippers. The door was opened by Xiao Qinkuai, whom we all called Little Fairy. Thick, bushy brows, big eyes, husky as an ox, but with a tongue so sweet it'd melt your heart. Chief Yang had said to him once:

"Little Fairy, since you're such a sweet talker, how about tricking that mynah bird up in the tree to come down."

"Mr. Zhang," I said as I walked into the living room, "Wu Min tried to kill himself."

That came as a shock.

"He isn't dead, is he?"

"He's at Taiwan University Hospital. He slashed his wrist. They're giving him a transfusion right now."

"Oh —"

A sigh of relief. He turned back to continue watching TV. The color screen showed Qingshan and Wanqu from the show "Night of the Stars" cuddling up and singing:

Pineapple, sweet as honey
Pineapple, just like you

Little Fairy slipped into the room and sat down next to Mr. Zhang, tucked his leg under him and rubbed his foot with his hand. They were quickly caught up in Qingshan and Wanqu's song, since they didn't blink as they stared at the screen. Qingshan had his arm around Wanqu's waist as they swayed back and forth on the stage. Their song was nearly over before the news seemed to register with Mr. Zhang. He turned to me.

"So Wu Min tried to kill himself. What do you want from me?"

Mr. Zhang, a man of about forty, owned an export company that specialized in plastic toys. He was a handsome man, with a nice straight nose and neatly combed hair with a touch of gray at the temples. But there was a deep, dark crooked scar to the right of his mouth, which seemed to give him a permanent sneer. As Wu Min was being wheeled into the emergency ward for a transfusion he begged me weakly, Please ask Mr. Zhang to come see me here in the hospital. But as I looked at the cruel smile on Mr. Zhang's face, my tongue wouldn't do my bidding, and I couldn't say a word.

"Well, it's a good thing you came. Wu Min left a bundle of clothing here, so you can take it to him." He turned to Little Fairy and motioned with his hand. "Go get that bundle of clothing."

Little Fairy jumped down off the sofa and rushed out of the room to fetch the bundle of clothing. It was filled with nothing but some yellowed, wrinkled underwear and a couple of tattered sport shirts. As Little Fairy thrust the bundle into my hands, his bulging eyes rolled smugly. I returned to Taiwan University Hospital, but instead of giving Wu Min the bundle of clothing, I told him that Mr. Zhang wasn't home.

"A-qing, you know I stayed home and behaved myself during

that year I lived with Mr. Zhang. I didn't go out on the prowl even once. I did everything he wanted, even though he had a terrible temper. He had a thing about cleanliness, so I got down on my hands and knees and mopped the floors every single day. And he was always yelling at me at first because I didn't know how to cook. But I taught myself with cookbooks, and one time he said, 'Wu Min, you make bean-sauce carp as good as Emei Restaurant.' You don't know how happy that made me, because I figured he really liked me. So you can imagine how shocked I was later that day when he blew up for no reason at all and ordered me to move out that very day. Up till then I wouldn't have believed he could be so cold-hearted. A-qing, I have to know if you saw him that day or not. Was he still mad at . . . ?"

Wu Min's words came out of the darkness, so shaky it scared me. The image of the deep, cruel scar on Mr. Zhang's sneering face flashed through my mind. I broke off Wu Min's whining:

"I saw him. He and Little Fairy were sitting together on the sofa watching TV, they were watching 'Night of the Stars'."

"Oh —" Wu Min gasped. After a moment he stood up.

"Gotta go. I'm gonna get something to eat."

He walked down the steps, his ghostly white face floating in the darkness.

It was already midnight when I got back to the lotus pond. The microphones had fallen silent and the park was nearly deserted. But our kingdom came to life in the darkness. The steps around the lotus pond were filled with shadows of moving figures. The young hustlers from Three Rivers Street were raising a racket with their wooden clogs. Lord Sheng, the revered oldtimer, was shuffling his way over from the gazebo. He hobbled up to Chief Yang and asked wearily, "Any fresh young kids?" Lord Sheng was already on his last legs and had a bad case of spinal arthritis. He liked getting fixed up with young boys to go out for a late snack or a glass of warm wine, and that's about all. He was an insomniac. The only way he could drive the loneliness out of his heart and get some rest was to feast his eyes on a youthful face; it worked like a sleeping potion. Lord Sheng was Chairman of the Board of the Eternal Youth Film Studio, which had produced several ultra-artsy love films that earned him lots of money. He was said to have been a romantic lead back in Shanghai who had acted with many famous female stars, but he himself commented emotionally, "What good are fame and fortune, anyway? Boys, youth is the greatest treasure in the world!" The young fellow tagging along behind Mousey and calling him "Rat Spirit" was Chef Lu, a famous chef at the Cornucopia restaurant. Weighing over two hundred pounds, when he laughed he looked like the Happy Buddha. Mousey was his favorite: "What I like about Mousey are those ribs of his. It's like feasting on duck wings. You can't beat 'em!"

Lots of people were standing off in the grove of trees, hiding like bashful schoolkids, including some college students from good families. The boys who hadn't even had time to change out of their uniforms were reserve soldiers from the outer islands on leave in Taipei; there were also some young hooligans with criminal records who had come to the park from the working-class suburb of Sanchong City to have some fun; then there were a few clerks from import businesses, tailor shops, and shoe stores in the commercial Westgate district. There was also a famous cardiologist, a judge advocate in the military, and a balding man in a beret who had once been one of the most popular celebrities in Taiwanese films; among them, too, was a once-famous artist who had put his heart and soul into the pursuit of beauty, but was now a wrinkled old man who was always saying things the rest of us could barely understand, like, "The human body is mortal. Art and art alone is immortal!" And so he painted portraits of all the pretty young men in our kingdom. Then, of course, there was Grandpa Guo the gardener, who'd been around the longest and had more experience than anyone. There he was, a white-haired old man, standing alone under the green coral tree gazing over at the flock of young park birds, a look of pity in his dim eyes as he watched us flit back and forth in the darkness, blindly, desperately. He owned a studio on Changchun Road called Youth Photo Studio, and had put together a thick album of our photos, which he named "Birds of Youth." My photo was number 87; the caption read "Little Hawk."

In this kingdom of ours there are no distinctions of social rank, eminence, age, or strength. What we share in common are bodies filled with aching, irrepressible desire and hearts filled with insane loneliness. In the dead of night these tortured hearts burst out of their loneliness like wild animals that have broken out of their cages, baring their fangs and uncoiling their claws as they begin a frenzied hunt for prey. In the dim light of the reddish moon above we look like a pack of sleepwalkers, frantically stepping on each other's shadows as we skirt the lotus pond, never stopping,

30

round and round, in crazed pursuit of that nightmare of love and lust.

In the darkness I climbed up onto the steps of the lotus pond and joined their ranks, as though in a hypnotic trance, having no control over my body, and began walking around the lotus pond, one endless revolution after another. In the darkness I saw pair after pair of eyes filled with the green light of yearning, desire, misgivings, terror, like a swarm of fireflies darting crazily back after one another. Dark though the night was, I was acutely aware that two of those eyes sparkled every time they met mine and seemed to burn holes in my face. I began to grow uneasy, my heart began to palpitate, but I couldn't evade those bright, shining eyes, staring so fixedly, so eagerly, as though they were exploring me with a sense of desperation, or imploring me for something. He was tall, slim, unfamiliar, someone I'd never seen in the park before.

"Go ahead, what harm can it do," Chief Yang whispered to me as he walked up from behind. "I've been watching him, he's had his eye on you all night."

The stranger had by then walked down the steps and was standing beneath the big coconut tree at the end of the gravel path, staring at me. He was just standing there, ramrod straight, without moving, but there was no mistaking that he was waiting for me to come to him. We normally stayed clear of strangers, to keep from linking up with the wrong person; the dangers were too great. We'd fallen into the habit of waiting until the chief had looked them over and given the okay before taking the chance. In sizing people up, Chief Yang hadn't been wrong yet. I walked down the steps and headed over to the gravel path that ran through the park all the way out to the main gate. As I passed in front of the stranger I pretended I didn't see him and kept walking toward the main gate. I heard his footsteps on the gravel as he fell in behind me. I passed through the gate and kept walking straight ahead toward Taiwan University Hospital, not stopping until I was under a streetlamp at the entrance to a deserted lane. I waited.

When the stranger caught up to me and was standing next to me under the streetlamp, I saw that he was nearly a head taller than I, certainly well over six feet tall. His sharp bones seemed to stick out all over his body. The dark blue shirt he was wearing looked like a tent thrown over an oversized skeleton. He had a long face, with high protruding cheekbones, sunken cheeks, a high, straight nose, long eyebrows that arched upwards at the ends, and uncombed thick black hair. He seemed to be in his thirties, an age when his face should be full, his features neat; but he was so gaunt he looked like a mass of withered muscles and flesh. His eyes alone, so singular in their deep recesses, looked like wildfires in a primeval forest, dancing brightly in the darkness, as though in urgent pursuit of something. When he looked down at me, a smile on his face, I broke the ice:

"Let's go to Yuanhuan," I suggested.

3

The window of room 25 on the second floor of the Yaotai Hotel faced the night market in Yuanhuan, from which sounds of talking and laughing came rolling over like waves; once in a while we heard the urgent sound of a horn, distant, drawn out, cracking, the signal that someone was selling "sea-dogs," an aphrodisiac. Flashing neon signs across the way sent their red and green lights into the room, which was incredibly hot and stuffy that night. The rickety old fan at the head of the bed rotated back and forth forcing gusts of hot air our way.

We lay next to each other in bed, naked. Even in the darkness I could sense his bright eyes, like two fireballs passing over my body in an urgent exploration, seeking something. He was lying on his back beside me, and as he stirred, his elbow bumped against me. The sharp pain made me cry out softly.

"Did I hurt you, little one?"

"It's okay," I replied vaguely.

"You see, I forget." He stuck his long arms up in the air, the fingers flared out, his hands looking like a couple of rakes. "There's nothing left of these spindly arms of mine but bones. It even hurts when I bump myself. But I wasn't always like this. I used to have nice broad shoulders like yours. Do you believe that, little one?"

"Yes."

"How old are you?"

"Eighteen."

"Yeah, when I was your age I was just like you. But in a single summer, three short months, my body wasted away until I was nothing but skin and bones. One summer, one single summer . . ."

His voice emerged from the darkness, distant-sounding, uncertain, as though rising out of a deep, distant cave.

Often, in the shadowy depths of late night, in some out-of-the-way hotel or inn, as we lie naked on a creaky old bed, two strangers afraid to reveal our names to the man lying next to us, we are suddenly so overcome by confessional impulses that we blurt out our most hidden feelings, things we'd otherwise never tell anyone. Unable to see each other's face, and knowing nothing of the other person's past, we abandon all concern over shame and bare our hearts to one another. The first person I ever took to the Yaotai Hotel was a high-school gym teacher, a northerner whose stomach muscles were as hard as rocks. He'd drunk a lot of strong wine that evening, and rambled on drunkenly all night long. He told me what a good woman his Peking-born wife was, so considerate, yet he still couldn't find it in his heart to love her. He was secretly in love with the captain of the school basketball team, a boy who had become his protégé in the three years of his tutelage, until they were as close as father and son. But he found it impossible to tell the boy how he felt about him, and the secret love burning in his heart nearly drove him out of his mind. He handed him his sneakers, got his jersey for him, even wiped the sweat off his body with a towel, but he never found the courage to approach him. Finally, just before graduation, the last intramural game was played, a heated contest that had everyone on the edge of his chair. During the game the captain argued about something with the teacher, who exploded in a rage and slapped the boy so hard he crashed to the floor. During all those years the one thing he had yearned for was a chance to touch the boy, to put his arms around him and hold him close. But he'd lost control instead and slapped the boy so hard he left welts on his face. They were like deep marks branded on his own heart that still ached from time to time. On and on he rambled, a husky gym teacher, until he began to sob and finally broke down and cried so hard it scared me. It was raining that night, and the window was streaked with meandering rivulets of water. The flashing neon signs across the way were little more than an intermittent blur of reds and greens.

"My father was buried five days ago."

"Hm?" I didn't catch what he said.

"My father was buried in the Eternal Repose Cemetery at Six

33

Plows five days ago." He was smoking, and the glow of his cigarette burned a hole in the darkness. "They say it was an impressive funeral. I saw the names of lots of high-ranking government officials in the guest book. But I've never been to the Eternal Repose Cemetery, I don't even know where it is. Do you know, little one?"

"At the end of Xinyi Road. The Eternal Repose Cemetery is on the top of Six Plows Mountain."

"You mean past Xinyi Road, Section Four. The streets in Taipei have changed so much I can't find my way around the city. It's been ten years . . ." He took a drag on his cigarette and heaved a long sigh. "I just returned from the States the night before last. I went over to see the house on Nanking Road where we'd lived, and it was completely surrounded by high-rises. I didn't even recognize the house itself. Back then there was nothing behind our house but rice paddies. Can you imagine what was in those paddies?"

"Rice."

"Naturally," he remarked with a laugh, waving one of his spindly arms in the air. "What I meant was egrets, little one. There used to be egrets in paddies all over Taipei. They'd shoot up into the sky like a white cloud when you walked by. In all my years in the States I never saw a single egret. Plenty of hawks, seagulls, wild ducks, but no egrets. There's a Taiwanese children's song called 'Egrets,' little one. Do you know it?"

"I've heard it, but I don't know it."

Egret
Honey bucket cart
Dump it at Xizai Pit

He began singing the ballad softly in Taiwanese. It is an innocent, sad little song, and as he sang his voice softened like a child's.

"You still remember it?" I laughed.

"I'd forgotten all about it, but as soon as I returned to Taipei it somehow all came back to me. A friend of mine taught it to me, a Taiwanese kid, years ago. The two of us used to run out into the rice paddies on Songjiang Road behind my house, where there were hundreds of egrets. From a distance they made the rice paddies look like they were covered with white lilies. While we were out there he sang that ballad over and over, and I just sort of picked it up. Now I'm back in Taipei, but the egrets are gone."

"Did you go to the States to study?"

"No, to save my skin." A heaviness crept back into his voice. "Ten years ago my father bought me a British passport in Hong Kong and took me down south to Kaohsiung, where he put me on a Japanese packet ship. I remember it was called the *White Crane*. I spent a month on that ship, eating almost nothing but pickled vegetables."

He took a couple of deep drags on his cigarette and grew silent for a while. Then he said very solemnly:

"Just before the ship got underway, my father said to me, 'I forbid you to come back as long as I'm alive!' So I didn't come back to Taiwan until my father passed away. For ten long years I stayed in the States, waiting . . ."

"I'll tell you, little one, the name on my passport is a strange one—Stephen Ng. In Cantonese the name Wu is pronounced 'ung,' so in the States everyone calls me 'ung, ung, ung,' with a nasal twang."

He barely got it out before he started laughing, and it sounded so funny to me that I quickly joined him.

"In fact, my name is Wang." He let out his breath loudly. "Wang Kuilong is my real name. The Kui in my name is a tough one to write, and I always got it wrong when I was a kid. I was told that in ancient times 'kuilong' was a sort of evil dragon that caused natural calamities wherever it went. I never did find out why my father gave me such an inauspicious name. What's your name, little one?"

I hesitated. We never told strangers our real names.

"Don't worry, little one," he said as he patted my shoulder. "You and I, we're in the same boat. Back in the States I never told anyone my real name, either, but now it doesn't matter anymore. I'm back in Taipei, and once again I'm Wang Kuilong. Stephen Ng, what a joke that was. Well, Stephen Ng is dead, and Wang Kuilong is alive once more!"

"My name's Li," I finally revealed. "They all call me A-qing."

"Then, that's what I'll call you, too."

"Did you live in San Francisco?" I asked. An assistant chef at Taipei's Five Blessings Restaurant, who'd once hung around the park, was hired by a Chinatown restaurant in San Francisco as their head chef. After he got there he wrote to tell us that the streets of San Francisco were filled with people like us.

"San Francisco? No, I didn't live there," he said before taking another deep drag on his cigarette. He sat up and tossed the cigarette into the spittoon by the headboard. Then he lay back down with his hands behind his head.

"New York, that's where I settled down." The sprightly quality had reappeared in his voice and was carried throughout the room by the electric fan. "New York is a city full of skyscrapers, and you can hide in their shadows so completely you almost never see the light of day. No one can find you if you don't want to be found. I hid in the shadows of those skyscrapers for ten years. Sometimes I hid in New York's darkest place — Central Park. Ever hear of it?"

"There are parks in New York, too?"

"You're kidding! Central Park is a hundred times bigger than our New Park, and hundreds of times darker. You can be in the middle of the city and feel like you're in the blackest depths of a bottomless lake. There are dark stands of trees all over the park, everywhere you look, and when you walk into them it's like you're in a maze. You wonder if you'll ever find your way out. When night falls, the people of New York won't step foot inside the park. There've been lots of murders there, and they even found a decapitated man there once, strung up in a tree. Another person, a young one, was found with more than thirty stab wounds . . ."

He sighed.

"American streets are filled with crazies."

"Are there people like us in Central Park?" I asked softly.

"Um, lots of them. On my third night in the city I went into Central Park and was dragged into the wooded area behind the bandstand by seven or eight people, I'm not sure just how many. There were a few blacks among them. Their hair was like steel wool. I could hear their heavy breathing in the dark, like a pack of hungry wolves fighting over a piece of meat. Their white teeth seemed to glow in the dark. That's how it stayed until the first light of dawn, as the sun's rays began to filter through the branches, when they grew suddenly alert and began slinking away, one after another, until the only one left was an ugly old black man kneeling on the ground and stretching out a trembling arm to grab my pantleg. As I walked out of the wooded area I was nearly blinded by the bright morning sun . . ." He stretched his bony, rake-like arm up above him and made a couple of grasping motions before continuing: "In one night I felt like they'd gnawed all the flesh off my arms, which were covered with ugly bruises. That summer I went as crazy as those American boys, crazy as hell. I could almost see the flesh fall away from my body, like flakes of dandruff. I had no feelings. I was like a leper. One day I was sitting in the middle of the street scraping my calf with a razor blade and bleeding like a stuck pig . . ."

"Huh? Why?" He was so matter of fact about it he might as well have been talking about scraping the skin of a dead chicken.

"I wanted to see if I had any feelings left."

"Didn't it hurt?"

"Not even a little. But I could smell the blood."

"Yow!" I shuddered. The gusts of wind coming from the electric fan seemed to prickle my skin.

"Some women saw what I was doing and screamed in terror. That brought the police over, who took me straight to a mental hospital. Have you even been in one of those, A-qing?"

"No."

"Interesting places."

"How's that?"

"Lots of good-looking male nurses."

"Really?" I laughed. My curiosity was aroused.

"The one they took me to was on the bank of the Hudson River, and I spent all my time there looking out the window and counting the sailboats out on the river. I remember there was a nurse named David, who was incredibly good looking, with shiny golden hair and eyes as green as the ocean. He must have been at least six-five — all the nurses in mental hospitals are tall, husky fellows. He smiled and tried to get me to take two tranquilizers, but I grabbed his wrists and brought his hands down on my chest. 'My heart!' I screamed. 'My heart, I can't find my heart!' He thought I was turning violent, so he twisted my hands backwards and pushed me down on the floor. You know why? Because I'd said it in Chinese, and he didn't understand me."

We both laughed.

"By the time I was released, summer was past, and the trees in Central Park had all shed their leaves. I bought a bag of breadcrumbs and fed pigeons in the park all day long."

He suddenly grew silent. I turned to look at him, and I could see his fiery eyes glowing in the darkness. The fan at the head of the bed kept sending gust after gust of hot air our way, and I could feel the clammy sweat on my back. More and more street sounds from Yuanhuan came in through the window. The raspy sounds of the "sea-dog" peddler's trumpet had grown shrill. For some reason the muted trumpet kept playing "Jasmine in June," one of the most lyrical Taiwanese ballads there is. I'd heard it often as a child, but the effect of hearing it on this raspy trumpet was comical and somehow disturbing.

"What about the water lilies, A-qing?"

"What?" His voice, suddenly breaking through the silence, startled me.

"The water lilies in the park, where'd they go?"

"Oh, those. They say the city government had them removed."

"Oh, that's too bad."

"Everybody who saw them said they were beautiful."

"New Park is probably the ugliest park in the whole world." He laughed. "Those water lilies were the only pretty things in it."

"They say they were red lilies. Is that right?"

"That's right. Bright, bright red. Every time they bloomed I counted them. The most I ever counted was ninety-nine. Once I picked one and placed it in a friend's hands. He stood there cupping that bright red lily, looking like he was holding a bowl of fire in his hands. He was your age, eighteen . . ." I felt his bony fingers gently combing through my hair, and his fiery, jumping eyes began roving over my body again, urgently, intensely, imploringly. I was suddenly gripped by a strange fear.

"I've got to go, Mr. Wang," I said as I sat up.

"Can't you spend the night?" he asked disappointedly while he watched me get dressed.

"No, I have to go back."

"Can I see you tomorrow, A-qing?"

"I'm sorry, Mr. Wang, but I have a date tomorrow."

I bent over to tie my shoelaces, wondering why I'd lied to him. I didn't have a date, but tomorrow I couldn't see him, at least not tomorrow. I was afraid to look at those eyes, those eyes that seemed to be asking me for something, so ferociously, so painfully.

"Then when can I see you again?"

"We'll run into each other at the park sooner or later, Mr. Wang," I blurted out as I walked out the door and ran down the creaky stairs bathed in darkness, out of the Yaotai Hotel, down the narrow, foul-smelling lane, and into the crowds at the Yuanhuan night market, surrounded by racks of dried squid, octopus, and greasy pig's heads. I stopped in the doorway of a café called the Drunken Genie to stare at all the sesame-oil roasted ducks hanging by their feet from hooks and dripping oil. Suddenly I felt ravenously hungry. I picked out one of the biggest, plumpest ducks and asked the woman who ran the cafe to give me half. I also ordered a bowl of steaming herbal chicken soup. I first gulped down the entire bowlful of soup, which had a slightly medicinal flavor and was so hot it scalded my tongue. My forehead was bathed in sweat that started to stream down my face, but instead of wiping it off, I tore off a drumstick with one hand and a wing with the other and began eating like a savage. In almost no time, all that was left on my plate was a pile of bones—I'd even sucked the brains out of the duck's head. My belly was bulging under my shirt, but my stomach, like a bottomless pit, still craved more. I ordered a plate of fried rice noodles, which disappeared like a pile of dead leaves in a windstorm. The bill came to a hundred and eighty-seven yuan. I reached into my shirt pocket and pulled out a wad of five hundred-yuan notes. No one had ever given me so much money before. He'd given me everything he had in his wallet, even apologizing, saying he'd only been back a short while and hadn't exchanged much money.

After I left Yuanhuan I headed slowly home to Jinzhou Street. Sun Yat-sen North Road was nearly deserted, and only the silent, shimmering fluorescent streetlamps kept me company as I walked down the pedestrian lane, the nails in my boots making a hollow, forlorn sound on the cement. I loosened my belt and untucked my shirt, which was sticking to my skin, then unbuttoned it. A cool breeze swept by, making my soaked shirttail flutter slightly. As my pores opened, a heavy satisfaction came over me, the sort of numbness that follows overindulgence.

4

BUDDY———

I sat up in alarm. I heard myself screaming. The floor was bathed in bright sunlight. It was noon already, and the room was as hot as a sweatbox. Sweat was pouring down my back, like so many caterpillars squirming, making me itch. A dark wet spot on the straw mat showed the outline of my body. It was going to be another scorcher. The place Little Jade and I rented together was a five-tatami room made out of plywood, so small that all I could fit into it were a bed and a couple of wicker trunks. Since it had a western exposure, the afternoon sun heated it up like a steamer, and made me gasp for breath.

I sat up in bed, feeling the numbed exhaustion of waking from a deep sleep. My throat was parched. I could hear girls laughing outside, probably some of the bar girls from Jinzhou Street who'd come into the lane to cool off and tease each other. The bars weren't open yet, but the radios were already blasting wild strains of jazz music. Gradually, vaguely, I recalled seeing Buddy just a moment ago. He was standing at the head of my bed, dressed in his Boy Scout uniform, the one with the shoulder straps. There was no mistaking that pale baby face of his. He stuck out his hand and said with a giggle:

"A-qing, where's my harmonica?"

The year before, on his fifteenth birthday, I'd given him a Butterfly brand harmonica I'd bought at the school co-op for 270 yuan, half my monthly earnings from the newspaper route. He loved it so much he wouldn't let it out of his sight, carrying it to school with him in his back pocket and putting it under his pillow at night, taking it out to play it for a moment before going to sleep. At first he could only play single notes, but I taught him some harmonies; he not only picked them up immediately, but was soon better at them than I. At school they were learning the song "Plum Blossoms in the Snow," a light, lyrical melody that he played every day at home. Sometimes, after we were in bed and had turned out the light, Buddy would take out his harmonica, pull the covers up over his head, and play it quietly to himself. One night he woke up Father, who came storming into the room and threw the covers back. Thinking he was in for a beating, Buddy quickly wrapped his arms around his head and made himself as small as he could. When Father saw him he actually laughed. It was the only time I ever saw a smile on Father's stern, wrinkled face.

I jumped out of bed, dragged out a wicker trunk I kept under the foot of the bed, and took out the Butterfly harmonica I'd given Buddy. Since I hadn't cleaned it for several months, the brass cover was turning yellow. I put it up to my mouth and blew—the sound was as sharp and clear as ever, although the harmonica had a mildewy smell. The day I left home, the harmonica was in my pocket; it was the only thing I took with me.

This was the first time in over three months I'd thought of Buddy. Those three months were a blur. We spent the daylight hours lying low, like snakes in hibernation in our private caves. We started coming to life as night fell, throwing its protective cover of darkness over us, and began flying through the Taipei nights like bats on the wing. In the park we were like damned souls, moving round and round the steps of the lotus pond in a ceremonial dance in frantic pursuit of each other long into the night, until dawn began to break. We fled to Nanyang Street, like a swarm of bees, filed into the New South Seas Theater, with its smell of urine, filling the back rows to spread our talons and paw the bodies of the faceless people. We went to the Westgate district, where we escaped the prying eyes of the neon lights by hiding in the fetid public toilets throughout the China Bazaar. We passed secret signals with our eyes, with hand motions, or by the way we walked, to attract the attention of people like us. In Wanhua, in Yuanhuan, on Three Rivers Street, on Sun Yat-sen North Road we made our sneaky way into one damp, remote lane after another, where we entered gloomy, decrepit little inns left over from the Japanese occupation. Late at night, in the wee hours, when everyone else had gone home, we slinked out of whatever corner we'd crawled into and made our way back to the streets. By then, the deserted, defenseless streets belonged only to us. Clutching wads of sweaty, grimy bills in our hands in the pre-dawn hours, we dragged our spent bodies through the streets, feeling wanton and near collapse, heading slowly back to our private dens.

Over the last three months my mind had been virtually empty, as though I'd had a lobotomy, leaving me devoid of thoughts and feelings. I hadn't even thought about Buddy, my beloved brother Buddy. But just a moment ago there he'd been, standing at the head of my bed, so close, sticking out his hand and saying with a giggle, A-qing, where's my harmonica? I remember I grabbed his hand. It was ice cold, just like that other night. Father had gone to bed, but I stayed there with him, all by myself. I took his hand in mine. It was ice cold, so cold it made me shiver. We'd put several bricks of dry ice underneath him. With all that vapor rising around him, it was like he was sleeping in a cloud of mist. At the municipal funeral parlor they placed him in a small casket, a tiny, thin box. When they weren't looking I slipped into the slumber chamber and opened the lid of his casket. Buddy was lying stiffly inside. He'd been made up with rouge painted lightly on his white baby face. His arms were crossed over his chest, his shoulders squeezed into a sloping position. He looked like he was pretending to be asleep, a mischievous look on his face, like he could barely keep from laughing. We took Buddy to the public cemetery at Green Lake, where two clumsy pallbearers banged his casket loudly on the rear door of the hearse as they took it out. I was so angry I went over and shoved one of them.

"Take it easy!" I growled. "You understand?"

"Aren't you up yet? The sun's gonna singe your butt!"

Moon Beauty stuck her head in the door and smiled. All she had on were bra and panties, with a pink satin nightie draped over her shoulders. Her hair was in curlers.

"Did Little Jade ever come back?" I asked her.

"That's what I'd like to know. I wonder where the little crystal boy did his hell-raising last night." Moon Beauty squinted as she looked at me and snickered. "A-qing, tell me the truth, did you land a big one last night? Was it an edible fish or a loach?"

"Is there anything to eat?" I ignored her comment.

"You still owe me for last month's food, and now you want me to give you more?"

"I'll give you a hundred now, how's that?" I took a hundred-yuan note out of my pants pocket, which she snatched out of my hand.

"Hurry up," she said with a laugh. "The rice porridge I made this morning has probably spoiled by now."

I followed her into her room next door, which was separated from ours only by some plywood. Back when she was living with Johnny, her American G.I. boyfriend, she used our room as a little parlor. But after Johnny dropped her and went back to the States, she rented it out to Little Jade for only four hundred a month, lunch included. Then after he met Old Zhou, he rarely stayed here, so he asked me to move in to cut his expenses in half.

Moon Beauty was Little Jade's cousin, and she adored him. She often pinched his cheek and called him her little crystal boy. Blessed with a stunning figure and natural flirtatiousness, she was the hottest attraction at the New York Bar, where the American G.I.s called her Lili—the Beauty. She got a kick out of cupping her large breasts in her hands and saying disdainfully,

42

"What's there to be afraid of when you've got stuff like this!" Sometimes she went to work in the daytime, and since Obasan had her hands full, she brought her three-year-old son, Johnny's bastard child, over for us to take care of while she was out. Johnny Jr., the little bastard, was a cute little kid, with milky white skin and deep green eyes, but a headful of wavy black hair. At first Moon Beauty put him in an orphanage, but when she found she couldn't bear to be away from him she took him back. She told us that the little bastard's daddy was a strikingly handsome American. She had a photograph of him, dressed in navy whites, on her dresser: smiling, sexy eyes. A cocky look. Moon Beauty lived with him, and took care of his expenses, for a year. She also bore him a little bastard before he hauled ass back to the States. He sent her a total of three letters and twenty U.S. dollars as a Christmas present for Johnny Jr. Moon Beauty gave an exasperated sigh: "Those American birds who wing their way over here, what do they do for a conscience?" But she said she didn't bear him any hard feelings, forgave him, in fact, and if he came back, she'd go to bed with him again.

"Wow! There's squid here, too!"

There was a plate of pickled cabbage and squid on Moon Beauty's kitchen table next to the bowl of rice porridge.

"Moon Beauty, you're wonderful!" I rubbed her firm, cool arm affectionately.

"Go to hell, and stop trying to kiss up to me," she said good-naturedly from her chair across from me. "I want you to tell me where Jade went hunting for his prey last night."

"Little Jade? He found himself an overseas Chinese sugar daddy, some guy from Tokyo."

"Shit!" Moon Beauty chuckled loudly. "That little crystal boy still likes sashimi best of all! Last year it was an overseas Chinese who ran a Chinese restaurant in Osaka. Jade fell head over heels for that guy and had cherry blossom dreams for months. Old Zhou came looking for him late last night, and I made up a story about his going to Sanchong City. But he refused to believe me, and poured out a torrent of woes in that Shanghai accent I can barely understand. I think that chubby old guy really has the hots for Jade."

"He spent fifteen hundred on a Seiko watch for him last week, automatic, with a calendar."

"I saw it. He wears it all the time to show it off." Moon Beauty sighed and smiled weakly. "That fat old guy has no one to blame but himself for falling for a heartless crystal boy like that."

"Mommy—"

Obasan brought Johnny Jr. into the room, and as soon as the little bastard spotted his mother he started weaving and laughing as he ran into her arms. Moon Beauty picked him up, opened the slit in the rear of his pants, and bit him on his smooth little butt.

"You wild little brat," she snarled, "you little bastard, you're gonna be the death of me yet!"

Obasan, a fat, hot-tempered woman, was still gasping for air after climbing the stairs. She was sweating profusely. She put two red candles, two packs of incense, several strings of tinfoil ingots, and a thick wad of paper spirit money down on Moon Beauty's table, then calculated what Moon Beauty owed her. Like a bolt of lightning it hit me—today was the fifteenth day of the seventh lunar month, Ghost Festival day.

"Who are you going to burn spirit money for, Moon Beauty?" I asked her.

"For dear departed Daddy!" she said with a sigh. She picked up a string of cash and shook it mournfully. "He was always borrowing money from me when he was alive, and now that he's dead he comes to me in my dreams asking for money. If I don't burn some for him, I'm afraid he'll start with his accusations in front of Yama, the King of Hell."

"Moon Beauty, would you let me have half of that cash? I'll pay you for it." I took out twenty yuan and handed it to her.

"Who do you want it for?" she asked me out of surprise.

"For Buddy."

"Has he been coming to you for money, too?"

"He wants his harmonica back," I said. "Today's his birthday—he'd be sixteen."

"Harmonica?" Moon Beauty laughed. "They must sell harmonicas where he's at, don't you think? They say everything we've got up here they've got down there, too. There must be plenty of bars, so when I croak I'll go down there and become a bar girl. I've got to think about all those G.I.s who died in the Vietnam War."

Moon Beauty laughed so hard at her own joke she could barely stand. Her breasts were jiggling like crazy. "Crystal ghost!" she pointed at me. "You'll be a crystal ghost! That's exactly what you and Jade will turn into when you die. Whatever you are on earth you turn into the same thing after you die, and there's no way to change it!"

I took the two strings of cash back to my room and put them down on the bed. Then I went in and took a cold shower and washed my hair. When I was finished I put on some new clothes — a pair of dark blue dacron slacks and a blue and white striped pullover. I combed my stiff, unruly hair neatly and put some of Little Jade's haircream on it. Just as I was walking out the door I stuck the Butterfly harmonica into my back pocket. When I walked past Moon Beauty's room she whistled at me and said:

"The way you're dressed up you must be going out looking for some company!"

I ran downstairs without turning my head and plunged into the outside world. Sun Yat-sen North Road looked like it was covered with something that was giving off clouds of white mist. The whole area shimmered in the heat. I quickly put on my mirror-lens sunglasses, which one of my dates had left on a hotel chest of drawers. Finders keepers, losers weepers. During daylight hours I wore them to hide my face from view. That way, if I happened to bump into someone I knew, I could pretend I didn't see him and just keep on walking.

I jumped onto a bus on Sun Yat-sen North Road and headed for the seats in the back. The bus was stuffy as hell. Since I'd just taken a shower, as soon as I sat down I was covered in sweat. I was heading for the Westgate district, and from there over to the old airport, which hadn't been used for years. That's where my mother lived. It had been over five years since I last saw her. The last news I'd had of her was that she was living with a guy who ran an underground teahouse near the old airport. That's what Buddy told me. He'd gone to see her two or three times. She'd taken him to the Dragon Restaurant in Westgate for some *jiaozi*, where they'd stuffed themselves. But she told him not to come back unless there was good reason. She didn't even know he was dead. I'd planned to go tell her more than once, but for some reason I never did. It had been so long since we'd seen each other I was afraid we'd feel awkward and not know what to say.

Thoughts of Mother, and of Buddy, got me thinking again about my broken, ruined home.

5

Our home was on Longjiang Street, all the way at the end, on Lane 28. You can compare where we lived by looking at a map of China and putting your finger on a barren spot of a land in Heilongjiang Province near the Siberian border. Located in one of Taipei's most remote districts, Longjiang Street is populated by people of very limited means. Given over mainly to living quarters for low-ranking employees of minor government agencies, our lane was lined on both sides by low wooden buildings, black with age and spotted with dry rot. The doors, windows, and eaves were broken or crumbling, making the buildings look like a huddled pack of ragged beggars with slumping shoulders and twisted backs. The first house on the left belonged to a staff officer named Qin. His front gate had been blown off during a typhoon, and never repaired. It looked like a gaping, toothless mouth. Staff Officer Qin used to sit on a bench in the open gateway pulling a bow across his *huqin* and singing. According to him, he followed the Qilin Tong school style of opera, although his voice was so raspy it sounded like he had a perennial cold. He'd suffered a stroke the year before, which twisted his face out of shape and caused one side of his mouth to hang slack; but he kept singing opera, filling the air with his desolate shouts of "Who tricketh the Emperor . . ." His drooping chin gave his face a pained expression. Squad Leader Xiao and Assistant Squad Leader Huang shared the first building on the right. Their wives had fought with each other for more than ten years, all because of the kitchen they shared. Often late at night, rhythmical sounds of a cleaver on a chopping board emerged from their kitchen, accompanied by high-pitched curses that raised the hair on your arms in the cold night wind. Mrs. Xiao, a big woman with a booming voice, always prevailed. Mrs. Huang, on the other hand, was a skinny, toothless woman who looked like a dried-up cucumber and always came away from these arguments with tears streaking her tragic face, as though Mrs. Xiao's curses had condemned her to perdition. I guess life was tough on everyone, and that's why almost all we ever heard were sounds of discontent. In all those years I can't recall a single time when tranquility reigned in our lane. The sounds of crying somewhere would barely cease before shouts and angry curses would erupt from somewhere else.

And yet it was hard to put thoughts of Lane 28, that dead-end of dead-ends, out of my mind completely: a unique smell of decay hung over the area, plus a unique sense of dilapidation and bleakness. The open ditches on both sides were repositories of rotting vegetables, ragged clothing, pieces of wicker and bamboo, and rusty tin cans. They were rivers of foul, black, stagnant water, and when the sun beat down on them, the overpowering stench floated in the air up and down the lane. The contents of the uncovered trashbox in the middle of the lane were an interesting mixture of filthy objects, piled high, occasionally including dead cats with horribly bloated bellies, staring, lifeless eyes, and bared fangs. They'd been poisoned and tossed there to rot. It was a breeding ground for huge green flies with red heads, which scattered in the air when anyone approached the box, exposing the maggot-covered cat corpse. The unpaved lane turned into a treacherous quagmire after every heavy rainfall. We walked through it, slipping and squishing in our bare feet, the mud coating our feet and returning with us to our homes. During dry spells, the wind sent sand swirling in the air and caused the tattered diapers, underpants, sheets, and pillows hanging from bamboo poles set up in the breaks in the fences to flap and fly excitedly in the sea of sand.

At the foot of the lane, the most tumble-down, the oldest, and the darkest little building was where we lived. Typhoon Daisy passed through the area the year before and took part of our roof along with it. Father and I patched the gaping hole with black oilpaper held down by bricks. But that didn't keep out the water when it rained heavily, and we'd put buckets, basins, even spittoons sometimes, under the leaky spots. If the rain kept up all night, we'd have to sleep amid a chorus of noisy dripping. Our place had lower ceilings than most houses, which kept the sunlight from finding its way in, so the cement floors were always damp, as though they were constantly sweating. It was deathly still inside our house as it quietly rotted. Blotches of green, yellow, and black dry rot, covered by a layer of fuzz, climbed the walls, all the way up to the ceiling. Our clothes had a strong mildewy smell that no amount of washing could ever remove.

And yet, Father told us we were lucky to even have a place like this to live in. Back in 1949, his army unit had been under attack at Dabie Mountain by the Communist Eighth Route Army for more than a week, and he'd been taken prisoner before help could arrive. He managed to escape and flee to Taiwan, where he was drummed out of the army. His old comrade-in-arms, Huang Ziwei, now Section Chief Huang, had pulled some strings to get us into this squat, tumble-down house, at least for the time being. Nearly every Sunday since then, Father had gone over to Uncle Huang's place in Lane 26, the next lane over, with a bottle of cheap wine and a bag of peanuts, and the two of them would sit there guzzling wine out of bowls and gobbling up the peanuts. Father was a taciturn man to begin with, and when he was drinking, you couldn't pry a word out of him. He'd just sit there silently, his face all red and puffy, his eyes bloodshot, until the sun went down and darkness invaded the room; then he'd stand up, cough drily, and say:

"Hm, it's getting late..."

"Why not stay for dinner," Uncle Huang would say as he got to his feet.

"Some other time."

Without waiting for Uncle Huang to respond, he'd march sharply out the door, showing the effects of his rigorous military training, his chest thrown out as far as he could manage, his head held so straight it was almost comical; his army boots, which he'd worn so long they were filled with holes, made a hollow flapping sound as he walked.

Apparently, Father had been decorated during the war with Japan. At least, that's what he said. Whenever he began talking about the victorious battle at Changsha, he'd suddenly grow very expansive and, in that heavy Sichuan accent of his, ramble on with precious little eloquence, saying all kinds of things we could barely understand. His dark, wrinkled face, so worn down by time and a lifetime of failures, would suddenly be infused with pride. Father told us that after that battle the rivers of Changsha ran red, and his sword was bent from cutting off the heads of Japanese soldiers. There was a photograph of him in full uniform on the desk in his room. He was wearing a leather belt diagonally across his chest and a pair of high-topped riding boots; holding a bullet-scarred helmet in his hand, there was a look of triumph on his face. The picture had been taken on a battlefield outside of Changsha, where the ground around him was strewn with the corpses of soldiers killed in battle. Father had just been promoted to regimental commander and decorated for heroism.

He kept his Order of the Precious Tripod – Second Class medal in a small wooden red box with a brass lock on his headboard.

One day, after I'd passed the high-school entrance exam, he called me into his room and solemnly carried the little red box from his headboard over to the desk, where he opened it with great care, to reveal a gold-plated copper star-shaped medal with an inlaid blue and white enamel tripod in the center. The gold plating had already started turning black and was flaking in places, letting the greenish copper backing show through. The red, white, and blue ribbon attached to the uppermost point of the star had begun to yellow. Pointing to the medal, Father said:

"A-qing, I don't want you to ever forget that your father was a decorated hero."

I was so intrigued by the medal that I reached out to touch it; but he stopped me and said with a frown:

"Stand up straight!"

Once I was standing at attention, my hands hanging stiffly at my sides, he picked up the medal and pinned it on the lapel of my school uniform. Then he, too, snapped to attention:

"Ready, salute!"

Instinctively, I raised my right hand to my forehead and gave Father a snappy salute. Although I felt like laughing, I forced myself to hold back when I saw the look of solemnity on his face. He said that his Order of the Precious Tripod would become mine on the day I graduated from high school. His cherished dream was that upon graduation I would enter the Army's Phoenix Mountain Military Academy to continue in his footsteps.

Having been a soldier nearly all his life, Father didn't know how to do anything else. That made finding a job in civilian life very hard. It was only through his personal relationship with Uncle Huang that he was able to land a sinecure in a credit cooperative under joint state-private ownership as a consultant, with a monthly salary of 3,000 New Taiwan Dollars. He didn't even have a desk at the office, which was all right, since there was no need for him to be there, anyway. But every day he put on the only decent dark blue serge Sun Yat-sen tunic he owned, picked up his black briefcase, whose worn zipper only went half way across, and stuck it under his arm, then trekked to the bus stop in a stiff military gait. The routine never varied, no matter how tired he was, no matter how bad the weather.

Father had cut himself off from all his old colleagues. Once, when a couple of his subordinates dropped by on an unexpected visit, he shut himself up in the bathroom, wearing only his underwear, and said to me softly from behind the door:

"Go out there right now and tell them I'm not home!"

Day in and day out, year in and year out, Father passed the time in his wicker-backed chair, worn shiny with age, sitting under a dim lamp in the hot, stuffy, mildewy living room. Bare-chested and covered with sweat, a pair of reading glasses resting on his nose, he'd read his dog-eared copy of *Tales of the Three Kingdoms*. One year, when a strong earthquake hit Taipei, some roof tiles came crashing down, and we ran frightened out into the lane. When we ventured back inside, there was Father, still sitting regally in his chair, his copy of *Tales of the Three Kingdoms* gripped tightly in his hands, the overhead light swinging back and forth like a pendulum.

Whenever Father sat alone in the living room studying the novel's great and universal principle of power—unity follows long periods of division; division follows long periods of unity— Mother would be outside on her haunches, all alone, bending over and washing the never-ending pile of dirty bedding and clothes that she took in to earn some extra money. There she was, the year round, nearly buried by mounds of dirty laundry, her back in a permanent curve as she scrubbed with all her might, over and over, her hands turning bright red in the soapy water. She squatted on the ground, the hem of her dress up around her knees, exposing her white calves; her long black hair was done up in a ponytail that fell across her back. Sometimes she'd casually hum a Taiwanese ballad while she scrubbed the clothes, then suddenly look up with a frown on her face and sing out loudly:

Ah——ah——this forgotten city——with its lonely, lonesome shadows——

Her voice was shrill and thin, and the shaky sound rising in the air sent chills down the spine of anyone who heard it. It was a sadder sound than Bai Ying, the Taiwanese blues singer, could produce from the song "The Mournful City."

Mother's origins and background were shadowy, to say the least. As far as we knew, she was the adopted daughter of a family that raised ducks in the Taoyuan countryside. Her adopted father was a cruel, abusive drunkard, and it was only because her adopted mother had a soft spot in her heart for her that she was spared some of the suffering. But one day her father threw a sickle at her, striking her in the forehead and leaving a deep gash. She fled to Zhongli, where she became a hostess in a low-class teahouse near the military base housing the First Army. Her conduct during those days must have been suspect, for she was the cause of several incidents between junior officers. On one occasion, two second lieutenants fought over her, nearly costing one of them his life. It was such a big scandal that she was forced to leave Zhongli. So she came to Taipei to find work as a housemaid. When Auntie Huang became pregnant, she hired Mother to help out around the house. That's how she and Father got together. Father was forty-five at the time, Mother a mere nineteen. Whenever Auntie Huang talked about those days, her mouth twisted into a laugh as she said:

"I told your mother to pass out the lucky red-dyed eggs to announce the birth of my child, and not only did your father keep the egg, but the messenger as well!"

Mother was probably quite a flirt in her younger days. You could tell she'd once had quite a figure, with a thin waist and slender limbs. Her satiny black hair was long and lush. When a smile appeared on her fair, baby face, the corners of her mouth curled upwards, giving her a childish look, reminiscent of a little girl who'd never grown up. But her eyes — so big, so deep, so dark — always had the look of a frightened deer, filled with indecision and trepidation as they darted this way and that. Every once in a while her brow would suddenly crease and her eyes would look like fireballs burning in her face, as though her heart had been ignited by the hatred stored up in it.

Mother barely came up to Father's shoulder, and when they went out walking together, he held himself straight and erect, like a soldier on parade, marching proudly, while she tagged along behind, trying to keep up as she glanced from side to side. The two of them — an aging, beaten, hulking man with white bristly hair, and a baby-faced, skittish woman following in his wake — were as incongruous a couple as ever walked down our lane, a husband and wife years apart in age who caused heads to turn whenever they walked together.

Father probably loved Mother with all his heart at one time, although you wouldn't have known it from his violent behavior toward her. Once, when she was joking around with a young vegetable peddler in the doorway, she playfully hit him on his bare chest with a turnip, and he responded by pinching her on the upper arm. Father saw it all, and when they were inside the house alone, he took down a whip from behind the door and, without a word, gave Mother three vicious lashes with it. She crumpled to the ground and curled up into a tiny ball, her shoulders heaving, her white calves flailing uncontrollably. Seeing her there on the floor reminded me of a hen we'd killed one New Year's as it lay on the ground with its throat cut, clawing the air, wracked by spasms, struggling to stay alive as its white feathers slowly turned red from the gushing blood. Mother didn't cry as she lay on the floor, nor did she shout. Her face was ashen, but she kept her mouth clamped tightly shut, as she looked up at him. Her eyes looked like they were about to leap out of their sockets. She stayed in bed the next day, and when Father returned home in the afternoon he placed a box wrapped in flowery paper next to her pillow, then turned and walked quickly out of the room. Inside the box was a brand-new dress made of fine green cotton with a peony pattern. Mother got out of bed, put on the new dress, went over to the mirror and looked at herself. Two welts the size of fingers were visible on her back just below the neckline, all red and swollen, like a couple of snakes crawling across her fair skin.

One day, when I was eight years old, Mother disappeared without a trace. She took all her clothes, including the dress Father had bought for her. She'd run away with a trumpet player in the Eastern Treasures Dance Troupe. She joined the troupe and performed with them all over the island. The members of the Eastern Treasures Dance Troupe originally lived in a dormitory on Changchun Road, and Mother had gone there regularly to pick up their dirty laundry. Once, when I was passing by the dormitory, I saw her inside singing along with them. The young musician, who was barely in his twenties, was wearing a crimson uniform with two rows of golden buttons down the front and gold stripes on the wide cuffs of his jacket. His white, gold-trimmed cap rested on his head at a jaunty angle above his long black sideburns. He was holding a shiny brass trumpet in his hands, playing it with so much enthusiasm his back was arched. Mother was standing with a group of women from the troupe who were having a rollicking good time singing "When the Spring Breezes Blow." She was wearing a man's white, gold-trimmed cap at the same jaunty angle, and I don't think I'd ever seen her look so happy.

The night Mother left, Father ran out of the house brandishing the pistol he'd worn as a regiment commander back on the Mainland, screaming that he was going to kill those two dogs in heat. He returned home in the middle of the night, so drunk he could barely walk. He woke Buddy and me up for a lecture we couldn't make heads or tails of, and before long he was wailing pitifully. His wrinkled, beaten old face was streaked with tears, making it the most terrifying, tragic sight I'd ever seen. Buddy was so frightened he cried and cried, while I just shivered uncontrollably.

I wasn't as sad as I thought I'd be over Mother's departure, probably because she'd never liked me; I only feared, never loved, her. I came into this world via a breech birth, and Mother lost so much blood she nearly died. She was convinced that my birth was retribution for her sins in a past life. She often smoothed the wrinkles on my forehead as she said:

"Don't frown like that, Blackie. Wrinkles on a child's forehead are an evil sign."

Mother called me Blackie and Buddy Whitey. I took after Father, big and dark, but Buddy, with his fair skin and baby face, was the spitting image of Mother; his dark eyes looked like they'd been taken right out of her head, except that they were free of hatred and filled with laughter. Mother said that when she was pregnant with Buddy she'd dreamt of Guanyin, the Goddess of Mercy, who was also the giver of sons. To her that meant that Buddy was a gift from Guanyin herself. That was why he looked so much like her. She made him a set of bright red satin clothes with her own hands, and put a silver-plated necklace with the twelve animals of the zodiac around his neck. As he crawled around the house, all those jingling little dragons, snakes, tigers, and rabbits set up quite a racket. Just watching him gave Mother such pleasure that she'd sweep him up in her arms and kiss him from the top of his head all the way down to his chubby little legs, as he giggled and flailed his arms and legs.

One day Mother was giving him a bath in the courtyard. Using her own bathsoap, she covered him from head to toe with suds as she squatted down beside the wooden tub, her back bent, her coal-black hair falling down to her knees. She scooped up water with her hands and splashed it all over his milky-white, chubby body as she sang "Jasmines in June" softly to him. Buddy was laughing, Mother was laughing, and their crisp, frolicking laughter floated on the rays of the sun. When Mother went inside to get a towel, I walked over and stood beside the tub. He playfully stuck out his arm. I grabbed it and sunk my teeth into it, leaving eight deep marks in his milky-white skin. Mother came running out, a pair of fire tongs in her hand. She hit me across the knee, leaving a nasty, swollen bruise that made me limp for days. The sight of blood and pus oozing out of my damaged knee actually filled me with the satisfaction of having gotten even, and I refused to cry or ask forgiveness. Mother's dislike for me grew more intense after that, for now she was convinced I was a demon sent to torment her.

But once Mother was gone, Buddy and I became inseparable. While Mother was at home, he had always slept with her, but on the night she left, he came into my room, climbed into bed with me, and huddled as close as he could, out of fear, no doubt. I was exhausted that night, and I hugged him close, patting him on the back, like Mother had done, until we both fell asleep.

I'd only seen Mother once after that, some four years later, when I entered middle school. The Eastern Treasures Dance Troupe had come to Taipei to perform at the China Splendor Theater in Sanchong City. Without telling anyone, Buddy and I took the bus across the Taipei Bridge to Sanchong City to see her. The China Splendor Theater, where Taiwanese opera was performed, was actually nothing more than a huge tent with plywood walls located in a small lane on Chongxin Street. The entrance consisted of two hanging cloth curtains, while the plywood walls were covered with posters that colorfully announced the current attraction: Eastern Treasures Dance Troupe — Hot and Steamy! The poster featured pictures of several bare-legged dancing girls. A man wearing a gaudy paper hat stood at the entrance, shouting through a bullhorn: Beautiful girls! Great action! Buddy and I walked up, bought two tickets, and pushed our way into the packed audience. The theater, nearly filled to capacity, was alive with activity. The dirt floor was covered with rinds, watermelon seeds, cigarette butts, and soft-drink bottles. The audience, which was squeezed onto long backless benches, was almost exclusively male, many of the men sitting there without shirts, sweat covering their upper bodies. Most were wearing wooden clogs instead of shoes, which they kicked off when they sat down, then curled their legs up under them. The rank air inside the theater was filled with the stink of sweat and dirty feet. I dragged Buddy up to the foot of the stage, where we squeezed onto a bench to the left. Just in front of the tattered red curtain was a row of footlights that lit up the entire stage. The musicians were seated stage right, five men dressed in crimson uniforms with gold buttons. They were already playing when we got there, and their racket reminded me of the drums and bugles at the Wanhua Market auctions. I spotted the young trumpet player Mother had run off with sitting in the second chair of the front row. His head was raised, his cheeks were puffed out, and his eyes were big as saucers as he played with great self-assurance, the trumpet in his hands glinting brightly in the lights. He wasn't wearing his hat, and his hair, shiny and black, was neatly combed forward. The announcer came out on stage, microphone in hand, to begin the show. After he'd cracked a few jokes, which were met by hoots and whistles from the audience, six dancing girls suddenly swept onto the stage, dressed in skimpy pink skirts that showed plenty of leg. They had shiny gold barrettes in their hair and glittering bracelets on their wrists. They moved to the middle of the stage, formed a chorus line, and, as the musicians struck up a new tune, swung their arms in unison toward the audience as they began singing a high-pitched song:

Taiwan girls are rare beauties —

The audience quickly got into the mood, shouting Dance! Dance! Dance! As the musicians picked up the tempo, the girls hooked arms, paired off, and began to dance, kicking their legs higher and higher with each step. They sang as they danced, their bracelets clanging noisily. The men in the audience clapped and roared their approval, while the announcer kept up the beat by shouting Hai! Hai! Hai! into the microphone, spurring the dancers on to greater heights.

Buddy and I were sitting too far to the side to see well, so I stood up and swept the stage with my eyes, until I spotted Mother, the first dancing girl on the left. All the girls were heavily made up, with lots of rouge and blue and purple eye shadow, which made it hard to tell one from the other. Mother was in her thirties by then, but she was so petite and so heavily made up she could have passed for eighteen or nineteen. She was shorter than the others, and her leg kicks were always a bit later than theirs. A forced smile on her face revealed her pretty white teeth between brightly painted lips. But she never stopped blinking those large eyes of hers, as though she were on the verge of panic. When I told Buddy that Mother was dancing on the stage, he jumped up onto the bench to see for himself. He spotted her.

"Mama — " he shouted as he stood on the bench, then began to sob.

6

Kenan Street, near the old airport, was lined on both sides by watermelon stands. Naturally, the ground around the area was strewn with melon rinds and seeds. Chunks of rotting watermelon drew hordes of flies. With the sun beating down mercilessly, the rotting fruit and rind gave off a sickeningly sweet odor. Mother lived in a slum area at the farthest end of Kenan Street in one of the strangest buildings I'd ever seen: a two-story cement structure left over from the Japanese occupation, with thick, sturdy walls in which there were small dark openings instead of regular windows. It was an ugly gray, like an abandoned fortress, although it had apparently been used to quarter Japanese troops. I walked into the building and up the twisting cement staircase, up and up into the darkness as though I were entering a black hole. Not only was the place dark, but it had the damp mildewy smell of an air-raid shelter. Confronted by a cacophony of human sounds — the shouts and curses of adults and the sobs and cries of children — I wondered how many people called this place home. The place was so dark that all I could see were shadows, no faces. Holding on to the cement bannister, I groped my way up to the top floor and over to an open door, where an old woman was sitting on a stool, fast asleep. She was wearing a faded cotton open-necked undershirt, which revealed a neck as wrinkled as turkey skin, sagging in folds. Her hair was pulled back in a bun, while her hairline in front had receded badly, leaving red spots where the hair had been. It looked like the skin on her forehead had been peeled away to reveal a layer of fresh pink flesh.

"Obasan, is Huang Lixia in?" I asked her as I removed my sunglasses.

"Hm? Who?" she replied loudly as her eyes snapped open.

"Huang Lixia. A-li."

Instead of answering, she cleared her throat and spat noisily on the floor, then looked me over with a scowl, and pointed to one of the rooms inside. I went in, walked down a corridor with a brick floor until I reached a doorway at the end, which was covered by a dark yellow door curtain. I pulled back the curtain and looked inside, but couldn't see a thing except a finger of light that shone in through the curtain. I groped my way into the oppressively hot room, where I was met by a horrible, rancid odor like the foul smell given off by a dead animal.

"Mother —— " I called out softly.

I stood there frozen to the spot for a moment, until my eyes got used to the dark. I saw the dim outline of a bed under a mosquito net in the middle of the room, and what appeared to be someone lying on it. I walked over and stood at the head of the bed and called out again:

"Mother, it's me, A-qing."

"A-qing, is that you?"

It was Mother's voice, all right — high-pitched and trembling — that emerged from the darkness. There was a rustling sound, then a click, as the lamp came on and cast a dim light. Mother was lying on her side in a curled-up position, a black wool overcoat thrown over her upper body and a comforter wrapped around her legs. Her head was pressed deeply into a pillow that was surrounded by mounds of yellow tissues. The mosquito net that hung from the ceiling was so filthy it looked like it had been thrown together from a bunch of old dirty rags. As I moved over to the head of the bed, she turned her head to look at me. I was stunned by how much she had changed. What had once been a round baby face was now a cadaverous skull with horribly sunken cheeks and eye sockets, separated by sharply jutting cheekbones; her big lovely eyes were now two deep, dark holes in her face, and the area around them was so discolored it seemed to be one massive bruise. Her skin was waxen and there were black medicine plasters over her temples. Her lush black hair was all matted from having been slept on for so long. Her bony fingers were tightly curled inward, like talons. Her once slight, seductive figure, which was buried under all that bulky bedding, had become the body of a dried-up infant. She reached out a spindly hand and grabbed me by the wrist. Her voice grew more plaintive than ever as she said urgently:

"You came at just the right time, A-qing. Hurry, pick me up. There's a spittoon next to the bed. See it?"

I pulled back the covers and picked her up off the bed. She had wasted away until she was nothing but skin and bones. With my hand under her back, I could feel every ridge on her backbone. The strong medicine odor from her body was mixed with the smell of sweat. I sat her down on the spittoon, which was half filled with a dirty yellow liquid. That was the source of the horrible smell that met me when I first walked into the room. As she sat hunched over on the spittoon she grumbled:

"I shouted myself hoarse for help, but nobody paid any attention. That old hag out there pretended she was deaf! As soon as they saw I was too sick to move they tried to make things hard for me. She had the nerve to stand in the doorway and say to her son, 'That woman in there's useless, so why waste time trying to make her better?'" Mother laughed drily and snarled, "To hell with her. I wouldn't mind dying, but I'm still here!"

After she finished, she wiped herself with some yellow tissue. Then I picked her up and laid her back down on the bed.

"I've got to keep warm, A-qing, so make sure I'm covered up," she said in a trembling voice. I wrapped the comforter around her. All the windows were closed and the curtains were drawn. My back was drenched in sweat.

"You know, A-qing, they're all waiting for me to die!" Mother said in a whisper. She stretched out her dark, cadaverous right hand so I could see the worn gold ring hanging loosely on her ring finger. "They can't wait for me to die so they can snatch this ring off my finger, but it'll be a cold day in hell before they get it! I'd swallow it before I'd let that vulture get her hands on it! But, A-qing, I don't even have enough money to buy a slice of watermelon ..."

She looked me over with her sunken eyes and smirked:

"Heh-heh, you're really dressed to kill, A-qing. You strike it rich or something? Be a good boy and give your mother some money so she can get something to eat. I haven't eaten all day. All they brought me was some pig slop. Did they really think I'd eat it?"

I took the two hundred from the night before out of my pocket and gave a hundred of it to Mother. Her bony hand closed tightly around the note and shook. Her hideous, ruined face started to come to life, as she smiled like a little girl. She quickly stuck the money under her pillow before anyone could see it and get the idea to take it away from her. Once the money was out of sight, she fluffed up the pillow and lay back down with a long sigh of relief.

"The doctor said the infection has entered my bones and that they'll have to be amputated..." She pointed to her legs. "He wants to take them both off, seven thousand a leg! I don't have that kind of money, and I wouldn't let him do it if I did. He said it's spreading, and when it reaches my heart I'm finished. But so what! What difference does it make if a woman like me lives or not?" She suddenly sat up shakily and looked at me with eyes that shone again. "A-qing, will you promise me something? I've never asked you for anything before, but I want you to promise me this, okay?"

"Sure," I agreed.

"I don't have long to live, and when I die, you go to the temple and burn some incense for me. Any temple will do. Just kneel down in front of the Buddha and put in a good word for your mother. I've done a lot of bad things in my life, but I want you to ask the Buddha to forgive me and not condemn me to an eternity of suffering. I can't make up for everything I've done! I'm not afraid to die, but I am afraid of having to answer down there for all my sins..."

Tears suddenly filled her sunken eyes and spilled out onto her cheeks. I picked up a couple of sheets of the coarse yellow tissue and handed them to her. After she dried her tears and blew her nose she lay back down. She was silent for a long moment, then sighed.

"Your daddy, he didn't treat me all that bad. Except that, except that..."

She frowned and clicked her tongue. Then all of a sudden her lips parted as she chuckled frivolously.

"Well?" she asked, "how is the old guy? Still hitting the bottle every day?"

"Don't know," I said, shaking my head. "I haven't seen him in over three months. Mother, I left home, too."

"Really?" Her curiosity showed. She blinked and patted the back of my hand. A nod, a sigh.

"So you ran away, too, huh, A-qing?"

"Daddy kicked me out," I said.

"Really?" she mumbled, looking up at me, her hand still resting on mine. In that moment it dawned on me that Mother and I were a lot alike in many ways. She'd spent most of her life running away, roaming, searching, only to wind up battered and broken in this bed under a mountain of sweat-soaked bedding and a filthy mosquito net, her body invaded by disease, just waiting to die. And me, I'm part of that same sinful flesh that has seen so much evil. I've followed in her footsteps, always running away, roaming, searching. At that moment I felt very close to my mother.

"So now your daddy only has Buddy, right?" Her trembling voice grew sad.

"Mother..." I had a lump in my throat, and couldn't get the words out.

"A-qing, Buddy's your own flesh and blood, so you've got to treat him well."

"Mother, Buddy's dead." I was finally able to blurt it out, like coughing up a lump of bloody phlegm. Mother looked at me, dumbfounded, as though she hadn't heard me. "Buddy died over three months ago, Mother."

I sat down on the bed beside her and held her claw-like hands tightly. My palms were all sweaty, my teeth were chattering, as I leaned over and rapidly told her that Buddy had died of pneumonia. Doctor Wu at the Kangfu Hospital on Changchun Road said he had a bad cold, so he gave him an injection to bring his fever down. Three days later Buddy was delirious, he coughed and hacked all night long, and ran a dangerously high fever. We took him to the emergency room at Taiwan University Hospital, where they put him in an oxygen tent. He spent the whole night gasping for breath and died at dawn. He died in my arms. When the hospital attendants wanted to take his body away, I kicked and fought to keep them from touching him. Finally, Father pulled me away so the attendants could cover Buddy up with a white sheet and take him away. Mother didn't make a sound as she listened to me, and when I was finished, the two of us just looked at each other without saying a word. All of a sudden, she wrenched her hands free of mine and bolted up into a sitting position. She pointed a trembling finger at me and screamed:

"You two killed my Whitey!"

"Mother..." I stood up.

"Pneumonia? What do you mean, pneumonia? I don't understand! You two killed my Whitey..." Mother's flashing eyes seemed about to leap out of their sunken sockets. I couldn't tell from her contorted face if she was going to laugh or cry. "I know it was you, with that black heart of yours, who killed my Whitey. Then you come here to lie to me and tell me he died of pneumonia. You're the one who killed my Whitey, and I'm gonna make you pay for it..."

She began pounding the bed with her claw-like hands as she wailed, louder and louder, her grief becoming greater and greater. The old woman sitting in the doorway rushed into the room, frantically waving her arms in the air and shouting:

"Crazy! She's gone crazy!"

I stepped back, then turned and stumbled out of the room and ran down the dark, twisting cement staircase as fast as I could, pursued by Mother's shrill wails. I ran out of the building, and kept running, unable to stop. The sun was beating down, white-hot, and I began to feel dizzy. I broke out in a cold sweat. I ran until I couldn't run any more. I was gasping for breath. I turned and looked back; that ugly gray fortress-like cement building with all those black holes in the walls, standing erect under the sweltering sun, looked like a huge prison.

7

The Barbarian coffee shop in the Westgate district was one of our meeting places. Sometimes, Little Jade, Mousey, Wu Min and I would leave messages there for each other: "New South Seas entrance, eight o'clock." "China Bazaar, second floor, Wu's Wontons, nine-thirty." It was four in the afternoon, and the August sun had roasted Taipei into submission. I threaded my way into the Barbarian basement, which was packed with people, all young, sitting in groups of two or three, shoulder to shoulder in bright shirts, making the place look like a huge sunflower. A cloud of white mist from the air conditioning floated through the dimly lit room, carrying with it the nearly suffocating smell of cigarette smoke. Rock music was blaring from the jukebox — it was the Beatles:

Yeah —— yeah —— yeah

I surveyed the room until I spotted someone sitting alone at a table in the corner next to the air conditioner. I walked over and asked:

"Is there anyone sitting here?" There were a couple of empty glasses on the table.

He looked up and shook his head. I took off my sunglasses and sat down across from him. He pointed to the empty glasses.

"They just left."

He was a boy of fourteen or fifteen in a school uniform, faded from countless washings. His shirt was unbuttoned and not tucked in, exposing his chest and abdomen. One of his shoulder straps had a button missing, and was sticking up in the air. He was sitting with his back to the air conditioner with his feet propped up on a chair. He was wearing sandals, and was wiggling his toes to the music. The glass in front of him was empty, the straw in it gnawed out of shape. He was holding a cigarette between his fingers, which he quickly brought up to his mouth as he watched me sit down, and puffed on it furiously; obviously, he'd just learned how to smoke.

"The two guys who just left stole an American's car last night," he said excitedly.

"What kind of car?"

"Mercedes!"

"Wow, top of the line."

"They took it for a joy ride up to Section Four of Ren'ai Road, where they crashed into a telephone pole. So they jumped out and ran like hell. They said the brand-new Mercedes looked like a squashed toad!"

He laughed. The image of the American's car smashed up against a telephone pole, looking like a squashed toad, made me laugh, too. He laughed and laughed, his large white teeth flashing in his round, sunburned face. His crewcut, not much more than an inch in length and just beginning to curl down over his forehead, showed he'd just begun his summer break from school. The patch on his left breast pocket said he was student number 593 at Hengyi Middle School.

"They're in the Westgate Brotherhood Gang."

"You a member?" I asked him.

"Nah!" He curled his lip in a sneer. "They're a bunch of punks!"

I ordered a glass of guava juice, and took a couple of sips through the straw as soon as it arrived. I noticed he was staring at me as he puffed away on his cigarette.

"Want some?" I asked him.

He hesitated at first, but finally pushed his glass over with an awkward laugh. I poured half my drink into his glass.

"I already had a glass of pineapple juice and a glass of mango juice, but I haven't had any of their guava juice yet. I've been hanging out here all afternoon, more than four hours already. I spent everything I had. I was gonna take in a movie." He smiled as he sipped his drink.

"What's so great about hanging around here all day by yourself?"

"Where else is there to go on a scorcher like today?" he said breathlessly.

"You could go swimming."

"I went over to the Eastgate Pool yesterday. They were packed in there like sardines. And the water stunk! At first I was going to stay home and read a martial arts novel. Hey, do you read martial arts novels?"

"I'm a master. I read *Heroic Tales of the Vulture Killer* when I was in elementary school!"

"Ha, ha. I just finished *Vulture Killer* myself." He clapped his hands and said loudly, "I read them every night in the school dormitory with a flashlight under the covers. I love 'em! One night Wu the Stooge caught me and took every *Vulture Killer* copy I had. He's our dormitory monitor. He weighs over two hundred pounds, and starts panting when he just talks. Well, he stuck his finger under my nose and gave me hell in that Shanghai accent of his: "You little runt, you're always breaking the rules!"

"You're not one of those Shanghai beggars, are you?" I asked him.

This really started him laughing.

"No, no I'm not," he said in a Shanghai drawl. "My stepmother's from Shanghai, and all she ever does is point her finger at me and say, "Damn little demon! Damn little demon!" She says if I get kicked out of Hengyi, she's gonna send me to the middle school up on Ali Mountain. Have you ever heard a woman from Shanghai bawl someone out? It sounds like scraping your fingernails on a piece of glass. As soon as she starts in on me, my dad slinks out of the room. He used to be a pilot, but even a jet engine comes in second to her grating voice."

"What kind of plane did your dad fly?"

"Bombers, b-25s, bomb——" He spread his arms and made a swooping motion like a dive bomber. "Now he raises chickens at home."

"What?" His voice was drowned out by a Tom Jones song blaring from the jukebox.

"I said he raises chickens!" he shouted. "We've got over five hundred leghorn chickens at home."

I started to laugh. I couldn't think of anything funnier than a bomber pilot staying home to raise chickens.

"Our house stinks all the time from the chicken shit! My dad spends half his time in the chicken coops gathering eggs, while my stepmother's inside playing mahjong. That's all she ever does, day or night. Do you know why she doesn't want me to hang around the house?"

"Because you're always up to something."

"No!" He smiled and shook his head again. "It's because she always loses when I'm there. She calls me 'Bad Luck.'"

"What's your name, Bad Luck?"

"Zhao Ying."

"Everybody calls me A-qing."

"What time is it, A-qing?" He reached over and turned my watch so he could see the time. He sighed.

"Shit, it's only four-thirty. My stepmother's playing mahjong, and she told me not to come home before eight o'clock."

"How about a movie," I suggested.

He reached into his pocket and fumbled around until he dug out a five-yuan note.

"I had fifty when I left the house, but I lost twenty in a game of pool." He stuck out his tongue to show his frustration.

"My treat," I said.

"Honest?"

"Let's go see *The One-Armed Swordsman* at New World."

"Great!" he exclaimed. "I think Wang Yu's the best swordsman there is."

"If we hurry," I said as I got to my feet, "we can make the four-thirty show."

We made our way out of the Barbarian as quickly as we could and ran down several of Westgate's busy streets to the New World Theater. It was the final day for *The One-Armed Swordsman*, and a Sunday to boot, so the best seats were sold out. We bought two tickets way up front in the third row, so we had to lean way back to see the screen. All the heads seemed bigger than normal, and the killing, the blood, the flying leaps through the air, the swords, the knives, everything seemed to come raining down on our heads. I went out into the lobby and bought some dried beef. I shared it with Zhao Ying as we watched Wang Yu perform his magical somersaults and all his martial prowess — a real pro. We ate it up.

"They ought to make a sequel," Zhao Ying mused with anticipation as we were leaving the theater.

"I'll write one," I said.

"Like what?"

"I'll call it 'The Armless Swordsman.' We'll take off Wang Yu's other arm."

"Then how'll he use his sword?"

"Dummy, haven't you ever heard of body magic?" I laughed.

Zhao Ying laughed, too. We were in a pedestrian crosswalk at the time, and a taxicab came whizzing up and stopped right next to Zhao Ying. He reached out and banged the top of the cab with a resounding slap. Assuming one of Wang Yu's theatrical poses, he pointed at the cabbie with two fingers and shouted:

"You there, watch your manners, the little swordsman is here!"

We ran across the street, leaving the cabbie's curses in our wake. Now that it was a little past six o'clock, Westgate started getting busier, and wherever we walked there were throngs of people. It was getting dark, people were everywhere. By then we were pretty thirsty, what with the dried beef and all, but since I only had about twenty yuan left, I bought a couple of popsicles at a refreshment stand. We ate them as we walked down Wuchang Street, heading toward the bank of the Tamsui River. The sun setting on the other side of the river was a red ball of flames that seemed to set the water on fire.

The area around Sluice Gate No. 5 of the Tamsui River was the outer fringe of the busy Westgate district. The rows of tall buildings started getting lower out here, until they turned into a line of run-down tenement buildings that seemed to have been pushed and shoved by the taller buildings until they were about to crumble and slide into the river. All the noise and bustle of Westgate petered out down here; the place was dreary. The people who lived in these squat tenement buildings were, for the most part, lumber dealers, so there was timber stacked up all over the riverbank, and lots more soaking in the water, covered with mold. Zhao Ying and I wound our way through the stacks of timber and climbed up to the bank. It was completely deserted. The water below was bathed in the red light of the setting sun, sparks shooting off the lapping waves. The sky above Sanchong City, on the other side of the river, was black with the smoke of burning coal, blurring the rooftops and giving the place the appearance of a huge, filthy dump. Beyond Sanchong City, Zhongxing Bridge stretched out across the river; it was filled with cars and trucks crawling back and forth like an army of gigantic black ants. A huge black barge, filled with coal sludge, was slowly chugging up the river, heading straight for that fireball in the sky.

"Look how red the sun is!" Zhao Ying shouted when he reached the top of the bank and started running toward the setting sun. His shirttails flapped in the wind, his reflection jumped and danced under the bright red sun. When he reached the end he stopped, turned, and signaled me with his arms to join him. I ran as quickly as I could, and he was still breathing hard when I reached him.

"Look," he said, "someone's fishing down there."

Alongside the river, not far from where we were standing, two fishing poles were stuck in the sand, but there was no one around. The poles were bent from the tug of the lines in the water.

"There's lots of fish in there. I've fished here before," I said.

"Really? What kind of fish?"

"Gold carp, plain carp, silver carp, all kinds."

"Did you ever catch anything?"

"Sure, lots."

"Honest?"

"I brought my little brother here once, and we caught two really big carp."

"Wow! Carp in bean sauce is one my favorite things to eat!" Zhao Ying said with a laugh.

"Carp are easy to catch. There's lots of 'em here because the water's so dirty."

"What'd you use for bait?"

"Worms. You can dig them right here on the bank. They're as thick as your finger."

"That's great!" Zhao Ying clapped his hands gleefully. He sat down on the bank. "Let's come here and dig for worms someday and catch some fish, okay?"

"Okay," I agreed. I sat down next to him. There was something hard in my back pocket. I reached back and took it out. It was the harmonica.

"What kind is it?" Zhao Ying asked when he saw the harmonica in my hand.

"Butterfly." I handed it to him.

"That's a good brand," he said as he examined it carefully.

"Do you know how to play?" I asked him.

"Sure," he said proudly, throwing his head back. "I'm the president of our school's harmonica club. I even represented the school at the Youth Day contest. Took second place."

"Let's hear you play something," I said.

"What do you want to hear?"

"What have you learned lately?"

"I know how to play 'You Are My Sunshine.' Ever heard it?"

"Oh, so you even know foreign songs!"

"You are my sunshine,

"My only sunshine,

"You make me hap—py

"When skies are gray——"

He sang the first few lines for me.

"An American priest who teaches at our school taught it to us."
He held the harmonica in both hands and tried it out, then
started to play. He played skillfully and with ease, all the harmonies pure and right on pitch.

"You're pretty good," I commented when he finished, clapping
and smiling to show my appreciation.

"Great harmonica!" Zhao Ying said. "I used to have a Guo-
guang that was just as good, but I left it in the dormitory and
some rat swiped it. Boy, was I mad! I couldn't eat for days. Guess
what my stepmother said when I told her I wanted to buy a new
one. 'I'm glad you lost it. That thing was the reason you neglected
your studies.' Is it any wonder I got mad?"

Zhao Ying kept fussing with the harmonica, cleaning it off
with his shirttail each time he played it.

"You can have it," I said.

"Honest?" Zhao Ying looked at me disbelievingly, his eyes as
big as saucers.

"If you'll play me one more song, you can keep it."

"No problem. What do you want to hear this time?"

"How about 'Plum Blossoms in the Snow'?"

"You got it!"

He wiped the harmonica off with his shirttail, tried it out
again, and began playing "Plum Blossoms in the Snow." He was
sitting on the ground with his legs tucked under him, and his
head was cocked as he skilfully slid the harmonica back and
forth past his lips, moving his cupped hand in and out. His round
face was shiny and red under the light of the setting sun, which
glinted off the harmonica in his hands. A warm evening breeze
swept across from the Tamsui River, carrying the strains of harmonica music up into the sky. Both Buddy and I had learned
"Plum Blossoms in the Snow" in school from our teacher, Wu
Aiyu. Buddy had a nice voice and loved to sing; when he was
taking a bath he sang happily from start to finish. He probably
inherited that from Mother. Wu Aiyu was very fond of Buddy,
and said he had musical talent. On her recommendation, he
joined a church choir, and every Sunday he put on a white choir
robe and sang hymns. I always thought it was funny the way he
opened his mouth so round when he sang. For our middle-school
commencement services, Wu Aiyu had Buddy come up on stage
and sing "Plum Blossoms in the Snow," with her accompanying
him on the piano. He was wearing his Boy Scout uniform with a
white scarf around his neck, held together in front with a silvery

ring, and his normally pale baby face was flushed bright red with excitement. He was so nervous his voice trembled. After he finished and came back down to his seat, he asked me, A-qing, how'd I do? Not so hot, I said. He was so anxious he broke out in a sweat. The teacher said he hadn't done bad at all. You were just too nervous. Your voice was trembling. Oh! Oh! Buddy kept stamping his foot in exasperation. Not bad. Really, not bad! Filled with emotion, just like Caruso, I said with a smile as I patted him on the shoulder. Really? He kept asking from behind me. Really, A-qing? Don't get so nervous, Buddy, I told him. I'll think of something, Buddy. A-qing, I don't want to go to Datong Vocational School. Buddy was sitting on the riverbank, holding his harmonica in his hands. I want to go to the National Academy of Arts and Music. Don't worry, Buddy, I'll come up with something. But Daddy says it's a waste of time to study music. Buddy lowered his head, his shoulders slumped, but he held tightly onto his harmonica. I'll think of something, I said, Buddy, wait a couple of years, wait till I've got a job, and I'll pay for your education. But Daddy says you can't make a living by studying music, Buddy's head drooped lower, rays of the setting sun glinted off his harmonica, flashes of red. Buddy, don't worry, I said. Daddy says that if I go to Datong I can get a job in a factory as soon as I graduate. Wait a couple of years, Buddy. I don't want to work in a factory, Buddy's voice was trembling. Wait till I've got a job, and I'll pay for your education. I want to go to the Arts Academy. Wait a couple of years, Buddy. Sparks flew from the harmonica in Buddy's hands. Buddy. Buddy. The nape of his neck shone bright red in the light of the setting sun. Buddy, don't worry. Buddy. Buddy. Buddy ——

"Hey —— "

He shouted in alarm. He was struggling with all his might. I wrapped my arms around him from the back and held him as tightly as I could. I pressed my face up against the nape of his neck. I was holding him so tightly my arms were getting sore. He jabbed me in the ribs with his elbow. The pain made me loosen my grip. He jumped away and turned to face me, fear written all over his face. He was breathing hard. After a moment, he threw the harmonica down at my feet, and said in a shaky voice:

"You, what the hell do you think you're doing —— "

The rays of the setting sun were so bright I couldn't open my eyes. All my blood seemed to rush to my head. My head ached, my temples throbbed, my ears were ringing. I saw Zhao Ying's body leaping rapidly in the light of the setting sun, and in a flash it was nothing more than a tiny dot disappearing at the far end of the riverbank. The bank was deserted. The harmonica was lying on the ground, glinting brightly. I bent over to pick it up and started following the river toward Zhongxing Bridge. Illuminated by fluorescent bridge lights, it looked like a white rainbow stretched out over the Tamsui River. I turned and looked behind me, where I saw the neon lights of Westgate distict lighting up the sky, a forest of brightly colored clouds.

8

It was dark inside. The light bulb was broken, so the only light in the room came from the neon signs of the China Bazaar filtering in through the window facing the railroad tracks. I could see his eyes in the dark, the urgent gleam of those cat-like pupils. The tall, heavy-set man was waiting anxiously in the middle of the room. I stood in front of the sink and turned on the faucets, then washed my hands over and over under the running water. The strong smell of ammonia rose from the toilet beside me in the heated air of the dark room. Several music stores downstairs turned up the volume on their recorded pop songs to see who could play it the loudest before closing up for the day. The water had been running for at least ten minutes when he began walking hesitantly toward me, heavily, searchingly.

I could see his balding gray head floating up and down in the surrounding darkness. That night, in the school chemistry lab, I'd also seen Zhao Wusheng's big bald head bobbing up and down urgently. The acrid smell of nitric acid permeated the lab. The top of the experiment table, occupying the middle of the room like an operating table, was pitted by the corrosive nitric acid, and it hurt my back when I lay on it. Test tubes filled with nitric acid, whose fumes stung my eyes and nose, filled the racks on either side of the table. I lay there on the experiment table that night, feeling as though someone were pounding the inside of my head with a mallet—bang, bang, bang—nearly knocking the top of my head off. I'd watched them drive five-inch nails into the lid of Buddy's light casket. Every pounding of the hammer caused a spasm in my heart. Those nails were so long, I was sure they were driving them into Buddy's flesh. They'd buried Buddy the day before. The pallbearers slowly lowered his light casket into the dark hole in the ground, and when it hit bottom, everything went black as I passed out cold. A train came rumbling down the tracks behind the China Bazaar, right through the heart of Westgate district. The sound was drawing nearer, getting louder, it was right beneath the window — suddenly, all the buildings in the China Bazaar began to shake. I looked out the window at the bright lights, and was nearly overcome by a desire to flee, to fly right out the window. But I didn't succumb to the urge; instead I stuffed the wad of warm, damp bills into my pants pocket without counting them, turned on the faucets again in the dark, and let the cold water run through the fingers of my dirty, sweaty hands.

9

LITTLE HAWK——

When I returned to the park I ran into the gray-haired gardener, Grandpa Guo, at the main gate. Dressed all in black, he greeted me from the steps of the museum.

I'd met Grandpa Guo my first night at the park, after being kicked out of my house. Since I didn't have any money on me, I wandered the streets of Taipei late into the night, before winding up in the park. I'd heard stories about the park before, but they sounded like old fantasy tales. That night, as I stood on the stone steps of the museum, just beyond the main gate of the park, and looked up at the curved dome rising majestically into the vast sky above, a row of thick stone columns guarding the doors, I felt like I'd entered a gigantic mausoleum. I walked through the darkened stands of trees inside the park, fearful, curious, even a little excited. After groping my way into the octagonal pavilion in the middle of the lotus pond, I huddled in a corner and held my breath as I looked out through the latticework in the dim red light of the moon. I saw, for the first time, the dark flickering shadows on the steps walking round and round the pond, never stopping. Hungry and exhausted, I curled up on the bench and dozed off.

"Son——" A voice next to my ear.

I woke with a start and sat straight up. It was Grandpa Guo, who'd come into the pavilion and awakened me.

"Don't be frightened, son," he said with a reassuring pat on my shoulder.

I was so cold my teeth were chattering, and I was unable to say a word. When Grandpa Guo sat down beside me, I could dimly see his white hair, combed back behind his ears like fine silver threads, and his powdery white eyebrows.

"Your first time here, I reckon," he commented with a nod of his head, a smile, a sigh. His voice was old and raspy. "No need to be nervous, we're all the same here. Sooner or later you all come flying over to the safety of this nest. I've been a gardener here for a long time. Everybody calls me Grandpa Guo. When you youngsters come here you always check in with me first. Say, look over there . . ."

He pointed to a tall, slender figure in black gliding round the steps of the lotus pond.

"That skinny devil over there is Little Zhao, but everybody calls him Death Angel Zhao. Twelve years ago, when he checked in at the park for the first time, it was me who met him."

"Twelve years ago?" I remarked in amazement.

"Ah," Grandpa Guo sighed. "Twelve years is a long time, isn't it? That's right, on a night twelve years ago, yep, he flew into this nest of ours, just like you. Back then he wasn't all wasted away, like an opium addict, but solid and good looking. Who'd have guessed that he'd waste away in a few years till he was a bag of bones. I'll bet he doesn't weigh a hundred pounds. I took some pictures of him back then, but if you saw them you wouldn't believe it's the same person . . ."

He shook his head.

"Have you ever heard of Youth Photo Studio?"

"No."

"Dumb little kid, how could you not know a famous studio like that!" He laughed. "It's on Changchun Road. I run it. I used to have a pretty good reputation as a photographer. But I just take pictures because I enjoy it. I like to find subjects with spirit, people with character. Like these babies here in the park. They may be wild, but they've got character. They're the type I like. I've got a thick album of their photographs."

He stood up.

"Son, this is no place for you to sleep, unless you want to catch cold. You come home with me. I've got some rice cake and some green-bean porridge there. Come with me and I'll show you my masterpieces. I'll tell you some stories about the park."

Grandpa Guo's Youth Photo Studio was in a lane off Section Two of Changchun Road. It was a two-story building, the studio occupying the ground floor. The display window was filled with beautiful portraits.

"That's Yang Feng. You know who he is, don't you?" He pointed to a photo of an extremely handsome young man. I shook my head. The young man, whose hair was combed neatly forward, had a broad smile on his face.

"He was a famous actor in Taiwanese films a decade or so ago. He starred in *Night in a Rainy Harbor* and *The Mournful City.*"

"I've heard of *The Mournful City,* but I never saw it," I said, recalling that my mother had gone to see the picture three times, crying after each time.

"Of course not, it's an old, old movie." He smiled. "Yang Feng still comes to the park once in a while, but now he always wears a beret to cover up his baldness. But what a figure he cut when he starred in *The Mournful City*! Everyone called him Taiwan's Takarata Akira. It's a good thing I took this picture of him and preserved his youth for all time."

Grandpa Guo led me upstairs to his living quarters. The living-room walls were covered with photographs of people and scenery, all of them black-and-whites. There were photos of age-worn temples and apricot blossoms, even close-ups of a wrinkled old face and the bare bottom of a newborn baby.

"I used to compete in photo contests, and even won grand prize for one of my portraits. But I'm too old now." He showed me his knotty, vein-covered hands. "Got rheumatism so bad I can't hold a camera without shaking."

He told me to sit down, then walked over to the refrigerator to take out a chilled plate of milky-white rice cake and pour a bowl of green-bean porridge. He set them down on the table in front of me. Without waiting for him to say a thing, I dug into the cake with my grimy fingers and shoved a big hunk into my mouth. The second piece followed before I'd even swallowed the first, and in no time the plate was empty. Then I picked up the bowl of porridge and slurped it so fast it ran down my chin.

"Tsk-tsk," he clicked his tongue. "You must have been famished. Probably haven't eaten all day, huh? Did you run away from home?"

I wiped my chin with the back of my hand, but didn't say anything.

"You aren't even wearing shoes!" Grandpa Guo said with a

sigh, pointing to my muddy feet. He reached down and picked up a pair of straw sandals, which he laid next to my feet. "You don't have to say anything. I can probably guess what happened. I've seen my share of wild little kids like you over the years. I'll go change my clothes, then I'll tell you some of the history of the park this old gardener's seen."

He hobbled into his bedroom and emerged a few minutes later dressed in a white silk bathrobe and a pair of black satin house slippers. He glided over and sat down beside me, holding something wrapped in blue cloth in his hands.

"Son, I'll show you this treasure of mine." He untied the cloth with shaky hands and opened it up to reveal a five-inch-thick photo album with a scarlet velvet cover stamped with the words "Birds of Youth" in gold letters. The velvet cover was turning black from age, the gold letters had begun to flake.

"The park's history is all right here..." He slowly lifted back the cover.

Every page of the album was filled with photographs, and all of them, big and small, were of young men; every imaginable pose and expression. Some were of seventeen- or eighteen-year-olds with their heads held high and their chests thrust out defiantly; others were cowering, their staring eyes filled with more pain and fear than they should know at their age; one had a harelip, another had his arm in a cast, many had an explosion of pimples on their noses. But there were some with regular features, intelligence written on their faces and in their eyes. Each photograph had a number below it, followed by the date and the subject's name.

"Ah, there's my little Sparrow," Grandpa Guo said as he rubbed his finger lightly over one of the photos, a look of tender affection spreading across his face. He had so many wrinkles that when he laughed his face seemed to crack. The photo was of a barefoot boy with a shaved head and dimples on his smiling cheeks. One of his front teeth was missing. The key below said #43, Hanzai, 1956.

"The little guy was only fourteen when he wandered off alone to Taipei from the little town of Yilan. He lied, he stole, everything, a kid who didn't know the meaning of the word shame. He pestered me day in and day out to buy him some ice cream. A master at blackmail, he refused to let me take his picture unless I bought him a whole tub of coconut ice cream. Then one day he

73

simply flew away. He left me a note: I've left, Grandpa Guo, I took fifty yuan..."

He shook his silver-gray head.

"I bumped into Sparrow again a couple of years later, hiding in a dark, remote lane off Three Rivers Street, alongside a stinking gutter. He was covered with syphilis sores."

He turned the page. There was a full-figure shot of a young man with an angry scowl on his face who was leaning up against a crumbling wall at the entrance to a mean-looking lane. He was wearing a sleeveless undershirt, with one hand on his waist to show off his bulging muscles. His bristly hair was standing straight up.

"That's him!" Grandpa Guo jammed his finger down hard on the picture of the young man.

"Look here." He opened the collar of his robe and showed me a three-inch zigzagging scar in the folds of his neck beneath his ear. "That little thug nearly cost me my life. His name is Iron Ox and he was meaner and more vicious than one of those evil owls! Last New Year's Eve he came to me for some money, so I gave him a hundred. But that wasn't enough, and he got so abusive I slapped him across the face. That's when the little assassin came at me with a knife!"

He puffed angrily.

"But I can't say the little sonofabitch didn't have any conscience at all, because he came back late that night, and since I wouldn't open the door for him, he jumped the wall and came in through the window. He threw himself down at my feet and cried like a baby, banging his head on the floor and begging me to forgive him and take him back. Grandpa Guo, he kept saying, Grandpa Guo. He was arrested a while back for going through the park demanding a 'love tax' and cutting the girls' dresses with his knife. After putting him through the mill, they were going to send him to a reform camp on one of the small islands, and it was all I could do to get him released to me. When I asked him why he didn't change his ways, he said it was because he hated women. 'You say you hate women,' I said. 'Well, what about your mother, she's a woman, isn't she?' You know what he said? 'Maybe she is and maybe she isn't!'"

He laughed and shook his head.

"Have you ever heard anything so perverse in your life? But there was some logic to what he said, since he had no idea who his mother was. He grew up in the gutters of Sanchong City and was quite a troublemaker. I hate to think about what he might do someday!"

Grandpa Guo got up and made a pot of strong tea. He poured me a cup, and as we sat there drinking tea, he went through the thick photo album page by page, relating to me one tale after another concerning the park, each one more interesting than the last, and each one more frightening...

"Ah, this one's Momotaro—Peach Boy. He does look a little like Kobayashi Akira, doesn't he? His father was a Japanese who died in the Philippines during the war. He may look delicate and refined, but he had an explosive temper. For some reason, he fell in love with a barber, Number Thirteen, from the Westgate district, and they went down south together, to Tainan. Number Thirteen was engaged at the time, so his family went down, brought him back, and forced him to go through with the marriage. Peach Boy attended the banquet, where he and the bridegroom drank one toast after another, until he was roaring drunk. Who could have imagined that when the meal was over, he'd walk over to the Zhongxing Bridge and jump into the Tamsui River? They never found his body. Number Thirteen went to the Tamsui River every day to pray, but Peach Boy's body never floated to the surface. People say there was so much hurt and anger in his heart that he sank straight to the bottom, where he stayed..."

"This one, this one here's Tu Xiaofu. I went to see him at the Taiwan Mental Hospital only last month. I took him some cookies. As soon as he saw me he grabbed hold of my sleeve and asked me with a giggle, 'Grandpa Guo, has the flight from the States arrived?' Five years ago Tu Xiaofu got involved with an overseas Chinese boy from the States who'd come to learn Chinese. They were a real hot item for a while, but then the Chinese boy from America went back to the States, and Tu Xiaofu's mind just snapped. Every day he went to the Northwest Airlines ticket counter at the airport and asked them, 'Has the flight from the States arrived?'"

"These little birds," he said emotionally, "are okay as long as feelings aren't involved. But as soon as they let their emotions take over there's trouble."

Grandpa Guo turned to a page in the middle of the album, and stopped. A single photo nearly filled the page. The key beneath it said:

#50. Phoenix Boy, 1960.

It was a 6×8 black-and-white glossy of a strange-looking eighteen- or nineteen-year-old boy taken from the waist up. He was wearing a black shirt with an upturned collar; all the buttons were missing, and the shirttails were tied together just below his navel. His exposed chest was covered with tattoos of phoenixes and kirins. Right in the middle of his chest was a one-horned dragon with its fangs and claws bared. The boy's black, bushy hair, like the mane of an angry lion, covered his forehead. Thick eyebrows ran arrogantly from one side of his forehead to the other in an unbroken line. A sharp, angular nose, thin lips pressed tightly together. His big, radiant eyes, sunk deep in their sockets, hid daintily under domineering eyebrows above a triangular, nearly chinless, pointy face.

Grandpa Guo stared at the photo for the longest time, as the light glinted off his silver hair.

"Of all these youngsters, his life was the most bizarre, and the most tragic..."

Grandpa Guo's aging, raspy voice suddenly turned mournful and began to flow very, very slowly.

10

"Phoenix Boy was born in the Wanhua District, near Dragon Mountain Temple. He was a wild kid with no father and no surname. His mother, a mute who wasn't very bright, always had a foolish grin on her face when she was around men, but there was something about the way she looked that made her appealing. She was a chubby girl with skin as fair as virgin snow, and everyone called her 'Sister Dumpling' because as a little girl she helped her father at his dumpling stand on Huaxi Street next to Dragon Mountain Temple. Her job was to stop potential customers with her grunting noises; everyone thought it was so cute they'd buy a couple of dumplings from her. Even after she grew up she did what she pleased, which included roaming to the brothel district, wearing wooden clogs and nibbling on pieces of roasted squid as she clomped noisily down the street without a care in the world. She'd smile at the men out looking for a good time. Some of the neighborhood thugs took advantage of the fact that she was a mute by dragging her off and raping her, and when she got home she frantically tried to tell her father what had happened with grunts and hand motions; when he saw that her hair was a mess and there was blood on her skirt, he beat her nearly to death. Every time he beat her she'd run off barefoot to Dragon Mountain Temple and sit on the curb to cry. When the neighborhood peddlers saw her crying on the curb they'd look knowingly at each other and comment with a laugh, 'Sister Dumpling's been stuck again !' When she was eighteen, she closed up at dusk one evening as a typhoon threatened and pushed her cart homeward. On the way she ran into a pack of thugs — five in all — who dragged her off, but this time she put up a fight, so they tied her up, knocking out one of her front teeth in the process. When they were finished with her they dumped her in a stagnant ditch behind Dragon Mountain Temple, where she lay in the filthy water with the storm beating down on her. She finally crawled out and dragged herself home. That was the night she got pregnant. Her father made her take a concoction of local medicine that nearly killed her, but no matter how bad the vomiting and diarrhea got, the fetus hung on. When her time came, she gave birth to a strapping, bawling son after more than two days of agonizing labor. Her father didn't waste a second in wrapping up the bawling baby in straw matting and delivering it to a foundling hospital that very night. Phoenix Boy grew up in a Catholic orphanage in the suburb of Zhonghe.

"Phoenix Boy was a gifted, clever child from the very beginning. He was so smart there was nothing he couldn't learn. The priests taught him the Catechism, and he had it memorized after one reading. One of the brothers at the orphanage, a Henanese named Sun who was particularly fond of him, taught him how to write and read him Bible stories. But with his volatile temper, you'd never know what Phoenix Boy would do; he ran hot and cold, and you couldn't predict if something would please or anger him. A loner by nature, he hardly ever mixed with the other kids, and if one of them angered him, he'd punch first and ask questions later. Eventually, they ganged up on him, but he just let them pelt him with dirt and rocks, without raising a finger in defense, then went over to the sink and cleaned himself off. When Brother Sun asked him why his face was bruised, he kept his mouth shut and didn't say a word. Phoenix Boy had a strange flaw as a child — he'd suddenly burst out crying, seemingly for no reason at all, and keep it up for hours. He'd cry so hard he'd shake from head to toe. Sometimes, in the middle of the night, he'd sneak off to the little chapel in the orphanage, sit down in one of the pews, and cry to himself. If Brother Sun found him there and asked why he was crying, he'd say he had a pain in his heart, and the only thing that drove it away was crying. As Phoenix Boy grew up, he became more and more perverse all the time. One Christmas night, the director of the orphanage took all the children to a mass in the chapel, but Phoenix Boy refused to go up and take communion. When the director chastised him, he exploded, running up to the altar and smashing several of the ceramic icons. The director restricted him to his room for a week because of what he'd done, and every day Brother Sun knelt with him as they recited the rosary. Phoenix Boy ran away from the orphanage when he was fifteen and never went back.

"Phoenix Boy showed up at the park like a wild stallion, charging about with that unbridled power of his, and no one knew how to tame him. Even me he listened to only about a third of the time. Not long after he first showed up he had a run-in with some young thugs with criminal records from Sanchong City, and got stabbed several times. I'm the one who brought him home and nursed him back to health. He'd lie there in bed, rubbing the angry red knife wound in his abdomen, and say to me with a smile:

"'Just a little deeper, Grandpa Guo, and you could've been spared a lot of trouble!'

"Phoenix Boy, he was really a child of the park, a wild phoenix, just like his name. He cruised the steps of the lotus pond, his black mane-like hair uncombed, his head high, his chest thrown out, like everybody else was beneath his notice. A lot of the oldtimers fell under his spell, including Lord Sheng from the Eternal Youth Film Studio. Lord Sheng wanted him for his own, so he took him to his home on Eight Virtues Road, where he made him over from head to toe; he took him to a Shanghai tailor shop in Westgate and ordered a custom-made gray flannel suit, then went to a jewelry store and bought him a Rolex watch with a silver case. Once he'd turned him into someone who looked like the young scion of a wealthy family, Lord Sheng took him to the best Western restaurants in town. He wanted to make something of the boy, and planned to send him to school to learn the ropes about movies and someday become a film star. But our young wild phoenix lived in Lord Sheng's home all of one week before he came flying back to the park. He'd pawned the suit and the watch for several thousand, so he took all his wild friends over to Chief Yang's restaurant, Taoyuan Spring, and ordered a meal for two tables. They ate and drank like there was no tomorrow, until they were stuffed *and* drunk. Then he climbed up on one of the tables and began to sing 'Flowers in the Rainy Night.' Just when everyone was clapping, shouting, and having a wonderful time, he jumped down off the table and walked out without a word.

"He was unpredictable, and the people in the park knew it, so they were careful not to do anything that might set him off. When he was eighteen, the fateful meeting occurred between him and the son of a high-ranking official, an only son named Dragon Prince, after the sign under which he was born. Handsome, well born, a college graduate who had a job in a foreign company and was planning to go overseas for more schooling, his future looked bright. Meeting up with Phoenix Boy was something no one could have predicted, particularly since sparks flew, and nothing could put out the fire. Dragon Prince rented an apartment at the end of Songjiang Road, where he quietly built a little nest to hide his Phoenix Boy. Back then, that part of Songjiang Road was no more than rice paddies, which extended right up to the building where they lived, giving them a panoramic view of lush green rice sprouts. The two of them would run out into the paddies, barefoot and shirtless, to dig up snails and loaches or sit down in the muddy field and share a muskmelon. Those were happy times for the two of them. But it wasn't in the wild phoenix's nature to stay in his nest like a good little fledgling, and sometimes he'd fly back to the park in the middle of the night to sit on the stone railing of the lotus pond and look up into the sky, counting the stars. Dragon Prince would follow him over and try to get him to come home, but he'd say, 'This is my home, so where do you want me to go?' Dragon Prince was as hot-tempered as he was, and without another word, the two of them would tear into each other, fighting until their clothes were in shreds. When it was over, they'd sit on the steps, holding each other and wailing. Everyone laughed and said they were 'love crazy.' Often, during those days, Dragon Prince would jump in a taxi and ride all over Taipei, asking everyone he knew, 'Have you seen Phoenix Boy?' Since some of the people he asked were either jealous or enjoyed seeing other people suffer, they'd make up things like 'Phoenix Boy went over to New South Seas' or 'Phoenix Boy went with somebody for a late snack at Taoyuan Spring.' 'Phoenix Boy? Didn't he go off with Lord Sheng?' Dragon Prince invariably believed them and went looking for him where they'd said, sometimes until the sun came up the next morning, when he'd drag himself back to the park, dejected and forlorn, and anxiously pace the steps of the lotus pond from one end to the other.

"Phoenix Boy came over here one night, his face ashen, his sunken eyes looking like they were going to jump out of their sockets.

"'Grandpa Guo...' The pain in his voice was unmistakable. 'I have to leave him. If I don't, he's going to reduce me to a pile of ashes. When I ask him what he wants, he says, I want that heart of yours. I tell him I was born without one. So he says, Then I'll give you mine. Honest, I'm really afraid that one day he's going to rip that thing right out of his chest and stuff it into mine. Grandpa Guo, you know I've spent most of my life running away. I ran away from the orphanage and came over to hang out in the park. I couldn't ask for a nicer place than the apartment he rented for me on Songjiang Road. And he sneaked a lot of things out of his home for me: electric fan, electric rice cooker, sofa, even his own TV, so I wouldn't be bored at night. But... but for some reason I can't stay there. All I think about is coming to the park. Grandpa Guo, I was fifteen when I started out. The first time I slept with someone I got a disease, and it was you who took me to Taipei Municipal Hospital for a penicillin shot, remember? Well, I ask him, This dirty, diseased body of mine, what do you want it for? So, he says, I'll lick every speck of dirt from your body, and I'll wash away all the disease with my tears. That's the talk of a madman, isn't it? I tell him, Not in this lifetime, but the next time around I'll get myself born into a good family and pay you back then. Grandpa Guo, I have to get out, fly away, start running again!'

"Phoenix Boy disappeared from sight for over two months, and Dragon Prince scoured the city for him, until his eyes were red and had the look of madness in them. Then late one night — New Year's Eve, it was — he found Phoenix Boy near the lotus pond. Phoenix Boy was leaning up against a stone railing, wearing a thin shirt in the cold night air and shivering. He was talking to an ugly, fat old man whose breath reeked of alcohol, trying to agree on a price. The old sot offered him fifty, and he was just about to go with him, when Dragon Prince ran up and blocked his way, begging him to come home with him. Phoenix Boy just shook his head and gazed helplessly into Dragon Prince's eyes. So Dragon Prince grabbed his hand and said, 'Then give me back my heart!' Phoenix Boy pointed to his own chest and said, 'It's here, take it.' Well, Dragon Prince took out a knife and plunged it into Phoenix Boy's chest. Phoenix Boy slumped to the ground, blood gushing out of his chest..."

Grandpa Guo stopped in mid-sentence; his eyelids began to close slowly, his cracked, wrinkled face seemed to be veiled by a cobweb.

"What happened then?" I asked haltingly after a long pause.

"What happened..." Grandpa Guo's raspy voice was trembling. "Dragon Prince sat down in the puddle of blood and held Phoenix Boy in his arms. His mind had snapped."

I stayed with Grandpa Guo for three days and listened to him relate a history of events of the park from beginning to end. He explained many of the unwritten laws of the park: who I could get close to, who I should keep my distance from, and how to recognize situations when I should stay away altogether. Grandpa Guo employed a photographer who took care of the regular customers in the Youth Photo Studio downstairs. But he personally took mine, upstairs, and developed it himself. Altogether he took more than ten shots, then chose one of them — shot from the waist up — to include in his "Birds of Youth." I became #87. Grandpa Guo said I resembled a little hawk, and when I looked into his mirror, I noticed that I did have a slight hook to my nose. Before I left, he handed me a set of old clothes, which Iron Ox had left behind; we were about the same size. Grandpa Guo stuffed a hundred-yuan bill into my shirt pocket, put his hands on my shoulders, and looked me straight in the eye as he said solemnly:

"Go on, A-qing, now it's your turn to fly. It's in your blood. All you wild youngsters who've grown up on this island have that strain of wildness in your blood, just like the typhoons and earthquakes that are part of this island. You're a bunch of fledglings who've lost your nest, like a flock of sea swallows crossing the ocean, struggling to keep flying ahead, with no idea where you'll wind up..."

11

"Well, he's back," Grandpa Guo mumbled as we walked up to the lotus pond.

"Who's that, Grandpa Guo?"

"That fellow you met last night."

"You know him?" I was surprised.

He nodded with a sigh.

"I knew he'd come back sooner or later."

When we reached the bottom of the steps, he stopped and pointed to the crowd of people at the top of the steps.

"Go on up," he said, "go listen to them. They haven't talked about anything else all night."

The scene at the top of the steps was like a moon surrounded by a galaxy of stars. A crowd of people was gathered around Chief Yang, who was talking animatedly. Everyone seemed pretty excited. Old Dick-Head, Death Angel Zhao, and a group of hustlers from Three Rivers Street were listening intently. The primitive A-xiong was standing behind Chief Yang, his head held high, his hands on his hips, looking bigger than ever and showing off like he was a bodyguard or something.

"Hey, you little queer, get over here!" Chief Yang snapped his two-foot-long fan in my direction. "Let me look you over," he bellowed, "to see if you're missing anything or if you've got any extra holes on your body."

As soon as I reached the top of the steps, he grabbed me and checked me out, front and back, then said with a laugh:

"Look's like luck was with you, since you came back alive. Do you know who you slept with last night?"

"His name was Wang Kuilong. He just came back from the States."

"Asshole!" Chief Yang smacked me on the back. "You don't know who Wang Kuilong is?"

"He doesn't know shit," Death Angel Zhao sneered. "Back then he was probably still wearing pants with an open crotch!"

Death Angel Zhao's gaunt, ugly face didn't seem as wide as my hand, and was resting atop a rail-thin body. He wore a black pullover and swished around, craning his neck as far as it would go. He'd been coming here longer than the rest of our crowd, and he never let us forget it, always bragging about how things were back then.

"My little precious," he said in a raspy voice that sounded

more like a raven's than a man's. His parted lips showed two rows of nicotine-stained teeth. "Last night you went to the Crystal Palace in the company of the 'Dragon Prince.'"

No event in the history of the park was better known than the story of "Dragon Prince and Phoenix Boy." It was passed on year after year, from one generation to the next, and had by now entered the legend of our kingdom. With the succeeding embellishments by the story tellers, Dragon Prince and Phoenix Boy had become supernatural characters. I was stunned by the news that the person lying beside me last night, stretching out his rake-like arms, was none other than the legendary, tall, handsome man who normally wore sky-blue shirts as he fell madly in love with the wild boy of the park — Dragon Prince.

"I had my suspicions last night," Chief Yang said as he fanned himself excitedly, "but he looked like someone who'd just crawled out of a furnace, so tanned his skin was almost black, and I didn't recognize him. But when he paced the steps, as though his heart was on fire, it was just like before. People say he's been in a mental institution all these years, but I've also heard he left the country right after it happened. Who'd have thought he'd burst back on the scene in the middle of the night, ten years later!"

"You said it!" Death Angel Zhao was thinking of the past again. "What I remember best was how he almost went crazy looking for Phoenix Boy. I shouldn't have tricked him by saying 'Phoenix Boy went home with Lord Sheng!' He dragged me into his taxi and made me take him to Lord Sheng's house and bang on his door in the middle of the night. Lord Sheng thought it was some thugs out there, so he called the police. Later on I asked Phoenix Boy, 'How come you're so cold-hearted?' But he just opened his shirt and showed me the tattoo of the single-horned dragon with its fangs and claws bared. 'Cold? You call me cold after I had him tattooed on my chest? What the hell do you know? One day he'll get the satisfaction he wants by tearing this to shreds!' We thought he was just popping off. Who'd have guessed that things would happen just like he said?"

"That guy Wang really thought he was hot stuff! So what if his father was a bigshot? He thought he was so much better than everybody else!" Old Dick-Head put in his own angry comment. His mouth was bright red from chewing on betel-nut. "One night he was sitting by himself on the steps, probably waiting for that little bitch of his, and since he looked kind of lonely, I walked over to chat with him out of the goodness of my heart. All I said was, 'Mr. Wang, I hear your father's a high-ranking official.' Well, he just walked away without giving me the time of day, like I was a leper or something."

"You shameless old fart!" Chief Yang cursed him with a smile. "If Wang Shangde wasn't a high-ranking official, I'd like to know what he was. Do you expect him to kiss up to an old ruffian like you? Just who the hell do you think you are, anyway? Why should he give you the time of day? Just another toad lusting after the flesh of a swan! I swear, you don't even have the shame to crawl off and die!"

We all laughed, while Old Dick-Head scratched the scaly ringworm on his neck without saying another word.

"Wang Shangde's funeral was on TV the other day," Death Angel Zhao said. "It was quite an event. The street was packed with mourners in white, and the guard of honor in front of the hearse was on motorcycles. Not your everyday funeral!"

I'd read about Wang Shangde's death in the newspaper; it was big news. Lots of important people had gone to his memorial service. His photograph and obituary notice filled half a page. He really looked impressive in his military dress uniform, and even though I didn't read the obituary closely, I noticed that it was packed with official titles.

"He got away with murder because he was the son of a high official," Old Dick-Head said spitefully.

"Got away with murder? His mind snapped!" Chief Yang shot back. "The judge said he didn't know the difference between right and wrong. I went to the trial, and when the prosecutor asked him why he did it, he just waved his arms and said, 'He stole my heart from me! He stole my heart from me!' If that's not the talk of a madman, what is it?"

"I remember the incident really caused a stir around town," Death Angel Zhao said as he lit a cigarette and took a deep drag. "There were stories in the Metro Section every day, and they ran pictures of Dragon Prince and Phoenix Boy. One newspaper ran a cutting headline, 'Phony Phoenix in Messy Affair; Boundless Lust Leads to Endless Hatred.' I was there when the trial began, too, at the courthouse across from the First Girls' High School. The place was packed, including lots of high-school girls. As soon as Wang Kuilong entered they started shouting, 'Dragon Prince, Dragon Prince...'"

"Boys!" Chief Yang suddenly raised his fan so that "Good

Dreams Are Gentle" showed. "Take off, here comes the fuzz!"

Off in the distance two policemen were swaggering toward the lotus pond. Their hobnailed boots were setting up a racket on the gravel path. We took off like frightened animals, running down the steps and spreading out to find a place to hide. Chief Yang, with A-xiong on his heels, expertly and calmly melted into the crowd of people in front of the loudspeaker stand. Our kingdom by the lotus pond suddenly ceased to exist, at least for the time being.

"A-qing!"

As I ran into the dark stand of trees I bumped into someone coming from the other direction. It was Little Jade.

12

"Tomorrow night, eight o'clock sharp, the Plum Orchard, don't be late!"

We were sitting in a loveseat on the second floor of the Great World on Hengyang Road, drinking lemonade. Little Jade's dancing almond-shaped eyes were shining with excitement. Great World was one of our favorite meeting places because it was so much more peaceful than the Barbarian Café.

"Where's the Plum Orchard?" I asked him.

"Jackass!" Little Jade punched me. "You've never heard of the Plum Orchard? Two lanes past the Ambassador Hotel on Sun Yat-sen North Road. The Taiwanese food there is better than Greenleaf or Plums. He's only taking the few of us there tomorrow night."

"What's so great about Taiwanese food? Since he's an overseas Chinese, why not get him to take us to a fancy restaurant like Five Blessings or the Cornucopia? That way we could have ourselves a real meal."

"Damn, don't you know anything?" Little Jade tried to sound very wise. "This is Lin *san*'s first visit after all those years, and what he's looking for is some regional, home-town food. Fancy restaurant? Don't you think there are businessmen just waiting to take him out? I like The Plum Orchard, because it's got atmosphere. Barbecued squid, abalone with hot dressing—dee-licious!"

Little Jade told me that the overseas Chinese from Japan, Lin Maoxiong, was a man in his fifties. He was born in Taipei, but during the war was conscripted into the Japanese army and sent to the China mainland to work in a military hospital in the Manchurian city of Changchun, where he served as an orderly for seven or eight years. While he was there he married a girl from Manchuria, who bore him a boy and a girl. After the war, he and a friend from Manchuria took their families to Japan, where they pooled their resources to start up a business. After years of hardship, it had finally begun to pay off. He was in Taipei as a representative of the Tokyo Seijyo Pharmaceutical Company, sent to set up a distribution outlet. This was his first opportunity to come back home after all these years.

"I spent all day with Lin *san* showing him around Taipei. We had a great time!" Little Jade's face was flushed with excitement. "A-qing, Lin *san*'s really a nice guy. Look —" He showed me his new red and black cashmilon pullover. "He bought me this."

"You little manipulator!" I said with a laugh. "Your eyes light up whenever you spot a Chinese from Japan. Don't tell me you're really looking for an overseas sugar daddy again!"

Little Jade sneered.

"What's wrong with that? My real daddy was an overseas Chinese. He's in Japan right now . . ."

"Oh?" That caught me by surprise. "Why didn't you tell me? You said your father's been dead for years, that he's buried near your home in Yangmei. The other day I heard you ask Old Zhou for some money so you could buy some incense for your father's grave. You could kill a person with your lies!"

"Tell you?" Little Jade snorted. "Why should I tell you? I've never told anyone."

The one thing we denizens of the park never talk about is our own family backgrounds. And even if we do, we don't say much, since every one of us has his own private anguish that can never be told to anyone.

"A-qing, tell me," Little Jade cocked his head with a mischievous grin, "do you have a father?"

"What kind of dumb question is that?"

"What's his name?"

"Li! What do you think!" I resented his question, but covered up my anger by taking a big drink of lemonade.

"Is that really his name? Do you really know who your father is? Hm?" The grin turned malicious.

"Fuck you!" I threw a punch his way.

"Heh, heh." He was extremely pleased with himself. "How can you get so mad over an innocent question like that?"

He bent over and silently drank his lemonade. After a long moment, his head shot up, snapping the hair that had fallen over his forehead straight back. His cheeks were flushed, his almond-shaped eyes flashed.

"Tell you guys? Tell you that I'm a bastard? I never laid eyes on my father, don't even know who he was. My name's not Wang, that's my mother's name. She told me my father was an overseas Chinese from Japan named Lin, Lin Zhengxiong. His Japanese name was Nakajima. On my I.D. card the line for father reads 'Deceased.' When people ask about my father, I say 'Dead.' 'Been dead for years.' I pretend I don't give a damn..." Little Jade shrugged his shoulders. "But I can't help wondering where that sonofabitch is. Tokyo? Osaka? Maybe out in the middle of the Pacific Ocean? He came to Taiwan on business, as a salesman for Shiseido cosmetics. He met my mother at a girlie restaurant, and that's how they got together. My mother says she was tricked by that sonofabitch! When he went back to Japan he told her he'd send for her in a month. She was already pregnant with me by then. The last thing she figured was that even his Tokyo address was a phony, but every letter she sent him was returned. Ever since I was a kid I told her, 'Mother, don't worry, I'll go get your Nakajima back for you.' I used to spend almost all my time running around to the tourist hotels—the Ambassador, the First Hotel, the Inn of the Sixth Happiness—every one of 'em. You know why?"

"Looking for customers?"

"Balls!" He laughed. "I went to the registration desk to look at their guest list and find out who came from Japan. Boy, that was tough! First I looked for his Chinese name, then his Japanese name. I often dreamed that one day my overseas Chinese daddy would suddenly return from Japan, rich as a lord, and take Mother and me back to Japan with him."

"Your cherry blossom dream again!" I said with a laugh.

"You just wait, A-qing, one of these days I'll fly off to Tokyo and make a lot of money. Then when I've got enough I'll come back for my mother and take care of her, let her enjoy her last few years and realize her lifelong dream of going to Japan. I want her to leave the man she's with now—that no-good son of a bitch who won't even allow us to see each other!"

"Why not?"

"Ai," he sighed. "I put some insecticide in his noodles one time."

"Aren't you the one! So you poison people, too!" I stuck out my tongue.

"That big guy from Shandong isn't all that bad, except he goes around all day saying 'Screw your mother,' 'I'll screw your mother.'" Little Jade laughed. "He's a driver for a transport company, drives a big truck. He used to be a driver in the army. He's from Shandong, and built like a bull. He just picks my mother up and carries her off to bed. I used to get along with him okay, and whenever he came back from taking some stuff down to Taichung he'd bring me a box of my favorite dried pineapple. And when he had a couple of drinks he'd entertain me by screwing up his nose and singing Henanese folk songs like a woman. But one time I was going down on someone at home and he walked in and caught us!"

"You shameless whore, how could you bring one of your Johns home with you?" I exclaimed.

"What's the big deal?" He shrugged his shoulders. "When I was fourteen I used to take guys home and do it in the kitchen. We lived in Sanchong City, and there were lots of old guys in the neighborhood who were nice to me. They bought stuff for me — pens, shoes, shirts — and every time they bought me something I went down on them. I called them my sugar daddies. One of them, a guy with a pock-marked face who sold beef soup, liked me the best. At night I'd go to his stall, where he'd give me a huge bowl of steaming beef soup, filled with meat and vegetables. It was just what the doctor ordered. He had a wife at home, so I took him home with me and sneaked him into the kitchen. It was just my bad luck that the guy from Shandong chose that moment to walk in and catch us red-handed. You know what he hit me with? A chain from his truck! 'Fag! Fag!' he screamed as he beat me with that chain. The only reason I'm alive today is that my mother ran up and stopped him. So what do you think, did I have a reason to poison him or not?"

He gazed at me with a helpless look.

"Luckily, it didn't kill him," Little Jade added with a sigh. "They took him to the hospital and pumped his stomach, then my mother rushed home, bundled up my clothes and put a gold chain around my neck, and said to me, 'Get out while you can.

He'll kill you if he comes home and finds you here.' And that's how I became a 'street angel.'"

He giggled as he finished his story.

"Old Zhou came looking for you last night," I said, suddenly recalling my conversation with Moon Beauty. "She said the old tub was fit to be tied, and if he knew you were out on the prowl again, it'd be a wonder if he didn't skin you alive."

"Fuck him." Little Jade got to his feet and picked the check up off the table. "That stinking old guy's more trouble than he's worth. Old pal, I beg you, make up something, say I had my appendix out, anything!"

Moon Beauty still hadn't gotten off work by the time I returned to Jinzhou Street, and Obasan had already put Johnny Jr. to bed and turned out the lights. I groped my way over to my room, where I saw the string of tinfoil ingots glinting in the moonlight at the head of my bed, where I'd put them that afternoon. I went over and picked them up, walked through the kitchen out onto the balcony, where a stick of incense in a tin can filled with sand was still giving off a few sparks. Obasan had probably put it there. I bent down, struck a match, and lit the tinfoil ingots in my hand, which began to crackle, as they quickly turned to ashes, which floated to the ground and formed a small pile. I raised my head and looked up at the festival moon, perfectly round and bright red, falling to the west, where it seemed to be pressing down on a tall building off in the distance.

I returned to my room and fell into bed without even taking off my sweaty clothes. Numb from exhaustion, I lay on the straw mat feeling as though my limbs had detached themselves from my body; I couldn't move. The bright neon lights from the neighborhood bars came wriggling through my window like colorful snakes. Surprisingly, I was getting more and more clear-headed. This was the first night in more than three months that I found myself suddenly missing Buddy so much I could barely stand it.

13

We arrived at the Plum Orchard on Sun Yat-sen North Road precisely at eight p.m. Chief Yang had only invited A-xiong and the two of us. Raven wouldn't let Mousey out, and Wu Min, who was feeling dizzy, stayed at Chief Yang's house. Chief Yang was dressed to kill in a blue-striped seersucker sportcoat bulging here and there like a dumpling made of glutinous rice, and a wide green and red paisley silk tie. He was sweating so much his white shirt stuck to his skin. He'd gotten A-xiong to dress up, too, in an ill-fitting checked suit whose sleeves were so short all you could see were the cuffs of his shirt. His sloping shoulders and curved back made him look like a circus bear dressed in a jacket. Before we went inside, Chief Yang admonished us:

"Mind your manners tonight, and don't make me lose face in front of this overseas Chinese!"

The Plum Orchard really did have atmosphere. It had a Japanese flavor, with an arch bridge over a murmuring stream and a man-made hill on the other side, with a green lantern on the top. The restaurant was bright and clean, the air was refreshingly cool. Fan-shaped lights set into the walls gave off a subdued red light and infused the smiling faces of the hostesses with a soft red luster. Someone was playing an organ at the far end of the restaurant, the soft strains of music filling the air. A hostess led us up to the individual banquet rooms on the second floor, pulling back the curtain beads of the second room, where Little Jade and the overseas Chinese, Lin Maoxiong, were already waiting for us. As we entered, Lin Maoxiong jumped to his feet to greet us, with Little Jade right behind him. Lin was in his early fifties, gray around the temples, and was wearing a pair of silver-rimmed glasses over his even-featured, long face. The corners of his eyes crinkled when he smiled. He was wearing a steel-gray suit and a dark striped tie, held by a silver, jade-inlaid tieclasp. Chief Yang rushed over and shook Lin's hand warmly, then introduced him to A-xiong and me. Lin Maoxiong had Chief Yang sit in the seat of honor, between A-xiong and me. When we were all seated, Chief Yang pointed to Little Jade with his fan and said:

"What do you say, Lin *san*? Quite a well disciplined little disciple, wouldn't you say?"

"Jade's a nice boy," Lin said with a smile as he looked over at Little Jade. He had a heavy Manchurian accent. Little Jade, who was sitting right next to him, smiled sheepishly. He was wearing a pastel green shirt with a white collar, and his long hair was neatly combed, looking like he'd just blown it dry. He had a freshly scrubbed look.

"Jade here has been my tour guide for the past few days. He's taken me to lots of places. Taipei's changed so much I feel like a stranger."

Lin smiled and put his hand on Little Jade's shoulder.

"I took Lin *san* over to Huaxi Road at noon today for some fresh seafood. He said it's a lot cheaper than Tokyo, and better, too!" Little Jade was beaming.

"What do you say, Lin *san*, how will you thank his leader?" Chief Yang snapped open his fan and began fanning himself with it. Even though the restaurant was air-conditioned, sweat was streaming down Chief Yang's pudgy face.

"That's right, that's why I've invited Chief Yang to drink with me tonight," Lin said with a smile.

"Just drinking's not enough," Chief Yang said with a shake of his head. "When we have a chance to go to Tokyo some day, Lin *san* will have to show us around and let us expand our horizons. I hear the boys in Japan are real beauties!"

"When Chief Yang comes to Japan I'll definitely be your guide. I'll take you to Shinjuku for a real tour."

"I'm afraid that one look at the chief's face would scare the wits out of those Japanese boys!" Little Jade piped up.

"Hmph! I'll show you, you unfilial little swine!" Chief Yang shouted with a wave of his hand. But he quickly lowered his hand and sighed. "Lin *san*, you don't know how hard it is to be the chief once your disciples grow up. It's enough to make you sick! These wretches are so dumb I'm embarrassed to let them be seen in public. All except this one here, who's got a bit of the devil in him, and a mouth that can be as sharp as a dagger or as sweet as honey. Not just anyone can handle him. I'll tell you, Lin *san*, I think you two were made for each other."

"Jade and I get along fine," Lin said with a smile as he patted Little Jade on the head.

A teenage waitress parted the curtain and came in with a tray of cool towels for us to wipe our faces. She handed each of us a menu. Lin deferred to Chief Yang:

"Chief Yang, you're the expert, so you do the ordering. Taiwanese food was Jade's idea."

"That's easy, I'll eat anything, even human flesh!"

We all laughed, including the waitress, who covered her mouth with her hand.

"Okay, then, let's have some mussels, what they call Xishi Tongues. We can see what the tongues of beautiful women taste like!"

"Hai!" the waitress responded as she wrote it down.

"What would you like, Jade?" Lin Maoxiong turned and asked Little Jade.

"Barbecued squid, I want some barbecued squid!"

Next, Lin turned to A-xiong, who giggled:

"Chicken, chicken..."

"Don't make a spectacle!" Chief Yang cursed light-heartedly. "Bring him some barbecued drumsticks."

"Hai!" the waitress responded again.

I ordered a plate of crispy shrimp, and Lin Maoxiong ordered a few more dishes, including roast eel, hot beancurd, and slices of fried pork stomach with salted pickled vegetables.

"Japanese don't eat internal organs, so I haven't had any fried pork stomach for years," Lin said with a smile and a sigh.

"What would the gentlemen like to drink?" the waitress asked timidly.

"Heat up some of your best aged rice wine," Chief Yang told her, "and put in some dried sour plums."

The waitress went out to heat up a carafe of wine, and came back with a tall bottle of dried sour plums. Just as she was about to pour the wine, Little Jade took the carafe from her:

"That's okay, I'll do it."

The waitress turned and walked out. Little Jade poured the wine into the bottle of dried sour plums, and after letting it settle, filled Lin Maoxiong's glass, then the others, before standing up and holding his glass respectfully in both hands to Lin Maoxiong:

"Lin *san*, you've given me a great deal of face today, so I'll drink this glass for you to show my respect."

He tipped back his head and drained his glass. His face turned beet red almost at once, and his fetching eyes and eyelids sparkled.

"Take it easy, take it easy! Don't choke," Lin reached out to stop him.

"This is the first time I've ever swigged wine like that," Little Jade said with a smile. "You don't know how happy I am tonight. So it's okay if I get a little carried away."

"Tsk-tsk," Chief Yang clicked his tongue. "Lin *san*, you've got a rare talent—you seem to have found a way to turn this little two-faced imp into a model of politeness!"

"Jade's always been polite," Lin Maoxiong said with a smile. He took a drink of his wine.

"I'm afraid not!" Chief Yang said with a wave of his hand. "With other people he's like a fighting cock, always ready to claw you. No, you've tamed him."

"The food will be here in a minute. Wait till it comes before you drink any more. Drinking on an empty stomach will get you drunk," Lin said to Little Jade under his breath.

"Okay," Little Jade answered with a nod.

The waitress brought in the first two dishes — barbecued squid and barbecued drumsticks. Lin Maoxiong picked up a piece of barbecued squid and placed it on Little Jade's plate. When A-xiong spotted the crispy, oily, plump drumsticks he reached out with his huge hand and grabbed one. Since I'd only had a couple of flatcakes all day, my stomach was growling, and the fragrance of those drumsticks made my mouth water; A-xiong's hand just barely beat my chopsticks, as I reached out and speared the biggest one.

"Hey, mind your manners!" Chief Yang shouted, then turned to Lin Maoxiong and said apologetically, "Lin *san*, you'll have to excuse them. It's just my bad luck to have taken in this little dunce, not to mention all these babes-in-arms who make fools of themselves wherever they go!"

"Let 'em be," Lin said with a laugh. "It's a treat watching them enjoy the food."

Lin took off his coat, which Little Jade quickly took from him and hung on the coatrack. Chief Yang took his coat off, too, and loosened his tie. Lin Maoxiong, holding his glass in both hands, toasted Chief Yang:

"To you, Chief Yang."

The chief quickly picked up his own glass and returned the compliment:

"Lin *san*, you're really the guest here, so I should be drinking to you."

After their toasts, Lin grew silent for a moment, then turned very serious and said to Chief Yang:

"Chief Yang, one of the reasons I invited you to dinner tonight was to discuss something. Jade here is a bright boy, and he seems to know the difference between right and wrong. But at the rate he's going now, he could be in for trouble . . ."

"Lin *san*," Chief Yang cut in as he banged his fan on the table, "you've put your finger on the very thing that's been troubling me! I'm his master, so to speak, and you know I've got his best interests at heart. Some of his previous sugar daddies were shopowners or ran trading companies, and for him to make something of himself and get a decent job would have been as easy as falling off a log. But this little imp has a perverse streak a mile wide and can't stick with anything. Sometimes all it takes is a single word for him to throw up his hands and walk off the job. He has no desire to improve himself, and there's nothing I can do, master or not."

"I know, I know," Lin smiled. "It's the master's place to look out for his disciples. It's like this: the Seijyo Pharmaceutical Company is opening a sales outlet on Songjiang Road, and we're going to be hiring. I'd like to give Jade a job there, give him something to do and a chance to learn a trade. It'll be good for him. I'd like your permission to go ahead."

"That sounds wonderful!" Chief Yang responded. "He's lucky to have Lin *san* go to all this trouble for him. Now the only thing is to see how he feels about it. I never know what that little imp is up to!"

"I've already asked him, and he's all for it," Lin said as he turned and smiled at Little Jade.

"I'll do my best for Lin *san*," Little Jade said earnestly.

"Okay, you're the one who said it," Chief Yang pointed at Little Jade. "We'll just wait and see. It's sure okay with me. From now on, if I ever catch a cold or have a headache, I'll go see Little Jade for some medicine!"

"We'll mainly be selling tonics like Popon S," Lin said with a laugh. "The Taiwan market is relatively small, and it's hard to compete with West German firms, so it'll be tough making a go of it."

"Connections, that's the key. You have to get the backing of major hospitals and reputable physicians if you want to sell medical products."

"We've already started advertising for salesmen. That's what I have in mind for Jade — sales."

"That sounds right, especially with that smooth tongue of his," Chief Yang said approvingly.

While they were talking, A-xiong and I had finished off the drumsticks, and by now the rest of the food had arrived. Lin Maoxiong kept telling us to dig in, to which A-xiong and I responded with busy chopsticks and spoons, filling our bowls with shrimp, eel, beancurd, and fried pork stomach. The food at the Plum Orchard was, in fact, better than either Greenleaf or Plums, much tastier. Since it might be a long time before I had another chance to eat in a place like this, I decided to put away as much as I could this time.

"I've been wanting to come back and see the place again for years," Lin Maoxiong said slowly as he sipped his wine, "but I never dreamed that Taipei would turn into the bustling place it is now, just like the Tokyo of ten years ago. Jade took me over to Eighth Avenue today—that's where I used to live—and now there are so many hotels and restaurants there it makes my head swim!"

"That district has really changed," Chief Yang said. "We used to have a place on Sixth Avenue called Taoyuan Spring, which was a real hot spot for a while—now the bar is owned by someone else, who calls it Ali Mountain. They've painted the entrance in gaudy colors, and it pains me every time I walk past it. Have you had a chance to visit family on this visit, Lin *san*?"

"The older ones are all gone," he sighed. "But there's a childhood friend of mine I'd like to see while I'm here."

Lin Maoxiong suddenly grew very pensive. His cheeks had turned red from the wine, and the dim light from the fan-shaped red lights on the walls cast a halo over his gray head. There was a slightly pained smile on his face, and the wrinkles at the corners of his eyes seemed more noticeable.

"His name's Wu Chunhui. We lived in the same lane and were best friends, just like brothers. We enrolled in the Taipei Technical School together, where we took up chemical engineering. We had a pact that we'd both go to Japan to study medicine, then come back here and open a clinic. But I hadn't taken into account that I'd be conscripted into the Japanese army and be sent to Northeast China, and that it'd take so long for me to get back . . ."

"I've been to Northeast China, myself. Talk about cold, my ears almost fell off!" Chief Yang interjected.

"That's right! When I first arrived in Changchun I had so many chilblains I could barely walk," Lin said with a laugh and a shake of his head. "I didn't learn until later that the Northeasterners line their shoes with a special grass to keep their feet warm."

"What about Wu Chunhui?" the ever-curious Little Jade asked.

"Ai!" Lin sighed. "The poor guy was taken by the Japanese to Southeast Asia to fight, and I never found out what happened to him. I don't know if he's dead or alive."

"What'd he look like?" Little Jade asked.

"I can only tell you what he looked like when he was young," Lin muttered. He looked over at Little Jade. "Come to think of it, you look a lot like him, at least around the eyes."

"Really?" Little Jade laughed. "Well, that should be easy. Lin *san*, I'll help you look for him."

"Little fool," Lin said as he scratched his gray head. "It's been thirty years, and I doubt that we'd recognize each other if we were face to face."

"That's okay. If we make up our minds, we'll find him sooner or later, even if we have to comb every street in every city there is," Little Jade said with unwarranted confidence.

"There's the little boy talking," Lin said with a smile.

Little Jade got to his feet and picked up some barbecued eel with his chopsticks, which he placed on Lin Maoxiong's plate. Lin took a bite.

"The barbecued eel here isn't bad," he said approvingly.

"They say that Tokyo's loaded with Chinese restaurants," Little Jade commented.

"The Japanese love Chinese food, and they have their parties at Chinese restaurants. The restaurant business is very lucrative in Japan. There's one called Liu Garden that's run by the Manchurian royal family. But it's so high class most people can't afford to eat there. Plain old crystal chicken costs 3,000 yen!"

"Lin *san*, why don't I go to Japan and work in a Chinese restaurant?" Little Jade volunteered.

"Can you cook?"

"I can learn."

"They have a lot of trouble finding chefs."

"Well then, I'll just enroll in a cooking school and get my chef's license," Little Jade joked.

"Why go to all that trouble!" Chief Yang said. "Lin *san* can just pack you in a suitcase and take you with him when he goes back! Lin *san*, they say that Tokyo has really gotten lively over the past few years."

"The city certainly has changed," Lin said with a sigh. "When we went there after the war, the place had nearly been bombed into oblivion, and everywhere you looked they were putting up tall buildings. Our boss was farsighted enough to buy a piece of land in Shinjuku's Banshu Street right after we got there, and that set him up for life. He's my wife's uncle, the one who took us to Japan to help him out."

"There's a bar on Banshu Street called Ichiban, where all the boys wear kimonos," Little Jade cut in.

"How did you know that?" Lin asked in amazement.

"The address is 75 Banshu Street," Little Jade giggled.

"You're quite the kid," Lin said as he ruffled Little Jade's hair. "You know Tokyo so well you'd think you'd been there several times."

"I have a map," Little Jade said. "I know almost all the streets of Tokyo, so when I go there I won't get lost. Someday I'm going to go to Shinjuku to see those Japanese boys in kimonos at the Ichiban . . . Lin *san*, how would I look in a kimono?"

"You'd look like a Japanese doll."

"Lin *san*, have you seen the movie *The Man Who Loved Love*?" Little Jade asked him. "It's a movie about the old days, but it's in color."

"*The Man Who Loved Love*?" Lin Maoxiong's brow wrinkled as he tried to recall. "Isn't it an old, old film?"

"It stars Ikebe Ryo," Little Jade replied. "In the movie he wears a white silk kimono with a black satin obi. Boy, what a looker! Do you own a kimono?"

"I have one that I wear around the house."

"What color is it?"

"Gray."

"Oh. I like white silk ones. I'm gonna get one someday. But I hear they really cost a lot. What if I wear a kimono in Japan and everyone thinks I really am Japanese? The only thing I can say in Japanese is ohayo gozaimasu — the chief taught me that. Will you teach me Japanese, Lin *san*?"

"That depends on how good a job you do for us," Lin said with a smile.

"Then I'll do a terrific job!" Little Jade laughed.

While this was going on, A-xiong and I finished off about half the food on the table. He was eating drumsticks with both hands, which glistened with oil. After he finished one he licked the oil off his fingers. Little Jade only ate a couple of pieces of the barbecued squid he'd ordered; I took care of the rest while he was talking. I liked them better than anything else we had — nice and crispy. As the meal came to an end, the only thing left was a fried shrimp, which I speared with my chopsticks and stuck into my mouth, swallowing it, head, tail and all. Having finished off the food, we drank what was left of the two bottles of wine, and left the restaurant.

14

"Lord Sheng's throwing a party!"

The news spread like wildfire. From morning on, it was disseminated throughout Taipei, in every corner of our secret underground kingdom. From Eight Virtues Road it spread to Sun Yat-sen North Road, from there to the Westgate district, where it crossed the Tamsui River and moved on to Sanchong City, then turned and headed back to the remote, hot, foul-smelling, filthy lane off Three Rivers Street in the Wanhua district. It was passed up and down major streets and small lanes, throughout the Barbarian basement, around the back rows of the New South Seas Theater, and ultimately, of course, filtered into our nest — the park. Whenever we met we happily confirmed the news:

"Lord Sheng's throwing a party."

"Eight Virtues Road, Section Two."

"Ten p.m."

By ten o'clock the small alley off Section Two of Eight Virtues Road was crowded with parked bicycles and motorbikes, even a couple of cars. From the outside, Lord Sheng's two-story Western-style garden home was completely dark — even the porch lights were out. All the doors and windows were closed, the curtains were drawn. Anyone walking by would assume that the people inside had turned out the lights and gone to bed. How could they have known that at that very moment a secret gathering was in full swing inside that quiet, peaceful big house? Only after you entered the living room did you become aware of the sounds of talking, laughter, and music. Rows of shoes of every imaginable type were lined up in front of the living room door: old fashioned pointed leather shoes with laces; white leather shoes with airholes; mud-covered, smelly sneakers; even some open-toed wooden clogs with high heels. Lord Sheng's living room was large enough to comfortably accommodate forty or fifty people, but there were so many people crammed in there now it was a sea of black heads. Red, green, and purple lights flashed from the rotating chandelier in the middle of the room in accompaniment to "Broken-Hearted Melody" playing on the phonograph, turning the room into a giant water vat with multicolored waves rising and falling. The people's faces and bodies kept changing from red to green, like colorful tropical fish floating to the surface then diving to the bottom. Everyone was shouting, laughing, dancing, but no one could hear what anyone else was saying over the roar of the 25,000 BTU air conditioner, which was turned up full blast. A strong masculine odor pervaded the sealed room.

Our host, Lord Sheng, was sitting in a sandalwood armchair on a raised platform at the far end of the living room. From his vantage point above the crowd, he took in the sights of all that hot youthful flesh with a mixture of interest and helplessness. The young men danced and flew around the room as though their lives depended on it. Lord Sheng was wearing a black silk sportshirt with a bright red crabapple flower embroidered on the left breast pocket. The few remaining strands of hair were neatly combed to cover his scalp as much as possible. His back was hunched over from chronic rheumatism, the pain eased somewhat by the two soft black velvet pillows behind his back. His Eternal Youth Film Studio had just released a film, *Body and Soul,* which had broken all box-office records in Taiwan and Hong Kong. He was so ecstatic he decided to throw a party to celebrate the success of *Body and Soul,* including the theme song "Broken-Hearted Melody," which had won a major award. Lord Sheng was a very generous man where we were concerned. Sometimes he'd take a bunch of us out for a meal for no reason other than he felt like it. As we dug into the food, he'd be there in the thick of things, patting us on the back and saying, "Eat while you can enjoy it, boys. Look at me, I can't even handle spareribs anymore." With a full set of false teeth, about the only dishes he could handle were shrimp and eggs and beancurd with chicken blood. One of his favorite pastimes was relating incidents from his glory days: back in Shanghai he'd been one of the mainstay actors for the Tianyi Motion Picture Studio, and had played opposite such luminaries as Xu Lai and Wang Renmei. To him, Xu Lai was so exquisite she should be called the "perfect beauty." We all laughed when he showed us photos of his performances. "What are you laughing at?" he demanded resentfully. "Do you mean you don't believe that's me?" How could we believe that the beautiful young man in the photos, with those captivating eyes, could turn into a shriveled, hunched-over, old man like this? The last time Lord Sheng had one of his parties, as soon as we'd eaten and drunk our fill, everyone left, since no one was willing to stay and share a late-night snack with him and be forced to listen to him relate ancient stories over a bowl of date and longan soup.

Lord Sheng was sitting alone in his armchair, looking dejected, the tea table in front of him piled high with a full ashtray, empty beer cans, candy wrappers, and melon-seed husks. He grew suddenly sentimental, as two big tears appeared in his rheumy eyes; he turned to Chief Yang and said with a sigh:

"Chubby Yang, it's sad to grow old and have no son to call your own."

As Lord Sheng's sole close friend, Chief Yang was the only person who understood what the old man was feeling.

"Don't think like that, Lord Sheng," Chief Yang said to comfort him. "You raise a son, and when he turns on you, it's all for nothing!"

"That's not a bad-looking piece of goods," Lord Sheng turned and said to Chief Yang, who was sitting on a bench to his left. His rheumy eyes were gazing at a boy in the crowd wearing a bright red skin-tight pullover. The boy had a wonderful physique, with nice long legs, a thin waist, broad shoulders, and a muscular chest. He was looking around, his head raised with a look of arrogance showing in the corners of his upturned mouth, somewhere between a smile and a sneer. Lord Sheng had an eye for star material: Lin Tian, the lead in *Body and Soul,* had become an overnight star after being discovered by Lord Sheng, and was now all the rage.

"You mean that butch queen?"

Chief Yang pointed to the boy in red with his fan, then leaned over and gave Lord a whispered account of his history:

Hua Guobao, but everybody calls him the Butch Queen. All he ever does is prance around showing off his muscles. Spent a year at a fine-arts academy and thinks he's a movie star already. You'll never find a sneakier, shallower peacock than him. That doesn't mean he's not bright or talented, and you're right when you say he's a piece of goods. See there, the man in the beret next to him who won't let him out of his sight—you know who that is? Yang Feng, the one-time star of Taiwanese films like *The Mournful City* and *Heartache.* He follows Hua around like he was chasing after his own past. Over the past couple of years, Yang Feng's soul has been worn away by this kid, I'm afraid. He pays for his room and board and his schooling, for which Hua Guobao pays him back by sneering, "I don't give a damn!"

Mousey, who was darting in and out of the crowd, snatched an unopened pack of Long Life cigarettes that had been put out for the guests and stuffed it into his back pocket, then grabbed a handful of foil-wrapped chocolates out of a sectioned red-lacquer candy dish on the marble-topped octagonal table; but just as he was putting them into his shirt pocket, Chef Lu of the Cornucopia grabbed his wrist. Mousey grinned a nicotine-stained smile and said helplessly, "Candy, Master Lu?" Fatty Lu laughed like the Happy Buddha and, sticking his paunch up against Mousey's chest, said, "Candy? No thanks. I'd rather gnaw on your bones!"

Wu Min, whose face was paler than ever, was huddling behind the black lacquer screen in a far corner of the room, wiping his sweaty forehead with a handkerchief. His left wrist was still bandaged, his white handcuff. Mr. Zhang had just walked in, wearing a handsome light-blue seersucker suit. His hair was neatly combed, he was freshly shaved, and the deep crease next to his mouth looked like a mean, cold-blooded sneer under the red and green lights. Little Fairy was right behind him, with his bushy eyebrows and big eyes, a big, burly ox who smiled when he saw someone he knew and said smugly, "We just came from seeing *Body and Soul*."

Dr. Shi, the famous cardiologist, had his hand on the chest of the youngster from Three Rivers Street. "Flower Child, your heart's off center, so no wonder you're so crooked." Dr. Shi tried to get us all to go over to his clinic for a checkup, free of charge; he even supplied penicillin. Someone had given him a sign for his clinic that read "Charitable Heart, Practiced Deeds." A kind-hearted physician who was deeply concerned with the state of our health, he often lectured us on basic hygiene.

Iron Ox was standing there with his hands on his hips, chest exposed, his bristly hair combed straight up. His tight black denims, which showed off his rippling leg muscles, were riding low on his hips, girded loosely by a belt. He exuded an aura of primitive masculinity, and the Master Artist said that it was Iron Ox's body that put him in touch with the primitive life-force of our island, like the howling winds of a typhoon. There was a terrifying natural beauty in both. He'd painted several portraits of Iron Ox, referring to them as his masterpieces. He had nothing but contempt for the college students who, he said, "had sacrificed their vitality to culture and education." "Know what they're like?" he'd sneer. "Artificial flowers!" The students, who had formed a clique, punctuated their speech with English expressions and danced the tango with each other.

In Lord Sheng's living room, behind closed doors and windows and drawn curtains, the air conditioner drowning out the other sounds, we twisted our bodies crazily as we danced, getting more and more carried away, wilder and wilder, with broad, exaggerated grins on our faces. We shouted like we were throwing down a challenge or wreaking retribution on the lawful world outside.

I looked at the helpless expression on Lord Sheng's aging face under the lights that were red one minute and green the next; at the mournful look in Yang Feng's eyes; at Hua Guobao's arrogant sneer; at Wu Min's ashen face; at the cruel sneer carved on Mr. Zhang's cheek; at all those faces — young, old, beautiful, ugly: in each there was a vague expression of loss, or of something concealed. Was it some dark hidden anguish? A bleeding wound in the heart that wouldn't heal? Under the revolving lights I saw the burnt copper face of the high-school gym teacher, whose stomach was as hard as a rock, the first person I'd ever taken to the Yaotai Hotel; he was holding his muscular arms out to me. I saw a sea of arms: Wu Min's ravished wrist covered with a white bandage; the blistered arm of Mousey, scarred by cigarette burns; Yang Feng's arm reaching out to Hua Guobao, only to be drawn back painfully, hesitantly. In this sealed-off, congested world of ours, we were all reaching out hungrily, desperately, violently, to clutch, scratch, tear, rend each other, trying to retrieve something from other's bodies that we'd lost in our own. The gym teacher held my wrist in a painful vise-like grip. He looked at me, his bloodshot eyes filled with anxiety, as though there were a thousand things he wanted to say. I smelled the alcohol on his breath — he was drunk again, just like that previous night, so drunk I could barely make out what he was saying as he related a tragic series of events before breaking down and crying like a baby, his toughness melting away. I felt so awkward I didn't know what to do, but I didn't have the heart to look at that burnt-copper drunken face streaked with tears. All the bodies in the crowded room were rubbing up against each other; I threw myself into a frenetic dance, overcome by a strange, powerfully oppressive sorrow. The room had suddenly lost its appeal, and the heaviness in my chest was suffocating. I broke free of the gym teacher's vise-like grip, pushed through the crowd of people, and rushed to the living room door, where I searched through the pile of shoes in the doorway until I found my boots with the flapping soles.

15

The heat of the park wasn't so oppressive now that it was midnight, and the camphor trees were giving off a refreshing pungent fragrance. It was the seventeenth, and the dying glimmer of the moon, perched on the tip of the tallest palm tree like a chunk of charcoal about to turn to cinders, was murkier than it had been on the fifteenth. The place was as still as death, except for there on the steps of the lotus pond, where solitary muffled footsteps, anxious and urgent, grew softer and softer, then suddenly turned and headed back, louder and louder, faster and faster. His tall figure moved through the night, back and forth. Bony, towering, he paced from one end of the pond to the other without stopping; he hesitated as his eyes met mine, and finally stopped. He rested his spindly hands on my shoulders and stared at me with eyes that looked like wildfires raging in a primeval forest.

"I've been looking all over for you, A-qing. For a long time."

16

"They all say I killed him, don't they?"

In the darkness, Dragon Prince's voice sounded like it was flowing slowly back to the surface after being buried in an underground spring.

"It wasn't Phoenix Boy I killed, A-qing, it was me. I plunged that knife into my own heart and I died. I've been dead for years..."

We were lying together on a sofabed covered with a cool woven rattan mat. We were in the room that had been his bedroom in the official residence of his father, an aging home left over from the Japanese occupation at the end of a lane off Section Three of Nanking Road. A coil of mosquito-repellent incense was burning at the foot of the bed, sending smoke curling up to the ceiling. Sleek leaves of the banana trees beyond the window screen behind us were rustling, their shadows weaving back and forth. Summer insects were setting up a racket in the garden behind us, tremulous, melodic, staccato, drawn-out.

"For years I hid myself in Manhattan, in the heart of New York, in an apartment on 72nd Street, across from Central Park. I was a living ghost who never saw the light of day. During the days I worked in an underground bar on Broadway to make enough money to get by. I didn't come out of hiding until very late at night, when I started walking the streets of Manhattan, from 72nd Street all the way to Eighth Street, until my legs seemed about to drop off. Then I'd sit down on the edge of the fountain in Washington Square, and just sit and sit and sit until dawn. Sometimes I'd ride the subway beneath the streets of New York, taking one line after the other, until I didn't know where I was. Then I'd crawl up to street level, into some darkened area I'd never seen before, and blindly walk in and out among the shadows of tall buildings. Once, about three or four in the morning, I stumbled into Harlem, the black ghetto. That summer the black neighborhoods had erupted into violence, and there were clashes between blacks and the police every night. I walked into a crowd of black faces and was clubbed and kicked by police, who threw me into a paddy wagon and dragged me off to the precinct station. But I didn't know what it meant to be afraid then, because I had no feelings at all . . .

"One stormy night, while I was standing beneath a tall elm tree in a park next to the river, soaked to the skin by the rain dripping from the leaves, I began sinking into the mud, deeper and deeper, until my shoes were covered with mud, and my feet were so cold they turned numb. I kept standing there staring off in the distance at the flickering lights on the Washington Bridge, completely forgetting that there was someone kneeling at my feet gnawing on my flesh. Then there was another night, in the middle of a winter snowstorm, when I was in a gay X-rated theater on Times Square, sprawled across the back row fast asleep. When I woke up — it was probably just before daybreak — I discovered I was the only person left in the dark theater. Naked bodies were writhing and twisting on the screen, but I didn't see them. When I looked down at my wrist to check the time, I discovered that the Rolex watch my father had given me as a present when I passed the college entrance exam was gone — someone had stolen it off my wrist while I was asleep. During the years I prowled the streets of New York I must have eaten a thousand hamburgers, but I couldn't tell you what a hamburger tasted like, because I'd lost my sense of taste, and everything tasted like sawdust. Once I bought a hamburger in Greenwich Village and gobbled it down so fast I bit my tongue. My mouth was filled with blood, but I didn't realize it, and I swallowed it along with the hamburger. Then one day I suddenly came to my senses again . . .

"It was Christmas night, and all the trees on the streets were decorated with colorful lights. People were singing 'Silent Night' all around me. It had snowed earlier that night, about five or six o'clock, and Manhattan had turned snowy white. Families were gathered in their homes to eat Christmas dinner. Me, too, along with a hundred or more other people, including old guys in their sixties and seventies whose bodies sagged so much they looked like human gunny sacks, and teenagers whose limbs were just beginning to fill out. There were people of all colors—white, black, yellow, brown. We'd come from all over the city to a dark, aging, three-story building on 22nd Street on that Christmas night to file into one steam-filled room after another, take off our clothes and huddle together for our meal. Silently but frantically we feasted on each other's flesh. When I emerged from that maze-like three-story Turkish bathhouse, it was already getting light outside, and snowflakes were swirling in the icy winds. Everywhere I looked there was blanket of white. I got on the subway to go home, and as I walked past the gate at Central Park, a dark figure suddenly darted out from behind a tree and started following me. On summer nights in Central Park there are nearly always shadowy figures scurrying around the wooded areas in pursuit of one another, and even in the winter you can find one or two lonely souls wandering among the icy winds until dawn. I was absolutely beat that day, so tired I was numb all over, but I quickened my pace anyway, heading toward 72nd Street, and home. When I reached the door to my apartment house, the person who'd been following me came up and asked in a shaky voice, 'Got any spare change, mister? I'm hungry." I turned and looked at him. It was a teenager wearing a black hooded overcoat that came down to his eyebrows, so I couldn't see much of his face. He was stooped over and shaking like a leaf. I told him I had some hot chocolate upstairs, and he followed me up. When we got inside, he took off his raincoat. All he was wearing underneath was a worn maroon pullover that showed how skinny he was. He had dark curly hair that fell down over his forehead, and spectacularly big brown eyes set deeply in his gaunt, pale face. They were sparkling like stars. I figured he was sixteen or seventeen, probably a Puerto Rican. I made him a cup of hot chocolate, which he held in both hands, like the heat didn't bother him. He drank it down without taking a breath. The color started returning to his cheeks. He sat on the edge of my bed, staring at me with those sparkling eyes as he waited. I knew what kids like that usually wanted—twenty or thirty bucks, enough to get them through another week. I reached over to start taking off his clothes. I wanted to get him out of there as quickly as possible so I could finally get some sleep. But when my fingers touched his chest, he yelped, and I quickly pulled my hand back. He looked up at me with a bashful smile and a furrowed brow, and there was such a pained look in his eyes they seemed about to pop out of his head. He slowly peeled off his shirt and sat there naked from the waist up. His pale, scrawny chest was covered with angry welts running in all directions, each of them as thick as a finger, all black and red, and converging in the center of his chest, like spokes, where there was a large infected area. It was all red and swollen, and oozing pus. He told me that a few nights earlier in Central Park he'd run into a sadistic biker in a leather jacket with brass chains and locks on his pants and belt. He took him home and strung him up with chains and whipped him like a dog until he was writhing on the floor. 'They're too tight, they're cutting into me . . .' The kid pointed to the nasty-looking wound in the center of his chest. He had an apologetic smile on his face as he told me what happened, and his eyes were flashing. At that moment, that very moment, while I was looking at the red wound in his chest, the knife suddenly flashed in front of my eyes, the knife I'd plunged into Phoenix Boy's chest. Because that was exactly the way Phoenix Boy had looked at me when he was lying on the ground bleeding to death, the pain so intense his eyes were nearly popping out of his head. But there was still that same helpless, apologetic smile on his trembling lips. For all those years I'd lived without memories, without feeling. But at that moment, that very moment, it was like I'd touched an electric wire, sending a jolt of excruciating pain straight to my heart, and I saw stars in the darkness that suddenly closed around me. I clutched the kid's ice-cold hand in mine and rubbed it with all my might. I knelt down in front of him and took off his wet, muddy boots, then lifted up his frozen, filthy feet and held them against my chest. I rubbed the backs with my cheeks until they were nice and warm. The poor kid didn't know what was going on, but I didn't care. I picked him up, laid him down on the bed, and took off the rest of his clothes. Then I took out a bottle of hydrogen peroxide and some cotton, and gently cleaned off the neglected injuries on his chest. When I'd finished I covered him with a heavy blanket and sat down on the floor next to him as he closed his weary eyes. After he'd fallen asleep, I got up and walked over to the window to look out at Central Park, which was covered with a blanket of pure snow, a blinding white under the rays of the early morning sun. I could feel the blood racing through my veins as I stood there at the window, could feel its warmth, and my face seemed to tingle. All the events of the past flashed in front of my eyes, like a kaleidoscope, and as I raised my eyes I spotted the reflection of a skeletal human being in the window panes. That was the first time in all those years I actually saw myself . . .

"The kid, whose name was Carlos, stayed with me for over three months. He was a Puerto Rican immigrant from San Juan who spoke fractured English mixed with lots of Spanish words. He told me that after his family had immigrated to New York three years earlier, his father couldn't handle the responsibilities of raising a family and just left. His mother went crazy and was committed to a mental institution in the city. One day when we were walking beside the East River, he pointed to a brick building surrounded by a tall chain fence on the opposite bank. 'That's where they've got my mother,' he said. He told me he'd been prowling the streets of New York for over a year, where he'd seen every type of strange person there was and picked up V.D. He had red lesions all over his penis, so I took him to a clinic, where they said he'd already entered the second stage of syphilis and gave him a series of injections. His underwear was always dotted with yellow stains, and I used to wash and disinfect them after he changed at night. Since we shared my narrow single bed, whenever I rolled over in my sleep my arm would invariably bump up against his ravaged chest, and the pain would cause him to wake up screaming. So finally I let him use the bed and I slept on the floor beside him, where I could listen to his deep, even breathing as he slept. Every day for three months I fed him eggs, beef, even vanilla ice cream—Carlos was thin, but he had an enormous appetite, and could put away a gallon of ice cream a day. Gradually, his cheeks began to fill out, and the wounds on his chest from the chains started to heal, leaving dark red scars. One day he told me he was going to visit his mother, and he never came back . . .

"So, A-qing, Carlos was gone, but there are thousands and thousands of kids like Carlos roaming the checkerboard streets of New York, day and night, night and day, prowling, hiding out, picking up diseases, and being devoured in the parks. So many, so very many, always being replaced by new ones from every town and city in America. Sometimes in the wooded areas of

Central Park, sometimes in subway station toilets, sometimes under the neon signs of 42nd Street, I'd suddenly spot a pair of flashing eyes, Phoenix Boy's eyes, nearly popping out of his head with pain. So I'd instinctively reach out and rub the kid's cheeks and ask him, 'Are you hungry?' I brought a thirteen- or fourteen-year-old Jewish kid home with me late one night—he was curled up on a bench just outside the park sleeping. I let him sleep in my bed, but some time before dawn he got up and went through my things. I didn't say a word as I watched him take my wallet out of my pants pocket and pick up a pair of sunglasses on his way out. Another time I brought home an Italian kid who was so hungry he could barely stand. I cooked some macaroni for him, and when he finished, he took out a push-button knife and demanded money. It just so happened that I was out of cash that day, but he thought I was lying, and was so mad he stabbed me in the chest. Luckily, he was off target and the wound wasn't as serious as it might have been. I fell down, but didn't cry out, and just lay there in my own blood, listening to it drip on the floor until I passed out. The next day, my landlady called an ambulance that rushed me to the hospital, where I stayed for a week and received 2,000 cc's of blood. Weak as I was physically, my senses suddenly grew frighteningly keen, as though all my nerve endings had awakened and even the slightest brush caused them pain. I was released from the hospital on a Sunday afternoon, and as I was walking past a park near 83rd Street I saw an old black man sitting up against a wall, a blind old beggar who kept blinking his sightless eyes as he played a beat-up old accordion. The wintry setting sun turned his wrinkled, shapeless face bright red. He was playing an old Negro spiritual called 'Going Home.' The sounds from his accordion quivered in the freezing night air. I walked along, the sun at my back, stepping on my own shadow, and suddenly an overwhelming desire swept over me: I wanted to go home, back to Taipei, back to New Park, back again to the steps of the lotus pond. But I had to wait two more years, two years, until my father passed away . . ."

Dragon Prince's voice, which had been flowing like a babbling brook, suddenly dried up and broke off. The dark red moon outside the window was sinking slowly into the plump banana-tree leaves, the insects in the yard chirped and sang their shrill, vibrant songs. My eyes ached so badly I couldn't open them, and I fell asleep. When I woke up, the first rays of the morning sun were filtering in through the screen. I was having trouble breathing, like there was a steel pillar crushing down on my chest; it was Wang Kuilong's spindly arm lying across my chest.

"What color shirt do you like, A-qing?" he'd asked on the way over.

"Blue."

"Let's go to Westgate tomorrow and get you one." As he was hanging my shirt on the back of the door the night before he'd noticed a hole in the elbow.

Wang Kuilong asked me to move in with him in his father's old house on Nanking Road.

"Give me another chance to take care of you."

He was pleading with me in the dark. He wondered how I could have the same kind of eyes, eyes filled with such pain they seemed about to pop out of their sockets. He'd spotted them that first night in the park. He reached out and combed his bony fingers through my hair. During the more than three months of wandering alone, never knowing where my next meal was coming from, when nights and days had been turned upside down, on more than one occasion I'd awakened in the middle of the night in some low-class hotel behind the train station, or in some stranger's bed in a filthy, sweltering inn in Wanhua, once even on the steps of the museum in front of the park, and in that first waking moment had felt a longing for some place I could call my own. But every time someone wanted to keep me, I always found an excuse to slip away. I'd only been cruising the park about a week when I met a decent, middle-aged man named Yan who managed the Silver Chariot in the Westgate district. He gave me a job waiting tables and took me home to his apartment on Jinhua Street. He said, It's not too late to turn things around, since you've just started, but once you get trapped into this kind of lifestyle, nothing can get you out. So I put on a spotless white uniform and waited tables, serving trays of coffee, tea, sour plum nectar, mango ice cream, spending ten hours a day mixing with customers who had come to Westgate to take in a movie or do some shopping. On the fourth night I went into the bathroom, changed out of my uniform into my own clothes, and slipped out the back door when no one was looking. I started running from Zhonghua Road toward Southgate, faster and faster, all the way to the park without stopping until I was on the steps of the lotus pond.

Suddenly I just knew I had to run away, to get out of this aging home that had been the official residence of Wang Kuilong's father. Not long before, I'd seen an American movie called *The Return of Frank James* about two outlaw brothers — Henry Fonda played the older one — who are lost in a swamp as they're running from the law. The older brother gets stuck in some quicksand, and while the younger one is trying to save him, he gets pulled in himself. The more they struggle the faster they sink, until finally all that's sticking out of the quicksand are four hands, frantically grasping the air. I gently lifted Dragon Prince's arm off my chest. While that spindly arm of his was on my chest, pressing down heavily, I was reminded of the outlaw brother desperately reaching out to pull me into the quicksand with him. I eased out of bed, put on my torn shirt, and walked out. The gate was locked, and the tall steel fence was topped by three-foot spikes. It took everything I had to get out of there, and I left with cuts on my legs.

17

At three o'clock in the afternoon, the heat turned Taipei into a mangy dog on its last legs, its panting tongue nearly touching the ground as it gasped for breath. The sun's merciless rays were scorching the people's scalps. I'd come to the red light district in Yuanhuan to meet Mousey. During Lord Sheng's party, he'd invited me to go see *The Hanging Tree* with him at the New South Seas Theater. He'd made a big score a few days earlier and was feeling pretty pleased with himself. He lived with his brother, Raven, in a loft behind the House of Fragrant Jade, above the home of Chen Zhumei, the madam. The prostitutes who worked in the House of Fragrant Jade were taking midday naps in their dark, gloomy dens; some of them hadn't even bothered to lower their door curtains, and as I walked by I could see mounds of yellow and white flesh piled up on the beds. In hot weather like this, the prostitutes shed their clothes and slept in bras and panties, and there was a strong odor of cosmetics and female bodies. I walked to the end of the corridor and out into the back yard. I whistled up to the loft — two shorts and a long, the secret signal Mousey, Little Jade, Wu Min, and I used. A window opened and Mousey stuck out his head, a broad grin on his face. After sneaking a quick look to his left and right, he signaled me to come up. I climbed up the long, narrow, steep cement stairs, only to find his door closed. Just then he opened the door a crack.

"Who is it?" Raven's voice.

"It's okay, it's only A-qing," Mousey said as he stuck out his tongue. All he had on was a pair of light yellow coarse cotton underpants. The drawstring was so long that even though it was knotted at the waist, one end still hung down to his knees and swung back and forth as he walked.

They were playing pai gow, eight or nine of them sitting shoulder to shoulder around the table, male and female. All the windows were closed and the bamboo curtains were drawn. The lights were on, as were two electric fans that were stirring up the air in the room. All the gamblers were smoking, filling the room with a cloud of smoke. Chen Zhumei was mixing the tiles vigorously when I entered. The madam, a big, fat woman, was wearing a linen vest over her large, sagging breasts, which rested on the table in front of her. Her dark leathery arms were a series of folds, like a leg of pork. Her oily, black hair was pulled back in a bun held in place by a thick, heavy, gold hairpin. She was wearing a yellowed tuberose behind her left ear. Raven, who was sitting in the "Heavenly Gate" position, one leg curled under the bench, was barechested, his rippling chest muscles exposed, his deeply tanned shoulder blades bathed in sweat. He was gambling with such intensity that his face was flushed bright red, the veins in his forehead were popping out, and his eyes were filled with a menacing glare. He kept rubbing his foot. Raven was a rock-solid six-footer with a physique perfectly suited to his job as chief bouncer for the House of Fragrant Jade. Mousey told us that his brother had been a blacksmith in Sanchong City. Once, when he was drunk, he'd threatened to brand Mousey on the cheek with a piece of red-hot steel. Everyone around the table, male and female, was caught up in the game: the men had taken off their shirts, the women had their hair pinned back and their collars turned down. There was a pile of money in the middle of the table. Sitting next to Raven, in a pink dress with a green border, was his mistress, Peach Blossom. The colorful bandana tied around her head forced the hair in back into a high ducktail. After Chen Zhumei had mixed the tiles, Raven, who was first, threw down a thick wad of bills. Chen Zhumei pulled a long face and arched her bushy eyebrows; her thick lips curled upwards, giving her a menacing look. She rolled the dice and pushed everyone's tiles away; when they turned them over, her lips parted abruptly, revealing a mouthful of gold-capped teeth. She slammed down her tiles and bellowed:

"A supreme, that beats you all!"

Everyone at the table cried out "Shit!" almost in unison. Then, as the others were showing their anger or regrets, or throwing down their tiles, or spitting, or whatever, Chen Zhumei sat there clucking like a hen that's just laid an egg, spread out her leathery, blubbery arms, and swept all the money into a pile in front of her. Raven and Peach Blossom looked at each other and cursed their bad luck with unpleasant looks on their faces. Mousey signaled me with his eyes to follow him into the kitchen, where he told me that they did some very serious gambling in there, with tens of thousands of yuan changing hands in a single night. Madams from all the whorehouses, bouncers, even some of the regular Johns were involved. Fights broke out some of the time. One time Raven caught one of the Johns cheating, and beat him up so badly he dislocated his jaw.

"As soon as I get them each a bowl of sweet-bean soup you and I can get out of here," Mousey said. There was a big pot of sweet-bean soup on the kitchen table with a chunk of ice floating on the top. He tested it with his finger. "Cold enough. Let's you and me try some first and get something out of the deal!"

He filled two bowls to the brim and handed me one.

"Drink it fast, hurry. If Rotten Peach sees us she'll raise a stink!"

Mousey called Peach Blossom "Rotten Peach." He'd seen her taking a bath once and said she looked like a rotten peach. We slugged the soup down so fast that Mousey's mouth was coated with it; but a quick lick of his lips with his tongue and the evidence was gone. He made a face and chuckled. I gave him a kick in the butt.

"You little sneak thief, what did you get at Lord Sheng's party last night? Let's see it!"

"Hey!" Mousey laughed, exposing his nicotine-stained teeth. "Take it easy, I'll show you. I really got some good stuff."

He led me into his room, a tiny, four-tatami baggage room off the kitchen, so filled with beat-up trunks and cages that there was barely room for the tiny bamboo cot. The windowless room was as hot as an oven, unbelievably stuffy, and stank of mildew. Mousey went over and turned on the forty-watt bulb at the head of his bed, then reached under the bed and pulled out a rusty metal box with a big brass lock. He picked it up and held it tightly against his chest.

"This is my treasure box," he said.

He unlocked the box with a key he took out from under his

pillow and opened it to show me: it was filled with colorful, dazzling objects, all things he had stolen. He emptied it on his bed like a kid playing house: two pairs of sunglasses, one with a missing lens; five fountain pens — a Parker 51, three Parker 21s, and a Sheaffer; two wristwatches — a Titus and a Bulova; seven assorted cigarette lighters; six nail clippers; four pairs of cufflinks; two tieclasps; two keychains, one gold and one silver, both rusty. There were several combs with teeth missing, shoe horns, every imaginable kind of ashtray, and a varied assortment of metal objects that defied description. Mousey sat on the bed with his legs tucked under him, surrounded by his beloved booty, and, with a look of sheer rapture on his face, told me the history of each item. He remembered it all — place, time, and victim. The pair of engraved, heart-shaped crystal ashtrays had come from the lobby at the Angel Hotel. The Sheaffer pen with the silver cap had come from the display case at the Chengyuan Stationers on Hengyang Road. He'd gotten his hands on one of the keychains at the New Day Theater, the other he'd taken from the uniform of a Boy Scout leader (there'd been a brass whistle attached to it) while he was asleep. The shoe horns were promotional gifts from the Shengsheng Shoe Store.

"Why don't you just go pawn this fountain pen?" I asked him as I picked up the blue Parker 51 with the gold cap. "Whatever you get for it we can use for a good meal at Wu's Wontons."

"Screw you!" He angrily snatched the pen out of my hand and clutched it tightly. "I'm not going to part with this! This pen's my favorite treasure."

He buffed the gold cap of the pen on his pants to clean off the sweat and grime.

"A-qing, have you ever tried Cantonese dim sum?" he asked as he examined the Parker pen.

"You kidding? I've been to the Malaya and to the Maple Grove."

"I never used to know what sachima was," he blurted out.

"That's because you're a hick."

"I can't keep up with you guys," he complained as he looked at me out of the corner of his eye. "You and Little Jade and Wu Min are high-rollers who always get taken out to restaurants by those rich guys. The only big restaurant I'd ever gone to was Fatty Lu's Cornucopia — until last week, when Mr. Huang took me to Ruby for some dim sum. That Mr. Huang's quite a guy. He ordered a tableful of food, and when we were finished, he bought me a box of sachima to take home for breakfast. He's the manager of a hotel in Kaohsiung, and he invited me to come down and visit him. This Parker 51 was his."

"You ungrateful little sneak thief," I laughed at him. "How can you steal from someone who treats you so good?"

"What kind of crap is that!" Mousey jumped to his own defense. "What do you mean ungrateful? I liked this pen so much I just had to keep it for a souvenir. People with that much money don't care, anyway."

"Okay, okay. Come on, show me the goodies you got last night. We'll divvy 'em up."

"Ah, my good brother, last night I hit the jackpot!" Mousey grinned as he picked up the Bulova wristwatch. "One of the rich daddies left this in the washroom. I never had anything that easy before! Look, fully automatic, and it even has a calendar."

Mousey shook the watch and put it up to his ear.

"How about the cigarettes?"

"What cigarettes?" He blinked his tiny eyes.

"You fucking phony!" I gave him a shove. "Last night I watched you stuff pack after pack of Long Life cigarettes down your pants. If you don't bring 'em out and split 'em with me I'll have to search you right now."

Mousey giggled as he reached under his straw mat and pulled out a squashed pack of Long Life cigarettes, which I snatched out of his hand. Then he felt around under the mat until he found two foil packets with English printed on them.

"Don't know what these are. I picked them out of some guy's back pocket. Probably coffee crystals. Let's brew ourselves some coffee."

He tore the corner off of one of the packets and something springy popped out. It was a semi-transparent latex sheath shaped like a baby's pacifier. After a pause, we both started laughing. I rapped him on the head and doubled up with laughter.

"You gutter thief, now you're even stealing these! You're not afraid of bad luck?"

He opened the other pack and put the thing on his thumb, then waved it around like he was putting on a puppet show.

"Don't laugh," he said. "These are worth something. I'll sell 'em to the Johns downstairs. 'American,' I'll tell 'em. 'Guaranteed safe'!"

"Mousey!" Peach Blossom yelled from the other room. "Bring in the sweet-bean soup."

He jumped down off the bed, scooped all his treasures back into his treasure box, locked it, and shoved it back under his bed, then rushed out of the room. He carefully put six bowls filled to the top with sweet-bean soup on a tray and carried them out to the game table. The players had just finished a round and were figuring up their wins and losses. The madam, Chen Zhumei, was counting a wad of bills, her face beaming. The pile of money in front of her reached up to her chin. A fat middle-aged woman wearing four gold rings and a twisted gold bracelet clapped her hands with a noisy jangle and bellowed:

"Where did the obasan's luck come from today? You've taken everything I have. I'd better check to see if my crotch is still there!"

Chen Zhumei, whose thick, dark lips were tightly pressed together, was too busy counting her money to respond to the comment. A man whose face was purple with rage picked up the dice and rolled them roughly in his hand, then spat out:

"Fuck! Fuck you! Fuck your ancestors!"

Peach Blossom was standing behind Raven grumbling and bitching:

"I told you not to play the Heavenly Gate position, but you wouldn't listen. You had the King of Heaven and you still lost! Like a rat licking a cat's whiskers!"

Raven sat there sulking, bent over, rubbing his foot with one hand and banging a tile on the table over and over with the other. Mousey walked up and handed a bowl of sweet-bean soup to each of the players. When he reached Raven, he stammered:

"Brother, A-qing and I are going to a movie."

Raven spun around, raised his hand, and glared at Mousey:

"Going to a movie? I'm going to send you to hell!"

Unable to defend himself, Mousey staggered backwards and spilled the bowl of sweet-bean soup all over Raven's back and Peach Blossoms's dress. Raven leapt to his feet and smacked Mousey across the mouth with the back of his hand, jerking his head to one side and sending him crashing to the floor. Raven then kicked him so viciously that Mousey screamed in pain and curled up into a ball. Raven was about to stomp on him when Peach Blossom pulled him back.

"You'll kill him! You'll kill him!"

The other people in the room rushed over to help hold Raven back and calm him down. He turned and walked off in a huff, cursing under his breath, his back dripping with sweet-bean soup. After Peach Blossom helped Mousey up off the floor, he stood there hunched over, his head cocked, looking at her, as blood trickled from the corners of his mouth, like he was growing a red beard. His gaunt, yellow face was all scrunched up as though he were about to cry, or laugh. Peach Blossom grabbed him by the ear and rapped him on the forehead with her knuckles.

"You zombie, you blind or something?"

"Forget it," Chen Zhumei walked over and said, rubbing his head and slipping him two ten-yuan bills. "The movie's on me."

Mousey straightened up and hobbled into the kitchen clutching the two bills, his drawstring swaying back and forth. He turned on the water faucet and splashed water over his face, then spat some bloody saliva into the sink. When he lifted his head, blinking like crazy, there were spots of blood on his face, like the rouge makeup on a Taiwanese opera clown. Several bruises had been raised on his washboard-like ribs.

"Ah, shit!" he grumbled after spitting out some more blood. He raised his rail-thin left arm and looked at it. "Infected," he mumbled.

Two of the dark, puffy burn blisters on his arm had gotten very big and were already oozing pus.

"You go to the movie by yourself," he said as he picked up the money Chen Zhumei had given him and handed it to me. "I don't feel like it."

"Me, either," I said. "I'm gonna go look up Little Jade."

The whores downstairs at the House of Fragrant Jade had gotten up from their nap and were making themselves up to go to work.

18

The offices of the Seijyo Pharmaceutical Company were on the ground floor of an office building on Songjiang Road. The clerical equipment was all brand new, the office was brightly lit by fluorescent lights, the air conditioner was humming. Large advertisements filling the display windows featured roly-poly babies with snow-white skin playing on the floor, and smiling young maidens in eye-catching attire. The cases beneath the ads were stacked with displays of potions like Popon S, Baonürong Hormones, and Ancibaile. I opened the door and walked in. There was Little Jade, picking up tea glasses and ashtrays from the desks. The women who worked at the desks were reaching into their purses for combs or lipsticks and making up their faces in their mirrors. It was quitting time. Little Jade was wearing the company outfit of a light blue shirt and dark blue pants, with a "Seijyo" patch sewn onto the breast pocket. His long hair had been replaced by a short crewcut; he fit the part of an office boy of a big company perfectly. I had to laugh. He gave me a sign with his eyes and walked over. "Keep it down," he whispered. "We knock off in five minutes, then I'll take you out for some ice cream."

When the desks were all cleaned up, he smiled at a pug-nosed, large-mouthed man wearing a suit and asked him:

"Manager Fan, is it okay for me to go?"

Manager Fan looked at Little Jade, rolled his eyes, and gave a snort. Little Jade nudged me as he turned and walked out the door. We went to an ice cream parlor on Nanking North Road, where we sat down and ordered two bowls of mango ice cream.

"You're not going to sell yourself to many customers with that haircut," I teased him.

"Knock it off!" he smiled. "Yours truly is now officially a salesman for the Seijyo Pharmaceutical Company, Ltd. Talk about selling? Now I'm selling Popon S."

"What about Lin *san*?"

"He's down in Taoyuan inspecting the plant. They've just installed the equipment and begin production next week. He told me to be on my toes at the office, so none of the other employees start talking. That's why I cut my hair."

"Tsk-tsk," I shook my head and sighed. "I never dreamed that Little Jade Wang could be such a good little boy. It looks like you've really found your overseas Chinese sugar daddy. No more living in sin, hm?"

"Worthy brother," he said as he patted me on the shoulder, "you're just starting out, so there are lots of things you haven't done yet. But me, Little Jade Wang, I've done it all at the park, and I'm not bragging when I say that I've been one of the stars there. Plenty of old guys have wanted to keep me, so I could have found a sugar daddy and stopped 'living in sin' anytime I wanted to. But there are two conditions: first, it has to be someone I like, and second, someone who really likes me. I'm not just a piece of meat that anybody who wants to can chew on."

"That's a bunch of baloney!" I laughed. "Doesn't Old Zhou really like you? A new watch, new clothes."

"Old Zhou treats me okay," he said with a shrug of his shoulders, "but I can't stand the way the horny guy's always pawing me. I had a cold once, so I said to him, 'Old Zhou, let's not do it tonight, okay?' So what does he do? He wakes me up in the middle of the night!"

"Don't be such a phony, you're as horny as they come." I laughed. "I suppose your overseas sugar daddy doesn't paw you?"

"I wouldn't lie to you," he swore to me with his hand raised. "The first night I went to the Inn of the Sixth Happiness to meet him, after we'd showered and were lying in bed, we drank beer, ate some peanuts, and talked all night long. I asked him all sorts of things about Japan, and he patiently answered every one of my questions. Lin *san*'s a good man, so I told him all about myself, and when I got drowsy I fell asleep in his arms."

Our ice cream arrived, and as I ate mine I asked him how things were going at Seijyo and how much they were paying him.

"Two thousand a month!"

"That's not enough to keep you in cigarettes."

"Hold your horses," he said with a smile. "Manager Fan said that if I get a good evaluation after six months I'll start getting a commission. You saw him, right? Damn, he's like a bulldog. He got on my case the very first day — say, you don't know anything about chemistry, do you?"

"Chemistry? Sure do. Got an 80 in my high-school chemistry class."

"Great!" Little Jade clapped his hands. "Teach me chemistry, will you? I only went through the eighth grade, and the only thing I remember about chemistry is that the old guy who was teaching us said, 'Sulfur smells like rotten eggs.'"

Little Jade fanned his hand under his nose.

"What? Don't tell me you want to become a student," I said in amazement.

"Here's the deal," he sighed. "Lin *san* says I won't be able to go far with Seijyo without any special skills. He'll pay for me to go to a technical school at night, and when I graduate I'll become a technician at the plant. That's how I'll get ahead. I checked out Kainan Technical School and they say I can take a test at the ninth grade level, majoring in chemistry. I think I can squeak through the other subjects, but if all I can remember about chemistry is rotten eggs, how am I going to pass? Now, if you'll help me brush up on chemistry so I can pass the test, I promise I'll do something really nice for you."

"Why wait till then? Let's go over and get something to eat at the Dragon."

"The Dragon? The Snake, if you want to. If it's dragon meat you're lookin' for, I'll find a way to get it for you," he said in a pleading voice.

"Well, as long as you're willing to work hard at it, we can give it a try. Now, since you're going to work at the feet of a master, let's hear you say the word."

"Master, Master. I'll call you 'Eminence' every day if you want me to. You've got to understand what's going on in here." Little Jade pointed to his heart. "This is the chance of a lifetime. I've been waiting for someone like Lin *san* for longer than I can remember. He's put so much trust in me, how could I not be willing to do anything to show he's made the right decision? Who knows, if I make my mark at Seijyo, maybe someday I'll have a chance to go to Tokyo and work with him in the company headquarters."

"Ah, so you're throwing out a long line to hook a bigger fish. I didn't know you had such a good scheme worked out." I smiled.

"What do you mean, scheme? What's wrong with trying to improve myself? I want to use the summer break to do some boning up so I can get into Kainan and start taking night classes in the fall. A-qing, tell me, do I look like a student to you?"

He rubbed his hand over his crewcut and giggled. I looked him over.

"Not bad. But those almond-shaped eyes of yours have that look that says 'street angel.' Go get yourself a pair of glasses to cover up the look of vice in your eyes."

Little Jade covered his eyes and laughed. As we were walking out of the ice-cream parlor I told him how Raven had beaten up on Mousey. He just sneered and said:

"Don't feel sorry for a low-class piece of goods like Mousey. That time he was whipped, I advised him to move in with me, and you know what he said? 'I've lived with Raven so long I'm used to it.'"

He scrunched his face up in that downcast look Mousey always wore, then spat loudly into the gutter on Songjiang Road.

"If that bastard Raven so much as laid a hand on me, he'd be seeing his maker with a bellyful of insecticide before he knew it!"

19

Two days later, after Little Jade got off work, he came home, just as he'd promised, with two junior-high chemistry textbooks, ready to begin the tutorials. He brought two bunches of lichees as a sly inducement. The room was so hot we stripped to the waist and sat on the floor. As I peeled the lichees I explained some of the basic concepts of chemistry to him, starting with the process of oxidation. Luckily, I'd used the same textbook when I was in junior high, and still remembered what was in it. Little Jade had been away from school so long he'd forgotten all the terms and symbols, and I could barely finish a sentence before he asked a question; he didn't even know the simplest molecular formula, and that made him so nervous he kept tugging on his ear and sweating like a pig.

"Damn you," I cursed as I hit him over the head with the textbook. "That little brain of yours is like a computer when you're working on some old guy, but as soon as we start talking chemistry it turns to mush!"

"What's so hard about working on some old guy?" he said, his eyes as big as saucers. He kept wiping the sweat off his face. "And what makes you think chemistry is all that easy? Everybody knows it's water, so why do they have to write H_2O?"

"I think you'd better forget about taking the Kainan exam, Little Jade. Just go to Taiwan University's Archaeology Department, and I guarantee they'll give you a scholarship without even requiring an exam."

"Why?"

"You dumb ass!" I laughed. "You know so much about antiques they'll probably hire you as a researcher. We'll have to start calling you Wang the Archaeologist!"

"What's wrong with antiques?" He had such a broad grin on his face his almond-shaped eyes were nothing but slits. "The older they are, the more valuable they become."

We kept at it for two solid hours, until we were both drenched in sweat and had managed to fix a few chemical symbols in his head. Moon Beauty came home while we were eating dinner. She'd just had her hair done, and the tight curls that nearly covered her ears bounced and flew as she walked into the room. She snickered when she saw Little Jade and reached out to rub his bristly hair.

"Jade, why not just shave it and go on up to Lion Mountain to become a crystal monk! I haven't seen you for days. A-qing tells me you found yourself a sugar daddy from Tokyo, some guy who's opened a pharmaceutical plant. From now on I won't have to spend a dime for my little bastard's vitamins. We'll just get them from his 'second cousin.'"

"I'll bring Johnny Jr. a few bottles of Popon S," Little Jade smiled, "and we'll see how fat he can get."

"Well, then, my little crystal boy, now that you've got a sugar daddy with a pharmaceutical plant, you ought to be in line for manager, huh?" Moon Beauty smiled and looked at Little Jade out of the corner of her eye.

"Are you kidding!" he giggled. "I'm just a salesman. I only started last week. Our offices are on Songjiang Road. Come over and take a look sometime, Moon Beauty."

She shook her head and sighed. "Aren't you something, now that you're back to work! That time I got you a job as a houseboy in Tianmu at the home of that American, you lasted all of three days before you came running home all pissed and saying the guy wasn't worth shit!"

"What did that Yankee have that qualified him to employ *me*?" Little Jade jerked his thumb at his chest.

"Oh, I guess only your overseas Chinese sugar daddy is qualified to employ you, right?"

"Lin *san*'s different. He's paying for me to go to school. A-qing was tutoring me just before you came home. I'm gonna take the entrance exam at Kainan."

"Now that *is* news!" Moon Beauty exclaimed with astonishment. "Next the sun will rise in the west. Auntie always used to complain to me, 'Our Jade played hookey again!' When was the last time you spent one full day in school?"

"Those little bastards in school used to call me Asaoka Yuriko, so why would I go to a shitty school like that?" Little Jade complained resentfully.

"Nobody asked you to tell them a pack of lies, like you were born in Tokyo," Moon Beauty said with a laugh. "Besides, you do look a little like Asaoka Yuriko."

Little Jade's face reddened with embarrassment.

"Obasan, come here, quick, we've got a student here!" Moon Beauty laughed and waved to Obasan, who was dragging Johnny Jr. up the stairs and gasping for breath. The fat old woman's blouse was soaked with perspiration. She raised her eyes and took a look at Little Jade. "Short hair's a good way to keep cool in hot weather like this," she said.

Johnny Jr., on the other hand, stared at Little Jade with his green eyes like he was dumbstruck.

"It's your uncle, little bastard, don't you recognize him?"

Little Jade reached down and swept Johnny Jr. up in his arms, and the little boy immediately started laughing and flailing his arms and legs.

"Obasan, what's for dinner?" Moon Beauty asked.

"Pickled cabbage with sliced pork stomach and mashed taro root."

"Make some soup with the rest of that chicken in the refrigerator. Let's celebrate Jade's return to school."

20

I'd told Wu Min I'd wait for him in my room. I was on the second floor, room 215, he was on the third floor, room 344. Chief Yang had told us to go to the Jinghua Hotel on Sun Yat-sen North Road, but he hadn't told us anything but the room numbers. My guy didn't turn on the light when he went out; he left the room key on the dresser and said softly in the darkness, The room's paid for. I never had a good look at his face, nor did I ask him his name. As he walked out of the room he looked to be a big man, probably a six-footer. The Seventy Seven Restaurant next door was open for late-night snacks, and even though it was the middle of the night, I could hear music through the wall. I was lying in bed smoking a cigarette when Wu Min knocked.

The two of us walked softly downstairs and slipped out the front door when the person at the front desk wasn't looking. We kept the keys. As soon as we were outside we started running in the direction of Yuanshan, not stopping to catch our breath until we reached a spot where there weren't many lights. There were no people out on the streets, none at all, and I walked with my arm around Wu Min's shoulder. We were walking at the same cadence, making a racket on the sidewalk.

"How's your wrist, Wu Min?" I noticed that the bandage was gone.

"It's already formed a scar." He stuck his hand into his pants pocket.

"You jerk, if Little Jade, Mousey, and I hadn't been there when you needed us, you'd have already gone to meet your maker. What's wrong with you? I can't believe that someone like Zhang is worth cutting your wrists over. No wonder Little Jade's unhappy with you. A couple of days ago he said he wants you to give him his blood back."

Wu Min shuffled along with his head lowered.

"That's not it," Wu Min said softly. "It's just that I lived at Mr. Zhang's home so long I began to consider it my own. Then when he kicked me out, I didn't know what to do, and that's why I did what I did. You know what Mr. Zhang's place is like — clean and comfortable. How do you expect me not to miss something like that?"

I recalled the occasions when I'd gone to Mr. Zhang's home in Guangwu Villa to see Wu Min. If he wasn't down on his hands and knees scrubbing the floor, he was cleaning the kitchen, keeping the place as neat as a pin. I used to tease him by saying that Mr. Zhang had got himself the perfect little homemaker.

"A-qing, I remember the first night I stayed at Mr. Zhang's home. I spent at least an hour in his bathroom." Wu Min shook his head and smiled.

"What could you find to do in a bathroom for that long?"

"You don't know what a neat bathroom Mr. Zhang has. It's all done in light blue tile, even the tub is blue. I've never seen a bathtub as pretty as that. He's got a gas heater above the tub, and as soon as you turn on the tap, hot water comes out. I filled the tub with hot water and just sat there soaking. I sat there so long I turned bright red. That was the most enjoyable bath I ever had."

"Listen to you! Talking about Mr. Zhang's bathroom like it was Paradise or something!" I said with a laugh.

"What do you know?" Wu Min sighed. "I told you before how I bummed around with my father ever since I was a kid, and none of the places we rented ever had a bathroom. In the summers we took sponge baths in the yard, and in the wintertime we went to a public bath every two or three weeks. I stunk so much it even made me feel like throwing up. When keeping clean is as important as it is to me, I'd like to know what Mr. Zhang's bathroom is if not Paradise."

Wu Min's father had been in a Taipei jail for over two years, after being caught dealing in heroin in the Wanhua district. He was a Cantonese, and according to Wu Min, he brought some gold bars with him to Taiwan, but he was such a compulsive gambler he lost them all in local games, and turned to dealing in heroin. The first time he went to jail, his wife was pregnant with Wu Min, who never once saw his father the first few years of his life. He grew up in the home of an uncle in Xinzhu. When his father got out of jail he came to get his son, and the two of them knocked around for several years, until he went back to jail.

"Being kicked out of a house is hard to take," Wu Min said dreamily.

"I know." I held him tighter around the shoulder. The day my father kicked me out of the house, I didn't have any money on me at all. I walked around Westgate all afternoon, looking at the pastries in bakery windows that had never attracted me before. The red-bean cakes and sesame biscuits made my mouth water and my stomach growl; I was so hungry I began to panic.

"In those two or three years with my father we moved seven or eight times, always getting kicked out for not paying our rent. Once we lived in a lane off Yanping North Road in a place owned by a really nasty woman. We stalled her for a couple of days on the rent, so she threw all our belongings out on the street. Wash basins and plastic glasses were rolling around in the dirt. The gambling tiles my father loved so much were strewn everywhere. Well, he split, leaving me behind to pick everything up, with all the neighbors watching. God, I wanted to crawl into a hole! So when I moved into Mr. Zhang's house I figured I had a home at last. That's why I was so careful not to do anything wrong. But that didn't keep him from kicking me out when he felt like it." Wu Min was feeling sorry for himself again.

We walked up to the entrance of the Yuanshan Children's Park and sat down on the steps. We took off our shoes to cool our feet as we sat there shoulder to shoulder. During the daytime this place was a beehive of activity, with the shouts and laughter of children filling the air. But now it was absolutely quiet, except for Wu Min's grumblings floating in the darkness.

"That night, when I left Mr. Zhang's house with only my beat-up suitcase, the more I walked the more confused I got, and I didn't know where I was going. I walked past a river, probably over by Shulan Street, and threw my suitcase into the river. If life itself doesn't mean anything, I thought, what good is a suitcase? It wasn't just something I did in anger. I hadn't done anything wrong, so why had Mr. Zhang been so uncaring?"

"What do you expect from a scarfaced bachelor like him?"

"What do you mean scarfaced bachelor?" Wu Min blurted out.

"When he smiles it looks like he has a knife scar on his cheek. That's what I mean."

"That's not fair, you shouldn't talk about people like that!" Wu Min objected.

"Oh, even after he was nearly the cause of your death, you jump to his defense!"

Wu Min wrapped his arms around his knees and hunched over without saying anything for a while.

"Mr. Zhang does have a temper, and you never know if he's going to run hot or cold, but that doesn't mean he doesn't have any feelings. It's just that he's not easy to get close to. The day before he kicked me out of his house he treated me better than usual. He even gave me a little transistor radio and complimented me on my bean-sauce carp. He was in such rare high spirits that night that he shared a whole bottle of sorghum wine with me before he said, 'Wu Min, you know you've been with me longer than anyone else. Do you think you could spend the rest of your life with me?' Of course I said yes, but he just sneered and said, 'There you go, lying again. You little queers are all the same. Give you an inch and you'll take a mile!' Mr. Zhang told me once about a boy who'd stayed with him, a kid he'd doted on. Well, the little sonofabitch not only didn't appreciate the kindness, but he even bit the hand that fed him by running off with as much of Mr. Zhang's stuff as he could carry. Just talking about it made him mad, so I said to him, sort of half-seriously, 'If you don't believe me, Mr. Zhang, I'll die for you!' He just sighed and, drunk as he was, patted me on the head and said, 'Wu Min, what do you know? A man in his forties can't afford to get hurt, and so he forgets what it means to be hurt.' A-qing, don't laugh, but I'd rather clean his kitchen and bathroom every day than live this kind of nomad life. A-qing, what about your home? Have you got a home?"

"My home's on Longjiang Street, Lane 28, Longjiang Street."

"Don't you miss it?"

"My house leaks, leaks badly, drip-drip-drip..." I laughed. "When Typhoon Daisy passed through a couple of years ago, it took a corner of our roof along with it."

I remembered that the day after the typhoon hit, our house was flooded, with muddy water covering the bed legs. It had to be at least a foot deep. Father had Buddy and me take off our shoes and strip down to our underwear, then we all began bailing out the water, Father using a big metal bucket, Buddy and me armed with wash basins. Father never stopped cursing while he worked, but it was all Buddy could do to keep from laughing out loud, as though bailing out the house was a game. After the water receded, there was a stench of rancid mud in our dark, damp, squat home that wouldn't go away, no matter what we did. Father brought some mugwort home, which he burned to disinfect the house, but Buddy was allergic to it and got a rash all over his body.

"How about your family? Don't you miss them?"

"I miss my kid brother."

"Where is he?"

"He's sleeping down there." I pointed to the ground.

"Oh . . ." Wu Min turned and looked at me. The streetlights painted a childish look on his delicate face. "Did he look like you?"

I hugged Wu Min and kissed him on the cheek.

"Actually, he looked a little like you, my pet."

"You're kidding." Wu Min laughed and struggled weakly.

I picked up my shoes and stood up. So did Wu Min. The two of us, still barefoot, dashed out into the middle of Sun Yat-sen North Road and started running, with me in front, all the way to the end without even spotting a car.

"Wu Min, are we Huns or what?" I shouted to him breathlessly as we ran along.

"Huh?"

"Didn't you say we were nomads?"

"Huns, I guess," Wu Min laughed.

"Who was the king of the Huns?"

"Chan Yu."

"Then I'll be Big Chan Yu and you'll be Little Chan Yu."

Wu Min pulled up even with me, breathing hard.

"Nomads look for a place with grass and water to make camp. What are we looking for, A-qing?"

"Fairies!" I shouted.

We burst into loud laughter that tumbled and floated in the air above the defenseless street.

21

It was two-thirty in the morning when I got back to Jinzhou Street, and I was surprised to see that my light was on. Little Jade had probably come home to spend the night. Over the past couple of weeks he'd been coming over to work on his chemistry as soon as he got off work, but when the lessons were over he went to be with Lin *san* and never spent the night here. But when I reached the head of the stairs I heard the sounds of an argument coming from my room, and I knew that spelled trouble—Old Zhou, this time he'd caught him for sure. He'd come by several times, but Moon Beauty or I had always stalled him with some story or other. Once I told him that Little Jade's grandmother had come down with cholera and he had rushed back to Yangmei as soon as he heard the news. That's what Little Jade had told me to say. The truth of the matter was, his grandmother had disowned both him and his mother. Old Zhou was standing beside my bed gesturing angrily. His puffy, pasty face was bathed in sweat and as red as a piece of raw liver. Every whisker on his dark chin was standing straight up, and there seemed to be sparks shooting out of his angry round eyes. The broad back of his satin peacock-blue Hawaiian shirt was nearly soaked through.

"You tell me!" Old Zhou screamed as he pointed at Little Jade, his Shanghai-accented Chinese even more than usually difficult to understand, now that he was so worked up. "Where've you been out selling it these past few days? How much did you get?"

Little Jade was sitting on the edge of the bed, wearing the red shirt Old Zhou had given him, which he left unbuttoned as he sat there barefoot with his legs crossed. A cigarette dangled from his mouth, which he puffed on ferociously without saying a word. After blowing a couple of smoke rings he sneered and said:

"Old Zhou, you aren't my pimp, so where I go to sell it is none of your business. And how much I get is my business. You don't expect a commission, do you?"

"You shameless piece of shit!" Old Zhou spat out hatefully. "Who do you think you're trying to fool? Everybody knows you've got yourself an overseas Chinese from Japan..." Old Zhou spun around and stared at me. "You little devils are all cut from the same cloth! Tell me," Old Zhou's stabbing finger nearly hit Little Jade in the head. "That overseas Chinese of yours, how much does he give you a night?"

"Lin *san*?" Little Jade took another drag off his cigarette before answering in measured tones, "I don't take any money from him."

"Did you hear that!" Old Zhou turned to look at me again, but this time he gave a fiendish laugh. "How low-class can a person get? Just because the guy's an overseas Chinese, he can't wait to wiggle his ass. But this time he does it for nothing! Do you think your value will go up because of your overseas Chinese? You'll still be a hooker, won't you? If you've got real talent you'll get your overseas Chinese to take you to Japan with him and keep you in a cage."

"Lin *san* told me he's taking care of the paperwork to get me an entry permit. After I get to Japan I'll think about whether or not I want to let him keep me."

Little Jade's face was raised slightly as he spoke, and the self-satisfied look on it was unmistakable. Old Zhou, who couldn't think of anything to say, just groaned loudly, as the glistening sweat on his face ran down in rivulets. Little Jade casually snuffed his cigarette out in a chipped soysauce plate, then jumped to his feet with a heavy look on his face and shouted at Old Zhou, pointing straight at him:

"What the fuck business is it of yours if I do it for nothing? You don't own a contract that tells me what I can do with my body, you know. Everyone knows I'm one of the most prized hookers in the park, so what makes you think I need you to advertise for me? I'm low class? How about you? If you're not, then why do you wiggle your ass for me?"

Smack! Little Jade's face was given a resounding slap, jerking it to one side. Smack! Another one. Little Jade jumped to his feet and screamed:

"How dare you hit me! I'll report you to the police!"

He drove his head into Old Zhou's chest, grabbed his collar, and starting dragging him outside. Old Zhou was beating on him with his fists, but Little Jade was holding on for dear life. They rolled around together. I rushed up and dragged Little Jade away. Old Zhou was gasping for breath and his voice was quivering as he said:

"What about all the things I bought you?"

Little Jade ran over, pulled a beat-up suitcase out from under the bed, opened it, and poured its contents onto the floor. He dug through the mess, picking out three pairs of slacks and six colored shirts, rolled them all into a bundle, and shoved it into Old

Zhou's hands. He took the Seiko watch off his wrist and tossed it over. Old Zhou was about to leave in a huff, his arms filled with his bundle of clothes, when Little Jade came up and tore off the red shirt he was wearing, and threw it at Old Zhou.

"Take it all!" he shouted.

Old Zhou had barely left when Moon Beauty came walking in, reeking of perfume. She was wearing a slinky black dress that showed lots of skin.

"What's been going on here? Police search or something?" She touched the clothes on the floor with the tip of her high-heeled shoe. Little Jade was standing in the middle of the pile, shirtless, his face bathed in sweat.

"Old Zhou was just here." I gave Moon Beauty a sign with my eyes.

"Oh," she laughed. "So the fat stud got jealous . . ."

She walked over to Little Jade and cupped his face in her hands. There were red finger marks on his cheeks. He quickly pushed her hands away and lowered his head again.

"He hit you," Moon Beauty sighed and shook her head. "That's what you get when you don't choose your sugar daddies carefully. Come over to my place, my little crystal boy. Obasan made some cassia and sour plum nectar. A bowl of that will cool you off."

"You're late tonight," I laughed. "Business must be good!"

"Good? It damn near did me in!" She unbuttoned her blouse and framed her breasts in her hands. "A black guy came to the bar tonight, must have been six-five and weighed a ton. He was like a tank! He wouldn't let me alone, and wanted to take me out for some fun. So I went into the bathroom and slipped out through the back door."

22

"A-qing."

"Hm?" I'd just dozed off when Little Jade nudged me awake.

"I can't sleep." He was lying in bed in the dark smoking a cigarette.

"If you can't sleep, why not go scare up some business at Baodouli?," I grumbled and rolled over.

"A-qing, Lin *san*'s gone."

By now, he'd pretty much ruined any chances I had of getting some sleep. He passed me the cigarette. I took a drag.

"When'd he leave?"

"This morning. He got a call from the main office a couple of days ago. They told him that things were getting busier there, and the boss was sick, so he had to go back right away."

"Sounds good to me. Now your overseas Chinese sugar daddy can send for you in Tokyo."

He rolled over and put his hands behind his head.

"Last night Lin *san* and I talked almost all night. He really thought of everything, took care of all my arrangements. He lined me up with another job in the company, as Manager Fan's assistant. Five thousand a month, double what I'm making now."

"Wow! You're really set up now, Jade!"

"He said he's going to send me money every month for my schooling. He wants me to do well on the exam."

"Then let's see how you're doing. What's the formula for sulphuric acid?"

"H_2SO_4."

"Great, son-of-a-gun, you're on your way."

"If I worked at it I could do okay in school. But I'm not going to take the test at Kainan!"

"What?" I blurted out. "Have you just been playing games with me with all those study sessions on those hot days?"

"And I'm not going to go back to Seijyo, either. You've seen Manager Fan, haven't you? He looks like the devil himself. I'm not gonna take any lip from an old bulldog like that, not for a measly five thousand. I can make more than that by undoing my belt, probably more."

"Boy, are you cocky!" I laughed. "You really think you're worth that much?"

"The only reason I went to work and did the studying was to make Lin *san* happy, and now that he's gone, what's the use? Last night he told me straight out that he'll come back to see me when he can, but he can't take me to Tokyo."

He took a deep drag on his cigarette and blew the smoke out slowly.

"That Manchu wife of his is no problem, since all she ever does is read Buddhist scriptures. But his son's a different matter altogether. He knows all about his father. Once, when he was taking a boy out of a bar in Shinjuku he bumped into his son at the entrance, and when they got home his son raised such a stink he didn't know what to do. This was just the chance the kid was waiting for to take over some of the family concerns. Now if he brought me to Japan, and his son found out about it, there'd really be hell to pay."

"It looks like your cherry blossom dream has gone up in smoke again, Jade," I said.

"I don't hold anything against Lin *san*. He wouldn't have told me the truth if he didn't care for me. He could hardly bring himself to leave when the time came, and he gave me the several thousand he had on him. He also gave me his Parker 61 to remember him by. A-qing, I wasn't with Lin *san* for very long, but I was happy every single day. No one has ever shown me that kind of affection before."

Little Jade put his cigarette out in the soysauce plate at the head of his bed and lay back down, his head pillowed in his folded arms. He was quiet for a while, then asked me all of a sudden:

"Did you see the movie *The Man Who Loved Love*, A-qing?"

"No, I hardly ever see Japanese movies."

"Ikebe Ryo is *so* good in that movie. He's wearing a snow-white kimono and standing under a cherry tree. When I go to Tokyo I want to wear a snow-white kimono like that and have my picture taken under a cherry tree."

"I think you'd look like Asaoka Yuriko in a kimono!"

"You know, A-qing, my mother took me to see *The Man Who Loved Love*. She saw it five or six times. She said that my Shiseido Cosmetics salesman-father looked just like Ikebe Ryo when he put on a kimono."

"Little Jade, I think your obsession with Japan is making you a little crazy."

"What do you know? People like you, who've got fathers, don't know shit! I won't rest, dead or alive, until I've found that goddamn father of mine!"

"Okay, let's say you do make it to Japan, and you find your father. What if he doesn't own up to it, then what'll you do?" Little Jade was being so serious about this that I couldn't help teasing him.

"Who says he has to own up to it?" he sneered. "I've got my pride, you know. If he doesn't want to admit he's my father, I'm not going to force him. I'll be content just knowing that he exists. So what if he doesn't look like Ikebe Ryo. I just want to see for myself what that sonofabitch looks like, if he's some weird-looking ogre or a freak!"

"What if he's already dead, won't all that time and energy be wasted?" One more little dig.

"So what if he's dead? His bones will still be around." Anger was creeping into Little Jade's voice. "I'll bring his bones back with me and bury them in our hometown cemetery in Yangmei. I'll put up an engraved marble headstone with gold letters that say, Resting Place of My Late Father, Lin Zhengxiong. Then each year, on Tomb-Sweeping Day, I can go clean off his grave."

"Jade, you might as well just go ahead and swim to Japan."

"I would if I could," he said with a sigh. "A-qing, if I get out of here someday and make it to Tokyo, I'm going to change my name and start over. I started cruising the park when I was fourteen, almost four years ago. You probably think it's a pretty good place to hang out, don't you? Well, look at Death Angel Zhao, he's not even thirty, and he looks like he crawled out of a grave. People say he'll go with someone for fifty yuan. Every time I see that opium-addict look of his it breaks my heart. You say the old antiques are easy to handle. Well, I spent a year with Old Zhou, and you heard what nice things he had to say tonight. Even if I was wrong to play around, if he had come over and said a couple of nice things, I'd have gone with him. Yeah, he treated me okay, but did you hear him call me a hooker? What a joke. He's no millionaire, you know. Does he think he can buy me for that little bit of money?"

Little Jade pounded the bed, then sighed and said in a lonely voice:

"You can only depend on your own flesh and blood. Even a considerate man like Lin *san* won't make the commitment."

"Forget it, Jade," I said to comfort him as I patted his shoulder. "After all, you're an archaeologist, so sooner or later you'll find your genuine antique."

"Won't be easy," he sighed with a soft laugh. "People are always misjudging other people."

"Go to sleep, Jade, it's nearly light out." I rolled over.

"A-qing," he said all of a sudden, as though he'd just remembered something. He rolled over and nudged me. "Do you like pig's ears?"

"Pig's ears?" I laughed. "I do if they're salted."

"I'll treat you to some salted pig's ears tomorrow. My mother sent someone over today with a note for Moon Beauty. She wants me to come to Sanchong City tomorrow for the Ghost Festival feast. That Shandong guy of hers is off making a delivery in Kaohsiung."

"Long live your mother!" I shouted. "I haven't eaten a holiday feast for a long time. Tomorrow I'll pour down a couple of glasses of good old wine."

"This time I'm gonna eat a goddamn pair of pig's ears!"

23

We slept till noon the next day and were covered with sweat when we woke up. After taking a cold shower, we changed into clean clothes and went outside. Our first stop was Westgate, where Little Jade bought some Shiseido cosmetics for his mother at the Today Department Store. He said that even though she was getting on in years, she still liked to use powder and rouge, and every time he went home he brought her some. He wrapped the cosmetics up in a cloth bundle with a pine tree and crane design. It was the same piece of cloth his mother had used to wrap his clothes in when he left home. He'd kept it all this time. His mother lived in a crowded lane filled with peddler stalls behind the Tiantai Theater in Sanchong City. When we reached her gate, Little Jade balked and took me around back to scout the house out. He stuck out his tongue and said:

"That Shandong guy's gone, all right. He told my mother, 'If I get my hands on that little queer, I'll split his mangy skull!'"

Little Jade cleared his throat, then called out:

"Mother, Jade's home."

She came running out from around back, and when she saw her son she rubbed her hands all over his face, then pinched his arm.

"How come you're so skinny? What do you eat? Has that whore Moon Beauty been mistreating you? I'll bet you're out on the prowl every day without eating right, aren't you?" She looked him over again. "At least your hair's short."

Although she was in her late forties, she was heavily made up, with a thick layer of powder on her face, plucked eyebrows penciled over with dark arches, and heavy lipstick. Her ample figure was covered by a green satin dress with a purple butterfly design, showing plenty of cleavage. She must have been quite a flirt back in her bar-girl days. Although there were lines in the corners of her puffy almond-shaped eyes these days, when she smiled they were as pretty as ever. Now I knew where Little Jade had gotten his eyes.

"Mother, I brought A-qing home with me for the feast," he said as he pushed me up in front of her.

"Wonderful," she said, putting her arm around his shoulder and turning to walk inside. She smiled at me and said, "Our old neighbor, Uncle Huowang, slaughtered a boar that weighed over 200 catties. We're all going over to his place tonight."

"What perfume are you wearing, Mother? It stinks." He put his nose up to her neck and sniffed deeply. She smacked him on the butt and scolded him:

"It's none of your damn business what perfume I'm wearing!"

When we were in the living room, Little Jade gleefully unwrapped the bundle he'd brought and spread the contents out on the table: perfume, vanishing cream, lipstick, and an eyebrow pencil.

"This is called Night Fragrance. Its delicate mint aroma makes it perfect for the summer. Smell it." He opened the green-tinted bottle and held it up to his mother's nose.

"Nothing special," she said with a slight curl of her lip. She eagerly opened the jar of vanishing cream. "But this is nice. I just ran out and was going to buy some."

Little Jade poured a few drops of the perfume on his palm, then dipped his finger in it and dabbed it behind his mother's ears. The rest he put in her hair.

"You're just like your damned father," she sighed and nodded. "He loved to work with cosmetics. All he left behind when he took off was you, my little seed of ruin, and twenty or thirty boxes of Shiseido powder. Since there was so much, I wound up giving most of it away." She massaged his cheeks and looked over at me. "He shouldn't have been born as a son," she said with a smile. "He used to pencil my eyebrows for me. If Jade had only been a girl, I used to say, he wouldn't have always been getting into trouble."

"A-qing, you know something," Little Jade giggled. "When Mother was pregnant with me she went to the Goddess of the Sea Temple and prayed for a daughter. Just her bad luck that the Goddess had a cold that day and couldn't hear very well, so she gave her a son, assuming that's what she wanted."

"You naughty little boy . . ." She laughed so hard she shook. She gave him a playful slap and went into the kitchen rubbing her eyes. She re-emerged carrying a tray of watermelon slices, which she laid down on the greasy dining table. She handed each of us a huge slice. We were so thirsty we gobbled it down in no time. Little Jade's mother sat down beside him and began fanning his face with a large palm fan. The room was dark, cramped, and windowless. There were two lit candles on the table and an incense offering to the gods. It was so stifling inside that sweat ran down our faces.

"How's that little whore Moon Beauty? Still hanging around the G.I.s?" she asked him.

"Moon Beauty's business is getting better all the time. She's the queen of the New York Bar. Sometimes she has so many customers she can't take care of all of them. She's always complaining about her sore back and asks me to give her a rubdown," Little Jade reported cheerfully.

"Ptui!" his mother spat on the floor. "That slut! A few years back she came crying to me, saying her G.I. boyfriend had left her, so I tried to fix her up with Uncle Huowang's son Chunfa. But that little whore complained that he was ugly, with his crossed eyes and pitted skin. Well, Chunfa's making lots of money in his shoe business now, and Uncle Huowang's entire family is in fine shape. She wouldn't listen to me when I told her to get an abortion, so now she's stuck with that little bastard, half yellow and half white, who's going to tie her down for the rest of her life!"

"Mother, why didn't you get rid of me when you were in the same boat? Now you're stuck with your own bastard for the rest of your life, and look at the life I live." He smiled and looked up at her. There were a couple of drops of watermelon juice on the tip of his nose.

She snapped the fan a couple of times and heaved a helpless sigh.

"It's all your damned father's fault, that Lin Zhengxiong, 'Nakajima.' I really fell into that wild guy's trap. He said he'd send for me in Japan within a month . . . well, we're still here, and you're already grown."

"Mother," Little Jade said with a cock of his head, "I almost found Lin Zhengxiong, your Nakajima!"

"Huh?" She was startled.

"I said *almost*." He patted her shoulder. "This guy's name was Lin, too, Lin Maoxiong. Only off by one syllable. The night he told me his name I thought my heart was going to pop out of my chest. I asked him if he had a Japanese name, if he was called Nakajima. But he said no. Too bad, huh, Mother?"

"Tell me about him."

"An overseas Chinese from Japan, from Tokyo. He came to Taiwan to open a pharmaceutical plant."

"Oh." She sighed and shook her head. "Another one of your overseas Chinese sugar daddies."

"Lin Maoxiong's different, he was good to me. He gave me a job in his Taipei office and wanted to put me through night school."

"Really?" That surprised her. "Maybe this time luck is finally with you. Jade, I don't like to say bad things about you, but you're never going to make anything of yourself by drifting around Taipei the way you've been doing. Now that you've met someone decent you ought to stick with him, learn a thing or two. You sure won't go hungry that way."

"But he already went back to Japan," Little Jade said with a shrug of his shoulders. "And I don't know when he'll be back."

"Ai..." A sigh of disappointment.

"Mother," Little Jade said as he moved close to her and looked up in her face, "tell me something truthfully."

"What's that?"

"How many guys named Lin did you sleep with?"

"You rascal!" She rapped him on the head and laughed. "How can you talk like that to your mother? And in front of other people! Aren't you afraid lightning will strike you?"

"A-qing," he said, pointing to his mother, "Mother used to be the star at Eastern Clouds. Lots of men were after her. She was more popular than Moon Beauty."

"Moon Beauty? What's she got?" his mother sneered contemptuously. "You could ruin your mother's reputation by just comparing her to Moon Beauty. When I was at Eastern Clouds I wouldn't give the run-of-the-mill customer the time of day. Certainly no little slut like Moon Beauty, who'll go to bed with anybody, black or white."

"But you told me there were three or four guys named Lin chasing after you."

"Ai," she sighed ambiguously.

"Mother, how many guys named Lin *did* you sleep with?"

"Naughty boy," she said with a gloomy look on her face. "It's none of your business how many guys named Lin I slept with."

"Well, if you slept with so many guys named Lin how can you be sure that Lin Zhengxiong of Shiseido is my father?"

"You foolish kid," she said as she rubbed his head. She just looked at him for a moment before going on. "Do you think *I* wouldn't know something like that?"

"Mother . . ."

He suddenly grabbed the front of his mother's blouse, buried his face in her bosom, and bawled like a baby. His head lolled back and forth between her full breasts like a grapefruit on the loose. He was clawing at her green satin blouse with both hands so wildly that the seams began to rip. His shoulders heaved and the hollowness of his sobs belied the unspeakable pain they contained. He was rocking her so hard she could barely hold him. The front of her blouse was wet from his tears, his runny nose, and watermelon juice. Her forehead and face were covered with drops of perspiration that made her makeup run and gave her face a blotched look. She kept patting him on the back until he began to calm down. Undoing the scarf she'd tied around her hair, she used it to wipe his face and blow his nose.

"Jade," she said, "listen to me. I told Uncle Huowang, 'My Jade's coming home tonight and he'll be over to see you. I'd like you to save that pair of pig's ears for him!' Business was good last year for Uncle Huowang and his family, and that's why he's spending money on this feast. He had a big grin on his face when I told him. 'If that boy of yours'll come by to see me,' he said, 'I'll give him ten pairs of pig's ears!' He showed them to me. You've never seen such big, meaty ears as on that boar. They're already salted and ready to eat!"

Little Jade's almond-shaped eyes were puffy and red and his nose was still running, but he nodded to his mother when she finished and sniffled loudly. His shoulders were still heaving.

By a little after six in the evening, the streets and lanes of Sanchong City were crowded with people from all over converging on the local feasts. The host families carried the food and drink outside, under the arcades. Up and down the lanes, table after table piled high with slabs of fatty pork quivering on the plates, like so many mounds of meat, the crisp brown skin glistening with oil, like it was sweating in the heat. Some families had just brought their offerings back from the temple and were resting in their gateway, a several-hundred-catty boar spread out contentedly on the sacrificial rack, red cloth draped over its back, shiny orange in its mouth, bristles plucked clean, eyes narrowed into slits, as though it were smiling smugly. Most of the food had been prepared the day before and was now being laid out on the tables, platter after platter of food giving off meaty smells that blended with the heavy smoke of incense candles. Not a breath of wind in the air; the black pall of smoke that hung over Sanchong City pressed down, covering the people's sweaty faces with a fine layer of soot. But that didn't affect their appetites. They ate with gusto and guzzled glass after glass of wine. Jubilation reigned.

Uncle Huowang's feast was truly sumptuous, with sixteen overflowing platters, not counting the seafood, barbecued squid, and abalone with hot dressing. There were three whole fishes, red and yellow, stretched out open-mouthed and wide-eyed. Uncle Huowang picked up a bright yellow, greasy pig's ear with his chopsticks and put it on Little Jade's plate; his lips parted in a toothless grin and his wrinkled face beamed as he said:

"Eat it up, Jade, maybe you'll grow a couple of ears as big as these!"

Little Jade rocked with glee as he picked up the pig's ear and shoved it into his mouth. His cheeks bulged. The tip of the ear still sported a couple of rigid bristles, which he swallowed along with the meat. Uncle Huowang picked up a duck drumstick and put it on my plate. He also put a bottle of wine in front of me, to share with Little Jade. He rubbed Little Jade's head with one head and mine with the other. By this time, Little Jade's mother had drunk so much wine her face had turned red. Her hair was done up with a scarf. She was playing a drinking game with Uncle Huowang's eldest son, the cross-eyed Chunfa. "Eight fairies, eight fairies," she shouted as she held up the sign for eight. She lost three rounds and had to drink three full glasses of wine, which she drained without spilling a drop, before turning her glass upside down and banging it proudly down on the table. There were roars of approval from the guests around the table. Uncle Huowang, his toothless mouth opened wide, shook his head spiritedly and shouted:

"Ha! Ha!"

Little Jade was playing the same game with Uncle Huowang's pimply-faced youngest son, Chunfu. The loser of each round had to drink a glass of wine. Little Jade told me to monitor the drinking, since Chunfu was a notorious cheat. Chunfu won the first round. He was so thrilled he ground his fist in his palm and handed the glass to Little Jade.

"What's your hurry? Let me take a bite of pig's ear first."

He picked up an ear and gnawed it for a long time, until the impatient Chunfu grabbed him by the neck and threatened to pour the wine down. Little Jade pushed him away and laughed.

"I'll drink, don't worry!"

Second round. As soon as he saw he'd lost, Chunfu tried to sneak another finger in.

"Little Jade lost again!" he said. "Little Jade lost!"

"Fuck you," Little Jade shot back, his face turning red. "You little liar. How can you lie like that!"

He poured a glass of wine and tried to force Chunfu to drink it. They struggled for a moment, then Chunfu looked up and blurted out:

"Look, Little Jade, here comes the Shandong guy!"

"Where?" Little Jade jumped to his feet and let the glass drop to the table, spilling wine all over, as he frantically looked around. His mother rushed up and gave Chunfu a shove.

"Little brat, what's the idea of scaring my Jade?" she screamed.

She turned and patted Little Jade on the back. "Don't be afraid, Jade. So what if he comes? He's not the king of the underworld or anything. If he so much as touches a hair on your head, he'll answer to me!"

"It's okay, everything's okay," Uncle Huowang stepped up. "Here, Jade, have some wine. Have another pig's ear."

Little Jade sat down without saying a word and started in on the second ear. Chunfu sat there enjoying a good laugh at Little Jade's expense, but Little Jade just ignored him as he poured himself a glass of wine and drank it straight down.

Little Jade's mother was almost completely drunk by the end of the feast. She stumbled home leaning on her son's shoulder. As soon as she was inside the door she kicked off her gold-colored sandals and took off her dark-green skirt. All she had underneath was a tight-fitting flimsy black slip cinched around her protruding belly. The scarf around her hair had loosened, and some straggling hairs were stuck to her sweaty neck. By now her makeup was all blotchy. She sat down on a bench, her legs apart, and fanned her face with her hand. She pulled Little Jade over and sat him down beside her. After gazing at him with her puffy, sleepy almond-shaped eyes for a while, she reached out and wiped the sweat off his forehead with her hand. She sighed and mumbled:

"Jade, you know I wanted you to come home."

"I know," he said with his head down.

"That Shandong guy has a nasty temper, but he treats me okay. He hands all his money over to me and doesn't play around with other women. You have to understand that your mother isn't what she used to be. I'm getting old, old and useless."

Little Jade kept his head lowered, holding onto the bench with both hands, his shoulders hunched up.

"He treated you okay too at first. You can't blame him after what you did..."

"Mother, I have to go." Little Jade got to his feet.

"Aren't you going to spend the night?" She stood up.

"No, I have to see someone in Taipei."

He picked his piece of fabric up off the table and started toward the door, but his mother grabbed it out of his hand and walked over to the spirit table, where she took down two plates of rice cakes and wrapped them up in the cloth. She tied a knot and draped the bundle over Little Jade's arm. As we walked out the door, she ran up to him in her bare feet and said:

"He's going to Tainan for a couple of days on the seventh of next month. I'll let you know. A-qing, you come along with him, okay?"

"Aren't you going to report in to the 'nest' tonight?" I asked him on the bus back to Taipei.

"No, I'm going over to see Boss Wu at Tianxing."

"Going back for seconds, eh?" I laughed.

Boss Wu, who ran an import shop in Westgate district, was one of Little Jade's old flames. He'd been nice to Little Jade, but his rotten teeth made his mouth smell so bad that Little Jade had ignored him.

"So what's wrong with seconds?" he sneered. "I'm not a thoroughbred, anyway. Wu once promised me a wristwatch, so now I'm going to take him up on it."

"You're a specialist in bleeding old guys," I said.

Little Jade stuck out his left arm for me—it was bare. In the past he'd enjoyed showing off the Seiko watch Old Zhou had given him and saying, "A present from Old Zhou."

"I remember when I was in the sixth grade, Uncle Huowang bought Chunfu a Seiko watch. He wore it to school every day and flashed it around, saying 'A present from my father.' One day he took it off before gym class and left it in the classroom, so I stole it and wore it one night. The next day I threw it into a sewer and watched it sink to the bottom. I've wanted a Seiko watch of my own ever since."

The bus reached the Taipei Bridge. Since there were so many people heading into town, the packed bus barely crept along. I stuck my head out the window and glanced back across the Tamsui River at the dim lights of Sanchong City reflected in the water. The sky was filled with the reddish light of the hazy moon hanging in the filthy air above Sanchong City. I was suddenly reminded of the time I took Buddy to Sanchong City's China Splendor Theater to watch the performance of the Eastern Treasures Dance Troupe, and I could picture Mother's dancing legs and her heavily made-up face, with its forced, painful smile. On the bus back to Taipei that night, when we reached this very spot, Buddy stuck his head out the window and watched Sanchong City fade slowly into the distance. I held his hand, which was cold and clammy.

"What are you looking at, A-qing?" Little Jade asked me.

"The moon," I said.

24

"Fifty yuan! Who'll give fifty yuan?"

As I walked into the park I saw a crowd gathered at the lotus pond, and even from this distance I could hear Chief Yang's raucous laughter. He was wearing a bright purple sportshirt, standing up straight and snapping his fan open and shut. A-xiong was standing behind him like an enormous apparition, holding a big paper bag in his hands, filled with food, which he was stuffing into his mouth as fast as he could. Old Dick-Head was standing in the middle of the crowd shouting the price in his Hunanese accent. He had a lecherous smile on his face as he held up the hand of a boy next to him. The boy, who was no more than fourteen or fifteen, had a shaved head and a pale baby face; he was wearing a coarse white low-cut undershirt that exposed his scrawny neck. His pants were loosely fitting blue twills faded nearly white from countless washings. He was barefoot. He was looking all around, an embarrassed smile on his face.

"You old muskrat," Chief Yang said as he hit Old Dick-Head with his closed fan. "What henhouse did you steal this little chick from?"

He walked up and pinched the boy's upper arm and rubbed his hand over his thin neck.

"He's still covered with down," he complained with a smile. "What do you think you've got here, you old fart, have you lost your mind? I don't know what rubbish heap you picked this up from, but I'm surprised you've got the nerve to drag it over!"

Old Dick-Head pushed Chief Yang away and complained with angry embarrassment:

"Screw your old lady. I'm not selling off your son or anything, so what's the problem?"

Chief Yang stumbled backwards and bumped into A-xiong, who roared with anger, raised his fists, and charged toward Old Dick-Head, who quickly retreated and begged:

"Chief Yang, call off the big bully! He'll break these brittle old bones of mine if he hits me!"

Chief Yang held A-xiong back and said approvingly:

"Spare him this time, my boy, for the sake of your Dada!"

Then he stuck his fan right up under Old Dick-Head's nose threateningly.

"You see that, you old asshole? The next time you lay a hand on me, that boy of mine'll make quick work of your mangy hide!"

A-xiong raised his head proudly, fished a piece of sesame candy out of his bag, popped it into his mouth, and began sucking it loudly.

"Fifty yuan!" Old Dick-Head raised the boy's arm again as he turned to Chef Lu of the Cornucopia restaurant — Fatty Lu — and smiled fawningly: "Chef Lu, since you like to gnaw on bones so much, why not take this scrawny thing home with you and try him out."

Fatty Lu, grinning broadly, transported his huge belly over alongside the boy, where he felt him all over, front and back, and clicked his tongue.

"Not a bad set of ribs!"

He tweaked the boy's ear and said with a smile:

"Little one, how'd you like to come to my place and go to bed?"

The boy looked up at Fatty Lu for a moment, then grinned as he pointed to the candies in A-xiong's hand.

"Candy," he said, "candy."

Once the effect had sunk in, everyone roared with laughter.

"Well, I'll be damned, he's a loony!" Fatty Lu shook his head and laughed ruefully.

A-xiong reached into his bag and took out some sesame candy.

"Here," he said, handing it to the boy.

The boy grabbed it and shoved it into his mouth — all of it. His cheeks bulging, he stared at A-xiong, exchanging foolish grins with him as the two of them sucked noisily on their candy.

"I found this little loony at the entrance to the park last night," Old Dick-Head said with a laugh. "Guess what he was doing there. He had his pants down around his knees and was taking a piss!"

Everyone laughed.

"I took him home with me, but he didn't know a damned thing. Every time I touched him he just giggled like an idiot." Old Dick-Head scratched the ringworms on his neck and sighed out of exasperation.

"Boys! The fuzz!" Chief Yang's fan snapped open.

Two policemen on night patrol were heading our way from the tennis courts. Their boots were making a racket on the gravel path. Knowing just what to do, we scampered down the steps and spread out. Old Dick-Head grabbed the boy by the wrist and dragged him toward the park entrance.

"I'll take him with me."

I stopped Old Dick-Head at the gate, pulled two twenties and a ten out of my pocket, and stuffed them into his hand.

25

I took the boy back to Jinzhou Street with me. Moon Beauty wasn't home from work yet, so I sneaked into the kitchen, opened the refrigerator, and took out one of Johnny Jr.'s cartons of milk and a big red mango, one of Moon Beauty's "forbidden fruits" — they were so expensive she wouldn't let Little Jade or me near them. When I went back into my room, the boy had already climbed up onto my bed and was sitting there cross-legged with his muddy feet, his cleanly shaved scalp shining under the light. He hopped down off the bed when he saw the carton of fresh milk in my hand and tried to snatch it away from me.

"What's your name?" I asked him, holding the milk up out of his reach.

"Sonny," he replied.

"You idiot," I laughed. "What's your name? You have to have a name."

He just stared at me with his mouth open. He stared at me with his big, dark, unblinking eyes.

"Son...ny...," he repeated. "Everybody calls me Son...ny."

"Okay," I laughed, "then that's what I'll call you. You can call me A-qing. Understand? A...qing..."

"A...qing..." He drew it out just as I had.

I opened the carton of milk and handed it to him. He drank it down as though it were an elixir, finishing half in a single swig. Some of it dribbled down the sides of his mouth and onto his white undershirt. He quickly drank the rest, then smacked his lips and sighed contentedly, holding the empty carton tightly with both hands, unwilling to let go of it. I sat on the floor and peeled half the mango, then took a couple of bites. It was sweet and juicy, tasting a little like an apple. While I was enjoying the mango I looked up and saw that he was back on the bed again, staring at me, his mouth opened slightly, his eyes following the movements of the mango in my hand.

"Greedy pig!" I grumbled good-naturedly. "You just drank a whole carton of milk, so how can you have that sad, starved look?"

He swallowed and blinked.

"Get down off the bed if you want some. If you get mango juice on the bed it won't wash out." I signaled him to come down.

He hesitated for a moment, then put down the empty milk carton, crawled to the edge of the bed, and jumped down onto the floor next to me.

"Your home, Sonny, where do you live?" I asked him as I peeled the rest of the mango.

"Wanhua," he replied after a thoughtful pause.

"The street and house number, do you know them?"

"Wanhua..."

"What street in Wanhua, Sonny?"

"Huh..." He shook his head impatiently.

"Is it Yanping North Road?"

He just looked at me without saying a word.

"If you don't even know where your home is, what are we going to do?"

He began to giggle. He had a weird laugh, a crisp, rapid-fire sort of gurgle that stopped as abruptly as it began; he'd open his eyes wide, with a dumb look on his face for a moment, as though nothing seemed to matter, then start in again, gurgling so hard he'd be rocking back and forth, his shiny head bobbing crazily in the air.

"What's so funny?" I rebuked him. "You're in trouble if you don't even know how to get home!"

He stopped laughing, then sighed emotionlessly.

"Ai..."

I handed the peeled mango to him, and he bit into it, leaving the tip of his nose and his chin covered with yellow mango juice. After finishing the fruit he sucked the pit dry. When I tried to take it from him he pushed my hand away and grunted unhappily:

"Hai..."

I noticed that his neck and back were covered with a fine layer of dirt, and his skin gave off the strong, disagreeable smell of sweat. He probably hadn't bathed in days.

"You're filthy! Let's get you cleaned up." I pulled him to his feet and led him by the hand into the bathroom, where I filled a bucket with water and helped him get undressed. I handed him a gourd ladle and said:

"Wash yourself off while I go get you a towel."

He held the gourd in his hand and looked at it as he stood there stark naked.

"Like this, dummy!"

I took the gourd out of his hand, scooped some water out of the bucket, and poured it over his head. He quickly tucked his head down into his shoulders and started laughing. I reached out and held him still and splashed some more water over him. Then I picked up a bar of soap and washed his back for him.

"Sonny, who do you have at home?"

He thought hard for a moment.

"Papa."

"What does your papa do?"

"Peach...guava...persimmon..."

He chanted the names, one after the other.

"What do you mean, peaches, guavas? I asked you what your papa does." I laughed in spite of myself.

"And longans!" He suddenly recalled and added proudly to his list. "Papa sells fruit," he added casually.

"Who else is there in your family, Sonny?"

"Grandma...Auntie Feng..."

"How about your mama?"

He froze for a moment, then turned and looked at me wide-eyed.

"Mama went up the mountain...Auntie Feng said Mama went up the mountain."

He laughed that gurgling laugh, his head bobbing, his shoulders twitching.

"Sonny," I said as I held his shoulders, "you shouldn't be running off like this. What if your family can't find you?"

"Cock-a-doodle-doo!" he crowed.

"What kind of chicken is that?"

"A...red...rooster..." Another chant. "Auntie Feng taught me: Red...rooster...with...long...tail..."

I laughed as I scooped up another gourdful of water and dumped it over his head. When I finished washing him off I handed him a towel from the rack, but as soon as I bent over to pick up the bucket, he tossed away the towel and walked out of the room stark naked. I reached out and stopped him, picked up the towel, and wrapped it around his waist before letting him leave the bathroom. Then I poured another bucket of water and took a quick cold shower. I dumped both his and my dirty clothes into a wooden washtub and added some soap powder. Obasan was pretty nice to me, and sometimes she'd wash my dirty clothes along with the others, but only if I'd put them in a tub of water to soak the night before—she wouldn't touch them if I'd just taken them off. When I walked back into my room, Sonny was curled up on my bed fast asleep, without a stitch of clothes on, the towel lying on the floor. He slept with his mouth open, and was slobbering slightly.

26

I was half asleep. I reached out and put my arm around his shoulder. His skin was cold and clammy, soaked in sweat. He had his back to me, his backbone arched because of the way his legs were curled up. It was getting light outside, and the early-morning sun's rays reflected off his shaved head. For a fleeting moment I thought it was Buddy sleeping beside me. Buddy had slept with me for a year after Mother left, since he only felt safe when I was holding him. As we got older and had our own beds, he still came to bed with me sometimes, and we'd lie there and talk about lots of things. He'd gotten all wrapped up in sword-fighting novels, which I'd introduced to him, starting with a cartoon edition of *Seven Swordsmen and Five Gallants*. We'd lie there talking all night long about how the Five Rats stormed the capital. He'd call himself the Bright-Fur Rat Bai Yutang and make me the Sky Rat Lu Fang. Bai Yutang was a handsome young fighter with great martial skills, which naturally made him the most appealing to Buddy; as the youngest, Bai Yutang displayed the same sort of youthful arrogance as Buddy himself. On cold winter nights, chilling winds would seep in through the window, making our room colder and colder as the night wore on, until our feet were nearly frozen. Buddy would snuggle up close to me under the covers, and we'd warm each other. We'd talk about how the River Rat cleverly caught the rapist, and I'd reach out and put my arm around him, like I'd done when he was younger, and hold him close to me.

I picked the towel up off the floor and softly wiped the sweat off Sonny's back. I was as sweaty as he was, and my throat was parched, probably because I'd had so much to drink at the feast. I wasn't feeling very clear-headed. I got up, went into the bathroom, and doused my head with cold water. By the time I'd drunk some water and gone back into the room, the sun was up. Sonny was still curled up on the bed, sound asleep. I covered him up with an old shirt, got dressed, and walked downstairs with a toothbrush mug to buy some soy milk. The bright sun was beating down on the street, and even the early-morning breezes were hot.

I walked over to the stall in the next lane and bought some soy milk and a couple of sesame cakes filled with oil fritters. I went upstairs, where I heard giggles and laughter coming from my room. It was Little Jade, Wu Min, and Mousey, who'd come over while I was out. They were standing around the bed, where Sonny was sitting up, stark naked, and smiling at them bashfully. Little Jade and the others were pointing at him and giggling, like they were watching a caged monkey at the zoo.

"A-qing, where'd you get this little loony?" Little Jade asked when he heard me coming in. He was laughing so hard he was bent over double. "When we came in we asked him, 'Who are you? What are you doing here?' And would you believe it, he stood up in bed, grabbed his pee-pee and said, 'Wee-wee.' So I hurried up and got him one of your wash basins to pee in."

"Damn you, why didn't you get your own wash basin?" I complained. I looked down at my enamel wash basin and saw that it was half-filled with urine.

Mousey noticed the soy milk in my hand and reached out to take it from me. I pushed his hand away.

"I bought it for him," I said.

"Well, now!" Mousey exclaimed gleefully. "A-qing's got a boy of his own!"

Wu Min walked up and rubbed the top of his head. "Look here," he said, "that's quite a shiny little head he's got!"

I pushed my friends away from the bed and handed the soy milk to Sonny. He lifted it up and took two long swigs, then sighed contentedly. I gave him one of the sesame cakes and oil fritters, which he took from me and ate with gusto. Just as I was about to eat the one I'd bought for myself, Mousey grabbed hold of my wrist and bit off a big bite.

"You damned rat!" I complained with a laugh. I told them how Old Dick-Head had auctioned the boy off in the park the night before.

"Damn that dirty old man!" Little Jade said indignantly.

"Dirty old man is right!" Mousey cursed as he chewed. "I'm going to shove a stick up his ass!"

"Those ugly ringworm scars on his neck!" Wu Min frowned.

Little Jade and the others had come over to get me to go swimming with them at the Eastgate Pool. They'd brought towels with them. But swimming in that crowded, filthy pool wasn't very appealing, so I recommended the headwaters at the Firefly Bridge. That would be a lot more fun. It sounded so good to them, they wondered why they hadn't thought of it.

"What about the kid here?" I pointed to Sonny, who was sitting on the bed again. "I was going to take him home today, but he's not even sure where he lives."

Little Jade walked over and took hold of the boy's ear. "You come with us to the river, little darling, and go swimming with us. You can wash your pee-pee, what do you say?"

Sonny stared dumbly at Little Jade with an apprehensive look on his face. Wu Min pushed Little Jade aside.

"Sonny," he said, "we'll take you with us to swim in the river, how does that sound?" He took a couple of strokes in the air to show Sonny what he was talking about.

"Pop...si...cle..." Sonny drawled.

"Okay, okay, we'll buy you a popsicle!" Wu Min assured him with a pat on the shoulder.

Sonny started gurgling, and was soon laughing so hard he was rocking back and forth, his shiny head bobbing in the air.

148

"Shit!" Mousey complained. "He's damned retarded!"

We agreed it would be a good idea to take Sonny swimming at the Firefly Bridge. I dug out some old clothes for him — a tattered white, loose-fitting shirt and a pair of khaki pants that were so long they dragged on the ground. I rolled up the cuffs and pinned them so they wouldn't roll down again. Since I had no shoes for him, we let him go barefoot. Little Jade and the others had rented bicycles, so the five of us headed out, with Sonny on the back of mine, Wu Min on the back of Little Jade's, and Mousey riding alone, with our towels on his rack. I told Sonny to hold me tightly around the waist. Little Jade was so unsteady he nearly crashed into the pedestrian island, causing Wu Min to shout out from behind him, "Careful, be careful!"

"Don't panic, little Wu, you'll be okay!" Little Jade shouted. "Slicing your own wrist didn't seem to bother you, so what's all the screeching about?"

Mousey was on a racing bike, leaning over the handlebars, his butt sticking straight up in the air. He whistled as he rode up alongside Little Jade and rubbed him on the face, then dropped back and gave Wu Min a kick in the leg. Little Jade's bike was wobbling worse than ever. His head bathed in sweat, a steady stream of curses emerged from his mouth, every word he could think of. Sonny was laughing happily behind me. We were hitting each other, cursing at each other, shouting, laughing, three bicycles whizzing grandly along, all the way to the headwaters at the Firefly Bridge. Our clothes were soaked by the time we got down off our bikes.

Since it hadn't rained in a long time, the water in the Xindian river was extremely shallow; the receding water exposed a lot of sandbars covered with gray pebbles and stones. The white powdery tips of reeds on the banks swayed in the wind and glared white under the boiling sun. The Xindian River was the only river in Taipei that hadn't suffered serious pollution, and it still had a green cast. In earlier summers, I'd often taken Buddy swimming there. When we'd finally leave to go home we'd be as red as lobsters. Within a couple of days Buddy would start to peel, beginning with the tip of his nose, which would become a white dot in the middle of his bright red face. Whenever a typhoon was on its way, we'd rush over and get in as much swimming as we could, because once the typhoon landed, the water would get all muddy as it rose higher and higher, with little whirlpools all over, making swimming impossible.

We walked our bikes down to one of the sandbars beside the river, walked in among the reeds, which rose above our heads, so we could strip down to our underwear without being seen before running down to the water. The pebbles and stones, which had been baked in the sun, burned the soles of our feet. Ouch! Ouch! Ouch! We ran and hopped along as fast as we could. Little Jade, who was wearing a pair of bright red nylon briefs, was in the lead. When Mousey caught up to him he patted him on the butt and giggled.

"Steal a pair of your mother's panties?"

Little Jade spun around and kicked him, catching him by surprise and forcing him to drop back a couple of steps.

"Rat Spirit!" Little Jade shouted at him. "Watch out or I'll kick you in the balls!"

Sonny, the slowest of the group, was bringing up the rear. The rocks were so hot he was having trouble keeping his balance, and before long he stumbled and sat down hard on the sandbar, screaming bloody murder. I ran back and pulled him to his feet, then dragged him down to the water's edge.

As soon as he reached the riverbank, Little Jade shoved Mousey hard and sent him sprawling into the soft mud in the shallow water, head first. He squirmed and crawled for a long time before he could get to his feet, clenching two fistfuls of mud. His face was caked with mud, and he was spitting the filth out of his mouth. We clapped and laughed at the sight, but he was fuming as he stumbled and ran after Little Jade to get even. Little Jade jumped into the water, splashing up a storm as he swam out to the center. He knew the breaststroke and was a fast swimmer. Mousey, who could only dogpaddle, couldn't keep up, and strained to keep his head above water as he inched along, barely moving at all. Before he'd gone more than a few feet, Little Jade was way ahead of him.

"Faster, Mousey, faster!" Wu Min and I called out from the riverbank.

By the time he'd made it out to the middle of the river, Mousey could see there was no way he'd ever catch Little Jade, so he turned and started back. By the time he crawled up onto the riverbank he was exhausted, his face bright red. He was gasping so badly he couldn't close his mouth.

"You're a real river rat now!" Wu Min teased him.

"Fuck you!"

Mousey's embarrassment quickly turned to anger. He bent

down, scooped up a handful of mud, and flung it into Wu Min's face. Not to be outdone, Wu Min kicked mud all over Mousey. The two of them broke for the river, stood in the shallow water, and began a water fight. Sprays of water flew up into the air, turning into strings of crystalline pearls under the bright sunlight. Mousey's upper arm was covered with dark welts from cigarette burns, Wu Min's wrist sported the bright red scar of a razor cut. The two combatants swung their injured arms in the air, as the fight grew fiercer and fiercer, until they were so tired they were about to drop; they drew closer and closer, finally falling into each other's arms, their heads resting on their opponents' shoulders, as they gasped for breath.

I was watching the battle so intently I forgot all about Sonny, who had been standing next to me, and before I knew it, he was out in the river where the water was up to his chest, waving his skinny arms in the air. His shaved scalp shone brightly in the glaring sun. I jumped into the water, which was so cool that the heat seemed to suddenly disappear altogether. As I drew up next to Sonny, he rolled over and started thrashing with both arms. His head went under and his legs began to kick, like a duck diving beneath the surface. He started to float, and actually began moving through the water.

"You little devil, so you know how to swim!" I said when his head broke the surface after he'd swum a few strokes.

"Hee, hee." He was taking in gulps of air.

"Come over here," I called to him. "I'll teach you the breast-stroke."

I stroked the water a couple of times to show him how it was done.

"Brothers!" Little Jade called out from the opposite bank. "Come on over here!"

He was standing on one of the bridge pylons, waving his arms at us. Mousey and Wu Min dove into the water and began swimming over to the opposite bank. Sonny pointed excitedly at Little Jade, eager to follow the other two.

"Hold on there!" I grabbed him. "You can't make it alone."

Growing suddenly obstinate, he began dragging me along, making grunting noises as he tugged.

"Sonny, listen to me!" I shouted. "If you're determined to cross the river, I'll take you over on my back. Hold me around the waist and kick like me."

I pulled his arms around my waist and we slipped into the water to give it a try. It seemed to work okay.

"Mousey, Wu Min, we're right behind you!" I shouted as Sonny and I started slowly across the river, his arms around my waist, both of us kicking. Mousey and Wu Min turned and escorted us slowly to the opposite bank, the four of us looking like a little flotilla. The water was shallow and smooth, without a ripple in sight. Having Sonny on my back didn't tire me at all. I remembered bringing Buddy here before he knew how to breathe while he swam, so the most he could manage was twenty or thirty meters, never all the way across. After I taught him how to do it, I swam alongside him the first time. We were about halfway there when he swallowed a mouthful of water and got scared. He wanted to turn back. But I yelled at him to stay where he was, then had him put his arms around my waist, and we made it to the other side. It was July, nearly sunset, and the sun, a bright red ball, was almost out of sight on the other side of the Firefly Bridge. There was quite a bit of wind that day, which made the going rough. We swam toward the setting sun, straining to move through the water, until we finally made it to the other side. Since it was the first time Buddy had crossed the river, as soon as he crawled up out of the water he began shouting excitedly, as the sun's rays turned his face a reddish yellow.

"Hooray!" Little Jade shouted as he reached out and helped Sonny and me up onto the bank. Mousey and Wu Min followed us up, and the five of us sat there on the pylon, dripping wet, to rest. There was a lot of noise from the cars and pedestrians on the bridge above and the street that paralleled the river; it was noon, and people were leaving work to rush home for lunch. The wind blowing beneath the bridge was cool and comfortable. Sonny sat there swinging his legs and humming a disjointed tune of some sort, happily, proudly.

"Little loony!" Little Jade patted him on the head. "I didn't know you could sing."

"'Little Mouse'—Auntie Feng taught me," he cocked his head and answered confidently. "And 'Red Rooster.'"

"Okay, Sonny," Wu Min said to urge him on, "that 'Little Mouse' of yours sounds nice. Let's hear it!"

"Sounds like a dumb song to me!" Mousey grumbled.

Lit—tle—mouse—
Poin—ty—mouth—
Stole an egg—stole some noodles—

Sonny sang one syllable at a time without taking a breath. He sang with enthusiasm, stretching his neck for effect. Little Jade, Wu Min, and I laughed so hard our bellies began to hurt. Little Jade was rolling on the ground and pointing to Mousey.

"This little mouse's mouth is even pointier, he steals pee-pees!"

Mousey ran over and kicked Little Jade a couple of times, then went over and grabbed Sonny's ear.

"Listen to me, you," he shouted. "From now on you'd better treat Mousey with respect! Understand? I don't want to hear that goddamn song ever again!"

"Then I'll sing 'The Red Rooster,'" Sonny said.

"Forget it," Mousey frowned impatiently. "You go back and sing those songs of yours for your A-qing here. We don't want to hear them. We're gonna go catch some crabs."

There were lots of little indentations in the bank beneath the Firefly Bridge, where crabs lived. Once Mousey caught seven or eight of them, which he brought over to my place and fried until they were bright red and smelled delicious. He shared them with Little Jade, Wu Min, and me.

Leaving Sonny alone on the cement pylon, the four of us scampered down onto the riverbank and started turning over stones. Mousey, always impatient, turned over a big rock before the rest of us were in place, exposing a big crab that easily got away. Mousey leapt and ran after it, but couldn't catch it, and by the time the rest of us had joined the chase, the crab was in the water and out of sight. Mousey stomped his foot and stormed around, turning over every rock in sight. We combed the area for a while, but all we managed to catch were two small soft-shelled crabs. Mousey took them, cursing and spitting in the sand, and threw them into the river. By then we were all getting hungry, so we decided to go over and buy some sticky rice balls. Just then we discovered that Sonny was no longer sitting on the pylon. In our anxiety we all began shouting:

"Sonny!"

"I wonder if the little loony fell into the river?" Little Jade mumbled.

"Let's go take a look on the bridge," Wu Min suggested.

We scampered up the stone path and pulled ourselves up onto the bridge, which was packed with cars and pedestrians. We spotted a crowd of people at the head of the bridge, pointing and laughing at something. When we ran over there we saw Sonny in the middle of the crowd, stark naked. No sign of his underpants anywhere. He had his arms crossed in front of his pale, thin chest, which was covered with a red liquid that was dripping down his body. He was staring blankly at the crowd of people, his lips parted in a foolish grin. But there was fear in his eyes, which were blinking rapidly. Most of the people were curiosity-seeking children and teenagers, including a few girls who craned their necks to see what was going on, then quickly ran away with open-mouthed astonishment. A couple of scowling young thugs in wooden clogs were standing in front of Sonny. One of them was throwing pieces of half-eaten watermelon at Sonny's chest. Mousey pushed his way into the crowd, ran straight up to the young thug, and shoved him hard.

"Who the fuck do you think you're hitting!" he snarled.

"He's crazy!" the young thug growled back.

"He was pissing on the ground!" the other one said indignantly.

"What the hell business is that of yours?" Mousey said with excited gestures. "As long as he didn't piss in your mouth, what're you worried about?"

The rest of the crowd burst out laughing, as the two young thugs doubled up their fists and moved menacingly toward Mousey.

"Brothers, a fight!" Little Jade shouted. We all pushed our way into the crowd and lined up in front of Sonny, ready for a fight. Seeing that they were outnumbered, the two young thugs quickly backed off.

"We're gonna call a cop," one of them shouted as they moved off, "and have him arrest the idiot!"

The four of us exchanged looks. Little Jade and I each took one of Sonny's hands and started running along the bridge, Mousey and Wu Min leading the way. When we got to the end we half-ran, half-slid down the bank to the river's edge. We didn't stop until we'd made our way into the clump of reeds where we'd stashed the bikes and our clothes. We collapsed to the ground and lay there without moving, lying on the hot sand gasping until we caught our breath. Suddenly, as if on command, we all broke out laughing.

"Fuck it all . . ."

27

"I'm not running an insane asylum, so why'd you bring that loony over here? What if something happens?"

Moon Beauty raised a stink when she discovered that I'd kept Sonny overnight.

"Don't worry, he doesn't know a thing and won't cause any trouble," I explained to her. Sonny was sitting cross-legged on my bed, his face and scalp sunburned. He was watching Moon Beauty and blinking rapidly.

"You make it sound so simple!" she said, pointing straight at me to emphasize her point. "He just walked away from home like a loony, and I'm sure his family is looking for him. How do you know they haven't already reported him missing to the police? You take him home right now, before the police come and accuse us of hiding a mental defective."

"Where'll I take him?" I smiled with my arms outstretched. "He's not even sure where he lives . . . all he knows is that it's somewhere in Wanhua."

"Ai, it's all your fault!" Moon Beauty said with an angry stare as she sat down beside Sonny and took a good look at him. She smiled and said coaxingly:

"Come on, Sonny, tell Moon Beauty where you live. What street in Wanhua? Guangzhou Street? Somewhere around Dragon Mountain Temple? Do you know what I'm talking about?"

He just sat there looking at her with his mouth open.

"You're not going to tell me? Your mother must be frantic by now. Is your mother looking for you, do you know?"

She reached out and rubbed the top of his head, which started him gurgling. He was soon rocking back and forth, a steady stream of grunts and other noises like baby talk issuing from his mouth.

"What the hell's going on?" Moon Beauty asked anxiously.
I laughed.

"He's telling you that his mother went up the mountain."

"Ai . . ." Moon Beauty sighed and shook her head. "He really is retarded."

"Fruit . . . fruit . . ." Sonny began shouting.

Johnny Jr. ran into the room just then, eating a peach.

Obasan was right behind him, breathing heavily and holding her stomach. Sonny scampered down off the bed and reached out to take the peach from Johnny Jr., who darted behind Obasan for protection.

"You trying to steal from a little boy!" Obasan raised her hand to hit him. Sonny tucked his head down between his shoulders and closed his eyes.

"Obasan, go get the little loony a peach from the refrigerator!" Moon Beauty said with a laugh.

"Have A-qing get one if you want it!" Obasan shot back. "The mango that was in there is gone, and a couple of Johnny Jr.'s milk cartons are missing. You ask A-qing what happened to them."

I ran out of the room, followed by Moon Beauty's curses:

"You tired of living, or what? How dare you touch one of my mangos! They're twenty yuan apiece! If you don't replace it by tomorrow, you can just forget about eating any more of my food!"

I brought in a peach and handed it to Sonny.

"Did you hear that?" I said to him with a laugh. "Your greedy mouth got me into trouble!"

Sonny took the peach from me, but seemed hesitant to eat it. He just turned it over and over in his hand, like he was playing with it.

"You listen to me," Moon Beauty said to me, pointing at Sonny. "You're the one who brought this trouble with you, so you figure out how to deal with it. I want you to take the little loony back tonight. I don't care where you take him, even if it's the police station or an insane asylum."

"Moon Beauty," I said with a smile, "you're a good woman. It's already too late tonight, so let him stay one more night. Tomorrow I'll take him to the police and let them find out where he lives."

"No!" Moon Beauty waved her hands in the air. "I let a couple of crystal boys like you and Little Jade live in my house, and that's trouble enough. People showing up looking for you, coming here for a fight! Now you've got this mental defective, and you're going to drive me crazy! Besides, you still owe me three hundred for last month's rent, and now you expect me to put someone else up. Get me mad enough and I'll send you packing, too!"

"I promise," I said, thumping my chest, "I'll get the money for the rent tonight. Then we can talk, okay?"

"I'll talk when I see the color of your money . . ." Moon Beauty's tone softened. She looked at me out of the corner of her eye and giggled:

"Throw your line out a little farther tonight and see if you can hook a nice big goldfish!"

Just before I left I very solicitously asked Obasan to look after Sonny for me and to give him some leftovers after dinner.

"You want me to take care of this little loony on a hot night like this?" she complained.

"Please, Obasan. I'll bring some lichees home for you."

Obasan could eat a couple of pounds of lichees all by herself. She once ate so many she had a nosebleed and had to drink some herbal tea to stop the bleeding.

"Make sure they're fresh!" she snorted. "Last time some of the ones you got were wormy."

I went over to the park to talk to Chief Yang, who was sitting on the railing of the lotus pond with A-xiong, so close they looked like a pregnant giant. I sidled up to Chief Yang, put out my hand, and asked him for a loan of five hundred yuan.

"Chief," I said with a smile, "it's really important. I promise I'll pay you back in a couple of days."

"You think I own a bank?" he asked with a scowl. "Everybody comes to me with their hand out. Tell you what I'll do, I'll find you a way to get the money. You go on over to the Great World and wait for me there. I'll go find you a god of wealth."

I walked over to the Great World on Hengyang Road, found a quiet corner, sat down, and ordered a glass of guava juice. I'd been waiting about a half hour when Chief Yang walked up with another man. He told the man to sit down next to me, then he sat down across from me.

"This is Manager Lai," Chief Yang introduced the man. He looked at Lai and asked him with a smile:

"Well, what do you think, Manager Lai? I was telling you the truth, wasn't I? Good looking boy, isn't he?"

The man named Lai moved closer to me and sized me up. He was a big, fat man around forty with a bright red face that looked sweaty and greasy in the rose-colored lights of the café. His hair was cut short, parted in the middle, and permed into soft waves. He was wearing a green Thai silk sportshirt with gold threads. His paunch stuck out when he sat down. He had a thick gold ring on the stubby middle finger of his left hand. While he was looking me over, his puffy eyes were smiling. I lowered my head and concentrated on drinking my guava juice.

"A-qing, Mr. Lai runs the Yongchang Apparel shop in the Westgate district." Chief Yang smiled at Lai and said, "Mr. Lai wants to give you a pair of dress slacks—custom made!"

"What's your waist size, little one? Here, let me measure it for you." He reached over and pinched my waist, and I moved away. He and Chief Yang laughed.

"Well built!" Lai said with a smile. "Do you work out?"

"This disciple of mine has all the skills down pat. He knows all the moves." Chief Yang and Lai laughed again. Chief Yang snapped his fingers for the waiter, who brought over two bottles of cold beer.

"What do you say, little one?" Lai said as he patted me on the shoulder. "Do you want mohair or dacron?"

I kept my head down as I drank through the straw.

"I recommend orlon," Chief Yang answered for me. "The last time I was in your shop I saw some new orlon suit material that looked nice. It's cool in the summer. I nearly had a suit made out of it, but when I heard the price—forty-five hundred—I got out of there in a hurry. We can't afford to have suits made in your shop." He sighed with a show of lament.

"A suit for Chief Yang is the easiest thing in the world. The Yongchang Apparel shop can certainly afford to express that little bit of appreciation." Lai thumped himself proudly on the chest. "I'll be in tomorrow. You come by in the morning and I'll give you a fitting."

"With a body like mine, I'm afraid your shop will take a loss." Chief Yang lowered his head and looked helplessly at the bulging spare tire around his waist.

"We'll make it a trade-off," Lai leaned forward and whispered in Chief Yang's ear, giving me a passing glance with his puffy little eyes.

"This disciple of mine can do it all!"

Chief Yang and Lai exchanged glances. Suddenly it felt as though there were caterpillars squirming all over my thigh. It was Lai's hand under the table, his fingers inching their way up my leg. I broke out in a cold sweat. Reaching under the table, I grabbed Lai's stubby hand, the one with the gold ring on the finger, lifted it up over the table and slammed it down so hard the beer bottles rattled.

"Chief, I have to go!"

I stood up and walked to the door without so much as looking back. Chief Yang ran after me, and I heard him call my name in a low, angry voice:

"A-qing..."

I left the Great World and headed for the Silver Chariot in Westgate to look up Manager Yan. He was a Hunanese from the city of Hengyang whom I'd met in the park the first week after leaving home. He'd taken me to his apartment on Jinhua Street and asked me to move in with him. Then he set me up with a job at the Silver Chariot as a waiter.

"Little one," he frowned, "you've just started out, so it's not too late to turn back. You need to get a decent job right away, because the longer you hang around the park, the harder it's going to be to ever find your way out!" I worked at the Silver Chariot for three days, and when I walked out I still had a key to his apartment in my pocket. I never found the time to return it.

I walked into the Silver Chariot and headed straight for the manager's office, where I bowed deeply and said:

"How are you, Manager Yan?"

"So it's you! How do you have the guts to face me?" Just seeing me shocked him. There was still anger in his voice as he said, "I thought they'd taken you to Taiwan's Fire Island!"

"I need a big favor," I said.

"So I can still be of some use to you," he sneered.

"I need a short-term loan. I desperately need five hundred." I straightened up.

"A loan? What makes you think it's that easy?"

"If I don't pay my rent I'm going to be evicted," I said imploringly.

Manager Yan nodded and sighed.

"A real piece of trash! I offered you a place to live for free, but you didn't know what was good for you. You chose the gutter instead...they say you're all the rage around the park! How could you be broke?"

I lowered my head and didn't say anything for a moment.

"If you lend me five hundred I promise I'll find a way to pay you back. If you've got some odd jobs around here, I'll do them for you and you can take what I owe you out of my wages."

"Sounds to me like you're trying to get back on the right track." He was softening up. "I'll give you another chance. It just so happens I need a replacement for one of our waiters, who's sick and needs to take three days off. Show up for work to-morrow at two o'clock."

He reached into his wallet and took out three hundred-yuan bills.

"It's up to you to make something out of yourself," he said. "I'll give you three hundred now and the rest when you show up for work."

I took the money from him, thanked him profusely, and ran out of the Silver Chariot. After buying some lichees at a fruit stand, I stopped at another stall and bought four turnip cakes fresh off the griddle, two sweet and two salty. This place was known for its turnip cakes, because of the way they made the outside soft yet crispy; and they used lard in the filling, so they smelled as good as they tasted. When I was going to night school at Yude, if I had money in my pocket on the way home, I'd get off the bus in Westgate and stop at this stall to buy four turnip cakes and take them home to share with Buddy as a late-night snack. On cold winter nights I tucked the newspaper-wrapped turnip cakes up against my chest and zipped up my jacket, so they were still warm by the time I got them home. If Buddy was asleep, I woke him up and the two of us would open the newspaper wrapping and eat our snacks in bed, leaving sesame seeds all over the sheets.

Sonny was sound asleep in bed, naked, his undershirt and underpants on the floor beside the bed. I walked over and noticed that the bottom half of the straw mat was soaked. I put down the lichees and the packet of turnip cakes and shook him awake.

"Get up, get up!" I picked him up under the armpits. He stared at me with sleepy eyes. The straw mat had left a red imprint on his left cheek.

"Look what you've done!" I said as I pointed to the urine-soaked mat. I picked it up off the bed. The mattress was also soaked with a yellow stain. He stood there without moving, his eyes darting back and forth. Unable to keep my anger in check, I smacked him on the butt.

"Wetting the bed at your age!"

I'd slapped him so hard he lurched forward and looked at me with fear in his eyes, rubbing his butt as he scampered over to the corner. I took the straw mat and mattress into the bathroom, and since I couldn't wash the mattress, I hung it up on the clothes rack, planning to take it outside in the morning and dry it in the sun. I scrubbed the straw mat with a soapy rag until the urine stain was gone. Then I took it out to the balcony and hung it up to dry on the clothes rack. When I got back to the room, Sonny was cowering in the corner with his arms around his knees, making himself as small as possible. He kept his mouth tightly closed as he watched me walk into the room; his eyes were as big as saucers. I picked up the packet of turnip cakes and sat down across from him, then opened the newspaper wrapping and put the cakes down on the floor.

"Look, Sonny, I bought some turnip cakes for you." I handed him one of the sweet ones, but instead of taking it from me, he just sat there staring at me.

"It's sweet, you'll love it." I smiled and held it up in front of him. He turned his head away.

"To hell with you. I'll eat it myself!" I finished it off in a couple of bites.

"Um, good!" I smacked my lips and looked straight at him. His eyes were fixed on my mouth.

"Want one?" I put a salty cake up to his mouth. He reached out and knocked it out of my hand. It hit the ground and left a trail of sesame seeds as it rolled around.

"You tired of living?" I rapped his scalp with my knuckles, stood up, and retrieved the turnip cake, which had rolled over to the foot of the bed. I blew off the dust. Sonny covered up his head with his hands, his lips began to twitch, and he was soon sobbing, tears dripping from his cheeks onto his scrawny, pale chest. I stood in front of the naked, crying boy, feeling miserable. I knelt down and patted him on the shoulder.

"I was just teasing you, little guy" I smiled. "It wasn't a real hit."

He ignored me, keeping his head protected as his shoulders heaved.

"Okay, okay, I won't ever do that again," I said as I rubbed his head.

Last year, on Buddy's fifteenth birthday, I'd hit him and given him a nosebleed. Buddy had always done whatever I told him to do, but this time he'd surprised me by losing his temper. It had been his turn to wash the dishes that night, but he'd stayed in his room sitting in bed and reading an illustrated edition of *Huang Tianba* I'd gotten from a rental library. He ignored me every time I called him out. When I tried to take the book from him, he knocked my hand away and said, "Get lost!" That made me so mad I reached out and slapped him hard enough to send him flying. It was the first time I'd ever gotten rough with him, let alone make his nose bleed. He didn't cry, he didn't make a sound. He just picked up a wad of tissues, raised his head, and wiped away the blood that was flowing from his nostril. I was shocked that I'd lost control like that. When we went to bed that night, I lay there in the darkness listening to him blow his nose. I didn't sleep at all that night. I felt absolutely miserable. The next day, when I gave Buddy the Butterfly harmonica I'd bought at the school co-op, he shouted his glee and started playing it right away, unwilling to put it down even for a minute. There were still a few drops of dried blood in the corners of his nostril.

Sonny finally stopped sobbing after I pacified him for the longest time. I went into the bathroom, soaked a washcloth, and wiped his face with it, then handed him the remaining sweet turnip cake. This time he took it and ate it greedily. In no time at all, he'd finished both of them off. A few sesame seeds stuck to the corners of his mouth.

"Did you like the turnip cakes, Sonny?" I asked him as we lay on the hard bedboard.

"Um," he replied.

"Which do you like better, sweet or salty?"

"Sweet...," he said after thinking it over.

"Then next time I'll only buy sweet ones, okay?"

"Um."

"But no more bed-wetting. If you do you can't have any."

"Ha, ha," he laughed.

"Did you have fun swimming today?"

"Fun."

"We'll go back there in a couple of days."

"Um."

"You know there's no swimming when a typhoon's coming," I said. I'd heard over the radio that typhoon Emily was heading toward Taiwan from the Philippines, and was threatening to sweep across northern Taiwan in a day or two if it didn't change course.

"Typhoon... big winds, whoosh, whoosh, whoosh, you know what I mean?"

"Whoosh, whoosh...," he copied me. I laughed.

"Let's get some sleep, Sonny," I said.

"Um."

I rolled over and put my arm around his thin, bony shoulder.

28

The weather had changed by the next morning, with the skies clear one minute and overcast the next. The barometric pressure dropped. I stopped sweating, and there was little doubt that Emily was about to hit. When I woke up, Sonny was still asleep, lying on his side, his skinny back a mass of lines put there by the bedboards. I walked into the bathroom, where I ran into Obasan, who was down on her haunches beside the tub washing clothes. When she saw me she pointed to the straw mat hanging above the tub and grumbled:

"You've got so many things hanging in this bathroom I could barely squeeze in here."

"I'll take it down," I said with a smile. "The little guy wet the bed last night. We haven't given you any extra trouble, have we, Obasan?"

"Enough of that talk!" she muttered. "The little loony may be skinny, but he eats like a pig. I gave him a plate of food, and after he gobbled it down he took Johnny Jr.'s hamburger before I could stop him. Last night Moon Beauty didn't know whether to laugh or cry with that little loony around."

"Why?"

She flipped the soapsuds off her hand and started to chuckle.

"Last night, Judy, Mona, and Lulu Wu from China Doll came over to see Moon Beauty. The crazy broads sat around nibbling melon seeds and chattering. While they were teasing Lulu Wu for having breast implants, your little loony walked in on them, naked as a jaybird, and sat down beside Moon Beauty. They were speechless. The little loony reached out and touched Moon Beauty's face with both hands and buried his head between her breasts. She laughed and said, 'You're going to be the death of me!' and pushed him over into Lulu Wu's lap. Lulu, Judy, and Mona tried to get out of his way, they screamed, and it was a wild scene. Finally, Moon Beauty managed to coax him out of the room with a piece of watermelon."

"I never thought the little guy would end up in a kingdom of lovelies!" I laughed.

"I think you'd better get him out of here quick," Obasan said with a sigh. "I wonder what his folks did to deserve a kid like that!"

"I'm trying to figure out where he lives so I can take him home," I said to calm her down. "Obasan, I brought some lichees home last night, big, juicy ones." I showed her how big they were with my hands.

"Oh," she muttered. "I don't believe you, let's see them."

I washed up and went back to the room. Sonny was sitting on the edge of the bed, looking around sleepily. The minute he saw me his lips parted in a broad grin. I reached under the bed and took out some old clothes. I handed them to him.

"Sonny," I said, "I'm going out for a while. You wait here for me, and don't leave the room, understand?"

"Um," he replied with a nod.

"And keep your clothes on," I said, tugging lightly at his shirt and giving him a gentle swat on the butt. "Running around bare-assed is a no-no, isn't it?"

"Ball, ball," he shouted gleefully, as a red, white, and blue ball came rolling into the room and bumped against his leg. He gave it a kick and sent it bouncing crazily around the room. Johnny Jr. rushed into the room, dressed in shorts with a split crotch, got down on his hands and knees, and crawled after the ball, laughing and having a great time. Sonny got down on the floor and joined him in his pursuit of the errant ball.

I picked up the lichees I'd bought the night before and took them into the kitchen to give to Obasan, who quickly peeled one and popped it into her mouth with a little moan of pleasure. I handed her two hundred yuan and asked her to give it to Moon Beauty.

"This is for the rent. I'll give her the rest in a couple of days."

I handed her another twenty and asked her to buy Sonny a couple of steamed buns when she was shopping for groceries. A light rain was falling outside and dark clouds were gathering. I looked up at the window of my room just as a shiny head popped out. Sonny was looking out the window. I waved to him, and he raised both arms and returned my wave.

"Say, little guy . . . ," I shouted.

"Ya, ya," he shouted from the window.

I rushed over to the Silver Chariot in Westgate, arriving just in time for the afternoon shift. Manager Yan praised me when he saw me:

"Looks like you're on the right track."

"I want to show you how much I appreciate your help," I smiled.

"When did you suddenly see the light?" he said with a slight frown. "Hurry up and put on a uniform."

I changed into a white waiter's jacket and black pants, and began serving trays of iced coffee, lemonade, red-bean soup, and sugar-cane nectar. The customers who came in to get out of the rain and the oppressive heat were all talking about Emily: the winds were picking up, the radius of the storm had expanded to five hundred miles, it'd probably hit Taiwan tomorrow afternoon. After the shops in Westgate closed up for the night, people busied themselves with boarding up shop windows. At ten o'clock, closing time at the Silver Chariot, Manager Yan divided up the tips and gave each of us thirty-five yuan. He called me into his office, where he took two hundred-yuan bills out of his pocket and handed them to me.

"This is the balance of what you asked me for yesterday, five hundred altogether. Go pay your rent—and this better not be another one of your lies."

I took the money.

"This time I'm telling you the truth," I swore. "I gave my landlady two hundred yesterday. I still owe her a hundred."

He looked me over and said softly:

"What are your plans after your three days here? Back to the park to take up where you left off?"

My face felt hot. I lowered my head and mumbled:

"Maybe I'll try getting a job . . . if you need some help around here, I'd be willing to come back."

"I don't have an opening now, but one of the boys is leaving next month, and I'll let you know," Manager Yan said earnestly. "Now, you'd better be going, the typhoon's almost here."

Before I left the Silver Chariot I went into the kitchen, where I took a bag out of the cabinet. In it were two chestnut cakes one of the customers had left behind in his hurry to get to the theater. I'd put them into a bag and tucked them away in the cabinet, planning to take them home for a late-night snack with Sonny. On the bus ride home I wondered how much longer I could keep Sonny with me at Moon Beauty's. Where could I take him after I'd run out of excuses? Maybe after my three days of part-time work I could tell Manager Yan I'd be willing to move back into his apartment on Jinhua Street with him—I still had that key I'd neglected to return to him. I could say that Sonny was my real brother and ask him to put him up for the time being. If I hired on at the Silver Chariot and did a good job waiting tables, he might be willing to go along with it. Manager Yan had treated me well, always trying to get me to return to the "straight and narrow." But what if he wouldn't go along? I thought of someone else — Mother's adopted mother, Wu Haomei. After Mother's adopted father died, she and her adopted mother began spending more time together. She'd taken Buddy and me to Longtan in Taoyuan county to see our adopted grandmother, a heavy woman in good health who'd never had her feet bound, and who had a faster, brisker walk than the ducks she raised. She was a good-hearted woman who had a soft spot in her heart for us. On the second morning of our visit she'd picked up her egg basket and taken Buddy and me with her to the duck pen to gather eggs after the hundred or more ducks had gone down to the pond. The piles of duck feathers and droppings on the floor concealed lots of green-shelled eggs. Buddy and I were so excited as we ran around noisily gathering the eggs that we didn't even notice the stench. Buddy, who still wasn't walking very steadily, stumbled around the pen, his hands covered with duck droppings. When Mother came over, Grandma smiled and said:

"A-li, why don't you let them stay here with me and help me with the eggs?"

Grandmother came to see us in Taipei last year, and she brought two breeding ducks with her. She gave me the black one and Buddy the white one. When Mother's name came up, she cursed her and shed a few tears. Then, when she was leaving, she said to me:

"Bring Buddy down to the countryside when school vacation starts."

The two ducks grew to adulthood that autumn, one black and one white, their feathers turning bright, the crests of their heads a bright red. Whenever there were people around, they quacked and waddled around in a show of bluster. We called them Whitey and Blackie, and feeding them was the highlight of Buddy's and my day. We often went over to the riverbank on Shulan Street to dig for worms, which grew long and fat in the fertile mud. When we'd filled a can with the worms, we'd take them home and feed them to the ducks, who soon grew so fat their tails nearly dragged on the ground. When Chinese New Year's came around, Father dispatched the two ducks. His objection was that the stench of their droppings, which covered the yard, drew hordes of flies. Besides, he didn't have the money to buy decent food for our New Year's dinner. So Blackie was turned into soup and Whitey a plate of crispy duck. Father handed one of the crispy drumsticks to me and the other to Buddy, while he ate the neck along with his wine. I ate mine with gusto, but Buddy just sat there looking woeful and didn't touch his. When Father asked him why, he said he had an upset stomach, but I knew he was grieving over his Whitey and couldn't eat it. After dinner I whispered to him:

"Silly, what's there to feel bad about? When vacation starts we'll go to Taoyuan and have Grandma give us a couple more ducks. We'll have her pick you out another white one, what do you say?"

But neither Buddy nor I ever went back to Taoyuan. I figured there'd be no problem taking Sonny to Grandma's house for a few days. I could help my uncle take care of the ducks, and Sonny could gather eggs with Grandma. That'd probably work out okay.

"Well, Moon Beauty, what do you say? Now that I've paid the rent, you're not going to kick us out, are you?"

The first thing I did when I got back to Jinzhou Street was hand Moon Beauty a hundred yuan to take care of the rent. I understood her well enough to know that no matter how generous she was to Little Jade and me, she wouldn't tolerate our not paying the rent. She and Obasan were discussing something when I walked in, and when she took the money from me she said:

"Sit down, A-qing."

"I'm working, Moon Beauty," I said. "At the Silver Chariot. But I don't make as much in a month as you do in one night."

"A-qing," she said as she took a drag on her cigarette, then continued slowly, "your little loony did something bad this afternoon."

"What'd he do?" I asked anxiously.

"He hurt Johnny Jr." Obasan answered.

"Here's what happened," Moon Beauty explained. "The two of them were fighting over the ball, and he shoved Johnny Jr. so hard he banged his head on the table and knocked out a tooth."

"The poor kid, his mouth was covered with blood," Obasan said, pointing to her own mouth.

"Damn him! I'll go teach him a lesson!"

"I already gave him a good spanking," Obasan said angrily, "but the little loony just laughed!"

I stood up to go into my room, but Moon Beauty told me to stay where I was.

"There's nothing for you to do. I already sent him away."

I was stunned. I stared at her without making a sound.

"Sent him away?" I said after a moment. "Where?" My voice was quivering.

"The police came over . . . ," Obasan interjected.

"The police sent over a car and took him away," Moon Beauty said. "Don't let it get to you," she added. "You're better off . . ."

"What gave you the right to call the police?" I shouted, suddenly enraged. "I want to know where you've sent Sonny!"

"You're as crazy as he is!" Moon Beauty shouted back.

"I'm going to go find him," I said as I threw the bag of cakes down on the table. "And if I don't," I threatened angrily, "I'm gonna hold you two responsible . . ."

I ran down Sun Yat-sen North Road into a strong headwind, pelted by an occasional downpour of rain. The first winds of the typhoon had arrived. The streets were nearly deserted, and the purple fluorescent streetlights shone dimly through the wind and rain. I didn't stop until I reached the Third Precinct stationhouse on Nanking East Road, where I explained the situation to the policeman on duty. He took me inside to speak to the duty officer, a thin, dark, and surprisingly pleasant man in his forties. He was listening to some Peking opera on the transistor radio on his desk. When he learned that I was there to find someone he slid a form over to me to fill out.

"Who are you looking for?"

I hesitated for a moment before answering.

"My kid brother."

"What's his name?"

"Sonny . . . ," was all I could think of to say.

"I need to know his name."

"Sir," I explained, "this kid brother of mine has a problem . . . what I mean is, he's not very bright, he's got the I.Q. of a three-year-old . . ."

"Oh," the officer sighed as he stopped me with a wave of his hand. "I understand. What you're saying is that your kid brother is retarded, right? Another one of those tough cases. Last month we detained a crazy woman near Yuanhuan who was hopping around outside with no clothes on. When we asked her her name, she couldn't tell us. She's still in the Taipei Mental Hospital, since no one's come to claim her."

"Sir, did my brother show up here?" I asked him.

"We don't have any record of it. Even if someone did bring him here we wouldn't keep him. In cases like this, the people are usually sent over to Headquarters, where they're committed to a mental hospital. If there aren't any available beds, they might send them to Xinzhu or Taoyuan..."

He stopped abruptly and turned his attention to the radio on his desk, where the announcer was broadcasting news about the typhoon: In the early morning hours typhoon Emily was located at twenty-four degrees north, one-twenty-four degrees east, traveling at a speed of ten kilometers an hour, heading straight for northern Taiwan...

"Young man," the officer said to me somberly, "Emily's going to hit pretty soon."

Seeing that his warning had produced no effect, and that I hadn't moved, he added reassuringly:

"Look, you go home, and we'll let you know tomorrow if there's any news. Your best bet is to go to Police Headquarters and check there. If he's already been placed in a mental hospital, you can rest easy, since he'll be well taken care of, and nothing can happen."

After I left the stationhouse I wandered the streets until I wound up at the Zhongshan Bridge. My shirt was billowing in the wind, but sweat was streaming down my back. The sky had turned black, and the city beneath the bridge had been swallowed up in a sea of hazy lights. As I stood there on the bridge a desperate loneliness began to settle over me.

29

Sir, did anyone send a boy with a shaved head and bare feet over here? Sir, do you have a mentally retarded boy here? Fourteen, fifteen years old. Barefoot. Sir, he would have been sent over yesterday. He's called Sonny...

I went out early the next morning, combing the city of Taipei for the little idiot boy. First I went to the Third Precinct, then the Fourth, and finally to Police Headquarters, but I came up empty. The Taipei Mental Hospital was my last hope. The male nurse at the reception desk wouldn't let me into the wards, so I had to stand behind a railing and look inside. He told me there were only two patients in my age group, both admitted three months earlier. One of them came out, a fat, pimply-faced boy of sixteen or seventeen, wearing horn-rimmed glasses and dressed in a green hospital gown. He looked like a sleepwalker groping through the dark as he held his arms, which had folds of fat, out in front of him.

"That's not him, is it?" the nurse asked softly as he pointed to the boy.

"No... sir..." I'm looking for a light-skinned, thin boy whose head is shaved like a monk's."

By noontime, Taipei was beginning to feel the effects of the storm, as the winds got stronger and stronger. The palm trees on both sides of Ren'ai Road were being buffeted so badly that many of the branches were snapped off and sent crashing to the street, where they were blown all about, adding to the noise of the storm. A telephone pole on Hangzhou South Road was bent at a 45-degree angle, its slack wires touching the ground. Policemen were directing traffic around the danger. Pedestrians were being blown around like rag dolls. A fancy plastic umbrella was whipped out of a woman's hand and up into the air, soaring and diving in the wind like a kite whose string had snapped. After a brief torrential downpour, Chungking South Road was completely flooded, creating a little river of muddy water that snaked its way rapidly down the asphalt. Signs above the arcade shops on Hengyang Street and Chengdu Road were groaning in the onslaught of gusting winds, as though thrown into a frenzy. The Three Cardinals' sign had been blown down, the sheet iron frame shrilly careening back and forth on the street. I took a bus to Westgate, but when I got there I found that the Silver Chariot had been closed all day. I was getting hungry, but the food stalls in the district were all closed. I headed into the wind toward Wuchang Street, where I hoped to find some open food stalls. A few fruit vendors had just packed up and were pushing their carts as fast as they could. Just then a strong gust of wind forced them to sprawl over their cartfuls of muskmelons and guavas to keep them from being blown away. The last vendor to leave was a slight young woman whose hair was flying all over. Her red skirt billowed up, exposing her milky white calves. Her cart was piled high with bright red persimmons. She was bending into the wind, her shoulders braced against the cart, but she was no match for the wind, which blew her backwards and sent her sprawling on the road. A dozen or so of the persimmons in her basket were blown to the ground, where they rolled around. I rushed over and grabbed the handles of the cart to steady it while she scrambled to her feet. When she saw her persimmons on the street, some of which had rolled into the filthy gutter, she sighed sadly.

She scooped up the hem of her dress, bent down, and gathered up the scattered persimmons, one at a time, cradling them in her skirt. After wiping the dirt off the undamaged fruit, she put them back onto the cart. But five or six had split open and were oozing juice all over the street. She picked up the biggest one and handed it to me:

"Let's eat 'em . . . can't sell 'em like this."

It was no time to be polite, so I thanked her and took a huge bite. It was as sweet as honey. She picked up one for herself, and we stood in the wind eating smashed persimmons. Apparently in her mid-twenties, she had sunken eyes and a pointy chin. Her pale face was now flushed from all the exertion, and she was watching me with keen interest, probably because I was eating so hungrily.

"Sweet, aren't they?" she asked with a smile.

She handed me another one. I hadn't eaten persimmons that sweet for years. I recalled how Mother suddenly began treating me with tenderness a couple of days before she left home; she'd bought a couple of ripe persimmons that day and surprised me by calling me outside to sit next to her on the bench and eat them with her. The fruit was so ripe the skin fell away as soon as she touched it. She peeled one and took a bite.

"It's *so* sweet!" she called out excitedly.

She handed it to me, and she was right, it was deliciously sweet, with just a trace of astringent persimmon taste.

"Good?" Mother smiled at me as she took out a handkerchief and wiped the corners of my mouth. Probably because she'd never done anything like that for me before, this sudden show of affection overwhelmed and, for some reason, embarrassed me.

"Blackie," she said, suddenly caught up in reveries, "did you know your mother once sold persimmons?" Mother seldom talked about her life in her adopted parents' home in the Taoyuan countryside, and when she did, it was usually to give vent to some pent-up anger. "We had about a dozen persimmon trees in our garden next to the pond. When the fruit ripened there was more than we could eat, so your grandmother told me to take them into town to sell. I always ate the leftover ones." She laughed. "Sometimes I ate so many I got a stomach ache."

As she laughed, her long, satiny black hair danced in the air. Just seeing her laugh like a carefree little girl made me laugh, too.

That was the only time Mother and I ever laughed together as though we hadn't a care in the world. Two days later she was gone.

"I'd like two catties of persimmons," I said to the girl.

"They're fifteen yuan a catty," she said as she looked me over. She picked out four of the biggest, reddest persimmons, put them on her scale, and showed it to me. The lanyard was flopping around in the wind.

"Two catties, two ounces. Call it two catties even," she said in a friendly tone.

"Thank you."

I handed her thirty yuan.

She put the money into the pocket of her skirt, picked up the handles of her cart, and strained against the wind, her hair blowing up over her head. Every few steps she turned and gave me a smile. I got on a bus, holding the persimmons in my hand, and headed for the old airport. These were for Mother.

When I arrived at the dark, dank fortress-like cement building on Kenan Road near the old airport, the same old woman opened the door for me. As soon as she saw me she said:

"You're A-li's oldest son, A-qing, aren't you?"

"I brought something over for Mother, Obasan," I said.

She let me in and led the way into the dark foyer.

"Wait here," she said.

She walked into the room and brought out a rattan chest. She dropped it heavily at my feet, then took off the lid and pointed breathlessly at the contents.

"Everything A-li left is in here."

The chest was filled with tattered old clothes, including the black wool coat with the smell of medicine that Mother had wrapped around her on my earlier visit. The old woman bent down and rummaged through the chest, holding up two soiled, yellowed sets of underwear Mother had owned. A strange, strong smell assailed my nose.

"Nothing here worth anything, but go ahead and take whatever you want," she said as she looked up at me.

"When did it happen . . . ," I asked with a sense of dread.

"When were you here the last time?" She cocked her head and squinted as she tried to remember. The scraggly bun of hair at the back of her head looked like it was about to fall off.

"The day of the Ghost Festival, the fifteenth day of the seventh month."

"That's right. It happened the very next day. She died in the middle of the night."

I was holding the bag of persimmons tightly in both hands as I watched her down on her haunches rummaging through the junk in the chest. After a few moments she straightened up, clapped her hands together, and began to grumble:

"A-li was sick for a long time. Confined to bed for over three months. That cost us a lot of money, if you know what I mean. We're not rich people, and it wasn't easy. It cost 3,000 just to have her cremated, which is what she wanted. I'll tell you honestly, my son treated her pretty good." She sighed and clicked her tongue. When it was obvious I didn't have anything to say, she stared at the junk in the chest and sneered.

"And that gold ring of hers, you know how much that was worth? Nothing compared to what we spent. Well, it's a good thing you came, because she left a message for you. No matter what, you're to claim her ashes and bury them next to her youngest son . . ."

"Where are her ashes?" I interrupted her.

"The Temple of Grand Compassion at Dragon Cavern. We already told the abbot there all about it, so all you have to do is go get them."

The Temple of Grand Compassion was a desolate, run-down temple surrounded by illegal shanties. Homeless old folks went there to get off the streets. As soon as I walked inside I noticed old people in rags huddling in clusters of three or four. Some of them were sitting dully on benches, others were engaged in whispered conversations. A young Buddhist novice led me in to see the abbot, an old monk in his seventies whose face was so wrinkled I couldn't distinguish his eyebrows, a shriveled little man whose cassock hung on his frame and nearly scraped the floor. I told him why I was there, but he was so hard of hearing he had to cup his hand to his ear to hear me. His toothless mouth never stopped moving the whole time. I shouted my mother's name in his ear several times before he finally nodded, apparently getting the message.

"Huang . . . Li . . . xia . . . brought over here a couple of weeks ago, right?" His raspy voice quivered.

"That's right, Abbot."

"They said she's waiting for her son, waiting for him to take her home . . ."

"I'm her son, Huang Lixia's son," I bent over and shouted in his ear.

"Oh!" He sighed and mumbled something. Then he waved at me and said:

"Follow me, son."

He shuffled out of the room, his cassock billowing in a gust of wind that rocked his frail body. I followed him into a room to the right, the Hall of Eternal Joy, where the ash remains were kept. The hall was dark. There was a three-tiered wooden rack against the main wall, filled with dark pear-shaped urns. An eternal-life oil lamp was burning dimly on the top of the rack. Each of the urns had an identifying tag. Some had gone unclaimed for so long they were covered by a fine layer of dust, and the names on the yellowing tags were barely legible.

"Huang Lixia is here."

The old monk walked over, bent over, and reached down with his trembling hands to the fourth urn from the left on the second tier. I rushed over to pick it up. It was new, and the light from the lamp glinted faintly on its surface. The tag was white. It said "Huang Lixia, Taoyuan." The black pottery urn was about a foot in height, had a rough surface, and was squeezed in between several others.

"Take your mother home with you," the old monk turned and said to me. I put the bag of persimmons under my arm, bent down, and picked up the urn with Mother's ashes in both hands.

"Abbot, I'd like to go into the main hall and light some incense." He nodded and his lips moved once or twice; then he turned and hobbled out of the room, across the corridor, and over to the main hall. When he reached the doorway of the Hall of Grand Compassion, he stopped and said:

"Son, leave your mother out here. She can't come in since the Buddha is in here."

I put the urn with Mother's ashes down on the floor beside the door of the Hall of Grand Compassion and entered through the door, above which hung a dark wood sign with the words, "Merciful Boat in the Sea of Bitterness" engraved in gold that was chipped and peeling. The wood itself was cracked. The idols in the hall were standing in dark, dusty alcoves. Owing to the dense incense smoke and years of neglect, the gold surface of the huge Buddha in the center was faded and blackened; even the pedestal was cracked and broken. Pieces of fruit and devotional candles were laid out on the offerings stand, the smoke curling upward in the gusts of wind that swept into the hall. I laid the persimmons I'd brought with me on the offerings stand and asked the old monk for a joss stick. It took three matches to light it in the gusty hall, but as soon as it was lit, a cloud of fragrant smoke rose in front of me, burning my eyes. Holding the joss stick in both hands, I stuck it into a blue porcelain incense pot, then retreated to the center of the hall and knelt in front of the Buddha. This was the first time I'd ever come alone to a Buddhist temple to burn incense or pray to the Buddha. But I remembered how, in my childhood, Mother had gone to the Guanyin Temple in Banqiao to burn incense each year on Guanyin's birthday. Once she took Buddy and me with her and told us to kneel beside her in front of the Guanyin statue. We watched her prostrate herself at the feet of the Guanyin bodhisattva, looking very small, her long black hair spread over the floor around her. She rose to her knees and clasped her hands in front of her as she began to mumble prayers, pouring out her heart. Her sunken eyes were more radiant than I'd ever seen them, filled with a light of unspeakable pain. When I'd gone to see her on the day of the Ghost Festival she'd clutched my hand and begged me to go to a temple and burn a joss stick for her, asking the Buddha to let her transcend death and forgive her for a lifetime of sins. Her eyes, which had become two black holes in her face, were filled with fear and trepidation. Mother had probably been afraid of something all her life for her eyes to radiate such fear, like a startled deer desperately seeking escape. She had lived in constant terror, always running away, always on the move. She'd gone with one man after another, drifting all her adult life, without ever finding the haven she was seeking, ending her days as a piece of human flotsam in a rickety bed, wrapped in a tattered quilt and surrounded by the smells of sweat and medicine, her body wasted by disease. She must have been unbelievably lonely and desperate in her final hours. But now her broken body had been turned to ashes and was resting in a crude urn just outside the hall. Was it possible that those ashes still contained the sins of her days on earth? I kowtowed to the statue of the Buddha and rested my forehead on the cold stone floor.

"Son, hurry up and take your mother home. The winds are picking up . . ."

When my prayers were over, the old monk spoke to me in a

shaky voice from where he was standing on the steps outside the hall. His cassock was billowing and shaking violently in the strong wind.

30

I told the taxi driver to stop at the entrance to Lane 28 of Longjiang Street, where our house was located. The lane was deserted and the doors and windows on all the houses were shut tight. Bamboo clothes poles were still sticking out from their anchorages in the holes of walls, but the tattered diapers and underpants had all been taken inside. Staff Officer Qin's gate was still broken — the remaining half was creaking on its hinges in the strong wind. There was the rubbish heap, piled high with yellow and black refuse. The flooded gutters were spilling their filthy water into the middle of the lane, turning it into a quagmire. Wind whistled through the ruined, dead-end lane, making it more bleak than ever and increasing the sense of chaos. I was holding the slippery urn with Mother's ashes close to my chest with sweaty palms, afraid of dropping it. The wind was so powerful, the footing so treacherous, that it took a great deal of effort to carry Mother's ashes safely home, one difficult step at a time.

The black oil paper was still in place on our roof, held down by bricks that were now covered with mold. Last year, when Typhoon Daisy swept across the area, taking a corner of our roof along with it, Father had covered the hole with oil paper the next day, with Buddy's and my help. I was up on the roof, while Father stood on the ladder passing up the bricks that Buddy handed him. But Emily was going to be much bigger than Daisy, and I wondered whether these emergency repairs would be able to withstand tonight's storm. I could see through a crack in the gate that all the doors and windows were closed and the lights were off. It wasn't yet six o'clock, so Father hadn't gotten home from work yet. As I stood there in front of the gate holding the urn with Mother's ashes, I momentarily forgot that I hadn't been here in four months and that my father had kicked me out. I put the urn down on the ground and climbed the wall. Then, after opening the gate from the inside, I picked up Mother's ashes and carried them into the house. As soon as I stepped into the darkened living room my nose was assailed by the ever-present smell of mildew that penetrated the walls and the floor of the dank, low-ceilinged room. That familiar old smell was all I needed to feel that I'd truly come home. I turned on the dim overhead light and put the urn down on the greasy, discolored dining table. Nothing had changed in the room. Father's well-worn rattan chair was exactly where it had always been, directly beneath the overhead light; his reading glasses were lying on the table next to it. On summer nights, when the rest of us were outside trying to cool off, Father would stay in the stifling room by himself, sitting barechested in his chair under the light, his reading glasses perched on the bridge of his nose, absorbed in his dog-eared copy of *The Three Kingdoms*. The only thing that broke his concentration was the mosquitoes; if one of them bit him, he'd reach down and smack his leg and look up with an angry expression. All of a sudden, the agonizing look on his face on the night Mother left flashed before my eyes. He was drunk, his face was streaked with tears, his wrinkles seemed deeper than ever, his eyes were bloodshot; he kept us awake all night with his drunken babbling. As long as I live I'll never forget that look of anguish, bordering on terror, and it suddenly dawned on me that I'd probably never be able to face that anguished look again. I believed that if he saw me returning Mother's ashes home he might take us back, for although he detested her fall from chastity, his feelings for her hadn't died. He'd taken the photograph of the two of them down off the wall, but a few years later, without any fanfare, it had reappeared in its old spot. If Mother had repented before she died, I believe that Father would have let her come back home. And me, well, I was his final hope as he entered his twilight years. It was his lifelong dream that one day I'd become a respected officer and vindicate him, wash away the shame of his being captured by the enemy and discharged from the army. When I was expelled from school in disgrace, this dream went up in smoke. It's not hard to appreciate the anger and resentment that must have filled his heart. Occasionally I wondered if he still held out a thread of hope that I might reject my sinful past and come home to start anew. He'd once had such high expectations for me that I refused to believe that his paternal affection could have dried up completely. And yet I knew I'd never be able to face that heart-breaking look of agony again. At that moment I knew why Mother had chosen the life of a fallen vagabond, never daring to return home — I'm sure the thought of coming home crossed her mind when things were going bad: she was probably as afraid as I to look into that agonized, ruined face. Only death allowed her to come home. Mother died, but her fears hadn't ended there; she was afraid of being left out in the cold to become a lonely ghost, a rootless spirit. She wanted me to bring her mortal remains, ravaged by sin, home to her final resting place; so she'd never stopped thinking about this ruined, chaotic home of ours after all.

I took a piece of paper out of my pocket, a sheet of stationery from the Jinghua Hotel, on the back of which was written the number 779741. My last customer at the Jinghua Hotel had given me his phone number. I turned it back over and wrote a brief note to Father, which I put on the dining table under the urn containing Mother's ashes:

Dear Father:
Mother died the day after the Ghost Festival. This urn contains her ashes. Before she died she left instructions that her remains be taken home and buried next to Buddy.

Your son, Qing

I had to get out of there before Father came home so I wouldn't run into him. But before I left I went over to the room Buddy and I had shared and walked around for a moment. Buddy's bed was gone, leaving only a single bamboo cot in the room. My straw mat and pillow were still there. My school uniform, my clothes, my shoes and socks were all folded neatly on the pillow. Even my school supplies were untouched. But everything in the room was covered with a layer of dust; it had been months since the last time it was cleaned. I left everything where it was, closed the door behind me, and walked outside. Wind was whistling down the lane, carrying rain along with it that pelted my face painfully. I ran down the lane into the wind, faster and faster, until it was the same scene over again. When I reached the end of the lane I turned and looked back. Just then I felt the sobs building inside me, and the tears began to flow. This time I really knew how miserable it was to give up your home.

31

Emily hit land at about ten o'clock that night, and all Taipei seemed to howl. The typhoon winds shook the towering, kingly palm trees in New Park until they looked like inmates of an insane asylum frantically trying to break out of their captivity, heads jerking, hair flying, teeth bared, straining against their bonds. Torrential rains, whipped by the winds, filled the night air, shooting in all directions, fast one moment, slow the next. Fighting the storm every step of the way, I made my way into the pavilion in the middle of the lotus pond in the heart of New Park, and sat down on the bench beneath the window. I kicked off my mud-filled shoes, which squished as I walked. I was soaked from head to toe, and every gust of wind chilled me. The winds were howling all around me, but I just sat there on the bench, my legs curled up under me, feeling desperately lonely. I hadn't the heart to return to my den on Jinzhou Street; I knew I couldn't stand the oppression of being cooped up in that little den on a night like this. So on this stormy, typhoon-wracked night, utter despair filling my heart, I chose to return to our kingdom, for this little strip of territory, protected by the darkness, held out at least a sliver of hope.

There appeared to be moving figures in the gazebos at each corner of the pond. Probably some of our people who, like me, had come over to this dark kingdom of ours to pass the night of the typhoon. Suddenly, a tall shape appeared out of nowhere at the far end of the pond, walking along the steps, struggling against the wind. His white raincoat was flapping high in the violent winds. I knew who that solitary tall figure was — Dragon Prince, Wang Kuilong. Was it conceivable that on this stormy, dark night he could find no peace in the aging official residence on Nanking East Road left to him by his father, and that he was compelled to burst through the iron gate and make his way over to this nest of ours? What was he looking for? Was he really that obsessed about finding A-feng, his wild phoenix? Phoenix Boy's death had long since become part of the legend of the park, growing more and more mysterious with each passing year, more and more fantastic. According to the hustlers from Three Rivers Street, who loved to tell ghost stories, on rainy nights a man dressed in black appeared beside the lotus pond, holding his chest and sobbing. They said it was Phoenix Boy, and that the knife wound in his chest was still bleeding after all these years. They'd point to some dark stains on the steps and say: That's Phoenix Boy's blood. Years of rain haven't been able to wash it away. On the night Wang Kuilong took me to the official residence on Nanking East Road, when we lay naked on the bed, shoulder to shoulder, he stretched his bony hands into the air and told me about the years he'd spent living in a loft on 72nd Street in Manhattan after his father, a high-ranking official, had forced him to go abroad. He'd crawl out of hiding late at night and roam the streets of Manhattan like a wandering ghost, drifting through the maze of streets and avenues in search of New York's boys of the night, whom he'd follow into the vast darkness of Central Park. He said that Central Park was ten times bigger than Taipei's New Park, and that the foliage in it was ten times denser. There were also ten times the number of dark shadows among the trees. But were there typhoons in New York? I was suddenly curious to know if they had dark, stormy nights like this. He told me it snowed there, and when it did, the trees in Central Park were dusted with white powder, turning them into huge white apparitions. Even on snowy nights there would still be some wandering ghosts lingering in the park, weaving their way through the snow-covered trees. He told me of that Christmas night when he met Carlos, the hungry, shivering Puerto Rican boy he took home with him and made him a cup of hot chocolate. The boy had wondrously big eyes and a bright red wound in the middle of his chest.

As Wang Kuilong emerged from the gazebo, I noticed someone else by his side, a slight person who limped as he tried to keep up. I recognized the awkward gait—it was Golden Treasure from Three Rivers Street, a boy with a club foot who seldom came over to the park; only very late at night or during a storm, when few people were out, would he slink out from behind one of the trees, hobbling along, his eyes darting this way and that, like a frightened deer. Dragon Prince opened his white raincoat and wrapped it around Golden Treasure's thin frame, and the two of them—one tall, one short—were quickly transformed into a single white outline that disappeared into the darkness of the night, the storm raging all around them.

I stayed where I was on the bench in the pavilion, one leg curled underneath me, keeping my solitary vigil among the howling winds. The night wore on, the rains fell harder; a large, bloated figure, dripping water, suddenly appeared in the pavilion, bearing down on me, slowly, clumsily, but with an awesome presence.

32

The typhoon moved on, taking with it the summer heat and the mosquitoes. The air was cool and damp, filled with moisture. The moon looked like it had been bathed and was now a hazy white orb shining through the inky, muggy darkness. The ground in the park was littered with twisted branches and fallen leaves. The kingly palms had been so battered by the winds that they cut a sorry figure; some of their long fronds had been ripped from the trunks and were hanging there miserably, revealing the leafless tips of the trees. Green corals that had been uprooted lay in clumps on the ground, their branches grotesquely intertwined. The park looked like a disaster area, a blighted piece of land.

Grandpa Guo was pacing back and forth on the stone steps of the museum at the entrance to the park, his hands clasped behind his back. He was wearing a black Chinese jacket, which contrasted sharply with his snowy-white hair. He was frowning deeply; he was worried. The night before, it turned out, just after the typhoon moved on, Iron Ox had been involved in a major incident. He had caught a young man and woman necking heavily in the pavilion in the middle of the lotus pond. The man was a reserve soldier back on leave from one of the outer islands, the woman a nurse. Iron Ox went crazy, cursing the couple, calling them dogs in heat, for invading our territory. What's the big idea, he bellowed, of a couple of outsiders behaving like dogs in *our* territory, *our* nest! When he began spewing filthy remarks at the nurse, the angry young soldier went after Iron Ox, who whipped out a knife and stabbed him in the belly, wounding him gravely. When the police arrived, Iron Ox was so out of control they had to beat him with their night sticks until he collapsed, bleeding profusely from the head.

"If I hadn't run over and held them back, they would have beaten the little shit to death!"

Grandpa Guo's emotions were bubbling over.

"As soon as he saw me he crawled up, wrapped his arms around my legs, and wailed: 'Grandpa Guo, save me, they're trying to kill me!' His face was covered with blood, and when the police tried to drag him away, he held on to my pants for dear life and sobbed like a little baby."

"This time," Grandpa Guo sighed, "they're going to send him to Fire Island for sure . . ."

On my first night in the park it had been Grandpa Guo who took me to his home to show me his "Birds of Youth" photo album and relate the history of the park. When he showed me the photo of Iron Ox he called him "The Owl" and predicted that he was a major accident just waiting to happen. According to him, it was in our blood, this wild streak, just as typhoons and earthquakes are a part of the island we live on.

"You're a flock of birds who've lost their nests," he said with a sad look, "just like sea swallows flying across the ocean, who only know how to struggle forward, even if they don't know where they're going . . ."

Saturday night, the typhoon had moved on, and all the birds of youth had flown back to the park, like bats that had been hiding from a storm in strange caves. Now, under the cover of darkness, they winged their way back to their own caves. We huddled together to get warm and to talk, relating all sorts of gossip.

As soon as I walked up the steps of the lotus pond I was met with a rap on the head from Chief Yang's fan.

"You want to know why I hit you, you little slave? You went and cut my balls off, that's why! From now on, don't expect me to look after you or help you find customers!"

"I really had a stomach ache that night," I said, "so I had to leave."

"Stomach ache, my ass," he sneered. "Maybe it was cholera you had. Boss Lai of the Yongchang Apparel Store is a man of means. He has several stores. The only reason I chose you was I figured you were special. And he was going to make you some slacks! Why, because you're hot shit? I'd like to know what makes you think that! As far as I'm concerned, you're nothing but scum! All you're good for is selling your ass in a place like this, cut-rate!"

"Dada, money, money," A-xiong said as he thrust one of his enormous hands out from behind Chief Yang.

"What do you want money for?" Chief Yang turned and screamed.

"Candy, candy," A-xiong said with a foolish grin.

"What happened to the bagful you just had?"

"Mousey ate it, and Little Jade, and..." A-xiong grinned as he rubbed his palm with his fingers, but before he could finish, Chief Yang reached out and slapped him resoundingly.

"Damned spendthrift!" Chief Yang said angrily. "One of these days Dada's going to go broke because of you! You're such a dumb little bird that those little queers can do anything they want with you!"

A-xiong shrunk back and dragged himself away from the scene. Seeing what a bad temper Chief Yang was in, I made myself scarce by mixing with the others.

"Damned thief!" I grabbed Mousey by the neck. "All for one and one for all. Where's the candy?"

Mousey giggled as he reached into his pants pocket and pulled out a handful of sesame candy, six pieces in all.

"That's all I've got left," he said with a click of his tongue.

"Chief Yang's gonna skin you alive for tricking that idiot out of his candy again!" I peeled the paper from one of the candies and popped it into my mouth.

"Aha!" Little Jade came over and snatched two of the candies out of my hand. "Chief Yang's been looking all over for you. He said when he found you he was going to castrate you. He said, 'We'll see what kind of a bird he makes without that pecker of his!' They say you refused to sleep with that old guy Lai. What's so bad about him? You can get a suit for a roll in the hay."

"His palms were all sweaty," I said, suddenly recalling that pudgy hand with the gold ring inching up my thigh, all cold and damp, like a bunch of caterpillars crawling up my leg. Little Jade and Mousey just stood there for a moment, then burst out laughing.

"Grandpa Lai's sweaty palms, A-qing's trembling butt." Little Jade laughed and clapped his hands.

Little Jade, Mousey, and I started walking around the lotus pond. The steps were covered with brown leaves and fallen branches. As we trampled on the broken branches and dead leaves, we joined up with the other troops who were performing their nightly march of pursuit. When we reached the first bend, a pale face appeared in the gazebo. In the surrounding darkness it looked like a sheet of white paper floating in the air. It was Wu Min. He jumped up onto the steps, waved to us, and yelled, "Wait up, wait for me."

We stopped and waited for him to catch up to us, breathing heavily. I put one arm around him and the other around Little

Jade, who put his arm around Mousey, and we strutted forward, four abreast. The taps on the heels of Little Jade's and my boots set up a clatter on the cement steps as we stepped on the shadows of the troops ahead of us; we looked like one of those carousel lanterns, always chasing, but never catching, the ones ahead. We passed the little bridge that led to the pavilion in the middle of the pond; every one of the steps was filled with hustlers from Three Rivers Street, including several new faces, probably fledglings on their first outing. Death Angel Zhao, dressed all in black, was sitting on the highest step, regally, a cigarette dangling from his mouth as he spoke of the past in a hoarse voice to the youngsters. He'd been hanging around the park a lot longer than we had, but we weren't intimidated by him and weren't taking what he had to offer; so he had to be content with showing off around those youngsters who had recently taken to the streets, regaling them with his exploits in the park in the past.

"Back then we were called the Four Titans..." He always started out like that. All the boys gazed up at him as they listened respectfully to his narration. "There was the bastard Peach Boy, the crazy little Tu Xiaofu, and then there was...then there was the wildest, the craziest of all, Phoenix Boy, the mad phoenix. The four of us made a mighty team, and we damn near turned the park inside out!"

"You kids don't know it, but Zhao the Elder here was an amorous titan, and it finally got so bad that the Great Jade Emperor sent him to hell, where he became the black Death Angel." Little Jade giggled from where he was standing on the step below, trying to get Death Angel Zhao's goat. This broke the kids up.

"You goddamn, nasty-mouthed, no-good sonofabitch!" Death Angel Zhao cursed Little Jade, shaking the hand that held his cigarette at him wildly. "Back when your Master Zhao here was having a wild time in the park, you barely had peach fuzz on your butt. You didn't know a goddamn thing!" He stared daggers at Little Jade, then turned back and continued to regale the kids with his tales.

"Boys, have you ever had your hair cut at the Red Rose in Westgate district?" he asked them. They all shook their heads.

"Go there the next time you need a haircut. Ask for Number Thirteen, then ask him, 'Number Thirteen, what about your Peach Boy?' As soon as you mention the name, your haircut will be free. Number Thirteen will sit you down and tell you the story of his ill-fated relationship with Peach Boy. On the fifteenth day of the seventh month, someone saw Number Thirteen standing at the edge of the Tamsui River, beneath the Zhongxing Bridge, burning spirit money. He was burning it for Peach Boy. They never found Peach Boy's body, and everyone says there was so much hate in his heart that his body refused to float to the surface." Death Angel Zhao took a deep drag on his cigarette, then said with a sigh, "I still remember the night he jumped into the Tamsui River. He came over to see me after leaving Number Thirteen's wedding banquet. He was drunk as a lord. He told me the bride was a real tub, big as an aircraft carrier, and you could play a game of mahjong on her butt. He didn't think Number Thirteen would be able to hold his own with her. He was laughing so hard when he told me this that tears were running down his cheeks. The last thing in the world I ever expected was that he'd go down to the river and jump in!"

"Then what happened?" one of the kids asked anxiously.

"Aren't you the clever one!" Death Angel Zhao barked. "After someone's dead, what else *can* happen? Number Thirteen went to the bank of the Tamsui River every year after that to offer sacrifices to him. He was afraid that if he didn't, Peach Boy would come looking for him. He got very sick once, after Peach Boy died, so sick that all his hair fell out. Someone said it had been plucked out by Peach Boy.

"You little runts will never have the wild times we had back then," Death Angel Zhao said contemptuously. "When those guys fell in love, if it didn't kill them at least it drove them crazy. Tu Xiaofu is in an insane asylum to this very day, and all because he fell passionately in love with that overseas Chinese guy! When his lover returned to the States, Tu Xiaofu couldn't bear to let go of the pillow his lover had used, and he walked around all day long holding it against his chest. Finally, he went crazy, and every time he heard an airplane he cried like a baby. Day in and day out he'd go over to the airport, straight to the reservation desk at Northwest Airlines, and ask them, 'Has the plane from the States landed?' The crazy little guy even asked them in English! That, my boys, is class!"

"What about the wild phoenix?" another kid asked timidly.

"You mean Phoenix Boy? Ah..." Death Angel Zhao took another deep drag on his cigarette, then sighed as he blew the smoke out. "That's a long story."

Death Angel Zhao's hoarse voice floated in the muggy night

air, and the story of Dragon Prince and Phoenix Boy, which had become a New Park legend, was once again related on the steps of the lotus pond, very slowly: Phoenix Boy was a fatherless child with no name.

"...yes, even before they were born, that fellow Wang was fated to take Phoenix Boy's life. Have any of you ever seen someone in the grip of passion like that before? Wang Kuilong would be here in the park at five in the morning waiting for him, right here, right where we're sitting. He'd pace from one end of the pond to the other like a caged animal whose only thought is to break out of its captivity. Then, when Phoenix Boy sauntered over after spending the night with someone else, Wang Kuilong would slap him so hard he'd make his mouth bleed. But then he'd quickly reach out and take him in his arms, and start crying miserably. Phoenix Boy would just smile. 'You say you want my heart? Well, I was born without one.' Now tell me, is that the talk of a crazed man or not? On the night it happened, New Year's Eve, as a matter of fact, we were all here, right here on these steps. Phoenix Boy, who was wearing only a thin shirt, was shivering, and Wang Kuilong plunged his knife right into the middle of his chest. He held his blood-soaked body in his arms and kept crying out: 'Fire! Fire! Fire!'..."

We walked over to the other end of the pond. The water was higher than normal, and black as ink, the hazy shape of the moon reflected on its surface.

"The pond used to be covered with lilies, bright red ones," I said as I pointed at the bare surface of the pond.

"The city sent workers over to take them away," Little Jade said.

"When the flowers were in bloom, there were ninety-nine of them," I said.

"Quit trying to show off," Mousey snorted contemptuously. "How would you know there were ninety-nine of them?"

"Dragon Prince told me," I said.

This piqued Little Jade's and Mousey's curiosity, and they peppered me with questions about Dragon Prince and Phoenix Boy.

"Once Dragon Prince picked one of the flowers and put it in the palm of Phoenix Boy's hand. He said the flower was as red as a ball of fire."

The four of us walked around the edge of the pond, one turn after another. I had my arms around Little Jade's and Wu Min's shoulders, holding them close as I told them everything I knew about that legend of the park. We walked late into the night, until the hazy moon disappeared behind the clouds on the horizon, until a police whistle suddenly rent the darkness and seven or eight flashlights lit up the area like bolts of lightning and shone directly on us. The sound of running boots on the cement steps; a dozen shouting policemen with night sticks in their hands surrounding us. Not a single one of us got away that night. We were all handcuffed as we fell into their net.

33

They lined us up at the police station detention center and searched us. All Mousey's hidden treasures were removed from his pockets: a dozen colorful matchboxes from the Ambassador Hotel, a couple of brass spoons, and a pair of salt and pepper shakers that also probably came from a hotel. A policeman put it all into a manila envelope and tagged it. Two young thugs from Sanchong City were caught with a dagger and an icepick, which were confiscated as weapons. The owners were taken away to be interrogated separately. After we were searched we were given forms to fill out, then we were fingerprinted and taken into the interrogation room in single file. We were cursing Iron Ox under our breath, since the police only began making secret raids on the park after the stabbing incident. Since the late-night curfew was placed on the park, we were all guilty of loitering. This made those with criminal records very nervous, afraid they might be sent to a prison on one of the outer islands. One of the hustlers from Three Rivers Street, who'd already been in a reform school twice, was right behind me. He sighed and mumbled, "This time I'm gonna be singing the 'Green Island Prison Blues.'" Our interrogator was a hulking, dark police officer with a booming voice. He was sitting on a platform that looked like an iron tower. His hair was closely cropped, his square face dark and leathery, and he was sweating heavily. He constantly picked up a white towel to wipe his face, and drank lots of water. The overhead fluorescent lights lit up the room like daylight and made our dirty, sweaty faces look like they were covered with a coat of shiny wax. The hulking officer barked an order. Mousey was the first winner. Two policemen came down and led him up to the platform.

"What's your name?" the officer asked in his booming voice.

"Mousey," he answered, the foolish grin on his face exposing his nicotine-stained teeth. He was slightly bent over at the waist, so that his body formed an "S."

"Mousey?" The officer's brow creased in a frown of astonishment. "I'm asking you what name is on your I.D. card."

"Lai A-tu," Mousey replied vaguely. The rest of us laughed when we heard that, since this was the first we knew that he had a comical name like that — "Lai the Hick."

"Just what were you up to, loitering in the park in the middle of the night?" the officer asked him.

Mousey, who didn't know what to say, squirmed.

"Tell me, were you engaged in immoral behavior?" the officer asked him in an officious tone.

Mousey turned his head and looked at us with an embarrassed smile. He suddenly seemed very ashamed.

"Do you sell your body in the park? How much do you get a trick?" The officer leaned forward threateningly. "Twenty yuan?" he asked.

"A helluva lot more than that!" Mousey shot back contemptuously. We all giggled. The officer's dark face also slackened.

"Well!" he bellowed. "Who'd have thought we had such a valuable piece of goods here!" He laughed. "Tell me, does your father know about your promiscuous activities in the park?"

Mousey's embarrassment returned, and he began to fidget again.

"What's your father's name?" The officer's face darkened.

"Sir," he said in a thin voice, "I don't know. My father died before I was born."

"Oh?" The police officer hesitated. He picked up his glass and took a drink of water, mopped his face with the towel, and stared at Mousey for a moment, as though he didn't know what to say next. So after asking a few routine questions, he signaled for the guards to take him back with the rest of us. Wu Min was next. The police officer looked him up and down, then came straight to the point:

"You're better looking than him, so you must come more expensive, eh?"

Wu Min lowered his head and said nothing.

"You must be the fuckee, not the fucker," he commented. The two guards snickered. Wu Min, whose face turned beet-red, dropped his head even lower.

"Tell me, have you ever scored a trick in the park?" the officer pressed the issue loudly. Wu Min kept his head lowered. The officer examined Wu Min's I.D. card.

"Is Wu Jinfa your father's name?"

"Yes," Wu Min replied in a quivering voice.

"Your home in Xinzhu?"

"That's my uncle's address."

"How about your father? Where's he?"

"Taipei," Wu Min answered hesitantly.

"Where in Taipei?"

Wu Min twisted his neck but didn't reply.

"You have to tell me your father's Taipei address!" the officer said threateningly. "We're going to tell him what you've been up to in the park, and have him take you home and straighten you out. Now you tell me, where is your father?"

"Taipei..." His voice quivered.

"Hm?" The officer stretched his neck forward.

"Taipei Prison." Wu Min's head was bent so low you couldn't see his face.

"Ptui!" the officer spat. "So your old man's in prison, too, is he? Well, that makes everything fine, because now you can have a reunion."

We laughed, and so did the police officer. He dismissed Wu Min, then interrogated a few of the hustlers from Three Rivers Street, all of whom had criminal records. The officer knew them all. He pointed at Flower Child.

"Up to your old tricks again, you little scum! Haven't had enough of the rubber hose, I see!" Flower Child made a face and giggled.

When it was A-xiong's turn, he stubbornly refused to go up to the desk.

"Go on, you dummy, it's okay," Chief Yang said comfortingly.

"I don't want to, Dada!" A-xiong howled.

"They won't give you any trouble as long as Dada's here. Now do as I say and go on up there." Chief Yang pushed him forward as the two guards came over to escort him up. A-xiong ran around and huddled behind Chief Yang.

"Sir, give me a couple of minutes with him," Chief Yang said as he held back the guards and smiled at the officer. But one of the guards shoved him aside and reached out to grab A-xiong, who was so enraged he raised his manacled hands and brought them down on the guard's shoulder, who had luckily ducked his head just in time. The guard screamed and stumbled backwards. His partner whipped out his night stick and brought it down hard on A-xiong's head, over and over. He groaned as his bear-like body swayed for a moment, then crashed to the floor like a pile of bricks. He began foaming at the mouth and clawing at the air with his manacled hands, thrashing around spasmodically. Chief Yang quickly knelt down, took a key out of his pocket, and thrust it into A-xiong's mouth. Then he turned to the policeman and said urgently:

"Quick, sir, bring some boiled water. He's an epileptic!"

There was a noticeable stir among the rest of us. The police officer rushed over with a glass of water and handed it to Chief Yang, who took a couple of pills out of his breast pocket and shoved them into A-xiong's mouth, washing them down with the water. The officer told the guards to take A-xiong outside to rest, then went to the phone and called for a doctor. All this commotion with A-xiong appeared to dull the officer's interest in the proceedings, and he just asked the rest of us a few routine questions before booking us. His shirt was soaked by the time the interrogation was finished. He stood up, wiped his face once more, and stepped down from the platform, one hand resting on his hip as he counted us with the other. Then came the lecture:

"The whole lot of you, young as you are, have no self-respect and no drive to better yourselves," he said in his booming voice. "Instead you get involved in cheap, shameful activities! How would your parents and teachers, who worked so hard to educate you, feel if they knew what you were doing? Sad? Pained? You're society's garbage, the dregs of humanity, and it's our responsibility to rid society of you, to put you away . . ."

The more he spoke, the more agitated he grew, and he began waving his hand in the air. His square, leathery face was sweating again. He was screaming himself hoarse. He suddenly stopped, took a long look at us, apprehension filling his eyes, and sighed.

"You seem to be intelligent kids," he said sympathetically, "but . . . but . . ."

He shook his head. He didn't know what to say.

We spent the rest of the night in jail, huddled against one another, reeking of sweat. A few were so tired they leaned back, closed their eyes, and slobbered as they slept. But Flower Child sat there singing the song "Three Sighs."

"You dumb fuck, go sing a dirge for your old lady. You trying to peddle your ass even in jail?" Little Jade said impatiently.

Flower Child tucked his head into his shoulders and shut up.

"This time it's reform school for sure," Mousey sighed.

"Which is better, the one in Taoyuan or the one in Kaohsiung?" Wu Min asked.

"I hear the one in Kaohsiung's better," I said. "They make you wear shackles in Taoyuan."

"What do you guys think, will they send us to Fire Island?" Mousey asked out of fear. "I'll bet Iron Ox was fed to the sharks after they sent him there."

"You little thief, if they send anyone to Fire Island, you should be first!" Little Jade laughed.

"If we have to go, the four of us'll stick together," Mousey smiled. "We're brothers in good times and bad."

"You cunt-brats!" Chief Yang blurted out as he glared at us. He'd been trying to get some rest. "You didn't kill nobody or set no fires, so why would they send you to Fire Island? Now shut up, all of you. I'm trying to think of a way to get us out of here!"

None of us went to prison, and only the young thugs who had criminal records were sent to the reform school in Taoyuan. Chief Yang got Fu Chongshan to get us released.

BOOK THREE

THE COZY NEST

Fu Chongshan, Papa Fu, was a well known humanitarian. Chief Yang often told us of his good deeds. He'd saved the skins of lots of boys in the park who were in serious trouble. About ten years earlier, one of the chief's favorite disciples, a boy named A-wei, got into a fight with a troublemaker in the doorway of the chief's restaurant, Taoyuan Spring. He beat him up so badly he was arrested and ordered sent to a reform school on one of the outer islands. Chief Yang went to Papa Fu for help, who hired a lawyer and got the boy out on probation. A-wei, the posthumous son of a man in the airforce, had first come to the park as an unruly boy of sixteen. Besides getting him out of jail, Papa Fu also paid for his schooling and worked hard to help him turn his life around. The efforts had paid off, for he was admitted into a maritime school, and the year before last had shipped out to Europe. We also learned from Chief Yang that after Wu Min tried to kill himself, Papa Fu had paid for all his expenses at Taiwan University Hospital, about 18,000 New Taiwan dollars. Chief Yang hadn't told us before, at the request of Papa Fu.

"What the hell do you know?" Chief Yang pointed at Wu Min. "You owe that scrawny neck of yours to Papa Fu!"

Fu Chongshan had been an official back on the Mainland, so he was known in military and police circles. During the war of resistance he'd been an assistant division commander, responsible for the Fifth Military District, and had waged a fierce battle with the Japanese at Xuzhou. He left the military when he came to Taiwan and went into business with some friends, opening a company called Bountiful Textile Mill. He was Chairman of the Board. Chief Yang told us that the textile business was very profitable back then, which allowed Papa Fu to live quite comfortably. He sometimes relaxed by going hunting with old war buddies, occasionally going all the way down to the mountains around Hualian to hunt wild boar. He also took in a lot of Peking Opera at places like the Eternal Joy Theater with friends who liked that stuff. His favorite was *The Orphan of Zhao*, sung by Hu Shaoan; he never missed a performance. But in the winter of 1958, tragedy struck, with the unexpected death of his twenty-six-year-old son, Fu Wei, a graduate of a military academy two years earlier who was serving as a platoon leader in charge of new recruits. One day Fu Wei's body was discovered in his bed, a pistol clutched in his hand and his face shattered. The bullet had entered his mouth and passed through his brain. The authorities concluded that the gun had gone off accidentally. The trauma of burying his own son was more than Papa Fu could take, and he suffered a heart attack. He was rushed to Veteran's Hospital, where he spent more than three months recuperating. He emerged from the hospital an old man who weighed half what he'd weighed before. His back was bent and he could barely lift his head; he looked like death warmed over. But the change in spirit was even greater. He resigned as Chairman of the Board of Bountiful Textile Mill and went into seclusion, refusing to see anyone, not leaving the house for nearly a year. Since his wife had died young, the only other person in the house was his aging servant, Auntie Wu. In fact, it was she who had related all this to Chief Yang some years afterward. She told him that Papa Fu spoke fewer than a dozen sentences during that entire year, spending every waking hour sitting alone in a daze. When he finally snapped out of it he severed all ties with friends and family, and devoted his time to visiting the Divine Light Catholic Orphanage in Zhonghe County to take care of abandoned kids. He went there three times a week, rain or shine. According to Auntie Wu, he missed his son so badly it nearly drove him crazy. That was why he wanted to do everything possible for those parentless children, including cleaning them when they dirtied themselves.

Papa Fu was not part of the gay community. Chief Yang said that he helped us solely out of the goodness of his heart, the same reason he took care of the children at the Divine Light Orphanage. Most of his good deeds were performed anonymously, and he seldom showed up in person, so we'd only heard that there was a "living Buddha" out there, and few of us had actually seen Fu Chongshan. Our chief's association with him was based on personal connections. They were from the same place in Shandong, and Chief Yang's grandfather had known Papa Fu back on the Mainland. When Chief Yang stole money from his father to pay A-xiong's hospital bills after he'd had an epileptic fit and been hit by a car, his father kicked him out. All during those hard times, Papa Fu had been Chief Yang's sole supporter, even letting him live in his home until he got a job as manager of a nightclub on Sixth Avenue. So Chief Yang always spoke well of Papa Fu, calling him a true humanitarian.

"Boys!"

Chief Yang waved his fan to get our attention.

"Listen carefully to what I have to say. Today I'm going to take you to see Fu Chongshan, Papa Fu, who's no ordinary person. He's the humanitarian who came to your rescue."

After we were let out on probation, Chief Yang decided we should pay a call on Papa Fu to thank him in person. He'd given us each a hundred yuan to go to the Red Rose for a haircut. We'd all changed into clean clothes, and just before we headed out, Chief Yang instructed us one last time:

"The old gentleman personally came out on a scorching day to rescue the lot of you, so when you see him, don't let me catch you forgetting to thank him, or slouching around like a pack of thieves, or you'll make me lose face! Where's Mousey?"

"Here!" Mousey stepped forward, squirming as usual. The chief frowned as he surveyed him. "I'm warning you especially, with those sneaky eyes of yours. You behave yourself when you're in Papa Fu's home, and if you get sticky fingers, I promise you I'll skin you alive!"

Mousey snickered. The chief called Little Jade out.

"I want you to keep your smooth tongue in check today. Don't you dare open that yap of yours to show off, you hear me?"

"With someone like Papa Fu? I'd like to know how a bunch of kids like us are gonna be able to open our yaps and show off at his place," Little Jade said defensively.

"As long as you're aware of that," Chief Yang sneered.

"If you don't believe me, I'll sew my mouth shut," Little Jade said with a laugh.

"It'd be my good fortune if you sewed that pussy-mouth of yours shut. It'd sure save wear and tear on my ears." The chief then gave Wu Min and me our instructions.

"You two aren't as quick on your feet, so when the old master asks you something, just tell him the truth."

"Right, Chief," Wu Min and I replied together.

Lastly, Chief Yang brought A-xiong up front, where he tucked in his shirt, wiped his sweaty face with a handkerchief, then led the five of us out in single file to call on Papa Fu.

2

Papa Fu's home was in a lane off Nanking East Road, not far from Songjiang Road. With all the highrises that had been built in the area, his single-story house was surrounded by tall buildings. It was an old wooden Japanese-style house that must have been a holdover from the occupation. The gray roof tiles were covered with moss and the red paint on the front gate was chipped and peeling. There was a large, spacious courtyard, with a row of tall cypress trees just inside the outer wall, which screened the house with their lush foliage. It was very impressive. Bougainvillaeas with prickly scarlet flowers grew in profusion above the front door, positively radiant in the late afternoon sun.

We were met at Papa Fu's gate by Auntie Wu. She was a small, white-haired old woman who'd probably had her feet bound for a time when she was a girl, for when she walked she rolled on the balls of her feet. She had a wizened face with indistinguishable features.

"Is Papa home, Auntie Wu?" the chief asked her with a broad smile on his face.

"He's been waiting for you all afternoon. Come on in!" She had the same Shandong accent as Chief Yang.

We followed the chief into the compound in single file, walking up to the front door on a stone path bordered on both sides by tall bamboo plants. As soon as we were inside we felt the coolness of the house. Auntie Wu closed the door behind us and hobbled up to Chief Yang.

"Is Papa well?" he asked her.

"Well?" She turned to him and muttered, "His old problem returned the night before last. His heart bothered him all night long, but he didn't go over to see Doctor Ding at Veteran's Hospital till yesterday. He simply refuses to rest. Early yesterday morning he went over to Zhonghe County. I don't know where a man his age, in his state of health, finds the energy to wait hand and foot on that bunch of kids hopping all over the place. But he won't listen to me, so what can I do?"

"Papa has the heart of a buddha, and those poor kids are important to him," Chief Yang said.

"Don't think I don't know that, Chief Yang." She paused in the doorway. "The old gentleman wants to do good deeds and store them up for the next life. Nothing wrong with that. But you don't live here, so you don't know how it is. At night, when his heart acts up, there are beads of sweat on his face as big as beans, and it frightens me so much I don't dare fall asleep. I shouldn't have to suffer like that!"

"The next time it happens I'll send one of my boys over to spell you, so you can get some rest. What do you say?" He tried to comfort her.

"That would be nice," she nodded and said approvingly. "That would give me a chance to rest these old bones. But I'm afraid you're just saying that to make me feel good, and you'll forget you ever said it later on."

"Auntie Wu, the next time it happens I'll send him over." He pointed to me. "He's got more on the ball than the others, and he's more dependable."

She walked up and looked me over. A smile spread across her wrinkled face. She nodded and said:

"He's a healthy looking specimen."

We stopped in the vestibule, where Auntie Wu took six pairs of house slippers from a rack and told us to put them on.

"Are they all here?" We were greeted by a hoarse, aging voice as we walked into the living room.

"I brought them all," the chief called out from the doorway. "They're here to pay their respects to Papa."

Auntie Wu opened the door, and Fu Chongshan—Papa Fu— shuffled into the living room. He was easily as bent over as we'd been told. Although not a small man, his back was bent so badly that his spine seemed to stick straight up like a mound rising up behind him, forcing his head down so low he couldn't look straight ahead. He was breathing hard from thrusting his neck straight out ahead of him; just walking obviously took its toll. He was in his seventies, at least, and his hair, which was combed straight back, was streaked with gray, as were his temples and eyebrows. He had a rectangular face, dotted with liver spots; his cheekbones protruded noticeably, and the wrinkles on his face looked as though they'd been carved with a knife, deep and dark. He seemed to have a problem with his tearducts, since his eyes were watery. He was wearing a gray satin traditional gown and black cloth slippers.

"Well, what are you waiting for? Kowtow to Papa!"

Chief Yang pointed his fan at us. We exchanged glances and fidgeted, not knowing what to do.

"Idiots!" the chief ground his teeth in anger. "Don't you even know what a kowtow is?"

Little Jade, who was always quicker than the rest of us, rushed up and got down on his knees in front of Papa Fu.

"Okay, no need for that," Papa Fu said as he reached out to help Little Jade up, at the same time signaling for us to sit down.

He sat down first, in an easy chair with a thick padded backrest, and Chief Yang took the seat to his left. The rest of us followed suit. Little Jade, Wu Min, Mousey, and I squeezed ourselves into a sofa directly across from Papa Fu, while A-xiong sat on an ottoman at Chief Yang's feet.

"Bring us some soft drinks, Sister Wu," he said to his servant.

"I made some sweet-bean soup and cakes, so what do you need soft drinks for?" Auntie Wu grumbled.

"That's even better," Papa Fu smiled. "These kids are probably famished."

He turned to Chief Yang and asked him our names, ages, and how we passed the time. He went into considerable detail, and Chief Yang answered each question. Papa Fu kept his watery eyes on us the whole time, nodding to the chief's responses. Finally, he seemed about to say something, but didn't; his lips quivered slightly, and he heaved a long sigh. "Ai . . ."

Papa Fu's living room was simply furnished. Except for the sofa, the chairs, and a coffee table, there was only a redwood offerings table against the center of one wall. On it was a bunch of white ginger flowers in a sky-blue ceramic vase. There was a bronze-colored dish beside the vase, filled with fresh fruit. Two large photographs in black glass-enclosed frames hung on the wall above the table. The one on the right was a shot from the waist up of Papa Fu in an officer's uniform, taken during his heyday on the Mainland. He was in full-dress uniform, with a leather belt diagonally across his chest; he must have been an assistant division commander at the time. His back was straight then; he had true military bearing and a dignified look. The photo on the left was of a young military officer in a lieutenant's uniform. It had to be Papa Fu's late son Fu Wei. There was a certain family resemblance in the square face and high cheek-bones, but Fu Wei had far prettier eyes than his father, and he lacked Papa's martial bearing. An officer's sword was hanging on one of the other walls; it had probably been there for years, since the scabbard was slightly rusted. The room was suffused with the faint fragrance of ginger flowers. Japanese paper-covered sliding doors lining the other wall of the room opened onto the back yard, where there was a man-made hill and a pond covered with duckweed. Water trickled from the hill into the pond.

"Yang Jinhai," Papa Fu said to the chief after a momentary silence, "now don't accuse me of saying bad things about you, but this time you went too far! These kids don't know anything, so why did you get them involved in a mess like this? Why was everyone taken down to the police station?"

Our chief, Yang Jinhai, jumped to his feet and defended himself animatedly:

"It's all a terrible injustice! Papa, this time you can't blame me. These creatures may be a reckless bunch, but they mind themselves around me. You won't catch any of them involved in any serious criminal activities. I won't even stand for cheating or scare tactics. Maybe this little thief here," he said, pointing at Mousey, "has sticky fingers once in a while, but only with little, insignificant things, and I've made him pay dearly for it. What got them into trouble this time was a jailbird called Iron Ox, a desperate ruffian who ran wild in the park and should have been sent to Fire Island long ago. If he had, none of this would have happened to these kids."

"You may not know it," Papa Fu said with a sigh, "but it took almost every connection I had to get you out this time. You're lucky you're not all off on one of the outer islands right now. I want you to understand, Yang Jinhai, that I've been retired from public life for a lot of years, and most of my old friends in the military and police have either retired or died. They've been replaced by a bunch of young Turks who don't owe me a thing. This was no easy matter, no indeed. I had to swallow my pride and look up an old colleague I hadn't seen in years before I was able to get you out on probation. If any of you get into trouble from now on, I'll probably be dragged into it right along with you."

"Papa, knowing how serious it is, you have my word I'll make them toe the line from now on," the chief replied respectfully. He sat back down.

Papa Fu sat there with a worried frown on his face and continued with a heavy heart:

"Yang Jinhai, letting these kids run loose in the park isn't the answer. Sooner or later they're bound to get into trouble. You ought to be trying to find regular jobs for them. That's the only way they're going to have any kind of future."

"Papa makes it sound so simple," the chief said as he smacked his fan into the palm of his hand. "Who's going to want to hire this bunch of slobs who've been driven out of the park? And that's not all. You can't underestimate the willfulness of this pack of desperate kids. The average boss can't handle them. I've gotten them jobs in hotels, restaurants, and theaters plenty of times, but within a couple of days they all come running back, without fail, saying things like, 'The outside world is no place for me. I feel more comfortable here in my own little nest.' So what am I supposed to do, Papa? Now the park is off limits, and they don't even have a nest to come home to. That's why I brought these pitiful vermin over today, to ask Papa to help them find a way to break out of this vicious cycle."

Papa Fu strained to raise his head. He scratched his thinning silvery hair and said with a laugh:

"I try to give you a scolding, and you turn it around to make it my problem! I shouldn't have been so soft-hearted when you brought A-wei to me that time. It'd take days to tell you what that cost me in time and energy. Somehow, I managed to get him straightened out and see him assigned to a ship. Now you expect me to get all tangled up with this bunch of kids. But even if I had the heart to try, I don't think I have the energy left to . . ."

Auntie Wu walked in just then, carrying a tray with bowls of sweet-bean soup and some little cakes.

"What's Chief Yang up to this time?" she asked. "Didn't I tell you when you walked in the door that Papa's heart acted up only two nights ago?" Chief Yang stood up and took the tray from her.

"Auntie Wu," he said with a smile, "I wouldn't have mentioned it if you hadn't brought it up. You know better than anyone that Papa doesn't like people to ask about his health."

"It was nothing, just something I've lived with for years," Papa Fu sighed and pointed to his heart. "I often have pains here."

"What does Doctor Ding say?"

Papa Fu laughed nonchalantly.

"What *can* he say? When someone reaches my age, the heart gets weak and the arteries start to harden."

"Then you have to take care of yourself," Chief Yang said earnestly.

Auntie Wu passed the bowls of sweet-bean soup around and handed each of us a glistening piece of cake on a small plate.

"That's what I've been telling him," she grumbled. "He has to take two buses to get to Zhonghe. What if he falls getting on or off the bus some rainy day?"

When all the snacks had been passed out, Auntie Wu picked up her tray and turned to leave the room, rolling on the balls of her feet. On her way out she said:

"There's more in the kitchen, a whole potful."

Chief Yang coughed drily and sat up straight. "I mean it when

I say we shouldn't have come over and disturbed you today in your condition. I brought these kids for two reasons: first so they could thank you for the kindness you showed them, and second, to let you in on something. You remember that tavern I ran some years ago, Taoyuan Spring, don't you?"

"Sure," Papa Fu nodded his head. "It was doing so well, why did you close it?"

"Hai," Chief Yang said with a stomp of his foot. "Because I had no behind-the-scene support, and if it wasn't a bunch of thugs causing trouble, it was the police. I'm not boasting when I say that Taoyuan Spring was all the rage for a while. The people in the park still talk about it with nostalgia, and they keep urging me to open another one and recapture the good old days. I've never completely given up the idea, but I haven't had the chance or the financial backing. But now the time has come! The park's off limits, and all these fledglings are in a state of panic, with nowhere to go. If I set up a new nest I don't have to worry that they won't come flocking over. I'll tell you the truth, I've already picked out the location, right here on Nanking East Road, Lane 125 . . ."

Chief Yang snapped open his fan and began rapidly fanning himself as he excitedly spelled out his plans to Papa Fu. The original idea had come from Lord Sheng, Chairman of the Board of Eternal Youth Film Studio, who'd said, "Chubby Yang, you can run the place, and I'll be your backer. If you open a tavern, we'll have a place we can call our own." Lord Sheng offered to lend him 200,000 yuan, while Chief Yang could set up a banking cooperative, at ten thousand a share, for those who were in a position to participate. Chef Lu from the Cornucopia and Boss Lai from the Maochang Western Apparel shop each agreed to take two shares, so finances wouldn't be a problem.

"If everything goes as planned, the grand opening will be on the Mid-Autumn Festival, the fifteenth day of the eighth lunar month." The chief continued in even greater detail: "I've gotten an estimate from an interior decorator. The mimimum cost for fixing the place up is 100,000. Everything costs money these days. I'm not lying when I say that these ruffians, who have nowhere to go, are the main reason I want to open the tavern. They're a lot better off waiting tables than cruising the streets . . ."

Papa Fu, who had been listening intently, suddenly raised his hand for Chief Yang to stop.

"What are you going to call the place?"

"That's where Papa comes in. I'd like you to honor us with a name," Chief Yang said with a smile.

Papa Fu sat there hunched over, his eyes half closed, as he thought for a moment. Then he smiled and said:

"Back in Nanking I lived in a place called Merciful Lane. There was a little tavern at the mouth of the lane where I used to enjoy a late-night snack once in a while. I still remember the name of the place — the Cozy Nest."

"The Cozy Nest! That's perfect!" Chief Yang shouted.

3

There were mainly taverns and restaurants on Lane 125 of Nanking East Road. Phoenix City, a Cantonese restaurant, was located at the entrance to the lane, with a sit-down restaurant upstairs and a food-to-go section downstairs. The display window was filled with glistening brown chickens and ducks hanging from hooks. Next door was the Plum Garden, a Japanese restaurant with dark red paper lanterns as big as watermelons hanging above the doorway. Next came a Korean barbecue called Alilang, which was directly opposite the Golden Angel, a Western restaurant with fat little winged cherubs floating above the glass door. The lane came to life when night fell. Neons signs lit it up from one end to the other, and the fragrance of barbecued meat filled the air. There were lots of pushcarts that sold lichees, longans, dried squid, even one where you could buy little roasted sparrows that were laid out in rows beside a wok. People crowded the lane, which was closed to car traffic at night. Our new haven, the Cozy Nest, was tucked away in a corner of this bustling lane where, unless you were one of us, you would walk right past it without noticing. There was no sign out front, and the front door was just to the left of the Golden Angel, so narrow that only one person could walk through it at a time. Once you were inside you walked down some steps under a single lamp that gave off a light so faint you had to hold on to the bannister as you groped your way along. When you reached the bottom of the steps you turned right. Two glass doors slid open automatically, and there you were — the Cozy Nest.

This basement tavern of ours was about 360 square feet in size. Mirrors set into both the eastern and western walls reflected the lights and human figures in an illusion of superimposed reflections. The lighting was amber color, bathing the interior in a dusky mist. A long bar was set up under the mirrors on the eastern wall, the front edge finished off in scarlet leather. The bar itself had a glossy laminated surface. By sitting on one of the twelve swivel bar stools you could toast your own reflection. The bar was stocked with everything from Johnny Walker scotch to Taiwan beer, from three-star Hennessey Brandy to Chinese medicated liqueur. A row of six high-backed booths, also in scarlet leather, lined the western wall. Each accommodated two people. Finally, there was a large round table in the corner that sat ten and could be reserved for parties. Just inside the entrance was a circular platform, equipped with a microphone, where customers could come up and sing. Since it was a basement, there were no windows, and the temperature inside was controlled by air conditioning.

Yang Jinhai, our chief, called us together a few days before the grand opening to give us our instructions, outlining the bar regulations and passing out individual assignments. Little Jade and I were to work behind the bar as bartenders. With his gift for gab, he could deal with the customers and have them eating out of his hand in no time. My job was to mix drinks. The chief reminded me that we made our profits off the drinks, not off the snacks that went with them. The success or failure of this venture rested mainly with the two of us.

"The people behind the bar are the keys to success," Chief Yang coached us. "No more getting on your high horse from now on. We're going to have customers from all walks of life who come in for a few drinks and some food. It's your job to welcome them with a smile and pretend you see and hear nothing. Those customers are nothing to us but wallets filled with cash, nothing else concerns us."

He lined several kinds of liquor up on the bar.

"Locally produced stuff has a fixed price and there's nothing we can do about it. But we have plenty of flexibility with the imported stuff. Even at a flat forty yuan a drink, there's lots of room for maneuvering."

He put some ice in a glass, picked up a bottle of Johnny Walker, and poured some in. A little soda, and he was finished. "If you pour too little, the customers will complain. Too much and we lose money. Play it by ear. You can go heavy on the soda and ice with an easy-going customer, but give the hard-nosed ones their money's worth. Some customers will want to buy you drinks. The standing rule is no drinking on duty. You don't want to get drunk and slip up somewhere. So if someone wants to buy you a drink, pour yourself a soft drink on the sly. The split for that is 60/40: you take sixty percent, the bar gets forty. That way, everyone's happy."

Wu Min's job was to wait tables, and Mousey was assigned to odd jobs like busing the tables, mopping the floor, and cleaning the toilets. A-xiong was to stand at the door to greet customers and give prospective troublemakers a reason to have second thoughts. Chef Lu from the Cornucopia agreed to send Little Ma, one of his assistants, over on a temporary basis to prepare the late-night snacks. Altogether we had four kinds: salted pork liver, buffalo wings, sliced pork stomach, and spicy beef strips. Once the demonstrations were over and the job assignments completed, our excitement level rose as we eagerly awaited the grand opening, when we could put on our new apricot-yellow uniforms with the red logo on the breast pocket, and start to work. Except for Mousey, that is, who moped around and grumbled to Chief Yang, looking at him out of the corner of his eye:

"How come I get all the shitty jobs like mopping the floor and cleaning the toilets? I know how to tend bar . . ."

Chief Yang cut him off:

"Hear that? He wants to make sure the customers get a good look at that sneaky face of his. With him behind the bar, our customers would spend all their time puking up last night's dinner. Now you listen to me. You're to clean those toilets, and clean them well. If I so much as smell urine, I'll pour Lysol down your throat! Little Jade, A-qing, Wu Min, you listen to me, too. Every broken glass and plate comes out of your pay, and while you're working there'll be no goofing off or flirting. I'll give you three warnings, just to show you I'm not heartless, then you're out the door. Understand?"

"We understand!" we all answered him.

4

The Cozy Nest opened its doors on the Mid-Autumn Festival, the fifteenth day of the eighth month. Floral wreaths had been sent over that morning, the largest from Lord Sheng, Chairman of the Board of Eternal Youth Film Studio. Standing six feet tall, it was

done in the design of a peacock fan, using hundreds of gorgeous red roses. The couplet on the red satin ribbon said:
Though storms may pound the lotus pond
At The Cozy Nest the good times roll on
Other congratulatory gifts were sent by Boss Lai of the Maochang Western Apparel shop and Old Man Wu of the Heavenly Import Store. Fatty Lu from the Cornucopia sent over a complete meal for twelve from his restaurant, all prepared personally by him and delivered in two large baskets by Little Ma.

At six o'clock everything was ready: the air conditioner was on, the amber lights shone from two walls, filling the basement space with a misty golden light. We were all in place, dressed in brand-new apricot-yellow uniforms with the words "The Cozy Nest" sewn in red on our breast pockets. We each wore a red boutonniere. Little Jade's hair, which was now about an inch in length, was combed down over his forehead, and his smiling, almond-shaped eyes gave him an especially fetching look as he stood behind the bar, every bit the dignified bartender. A-xiong looked positively cocky as he towered over his dominion beside the door, manning his post with dead seriousness. Mousey and Wu Min were kept busy doing all sorts of things for Chief Yang, like moving stuff back and forth. The chief was dressed in a brand-new fitted black orlon suit—a present from Boss Lai of the Maochang Western Apparel shop—that showed off his bulging belly and protruding rear end. He was wearing a white shirt and a bright red string tie tucked up under his double chin. Sweating profusely in spite of the air conditioning, he kept fanning himself.

At precisely eight o'clock, the automatic doors of the Cozy Nest slid open to admit the spirited birds of the park who came flying in one after the other, and in no time at all, our new nest was filled with bobbing black heads. Virtually every dignitary in our circle was there. Standing in the middle of the room, where you couldn't miss him, was Hua Guobao, surrounded by a circle of admirers. He'd become more of a butch queen than ever since Lord Sheng had, as expected, fallen for this "piece of goods" and given him a role as supporting male lead in his latest movie, *Feelings and Desire*. With the incredible box-office success of *Body and Soul* in Taipei, Hong Kong, Singapore, and Malaysia, he had moved quickly on the sequel. Hua Guobao was dressed in a long-sleeved electric-blue shirt, with the sleeves rolled back; a wide silver bracelet hung loosely on his left wrist. His muscular chest was exposed beneath the unbuttoned top of his shirt, and adorned by an agate necklace. He was wearing white bell bottoms, cinched tightly at the waist by a maroon leather belt. Always the proud peacock, he held his head high, as though he were the only person in the room. The balding Yang Feng, in his customary beret, was seated on the end stool, gazing at Hua Guobao with a look of melancholy. The young hustlers from Three Rivers Street, led by Flower Child, pushed their way through the crowd up to the electric organ to make requests. "Play 'Every Day Is Spring,'" one shouted to the organist. "'I Can't Control My Feelings,'" another shouted. "No, play 'I Don't Know, I Don't Know,'" another demanded. The organist, Yang Sanlang, had been a respected music teacher during the Japanese occupation. He'd composed a few songs that nightclub singers had made popular all over Taipei. Yang, who was nearly blind, wore dark glasses even at night, and there was always a distant smile on his otherwise expressionless face. Once he'd programmed the accompaniment, he raised his head and the organ music began to float in the air above the sounds of talking and laughter. The four military reservists sitting at the table nearest to the organ raised their voices. One of them was gleefully telling the others how his old platoon leader got him drunk and took advantage of him. They all had crewcuts and deeply tanned faces; one of them, still in uniform, had come straight from the train station when he arrived in Taipei, without even stopping to change into civvies. The next table over was occupied by college students; two of them were sociology students who were talking about a project they hoped to undertake someday on migration habits of the young birds of New Park. They'd come to the Cozy Nest to have a farewell party for one of their friends. They hoisted their glasses and wished bon voyage to an overseas Chinese student from Malaysia who was returning home to Penang. He was sad to leave Taiwan, where, during his four exciting and heart-breaking years, he'd fallen hopelessly in love with a handsome aborigine singer named Blue Water. Every member of our little community knew the story. Everyone had shown up: shopowners and their employees from Westgate district; the renowned cardiologist; the judge advocate . . . The Master Artist was sitting off in a corner sulking. He hadn't been able to complete his portrait of Iron Ox, and when he was sent to Fire Island, the artist's inspiration had turned to cinders. Where was he going to find another subject like Iron Ox, so primitive, so wild, so masculine it made your blood race? He was lamenting the loss. Another middle-aged man was sulking off in a corner of the bar. He had a deep crease above his mouth, like a dark scar branded on his face. Mr. Zhang of Guangwu Villa had come after all. There were two schools of thought as to why he was always sulking. One was that he'd kicked Little Fairy out of his house because he didn't keep himself clean and because he'd stolen Mr. Zhang's Canon camera. The other version had it that Little Fairy had left Mr. Zhang for a German businessman who'd gotten him a job in Hong Kong with Lufthansa. Whatever the reason, Mr. Zhang was on his own again, and was sitting there crying in his beer. The pot-bellied, high-spirited Chef Lu of the Cornucopia was trying hard to find his little "rat spirit." The Cozy Nest was so packed you could hardly turn around. The mirrors on the facing walls reflected the people's figures back and forth, doubling and redoubling the number of people, who, in the amber light, bobbed and weaved like a flock of excited penguins in a red sunset.

Lord Sheng, Chairman of the Board of Eternal Youth Film Studio, made his entrance, but, because of the crowd of people, could not get through the doors. Chief Yang, seeing what was happening, quickly cleared a path and escorted him inside, half pushing and half pulling. When they reached the bar, the chief called out to Little Jade:

"Brandy and a pack of State Express, and make it quick."

Then he turned to Lord Sheng.

"Lord Sheng, we've had our eye out for you all night. We were afraid we wouldn't have the pleasure of your company."

"On a night as important as this? I wouldn't have missed it even if I'd had to come through a hailstorm!" He laughed. "I went to Five Blessings for dinner tonight and couldn't get away. Finally, I had to fake a stomach ache."

He was wearing a red Hawaiian shirt with big white flowers, white slacks, and white leather shoes with air holes; the few straggling hairs on his head were slicked down with oil and combed from one side of his head to the other.

"Lord Sheng is ravishing tonight!" Little Jade complimented him with a giggle. He handed him a glass of brandy and lit his cigarette.

"Did you all hear that? He's got his eye on these old bones of mine." Lord Sheng's face was scrunched up in a hearty laugh.

"You can't get more nutritious bones than Lord Sheng's. Feast on them and you're guaranteed longevity!" Little Jade responded.

Lord Sheng laughed till tears came to his eyes. He turned to Chief Yang and said:

"With a naughty little boy like this, the Cozy Nest is sure to do a land-office business!"

He reached into his pocket and pulled out two hundred-yuan bills. He tossed them over to Little Jade.

"Good boy, keep it up and there'll be good things in your future."

Little Jade picked up the money and laughed:

"If we have the pleasure of Lord Sheng's company every night there'll be all the good things we could ask for."

"Chubby Yang," Lord Sheng said with a broad smile and a nod of his head, "it looks like you got your wish. You've recaptured the glory days of Taoyuan Spring tonight."

Chief Yang clasped his hands in front of his chest and bowed.

"You made it all happen."

Chief Yang picked up Lord Sheng's drink and cigarette and politely cleared a path for him over to the big round table, which was filled with young men, including Hua Guobao. As soon as Lord Sheng approached the table, they all got to their feet and offered him their seats. Having heard that two supporting male roles in *Feelings and Desire* weren't yet filled, they harbored dreams of becoming a movie star. The best way to realize that dream was to be discovered by Lord Sheng.

Little Jade stuffed the two hundred yuan into his breast pocket as Death Angel Zhao glided up to the bar. He looked Little Jade up and down and sneered:

"So, you've already hung out your shingle! Do you have a seal of approval from the Department of Sanitation? Got your license yet?"

Death Angel Zhao, all in black, as usual, his gaunt horse-like face powdered a deathly white, smiled, exposing his nicotine-stained teeth.

"At least we still need seals of approval," Little Jade shot back with a giggle. "But some old whores have been around so long they must be immune to V.D.!"

He set a glass of beer down in front of Zhao, slopping some of the foamy head on the bar.

"Here, wet your whistle. It's on the house, compliments of the Cozy Nest!"

Without waiting for a response, Little Jade walked to the end of the bar, took a glass of Johnny Walker out of my hand, and set it down in front of Doctor Shi, the cardiologist.

"Doctor Shi, I've got a disease," he said.

"What do you have, Little Jade?" Doctor Shi asked as he puffed on his pipe, his interest piqued. "Come to the clinic tomorrow, and I'll give you a check-up."

Doctor Shi was always doing that for us. He was a thoughtful man who made his living off the rich and took care of the poor. We heard that Lord Sheng went to see him once and paid five hundred just to have his blood pressure checked.

"Heart disease," Little Jade said, pointing to his chest.

"Heart disease? That's my specialty. I'll give you an EKG, and we'll see what your heart looks like."

"You won't be able to see anything," Little Jade sighed. "This heart disease of mine is pretty strange, and I doubt if even a famous doctor like you can cure it. Whenever I lay eyes on a gorgeous man like you, my heart starts beating like crazy. What can I do? Think you can cure me?"

"That's a wanton disease!" Doctor Shi laughed loudly. "We don't have any medicine here to cure what you've got. I've heard there's an electric shock procedure that some foreigners use — they show you a picture of a man and give you an electric shock, and keep doing it until just the sight of a man makes you feel like throwing up."

"Oops, forget that!" Little Jade shouted, holding both hands over his chest. "My heart would stop from the shocks before they managed to cure me."

Mr. Zhang had already finished three drinks, all served by Wu Min. This time there was no perspiration on Wu Min's forehead because The Fairy hadn't come along. Wu Min gave Mr. Zhang a glass of brandy, then very attentively handed him a lightly per-fumed cold hand towel. Mr. Zhang snatched the towel out of his hand and wiped his face roughly, although he couldn't wipe away the cruel scar-like crease above his mouth.

"Look at that cheap thing!" Little Jade whispered in my ear. "He's going back for seconds."

Chef Lu reached out and grabbed Mousey's ear.

"Rat Spirit, I came here tonight to sing your praises, but you haven't so much as said hello." It was more than just a playful comment.

"Master Lu," Mousey pleaded, cocking his head and screwing

his face up, "don't you have any pity at all? I haven't had a minute's rest all night. My legs are about to drop off."

Fatty Lu pulled Mousey's ear down next to his mouth and whispered something to him. Mousey cackled gleefully, freed himself from Chef Lu's grasp, and slipped quickly in among the crowd.

There was a lot of activity at Lord Sheng's table, where young men dreaming of stardom were listening attentively to what he was saying about the rise and fall of movie stars back in the 1930s and 1940s.

"Have you heard of Xu Lai, the Perfect Beauty?" he asked.

The youngsters exchanged glances.

"They were no more than glints in their daddies' eyes then, so how could they know?" commented Chief Yang, who was sitting beside Lord Sheng. "Lord Sheng, I've seen the movie *Willows on the Road, Flowers on the Wall*, with you and Xu Lai. You were a real charmer in that one!"

A smile that had a trace of embarrassment blossomed on Lord Sheng's wrinkled face. He rubbed his nearly bald scalp and sighed.

"Chubby Yang, I'm glad you remember that movie. That became the hallmark film of Bright Star Studio and saved the company from bankruptcy."

The chief had told us that Lord Sheng had been a dashing star of 1930s films, a handsome romantic lead. His autographed photos were fought over by girls in Shanghai and Nanking, who hung them up in their rooms. Lord Sheng always got sentimental when he talked about those days, and was always looking for young talent, particularly pretty boys like Hua Guobao, whose peacock looks reminded him a little of himself back then.

Lord Sheng had his listeners riveted to their seats with stories about the lives of old movie stars, but just when everything was getting more enthralling than they could bear, he stopped abruptly and took a long look with his rheumy eyes at the young men gathered around him, then sighed and continued, "Your youth is the best capital you have. Boys, you must treasure it!"

The Cozy Nest's air conditioning was becoming less and less effective, owing to the pervasive body heat, the increasing level of excitement and stimulation, and the alcohol in the air. Under the cover of all that clamor, we formed little groups or paired off in our new amber-colored nest, whispering, pouring out our hearts, telling secrets of which the outside world was totally ignorant.

On the night of the Mid-Autumn Festival, we had migrated to this basement room from all over, spontaneously forming a single body, with no concern for age or social station. Even the pain, sorrow, melancholy, and remorse hidden deep down in individual hearts gave way to all the laughter, the banter, the madness, and, of course, the wild music coming from Yang Sanlang's electric organ. His head was raised high; there was a distant smile on his well-worn face beneath his dark sunglasses. He switched to a new beat and began playing the song he'd written during the Japanese occupation, "Taipei Bridge Blues."

5

All the neon signs in Lane 125 had been turned off. The restaurants and nightclubs were closing up for the night. Only the watermelon-sized lanterns swaying in the doorway of Plum Garden still gave off a pale red light. It was, after all, mid-autumn, and the lane was cooled by night breezes as the last few customers finished their late-night snacks, came out of the Japanese restaurant, and climbed into taxis. They drove out of the now still lane. All of a sudden, a huge, radiant full moon climbed into the sky above Phoenix City at the head of the lane. It had been years since I'd given more than a passing glance to the mid-autumn moon. How could it be so big? So bright? It was like a searchlight suspended above the entrance to the lane. We hadn't celebrated the Mid-Autumn Festival at home since the year Mother left. Before that, it had been one of the big events of the year, a time when Mother paid reverence to the Moon Goddess. Late at night, when the moon was directly overhead, she would take Buddy and me out into the back yard to light incense, which she offered up to the Moon Goddess as she prostrated herself on the ground. While her attention was diverted, Buddy and I would snatch mooncakes off the devotional table and start eating them. Since Father never came out with us, when Mother was finished outside, she'd cut up a mooncake and take it inside to him. Only once did the routine change, and that was on Mother's last Mid-Autumn Festival at home. That year, Father surprised us by joining us in the back yard to enjoy the view of the moon. The cooperative he belonged to had paid a dividend that year, so we were each given an extra mooncake. The moon seemed brighter than ever that night, so luminous that the cement covering the yard was as white as snow, Mother's long black hair shone like satin, and Buddy's pale shoulders glistened. Father was in such high spirits he made lanterns out of grapefruit peels for Buddy and me. We were astonished that those big hands, with their protruding veins and swollen knuckles, could make such nifty lanterns; he scooped out the grapefruit without leaving a scratch on the inside of the peel, then used a pair of kitchen shears to cut out a human face on each one, complete with eyes and nose. The mouth on Buddy's figure curved up to the left, mine to the right, so when the lanterns were put together, the two round faces smiled at each other. We lit red candles and stuck them inside the lanterns, then hung them from the eaves to watch the light glowing through the carved eyes and mouths. When the moon was directly overhead, Mother lit incense and chanted some prayers; when she finished she sat down in her rattan chair, lifted Buddy into her lap, and rubbed his back to get him to fall asleep. He'd already eaten one whole mooncake and half of another, so he lay his head against her breast, yawned sleepily, and fell into a contented sleep. Father paced back and forth in the yard, his hands clasped behind his back. He hadn't said a word all night. He walked over to the hanging lanterns, raised his graying head, and stared at them for the longest time, before mumbling to himself:

"The grapefruits we had in Sichuan were a lot bigger than these."

I walked out to the head of the lane and looked up into the sky. The moon was pouring out its rays like water from a bucket, cascading down and bathing me. I shivered and felt my pores open in the cold air.

6

I bumped into Wu Min at the entrance of the South Seas Department Store in Westgate, where I'd gone to buy some underwear. My undershirts all had holes in them and the elastic drawstrings of my underpants were shot. When I hung them out to dry, all tattered and torn, Obasan complained about how it looked and threatened to take them down and use them for rags. The South Seas Department Store was having a big three-day autumn sale; the sign over the entrance said: Shirts, Pajamas, Underwear, 30% Off! As Wu Min started to fidget, I noticed a middle-aged man standing next to him. He was about fifty, had a shaved head, and was little more than skin and bones. His gaunt, pale forehead was streaked with bulging veins, his sunken eyes were dull and lifeless, and his sockets were dark and unhealthy looking. He looked like a cadaver. He was wearing a white shirt that was turning yellow and had a frayed collar. His baggy black pants, cinched tightly around the waist, flapped when he walked. He had on black plastic galoshes, one of which had a big hole in the toe.

"A-qing..." Wu Min smiled as he greeted me.

"Where are you headed?" I stopped in the entrance.

"Same place you are. I need to buy some things..." He paused before introducing me to the middle-aged, sickly man beside him.

"A-qing, this is my father."

I quickly nodded a greeting.

"Uncle."

Wu Min's father smiled shyly and looked over at his son, as though waiting for him to say something to ease his embarrassment. But Wu Min didn't say anything. He opened the department store door and walked in, his father right at his heels. They headed straight for the shirt department, where the counter was piled high with sale items. Bargain hunters were digging through the merchandise, tossing the shirts all over the place. Wu Min pushed his way in and picked out two shirts, a blue one and a gray one. He looked at his father and asked:

"Papa, what size do you wear, fourteen and a half or fifteen?"

"Either one's okay," he said.

"What about these colors?"

Wu Min handed the two shirts to his father, who looked them over carefully.

"This gray one's fine."

He handed the blue shirt back to Wu Min, who shoved it back into his hand.

"We'll take them both. They're on sale, after all."

After they paid for the shirts, Wu Min took his father to some of the other departments, where they bought underwear, handkerchiefs, socks, slippers, everything he needed, including sundries like toothbrush and toothpaste, razor blades, as well as a bottle of Three Flowers hair-growing tonic. Wu Min paid for the purchases and carried the shopping bags. After the first time or two, he even stopped asking his father's opinion, and just bought whatever he thought he needed. I picked up four sets of underwear and a blue and white striped sale shirt. As we were walking out of the department store, Wu Min leaned over and whispered in my ear:

"A-qing, come to the train station with me to see my father off, then we'll go get something to eat."

Wu Min's father had a ticket on the 4:30 local to Xinzhu. After Wu Min bought me a platform ticket, the two of us accompanied his father to platform number two to wait for the train. Wu Min's hands were filled with bundles.

"If you need anything else," he said to his father, "just drop me a line."

His father mopped his brow. He had the eyes of a dead fish.

"This is plenty," he said after a long pause. "I don't need anything else."

Another moment passed, then he rolled up the right sleeve of his shirt and raised his rail-thin wrist to show his son.

"I've had this ringworm for two years. It won't go away. The itching drives me crazy. Do you know any medicine that'll take care of it?"

His wrist was covered with scaly ringworm circles, some of which had dried up and left deep red scars. The skin over the others was newly broken, exposing the pink flesh underneath. Wu Min frowned and said:

"Why didn't you say something earlier? The Sino-American Drugstore is right across the street from the South Seas Department Store. They sell a salve that works wonders with ringworm. Tell you what, I'll buy some and send it to you at Uncle's house."

His father looked at him and nodded, then rolled his shirtsleeve back down without saying another word. We waited quietly on the platform for a while, then Wu Min said thoughtfully to his father:

"Papa, when you get to Uncle's, even though he's easy to get along with, you know how Auntie is. So don't do anything that'll get her angry."

"I know."

"Now remember, as soon as you get there give that bottle of hair-growing tonic to Auntie and tell her I bought it for her. She always uses Three Flowers."

His father nodded again, just as the train entered the station. Once his father had boarded the train and found a seat, Wu Min handed the bundles to him through the window. After he was all settled, he stood up and stuck the top half of his body out the window, pointing to his right wrist.

"A-min, the ringworm medicine, don't forget, the itching drives me crazy . . ."

"Don't worry," Wu Min frowned. Then he added, "I'll send it to you."

The train headed slowly out of the station. Wu Min stood there without moving, gazing at the departing train.

"My father," he said placidly, "just got out of prison this morning. He spent three years in Taipei Prison."

7

"I saw my father for the first time when I was seven."

Wu Min and I had walked over to the Old Prosperity Western restaurant on Guanqian Street near the station, where we ordered ham and egg sandwiches. There were hardly any customers on the second floor at that hour, 4:30, which was too late for lunch and too early for dinner. The lights were turned down and soft music drifted up from downstairs. After we'd finished our sandwiches, we ordered some coffee. Wu Min took out a mentholated cigarette, lit it, and took a deep drag.

"I was scared the first time I saw him. He wasn't all wasted away like he is now—he hadn't started using drugs then—and he looked pretty spiffy with his hair all neatly combed. He and Auntie started arguing right after he got there, because he wanted to take me away. He'd been sent to prison for the first time when Mother was pregnant with me. I was born at my uncle's house. As soon as I saw that tough look on his face I high-tailed it into the rice storeroom. My uncle ran a little rice mill, and the storeroom was filled with baskets of rice husks. I hid among those baskets and refused to come out. So Father came in to drag me out, and I fought and kicked until I was covered with rice husks from head to toe. Auntie laughed and teased me, "You look like a rat that's been stealing our rice!"

Just thinking about it made him laugh.

"You don't mess around with those Hakka women!" He shrugged his shoulders as though to mask some hidden fear.

"Is your uncle afraid of her?" I asked him. "They say Hakka men are all afraid of their wives."

"Him? All she has to do is raise her voice for him to turn pale.

What do you think?" He laughed. "She comes from a prominent Hakka family in Xinzhu. The rice mill was her dowry. My poor uncle looks like he's half her size when he's standing in front of her. He sure has my sympathy, since she yelled at me every single day, from one end of the room to the other. I felt like I was walking on eggs all those years I lived in her house. The clearest memory I have is the night Auntie kicked my mother out of the house. She told me to go sleep in her room, and I woke up in the middle of the night with a bladder so full I thought it was going to burst. But I was afraid I'd wake her up if I got up to pee, so I wet my pants..."

"Poor little thing," I laughed and shook my head. "Just like a little child-bride."

"What was I supposed to do?" He took a drag on his cigarette. "It wasn't my fault my parents were losers. My father was in prison, my mother was sleeping around—some millworker got her pregnant, and Auntie kicked her out of the house without a second thought."

"Did you ever see your mother after that?"

"No." He shook his head. "I don't know where she is, but I heard she married some blue-collar guy, and she's probably doing okay."

"A-qing," Wu Min blurted out after quietly putting out his cigarette, "have you ever heard of someone cutting off his finger to keep from gambling?"

"Sure," I laughed. "Some people cut off two or three!"

"My father's such a gambling addict he'd find a way to play if he had nine fingers cut off!" He shook his head and gave an exasperated laugh. "He can sit at a Taiwanese poker table non-stop for three days and nights. He's gambled his whole life away. I'm not saying this just to be mean. Okay, so he was sent to Taipei Prison, at least I could go see him from time to time and take care of some of his needs. But now he's out, and it won't be more than three months before he gets the gambling urge again. God only knows what that'll lead to. A-qing, why's life so hard? It's tough getting through life!"

He looked at me with a helpless smile.

"Who doesn't know that!" I said. "You're not thinking of doing youself in again, are you? Little Jade said he's not gonna give you any more blood, even if you cut off your pee-pee!"

"No, that's not it. You won't catch me doing a stupid thing like that again." He lowered his head out of embarrassment.

"A-qing, last night Mr. Zhang asked me to move in with him again."

"What did you say?"

"I said I would."

"No wonder Little Jade calls you cheap! How can you let your soul fly away the minute Old Scarface wiggles his little finger? What do you want from him? That fancy apartment of his in Guangwu Villa?"

I thought back to when he told me how he'd spent an hour soaking in Mr. Zhang's blue tile tub his first night.

"I didn't say I'd move in with him right away," Wu Min defended himself. "I went over to see him last night after we closed up the Cozy Nest. I knew he was drunk. He never could hold his liquor."

I remembered the time I went over to Mr. Zhang's, and how he'd told Little Fairy to get the bundle of old clothes Wu Min had left there so I could give them back to Wu Min. It was probably at that moment that I first noticed the crease above Mr. Zhang's mouth, like a deep knife scar. The first thing I thought of was Long Fei, the movie star who was always the bad guy in movies. He played a mean, sneaky character with a knife scar on his face.

"Is a cold-hearted guy like that worth it?" I was suddenly struck by the feeling that the 500 cc's of blood I'd given Wu Min were wasted.

"I feel sorry for him," Wu Min looked at me and said.

"You feel *sorry* for him?" I sprayed the mouthful of coffee I'd just sipped. "My little darling, I think you ought to feel sorry for yourself first. You damn near died because of him."

"You don't realize it, A-qing, but Mr. Zhang's a lonely man. When I was living with him he was very stand-offish and didn't talk much. But as soon as he had a few drinks in him he came out of his shell. At first he'd get mad and yell at me for no reason. Then he'd close himself up in his room and fall fast asleep. He got so drunk once he threw up all over his room, so I ran in to help him into some clean clothes. He was so drunk he probably didn't even know who I was. He threw his arms around me and buried his face in my chest and wailed. I've never seen anyone cry that hard. Have you ever seen anything like that, A-qing? Have you ever seen a grown man cry so hard it scares you?"

I said I had. I thought of the gym teacher I spent the night with in the Yaotai Hotel, that big, strapping guy whose stomach muscles were as hard as rocks, and who kept telling me to feel them. But that night, when he was lying next to me he cried so pitifully I didn't know what to do. He was very, very drunk that night, too; he reeked of alcohol.

"I used to think that grown men didn't cry, especially people like Mr. Zhang, who kept their feelings hidden. I couldn't believe it when I saw those hot tears streaming down his face, splashing on the back of my hands. Mr. Zhang doesn't get along with people very well. He's mean, suspicious, and stingy. He doesn't have many friends at all, and none of the boys who've lived with him really cared for him, so they didn't stay long. And when they left they took whatever they could get their hands on. Little Fairy was the worst of the lot. Mr. Zhang told me that not only did he walk off with his Canon camera, but he took Mr. Zhang's favorite Sanyo stereo set, too. Then to top it off, he warned Mr. Zhang that if he went to the police, he'd tell them all about their relationship. When this happened, he thought of me, probably because I was the only one he could trust. That's why he asked me to move back in with him."

"Then why not just go ahead and do it? That way you can be Old Scarface's slave again."

"No, now I'm thinking more clearly. We'll do it my way this time. Mr. Zhang's got a strange temper. When he's lonely he wants me back. But if he regrets it later, that'll really make me look bad. Besides, I don't have to worry about a place to live now. The chief wants me to spend the nights at the Cozy Nest to watch the place. So I told Mr. Zhang I'd move in with him when I thought he really needed me."

Wu Min paused and looked at me before going on:

"A-qing, I know Mr. Zhang isn't a very likable person. But I was with him for a long time, and even though he broke it off, if there's something I can do for him I'll do it. No matter what you say, he put me up in his house for all that time. The truth is, the happiest days of my life were the ones I spent with him."

There was the hint of a smile on Wu Min's lips. He looked up at the clock on the wall, picked up the check, and stood up.

"It's six o'clock. Time for us to go to work at the Cozy Nest."

8

Business at the Cozy Nest was booming from the very beginning. The place was packed every night for the first week. The flock of birds that had once nested at New Park were only too happy to spread their wings and fly straight to their new home at the Cozy Nest. There were a number of new creatures as well, those who'd been afraid to show up at the park. Potential dangers in the open-air park were too great for the timid souls, who couldn't screw up the courage to penetrate the borders of that dark kingdom of ours. There were, for example, the pampered college students who'd never had to fight for anything. Born into good families, they were either afraid to set foot in the park, or sneaked in and hid in the bushes to peek out at what was going on. But this new nest of ours was like a paradise to them. They swaggered in the door, confident in their safety. The amber-colored lights, the organ, the foamy beer—it was all perfectly suited to these youngsters who were seeking a little romance. They came to the Cozy Nest as they would to a college party. There were a couple from Tamkang University, one or two from Soochow University, several from Fu Jen Catholic University, and quite a few from the Chinese Culture College. They also included an athletic boy from the College of Physical Education who always wore tight blue jeans and white Adidas sneakers; he was captain of the Golden Dragon basketball team. Another boy with long, curly hair and a moustache, was a promising singer from the music department of the Academy of Arts. He'd written a song called "Your Shining Eyes," and one night after closing time the college students stuck around to listen to him sing as he sat at the organ:

> Your shining eyes
> Have singed my heart
> Your shining eyes
> Have ignited my soul
> I raise my hands
> Cradling the cinders of my love
> The heavens are deserted
> The earth has grown old
> The mountains have crumbled
> The seas are empty
> And yet
> Why can't I

Control my feelings
Why doesn't my love die

He sang with passion, with affected sadness, as he cocked his head, his hair falling to the side. His eyes were closed, his brow was furrowed, his cheeks were on fire, as though he could no longer bear the pain in his heart. The other students crowded around him, gaping with open mouths, as though transfixed by his song. Little Jade and I, brooms in hand, swept the littered floor. Little Jade was grumbling under his breath, wishing they'd go home so we could close up and get some rest. Many of the college students were couples; those who were alone were probably suffering through a recently ended affair. The singer's boyfriend, an overseas student in the Department of Foreign Languages at Taiwan National University, had left him a month earlier to return to Singapore. Everyone said he was a handsome boy with shining eyes.

Some of the other customers were socially prominent, respectable men with families. The violence, blackmail, and frightening incidents that occurred in the darkness of the park scared them away. But at the Cozy Nest, amid the gentle amber-colored lighting, these chairmen of the board, managers, and professors felt right at home. They could leave their daytime professions and troubles at home at the door and enjoy the intoxication of this nest of ours. These middle-aged men with their bulging wallets were our favorite customers. The chief made sure we fawned all over them, unlike the college students, three of whom would share a bottle of beer, and whose pockets were so empty it was impossible to squeeze a tip out of them. They were like pretty ornaments put there for the viewing. Chief Yang, who'd walked around for days with a broad grin on his face, bought a gold-filled Ronson lighter for me and one for Little Jade. Whenever one of our wealthy customers took out an imported cigarette, we'd whip out our shiny Ronsons and light it for him — deferential, with a touch of class. While they were pouring out their complaints, only part of which we could understand, we'd be pouring out a glassful of the most expensive Napoleon brandy. All it took to get these successful middle-aged family men, with their bulging wallets, to talk about their surprising unhappiness was a couple of drinks.

After finishing off half a bottle of brandy and nearly a whole pack of cigarettes, the fat, balding chairman of the board of an acrylic-plastic factory in Banqiao, Ke Jinfa, grabbed my wrist and poured out his woes to me for what seemed to be half the night: he had three sons: one a mahjong addict, one who spent all his time chasing pop singers, and one — the youngest — who'd just been expelled from school. Three useless sons whose only talent was in spending their father's hard-earned money. He ground his teeth and lamented, "It's my horrible fate to have three spendthrift sons!" I kept his glass filled and his cigarettes lit until he'd said all he could about his family tragedies. He gave me a hundred-yuan tip and complimented me on my service to Chief Yang.

Little Jade was particularly spirited those days, because Chief Yang had turned a very important customer over to him. He was captain of the *Cuihua*, one of the ships in the Yongxing Freight Lines. The captain, whose surname was Long — dragon — was around fifty. He was six feet tall, broad-shouldered and muscular, and when he stood in the bar, it was like someone had put up a solid door there. He was deeply tanned from all his time out on the sea, and his leathery skin, which looked like a steel mask, gave him a look of power. The first night he dropped in, Little Jade joked in a low voice, "Here comes the Dragon King!" Captain Long did have a big head, a rugged face, high cheek-bones, a large nose, steely eyes, and two rows of straight white teeth — the face of a dragon. Yet he was a straightforward, warm-hearted man who took Little Jade's face in his hands and laughed. He called Little Jade "Little Honey." He had a heavy southern accent and spoke Mandarin like Little Jade's former patron, Old Zhou. The *Cuihua* was an oil tanker that steamed from the Persian Gulf to Japan. Captain Long had just returned from Japan for a vacation, so he was free to come to the Cozy Nest every night and get drunk. The chief said to make sure he got strong drinks and all the snacks he wanted, free of charge, for he knew this was one of those priceless customers who could make or break the Cozy Nest. The plan was to ask Captain Long to bring duty-free liquor in on his ship, which could save us two hundred on a bottle of Johnny Walker, three hundred and eighty on Napoleon brandy. It would take a lot of drinks over the bar to clear those kinds of profits, since imported liquor was where we made our real money. So Chief Yang said to Little Jade:

"Jade, he's an important man, so take good care of him. Don't let this fish get away."

"Don't worry," Little Jade smiled. "Once I get the Dragon King's balls in my hand I won't let go."

Among the old friends and new faces in the Cozy Nest, there was one who didn't like our new nest. He missed our old home, missed the lotus pond that had been picked bare of flowers, missed the intertwining branches of the green coral trees, missed those shining, lust-filled eyes, like fireflies darting back and forth in the darkness. The Master Artist said that our old nest had a primitive quality, that it was filled with wild, raw life forces, that it was a mysterious, frightening underworld that made your soul take flight. For him, only our dark kingdom was stimulating enough. Our new, man-made nest was too common, too peaceful. He didn't like it. The gentle music, the soft lights, the clinking glasses, the new faces. He was critical of the college students, finding them spoiled, shallow, and full of themselves. He gained no inspiration from their cultured existence. What he longed for were the wild kids who fled to the park from Huaxi Street, from Sanchong City, and from the stormy fishing port of Hengchun. They were the true source of his art. The Master Artist told us he'd traveled in Europe and America, had lived in Paris and New York for years, but had come home to Taiwan, to the old nest in the park, for only the wild kids around the lotus pond had the power to inspire his desire, his passion for life. He painted their portraits to record his "Rhapsody of Youth."

A commercial painting had been hung on the right-hand white wall behind the organ, just inside the entrance to the Cozy Nest, by Shengmei Interior Designs, the company that had decorated the bar. It was a still life with red flowers and green leaves in a vase. The Master Artist frowned when he saw it. "Vile trash!" he'd called it. So Chief Yang asked him to donate one of his own creations to hang in its place and lend a more artistic atmosphere to the bar. The Master Artist replied that he'd never donated one of his paintings to anyone, but he'd make an exception in this case to increase the appeal of the Cozy Nest. He'd let Chief Yang display one of his paintings for a month. We never expected that he'd lend us his masterpiece, "The Call of Wildness." It was a huge oil portrait, three feet wide by six feet high, whose background was a hazy ghetto district, complete with canopied stalls, criss-crossing lanes, and a temple with upturned eaves. It looked like the Dragon Mountain Temple district around Huaxi Street at dusk, the temple's eaves bathed in a blood-red sunset that turned the filthy houses and lanes deep red. A boy all in black stood in the middle of the street, his body elongated into a thin line. His hair was matted like the mane of a lion, completely covering his forehead. The eyebrows consisted of a single straight line, and his eyes, those strange eyes, seemed about to leap off of the canvas, like two dark wildfires. His face was triangular, his mouth tightly closed. The boy was barefoot, his shirt was open to reveal a savage tattoo on his chest. There was such a violent aura about him that you felt he might jump down out of the painting at any time. When I first saw it I blurted out in alarm:

"It's him!"

"It *is* him," The Master Artist replied. A look of unspeakable sadness suddenly came over his wrinkled face.

"The first time I saw him was on the steps of the lotus pond in the park. He was striding along with his head held high, like he was the only person in the world. He made me think of a wildfire raging through the mountains, consuming everything in its path, inextinguishable. I knew I had to paint him at once, for I had a premonition that this wildfire's days were numbered, and that once it had moved on it would leave only charred remains behind. He agreed, and didn't ask to be paid for sitting. His only condition was that I include the Dragon Mountain Temple on Huaxi Street in the painting. That was where he was born, he said. I think it's one of my best paintings."

The Master Artist's masterpiece was hung on the wall of the Cozy Nest. The radiant eyes blazed like two black wildfires glaring down on the people in the Cozy Nest, filled with fury. So in the misty amber lights, with Yang Sanlang's organ music floating above their heads as they held their whispered conversations, the customers of the Cozy Nest, this new nest of ours, once again began spreading the park legend of Phoenix Boy, lending it more and more mystical airs.

9

"The Dragon King's a nice old guy!" Little Jade informed me gleefully.

For several nights, he'd come home with me to Moon Beauty's place on Jinzhou Street to sleep. After washing up, as we sat there smoking and talking, he excitedly filled me in on some of the details of Captain Long's fabled life. Moon Beauty called the Cozy Nest the Crystal Palace. The way she figured it, we crystal boys had moved up a rung, increased our value, and become "underwater crystal boys." After warning us she was going to raise our rent, she smiled, pointed at Little Jade, and said:

"Jade, that was a stroke of luck, your running into the Dragon King of the Sea in the Crystal Palace. You'll probably turn into an immortal pretty soon!"

Little Jade told us that the Dragon King was from Ningbo, near Shanghai. He'd spent his youth hanging around the Shanghai Bund, where he caught the fancy of an old Jewish fellow who taught him some pidgin English and got him a job as a steward on a foreign ship. He was eighteen when he went to sea on a fancy Italian steamer that regularly set anchor in Shanghai and Hong Kong. He'd never seen such elegance. He said that when he served the rich old ladies and gentlemen in the salon he wore tails, white gloves, and black leather shoes so shiny you could see your reflection in them. The leather soles resounded when he walked the decks. I couldn't imagine Captain Long in tails, but I'm sure he made quite an impression with that large head of his. And the menu—there would be ten or more kinds of soup alone, all listed in French. Some of the Shanghai merchants who went aboard to show off their wealth would often order two or three different soups. The Dragon King spent several years aboard the ship, and after he learned the ropes he hired on to the infamous Pacific Liner as third mate. He'd only been aboard for a year when the communists attacked Shanghai. The Pacific Liner made its last run from Shanghai to Hong Kong in the winter of 1948, packed to the gunwales with wealthy Shanghai residents, most of them taking all the jewelry and U.S. dollars they could carry.

The ship struck a reef as it was sailing out of the harbor and sank to the bottom with no survivors. All those rich Shanghai passengers carried their treasures with them to meet the real Dragon King of the Sea, while our Dragon King escaped with his life—the sole survivor.

"How'd he manage that?" Moon Beauty and I wanted to know. Little Jade, smug in his role as story-teller, explained:

"Just before the ship sailed, the Dragon King was on deck supervising sailors who were loading some freight. Suddenly his feet slipped out from under him, like someone behind him had given him a shove, and he hit his head on the steel railing. The lights went out. When he came to and opened his eyes again, all the sailors had no heads."

"Jade!" Moon Beauty shouted at him. "We've just gotten

through the Ghost Festival, so no more of those ghost stories, especially in the middle of the night." Moon Beauty had but one fear — ghosts. Every time she dreamed of her late father she went out and bought devotional candles and spirit money to burn for him.

"It's true!" He said smugly. "The Dragon King told me himself. He said the sight of all those headless sailors in their white uniforms made him sick to his stomach. So he got off the ship and was saved from oblivion."

"You're getting carried away with your story. I think you ought to tag along with your Dragon King when he goes out to sea, so you can see those headless ghosts for yourself." Moon Beauty got to her feet and walked unhappily out of our room. Little Jade and I laughed and clapped our hands. My relationship with Moon Beauty had suffered since she'd kicked Sonny out, and every once in a while I did something to get even. Naturally, seeing Little Jade get her goat gave me a measure of satisfaction.

"Little Jade, the chief ought to give you a prize!" We'd turned out the light and were lying in bed. "These last few days you've really been pouring it on thick with the Dragon King, and now you've got him eating out of your hand. This time you've really let out all the stops. The only thing you haven't done is lick his balls!"

"I'd lick 'em if he wanted me to!" Little Jade shot back.

"You'd really stoop that low?" I laughed. "What can the Dragon King do for you?"

"What the hell do you know?" Little Jade sneered. "Don't you realize how important he is?"

"The chief wants to get him to smuggle in some liquor."

"Smuggling in liquor doesn't mean shit to me!" Little Jade spun around in bed. "I'll tell you, A-qing, the Dragon King might just be the savior I've been waiting for!"

"What goofy idea have you got now?" I knew he was always scheming, always throwing out a long line to catch bigger and bigger fish.

"It's too early in the game. I wasn't going to tell you, you old jackass." He sat up in the darkness, fished around for a cigarette, and lit it with his lighter. "Yesterday morning I signed up for a crash course at the China Culinary Academy. I can get a certificate in three weeks. I had my first class today on how to use a butcher knife. I tried it all, chopping, mincing, slicing, paring, dicing. Let's see what you know. How do you cut tripe, with the grain or against it?"

"With the grain."

"Idiot!" He laughed gleefully. "If you cut it that way it's as hard as shoe leather. We were also taught how to prepare crystal chicken today. When the teacher tasted the results, she said mine was the best. I didn't tell her that making crystal chicken comes naturally to citizens of the Crystal Palace."

"Why do you want to learn to cook?" I sat up.

"Nothing wrong in learning a skill, is there?" He handed me his cigarette. "When I get old and ugly and no one wants me anymore, I can go cook for someone. I'll tell you the truth, A-qing. The Dragon King's ship, *Cuihua*, is looking for a galley helper..."

"Hold on there," I interrupted him. "How's a dainty little thing like you going to handle all the rigors of shipboard life? The only thing you'll get from going aboard ship is gang raped by all those sailors!"

"Shit, I knew I shouldn't tell you!" He was getting agitated. "How about letting me finish before you pop off! Who do you think I am, someone who's going to roll over for all those stinking sailors? The night before last the Dragon King casually remarked that a galley helper turned up missing. He'd jumped ship in Tokyo. I almost passed out when I heard that, but I didn't let on. He said sailors are always jumping ship. The owner of a Chinese restaurant in Shinjuku was a galley helper on the *Cuihua* who jumped ship. A-qing, if other people can do it, why can't I? If I got to Tokyo I'd be the first one off!"

"Tsk-tsk," I sighed. "You won't give up, will you, Little Jade? You're still chasing your cherry blossom dream, aren't you?"

"Why should I give up? Why should I, huh?" he shouted. "I won't give up, even after I'm dead! I'm going to fly across the Pacific, even if I have to wait till I'm a ghost to do it! Sure, I was disappointed when Lin *san* from the Seijyo Pharmaceutical Company didn't take me to Japan. And you probably thought I just gave up after that, right? Not on your life! I never stop thinking about it, and when the day comes, nothing will stop Little Jade Wang, not a mountain of knives or a vat of boiling oil. Certainly not a few hardships aboard ship. I went to Sanchong City this afternoon to tell my mother. She said, 'You've got a good job now, so why not stick it out instead of hatching all these crazy schemes? Let's say you jump ship but get caught by the Japanese, and they put you in jail. Then what?' By then she had tears running down her face. But when she was finished crying she took off her gold bracelet and handed it to me. Lin Zhengxiong, that goddamn father of mine, who worked for the Shiseido Company, gave her that bracelet as a present when he was chasing her at the Eastern Clouds. He had it engraved on the inside with her name, Wang Xiuzi, and Nakajima, his Japanese name. When she handed it to me she said, 'If you make it to Tokyo and find Nakajima, show him this bracelet and he'll know who you are. If you don't find him, you can sell it to pay your way back home, so you won't be stranded in a foreign country.'"

Little Jade excitedly told me his plans as though he'd be jumping ship tomorrow.

"A-qing!" We'd talked for a while longer, then I'd fallen asleep. He woke me up. I almost never got any sleep when he spent the night.

"What now? Isn't jumping ship enough for you? What do you want to do, jump into the ocean?"

"Next month I'm going to Taiwan University Hospital to have my appendix out."

"Why don't you have them take out your intestines while you're at it?" I grumbled. But curiosity got the best of me. "Why do you want to do that?"

He sighed and said:

"The Dragon King said that all new crew members have to have their appendix out before they report on board. Otherwise, if someone had a case of appendicitis out at sea, there wouldn't be anyone to do the operation."

10

Auntie Wu, Fu Chongshan's aging servant, fell while she was grocery shopping and broke her right leg. She was rushed to the hospital, where the leg was set and put into a plaster cast. She was told to stay off it for a month, so her son, a soldier, came and took her home with him. This left all the chores around the house to Papa Fu himself. When the chief went to pay a call on him he found him scrubbing the living room floor on his hands and knees, his hunched back arched high in the air. He was exhausted from the drudgery and sweating profusely. Chief Yang quickly helped him up off the floor and urged him to find a temporary replacement for Auntie Wu. He gave him my name as someone reliable. Unwilling at first, after listening to Chief Yang give him a song-and-dance story about how I'd been kicked out by my landlord and was looking for a place to live, he gave in, since he was convinced he'd be helping me out. Moon Beauty hadn't kicked me out, but she'd doubled my rent and increased my meal costs by thirty percent. One of the other girls from the New York Bar ran off with the money in the banking cooperative, and Moon Beauty lost over 20,000 yuan. It devastated her. All day long she cried and lost her temper, lost her temper and cried. On top of that, Obasan was demanding a raise, threatening to go to work as a cook in Lulu's China Doll bar. All these financial problems put Moon Beauty in a terrible mood. When she raised my rent she said, in a none-too-friendly tone, "If you think that's too much you can move out." But when I told her I was moving into Papa Fu's place, she suddenly grew apologetic and told Obasan to make a few of my favorite dishes, even calling Little Jade over to share the farewell meal. She put a big spoonful of fried squid and pickled vegetables on my plate and said:

"You have to admit, A-qing, that I never treated you bad while you lived here. Now that you've got somewhere else to stay, make sure you don't burn your bridges behind you by saying bad things about me to others."

"Why would I do that?" I quickly defended myself. "Ask Little Jade if you don't believe me. I always say nice things about you."

"A-qing tells everybody that Moon Beauty is our Goddess of Mercy!" Little Jade snickered.

"I don't believe you," she laughed. "You two little crystal boys cooked it up together. A-qing wouldn't be in such a hurry to move if he didn't have a grudge against me. He hasn't been very friendly with me lately."

"He lost his lifeblood because of you, so how can you expect him not to have a grudge?" Little Jade said.

"What lifeblood?" Moon Beauty was puzzled.

"You got rid of his little retarded friend, and that almost broke his heart."

"What!" Moon Beauty shouted. "That little loony wasn't even housebroken. He was pissing and shitting all over the place. And he hurt Johnny Jr. How can you keep someone like that around? I'd like to know what makes A-qing think he could take care of a loony like that."

"Don't listen to Little Jade," I said, feeling a little embarrassed.

230

"The only reason I'm moving is because of Papa Fu. He's all alone, in poor health, with no one to take care of him. Since he got us out of jail, it's only right that I go over and stay with him."

Moon Beauty looked straight at me and nodded her head with a sigh.

"I wouldn't have figured a crystal boy like you could have a conscience, too."

I reached under the bed and pulled out Little Jade's beat-up suitcase, dumped all his junk onto the bed, and stuffed my clothes and things into it. Since the latch was broken, I borrowed some twine from Obasan and tied it up so it wouldn't fall open. Obasan went out and got a net bag, into which she put my wash basin, plastic cup, and two pairs of old shoes. Then she wrapped it up, tied a knot at the top, and draped it over my left arm. Moon Beauty was holding Johnny Jr. in her arms as she saw me to the door. She lifted up his chubby, light-skinned arm and waved it to me.

"Bye-bye," she said to him, "tell Uncle bye-bye."

"Bye-bye," Johnny Jr. said with a giggle. His green eyes were blinking a mile a minute as he laughed.

"Bye-bye." I couldn't help laughing.

II

As the sun was setting, I took my beat-up suitcase and net bundle over to Papa Fu's house. I left them in the vestibule, then ran over to the Cozy Nest to go to work. Chief Yang let me off at ten that night, two hours early, since Papa Fu was waiting for me. The first thing he had me do was move my things into a six-tatami room next to his bedroom. It was furnished with a table, a chair, and a bed, which had a mattress and fresh sheets and pillowcases. The room was neat and tidy. It would be the most comfortable, most presentable room I'd ever stayed in. After leaving home, I'd spent several months in that austere little den on Jinzhou Street, always feeling it was a temporary shelter I'd be leaving at any time. Besides, I wasn't there most of the time, anyway, since I spent so many nights drifting from one stranger's bed to another.

"This is your bedroom," Papa Fu said as he followed me in. "There's nothing much wrong with it, except that window facing west sometimes makes the room pretty hot in the afternoons. I found you a bamboo shade. You can hang it up tomorrow."

He pointed to a rolled up bamboo shade lying beneath the window. It must have been pretty old, since the green paint was already flaking. He bent down and, with considerable effort, took a little dish for burning mosquito incense out from under the bed. There was already a coil of incense on the metal stand.

"There's a pond in the yard, and lots of mosquitos," he said. "So make sure you burn this when you go to sleep at night." He took a turn around the room, touching this and looking at that, and when he was satisfied that everything was all right, he said:

"Try it out. If you think there's anything missing just let me know."

"Papa doesn't have to worry on my account," I replied quickly. "The room's terrific!"

He walked over to the bookcase and stopped. There was a set of English books on the case, a radio, an alarm clock, and a brass model of an artillery cannon.

"This was my son's room, these things were all his..." He stopped in mid-sentence. He was all hunched over, his back to me, his gray head bowed low, as he leaned across the desk. "Feel free to use them."

Then he turned and shuffled over to the closet. He slid open the paper screen door. Half the closet was filled with clothes. Papa Fu lifted up some of them, looked them over, and mumbled:

"I ought to take them out and air them. They smell like mildew."

He turned and sized me up.

"You're about the same size as Fu Wei. You can wear these clothes if you'd like."

"That's okay," I quickly begged off. "I've got my own."

"Winter clothes, too?" he asked me.

I hemmed and hawed for a moment, since all I had in my suitcase were a few changes of thin clothes. Papa Fu reached in and took out a brown wool suit. He told me to try it on. I slipped the coat on, and he looked me over.

"Not bad," he said. "Except the sleeves are a little long. I gave away most of his clothes. This is all I kept, but it's enough to get you through the winter."

I noticed an olive-green overcoat and a black leather jacket in the closet, plus some old sweaters that probably hadn't been worn in years, since they smelled of mothballs. I put the suitcoat back on its hanger, and Papa Fu slid the screen door closed. He led me back into the living room.

"A-qing."

After we sat down, he picked a glass of tea up off the table and took a sip. He called my name as though he had something on his mind.

"You make yourself at home here, I don't want you to feel ill at ease."

"Thank you, Papa," I replied.

"Yang Jinhai told me several times that you're a dependable boy, and he recommended you as a companion. Auntie Wu's an old woman, and she took a pretty bad fall. I think it's going to be a long time before she's up and around again. My health hasn't been very good lately, either, and heavy chores are too tiring. You can help me a lot while you're here."

"Whatever you want me to do, just tell me."

"There's really not much to do around here. A couple of meals a day, cleaning the yard, things like that. But I don't know if you're used to that kind of work."

"When I was at home I helped my father with the housework," I explained. "But I'm not much of a cook . . ."

"That's all right," he smiled. "I don't eat fancy food. A couple of vegetarian dishes, maybe a little bean curd, that's all I need."

"I can handle that," I smiled in return.

"I hear you're the son of a military man," he looked up and said after a thoughtful pause.

"My father was a regiment commander back on the Mainland. But he was drummed out of the service when he came to Taiwan because he'd once been taken prisoner . . ." Just talking about Father made me uncomfortable, and I began to stammer a little.

"Do you know what army he was in?"

"I'm not sure," I shook my head. Father had mentioned it, but when he got to talking about how gloriously they'd fought against the Japanese he was so excited we could barely understand him. "All I remember is that his commanding general was someone named Zhang Kan."

"Oh, Zhang Kan's army." He nodded. "They were Sichuan soldiers who did themselves proud against the Japanese. They fought a great battle at Changsha."

"My father was decorated at the Battle of Changsha," I said, suddenly recalling Father's little locked case with the rusting Order of the Precious Tripod inside.

Papa Fu sighed.

"That army ran into some bad luck against the communists."

"Father told me that even Commander Zhang was taken prisoner."

"That's right, his whole army was wiped out." He sighed again, with even greater emotion.

"Who else is there in your family?" he asked.

I told him that Mother and Buddy were both dead, so Father was all I had left.

His steel-gray eyebrows knitted into a frown.

"Yang Jinhai tells me you and your father had a falling out."

I lowered my head to avoid having to look into his teary old eyes.

"Your father just blew up, but time will take care of that. You ought to go see him."

I kept my head bowed and didn't say anything.

"Go wash up and get some rest," Papa Fu said as he stood up, walked over beside me, and patted me on the shoulder.

After washing up I went into my room and put away the things I'd brought over. I lit the mosquito incense, turned off the light, and climbed into bed. The luminescent dial of the clock on the bookcase said twelve-thirty. I had trouble getting to sleep, maybe because it was my first night there. I heard the sound of frogs croaking through the window, probably from the pond outside, which was covered with calabash flowers. In the next room over, it sounded like Papa Fu was restless, too, since he got up two or three times to go to the bathroom. I heard his slippers shuffling across the floor. I thought about home, and how I used to hear Father's footsteps in the middle of the night in the next room. Our walls were so thin I could every sound he made while I was in bed. For the first couple of years after Mother left, his behavior was eccentric and unpredictable. Sometimes he'd leap out of bed in the middle of the night like a man possessed and pace back and forth, back and forth. His footsteps were so urgent, so heavy, like those of a caged animal, as he walked round and round. I'd be lying in the dark, holding my breath as I listened to the *clomp, clomp, clomp* in the next room, and suddenly feel unspeakably nervous. Even in the dead of winter my forehead would be covered with sweat.

12

It was eleven o'clock when I woke up. I threw on my clothes and rushed into the living room, where Papa Fu, wearing his reading glasses, was reading the newspaper. He was wearing a dark blue button-down jacket, apparently ready to go out.

"You were sleeping so soundly I didn't have the heart to wake you," he said with a smile as he laid his paper down.

"I can't imagine why I overslept." I was feeling a little embarrassed. I hadn't actually fallen asleep until nearly dawn.

"I've already been out for a walk this morning. I bought a couple of cans of Klim powdered milk in a store in the lane. Go make yourself a glass. I put it on top of the refrigerator. There's boiled water in the thermos."

"Would you like some, too?"

"I don't drink milk," he said with a wave of his hand. "It's nearly lunchtime."

"I'll make lunch," I quickly volunteered.

"Make it simple, noodles will be fine. There are some leftovers in the refrigerator. Your chief brought some food over last night. Just heat it up."

"Right away."

"No hurry," he stopped me. "Have some milk first."

"Okay."

I went in and fixed myself a glass of thick milk. At home, our neighbor Auntie Huang would sometimes send over a can of powdered milk. It was part of her pension, given to the government through American aid. Since Father didn't drink milk, it was all for Buddy and me. It was awful, all bland and watery. Klim powdered milk was different. It was real American powdered milk that was sweet enough you didn't have to add sugar. As I was finishing the milk, Papa Fu came into the kitchen and started looking for something in the pantry.

"Auntie Wu always puts things where I can't find them," he grumbled. He was standing on his tiptoes, hunched over and breathing hard as he opened the cupboard doors.

"Here, let me do it." I rushed over and opened it for him.

"I remember she always put the noodles on the top shelf."

I reached up and felt around until I found a package of dry noodles.

"She was afraid cockroaches would get to them, so she put

235

them up there. But cockroaches have wings, so that doesn't do any good." He laughed.

I heated up the water and dumped in the noodles. Then I took the leftovers out of the refrigerator and heated them up in a skillet. When the noodles were done, I filled up two bowls and sprinkled a little sesame oil and soy sauce on the top.

"You're no stranger to a kitchen," Papa Fu said.

"I did most of the cooking at home when Father was working. Since I went to night school I was home during the day." I smiled. "Noodles was his favorite, too, so we had them a lot, usually mixed with spicy peanut paste."

Papa Fu and I sat down at the kitchen table and ate lunch. He told me he was going over to the Divine Light Orphanage that afternoon to take care of the little orphans. The director had asked several old folks to volunteer some of their time. Most of them had come from the Mainland. Some had left children behind when they came to Taiwan, while others had already raised their children, who were now out on their own. They were financially independent, but had grown lonely and needed a place like the orphanage to boost their spirits.

"I started going there three years ago," he said slowly after he'd finished his noodles and drunk some hot water. "The director spends a lot of his time soliciting contributions and inviting people like me to visit the orphanage. They're a bunch of lively, healthy children, and you can't help but like them. But then I spotted a deformed child off in a corner. He didn't have any arms, and his empty sleeves just flapped when he moved. He still couldn't walk very well, since he was only three, and I watched him fall down. Without any arms, he couldn't get up, and just rolled back and forth. There was panic in his eyes. I rushed over and picked him up, and he buried his head in my arms and cried like he was ridding himself of all the unfairness he'd experienced in life. The director told me he was an abandoned child. His parents had just bundled him up and left him on the orphanage doorstep. Such a strange little baby—he just sat there with no arms. I felt so sorry for him I donated ten thousand on the spot, with instructions that it be used for him."

A sad smile spread across Papa Fu's wrinkled face.

"I know it sounds strange, but after I got home I couldn't get that deformed child off my mind. The director had rolled up his sleeves and shown me that there was nothing at all below his shoulders. It was like both arms had just been snapped off. Just thinking about it made me sad. A couple of days later I went back to see him. I never expected to get involved, and now it's been three years . . ."

He shrugged his shoulders and smiled as he walked through the living room to the front door, picked up his cane, and hobbled down into the vestibule. I saw him out the door, and as he was leaving he added:

"He didn't have a name, so I call him Heavensent Fu."

13

I spent the afternoon working around Papa Fu's house. After mopping the living room floor, I cleaned the stove and took out the trash before changing clothes and heading for work at the Cozy Nest. When the chief saw me he came up and said sternly:

"I recommended you highly as Papa Fu's companion. This time you do things right and don't make me lose face, no matter what. You get a place to stay and all you want to eat. In other words, paradise. Use your head. A youngster like you should be fast on his feet and get things done. It won't kill you."

"I already mopped the floor and cleaned his kitchen before I came over here. If you don't believe me go ask Papa. I even made lunch for him!" I was smiling.

The chief screwed up his mouth and said:

"Even a new latrine doesn't stink the first few days! You just got there and you're trying to put on a good show. But I want you to put your heart into taking care of the old fellow. Try to sleep a little lighter at night. That way, if he calls you, you'll hear him."

"I know," I said. "Give me a month to prove myself. If I do anything wrong, you can come over and fix my wagon."

"Don't be so pleased with yourself!" the chief said. "If I hear one bad word from Papa, you know damned well I'll find some-body else!"

"If you're looking for somebody else, how about me?" Little Jade piped up. He was drying glasses behind the bar.

"You?" the chief sneered. "Save your silver tongue and cute moves for that old butterfly Lord Sheng. Papa Fu's too respect-able for your shenanigans."

"The chief's wrong there," Little Jade laughed. "I can make myself respectable, more respectable than anybody. You've just never seen me. If I went over and took care of Papa, I wouldn't be surprised if I was more filial than his own son!"

"You've got an important job of your own right now. Tell me, did you find out what I wanted from Captain Long?"

"No sweat, Chief. He said his company always has ships tied up in Keelung Harbor. Last month a ship anchored out in the harbor kicked two cases of Johnny Walker into the harbor. There's plenty more where that came from. The next time one of his ships comes into the harbor, he'll keep his eye out for us."

"Tell me as soon as you hear anything. I'll work out the price with Captain Long."

The chief told Wu Min to wash the ashtrays. When he counted them he discovered that a porcelain ashtray in the shape of a grape leaf was missing. Wu Min admitted he'd broken it.

"Thirty-five yuan. It'll come out of your wages." The chief didn't even look at Wu Min. He walked to the back of the bar and yanked open the toilet door.

"Where's Mousey?" he shouted through the door.

"He hasn't shown up for work yet," Little Jade called out from behind the bar.

The chief rushed angrily back in, cursing up a storm:

"When that goddamn little thief shows up I'm going to stuff him down the toilet and drown him! He didn't bother to tell anyone the toilet's stopped up! The room stinks to high heaven! He'll single-handedly ruin the Cozy Nest's reputation!"

The automatic doors opened just then, and Mousey stepped in. The chief walked up to him and raised his fan to hit him over the head, but his hand froze in mid-air. We all dropped what we were doing. Mousey was hugging his treasure box tightly in his arms, swaying unsteadily as he walked, like he was drunk. He was quaking.

"My god!" the chief blurted out.

Mousey's white shirt was in shreds, and there was blood splattered on the front. His face was a mess, with puffy, bloody lips; his left eye was all swollen and cut, like a piece of rotten fruit. His nose was spread all over his face, and the rest of his face was a mass of cuts and bruises. We crowded around him. His swollen lips parted slightly, his teeth chattered, and he muttered in a cracked voice:

"Raven...Raven...Raven..."

His spindly arms were wrapped tightly around his treasure box. His head was tilted at an angle. He raised his swollen, bloody face pathetically and whimpered incoherently, as though he didn't know who he was.

"We can't let anyone see you like this," the chief frowned. "Get into the kitchen, the customers will be arriving any minute. You've been asking for a beating, you little thief, but that hooligan brother of yours has gone too far this time."

"Chief, I'll take him over to Papa Fu's to rest up," I suggested.

"Okay," the chief said after thinking it over for a moment. "But don't make it sound too bad to Papa. Make up something."

I hailed a taxi and took Mousey over to Papa Fu's house. Papa Fu had probably just gotten back from Zhonghe, and when he saw what a mess Mousey was, he dragged him over under the light and examined him closely.

"I have something to put on that," he said. "I'll go get it. It'll stop the pain."

He hobbled into his room and came out with some herbal powder.

"A-qing," he said to me, "get me the bottle of rice wine from the kitchen. It's on top of the stove. And bring me a glass and a soy sauce plate."

After I brought him what he asked for, he sprinkled some of the powder into the soy sauce plate, added a little wine, and mixed it until it thickened. After applying it to the wounds, he poured half a glass of wine, added some more powder, and told Mousey to drink it.

"Sit down and drink this slowly. It'll thin your blood to help the swelling go down."

At first, Mousey wouldn't let us take his treasure box from him. He clutched it tightly against his chest. So I went over and whispered in his ear:

"Give it to me, no one here's going to take it away from you."

Mousey looked at me and handed over his treasure box, then took the glass of wine from Papa Fu, sat down in the chair, and slowly drank the potion down, sighing after each swallow. Papa Fu stared at him and asked:

"Who did this to you?"

I told him how mean and vicious his brother Raven was.

"You go back to work," Papa Fu said to me. "Let him stay here and eat with me."

239

14

There were several customers in the Cozy Nest by the time I got back there. I reported in to the chief, then went behind the bar to help Little Jade, who was running around mixing drinks and chatting with the customers. As soon as I got there, he handed me the bottle in his hand and said:

"Whiskey and soda." Then in a low voice he asked, "How's Mousey? Raven really beat the shit out of him this time. I knew it'd happen sooner or later. He's lucky he's not a cripple."

"Papa put some medication on him. I think he'll be all right. Give him credit, he brought his treasure box along."

"That's his lifeblood. You think he'd leave it behind?" Then Little Jade whispered in my ear, "Mr. Yu's been asking for you. I told him you'd be right back, but he's still antsy. He's got you on his mind. 'Will Li Qing be coming back tonight?' he keeps asking. I think you'd better go over and say hello."

I looked up and saw Yu Hao sitting on a barstool at the far end. He was smiling at me. I walked over and said hello. For several nights now he'd come over to talk with me at the Cozy Nest. He was an English instructor at a technical school. He was in his mid-thirties, a tall, well-built man with broad shoulders and confident airs. He'd participated in school athletics and was an excellent swimmer. He was Sichuanese, from Chungking, and when I told him I was half Sichuanese, he began calling me "My Little Qing." I'd learned some Sichuan slang from my father, who used it when he was angry, things like "fuck off!" Mr. Yu laughed when he heard me, and said I spoke Sichuanese with a Taiwanese accent.

"My Little Qing," he said, "look what I brought you."

He handed me a thick manila envelope. I opened it. It was a four-volume set of the martial-arts novel *Revenge on Great Bear Mountain*, by Zhuge Jingwo.

"Wow, Mr. Yu, they're great!" I screamed excitedly. We'd talked about martial-arts novels the last time he was in. He said he was a big fan, too, and asked me which authors I liked. I mentioned several, including Zhuge Jingwo. I'd only read the first two volumes of this set, which I'd gotten at the lending library on Longjiang Street that specialized in martial-arts novels. Buddy and I had read them in turn: he read volume one while I read volume two, then we traded. But we never had time to borrow the last two volumes before Buddy took sick. So I'd never read it all the way through, and it was Zhuge Jingwo's most famous novel. It's set in late Ming China, when the Manchu troops poured through the pass at the Great Wall. A swordsman named Ding Yunxiang, whose nickname is the Flying Roc, leads his family and retainers out of the capital, but on the road his youngest son is lost. So he flees to Great Bear Mountain on the border between Yunnan and Guizhou, where he works to unite all the famous swordsmen in the south to defeat the Manchu government of the Qing and restore the Ming. Meanwhile, the youngest son has been captured by the Qing general E Ersu, and had his name changed to E Shun. Twenty years pass, and E Shun becomes a valiant general who leads a Qing army to Great Bear Mountain in an assault on the Ding headquarters. The second volume ends with the first battle between the Flying Roc and his son.

"What happened after that? Did the Flying Roc win or lose?" I asked impatiently as I flipped through the third volume of *Revenge on Great Bear Mountain*.

"Take it home and read it. I don't want to ruin it for you." He smiled. "I spotted this at a bookstall this afternoon and remembered you'd mentioned it. So I bought it for you."

"Thank you, Mr. Yu," I said with an affected bow. "Zhuge Jingwo's my favorite author. I read *The Legend of Heavenly Mountain* and *The Cosmos in Turmoil*.

"My Little Qing, you're quite an expert. I've read those, too, but they're not as good as *Great Bear Mountain*. The tragic, bloody battles between Ding Yunxiang and his son are the most gripping I've ever read."

"Mr. Yu, you just got through telling me to take it home and read it, and now you're trying to tantalize me!" I couldn't wait to devour the third and fourth volumes of *Revenge on Great Bear Mountain*.

"Okay, okay, I won't say any more," he laughed. "My Little Qing, go get a bottle of beer and join me in a drink, what do you say?"

"We're not allowed to drink while we're working," I said in a low voice. "One of the rules of the house."

"Don't worry about it," he said with a wave of his hand. "If your boss gives you any trouble, I'll take care of it."

I went over and got a cold bottle of beer and another glass. I filled up both glasses, then raised mine and toasted Mr. Yu:

"Here, Mr. Yu, let's drink to the Flying Roc!"

He laughed loudly, then we drained our glasses. I went over and got a dish of oil-fried peanuts, sat back down, and chatted with Mr. Yu over the beer. The noise level at the Cozy Nest was increasing. Little Jade was sitting with Captain Long, who'd brought a few of his sailors with him. They were engaged in loud drinking games. Lord Sheng, who had been bothered by a cold for several days, was wearing a thick vest. The chief brewed him some ginger tea and sat down with him to talk. Yang Sanlang, wearing his dark sunglasses and raising his head high, was playing old Taiwanese folksongs that no one was listening to.

"My Little Qing," Mr. Yu leaned over and whispered as he was leaving, "I'll take you to Sichuan Noodles in a couple of days."

"Long live Mr. Yu!" I whispered back to him.

15

I didn't get back to Papa Fu's home until after midnight. He was already in bed, so I went straight to my room. There I found Mousey, still awake and sitting cross-legged on my bed in his underwear. He'd dumped out all the junk from his treasure box and was rummaging through it to make sure it was all there.

"Damn her," he mumbled angrily, "she must have stolen it."

"Who are you talking about?"

"Rotten Peach, who else!" he looked up angrily. His left eye was nearly swollen shut, but the right one, which was wide open, glared angrily. His cut and bruised face had dabs of medication all over it, and his swollen lips seemed to turn outward.

"What is it with you? How could someone steal anything from a sticky-fingered thief like you?"

"A-qing, you remember that gold-filled Parker 51 of mine?"

"You mean the one the restaurant manager from Kaohsiung gave you?"

"It's not here, I can't find it!" he lamented.

"I told you to pawn it a long time ago. We could have spent it on a feast at Wu's Wontons. But no. So now it's gone and you've got nothing to show for it." I sat down on the edge of the bed.

"I take inventory every single day. This morning I noticed that the lock had been picked. I had a Bulova watch, some rings, a necklace. They were all gone, and I really freaked out. I didn't care so much about the other stuff, but that Parker 51, my Parker 51 . . ." He was nearly crying.

"How do you know Rotten Peach stole it?"

"Who else could it be?" he spat out hatefully. "Raven may be mean, but he's no thief. She's the one who comes into my room all the time, but when I asked her about it, she reached out and slapped me across the face. Then she ran into my room and picked up my treasure box to throw it out the window. So I hit her, and kicked her, and I grabbed my treasure box out of her hands..."

He raised his spindly, blistered arms and said defiantly:

"I'll fight anyone who touches my treasure box..."

"Hey!" I held him down. "Not so loud, Papa's asleep."

He was so worked up he could barely catch his breath.

"Raven thinks I'm scared of him. Well, I'm not! I'm not scared of anyone!"

He struck a pugnacious pose.

"He came in to help Rotten Peach take my treasure box away from me, so I bit a chunk out of his arm. Then they both started hitting me, and hitting me..."

He began hitting himself hard on the head.

"The only way they'll get my treasure box is to kill me!"

"Heh, heh," he laughed with evil satisfaction.

"Raven saw there was nothing he could do, so he kicked me out."

"Fine, welcome to the ranks of the homeless."

"That doesn't scare me," he said, growing more defiant. "You don't think I'm going to starve, do you?"

"The chief says he wants you to start spending your nights at the Cozy Nest tomorrow. You can help Wu Min watch the place."

He muttered to himself for a moment, then said to me:

"A-qing, will you do me a favor tomorrow?"

"What's that?"

"Will you go to a hardware store and buy me a new lock? A good, strong one."

"To lock up that treasure box of yours? If someone wants to steal it, why can't they just take the whole thing?"

"That's right," he said as he gazed up at me with a pleading look on his swollen, misshappen face, "so that's why I'm begging you to keep it here for me and look after it. What do you say? There are too many people and too much going on at the Cozy Nest. I won't stop worrying about it if I take it with me."

"What's in it for me?" I asked playfully.

"No problem," he said slyly, his swollen lips parted in what passed for a grin. "Tell me what you want. I'll give you the moon if that's what you want."

"Forget it," I laughed. "Sooner or later the police are going to catch you with your hands where they don't belong, and then it's Fire Island for sure."

He jumped down off the bed, carefully scooped all his loot into his treasure box, and slid it under the bed. He let out a sigh of relief and touched his bruised, swollen face with his hands.

"That powder of Papa Fu's works. It doesn't hurt anymore."

16

The chief called us all together to discuss how we should celebrate Papa Fu's seventieth birthday on the eighteenth day of the ninth lunar month. Business at the Cozy Nest had been terrific during our first month, and the money was rolling in, so the chief decided to close up on the eighteenth and throw a birthday party. But he warned us not to breathe a word to Papa Fu beforehand, since he knew Papa wasn't one to celebrate birthdays. He wouldn't allow it if he knew. Since Papa Fu was family, the chief didn't want to go to any special lengths; we'd just prepare some food at the bar and take it over to his house. The chief talked Fatty Lu of the Cornucopia into coming over to cook some of the restaurant's specialties: snowflake chicken, battered duck in lotus leaves, and stuffed sea cucumber. Chef Lu also volunteered to make his famous Eight Immortals birthday cake. Altogether there'd be ten dishes, including two steamers of longevity peaches. Little Jade tied on an apron and insisted on being Chef Lu's assistant. Having learned how to cook a few things at the culinary academy, he'd been looking for an excuse to practice his skills. He begged Chef Lu to let him make a "squirrel" croaker. The rest of us crowded around to watch, and the first thing we noticed was that he'd taken on some of Chef Lu's airs. One minute he'd be ordering Mousey to wash the pot, the next he'd be telling Wu Min to slice up some ginger or asking me to hand him the oil and salt. He ran our legs off. Mousey was going to raise a protest, but Little Jade stopped him:

"Those are the rules of the kitchen. Since I'm the chef, you guys have to do the odd jobs. Who'll do it if you don't?"

He sprinkled on some sugar and vinegar, then slid the fish into the hot oil. He waved his spatula in the air and shouted:

"Look, you guys, doesn't that croaker look like a squirrel? Just wait, it'll even stand up!"

When everything was ready we put the food into baskets, while the chief went out to buy several packages of birthday noodles and six bottles of good rice wine. After hailing two taxis, the six of us drove over to Papa Fu's to wish him happy birthday. He'd just returned from spending the morning at the Divine Light Orphanage in Zhonghe, and was sitting in the living room resting his eyes. His old gray head was resting on his chest. There were fresh white chrysanthemums in the vase on the table against the wall. A black pottery incense burner had been set out on the table. The fragrant smoke from the sandalwood incense curled up the wall to the framed photographs of Papa Fu and his son Fu Wei in their military uniforms. We all crowded into the living room, startling him out of his snooze. He didn't know what to make of it. Chief Yang quickly went up and apologized for bursting in on him like this and tactfully explained why we were there.

"Papa, it's all these kids' idea." He turned and dragged or pushed us up in front of the old man. "They knew today was Papa's birthday and they insisted on coming over to pay their respects. I couldn't have stopped them if I'd wanted to."

Papa Fu wasn't terribly pleased and started to voice his displeasure. But when he saw the food baskets in our hands, and the bottles of wine, not to mention the two steamers of longevity peaches held high in A-xiong's hands, a smile appeared on his wrinkled face. He sighed.

"Yang Jinhai, this is too much. You know I don't go in for this kind of thing, especially putting these kids to all this trouble."

"We make out like bandits," Little Jade giggled. "Would the chief have given us a day off if it wasn't such a special day?"

"All right," Papa Fu relented with a smile. "You've been pretty busy lately, so maybe it's time you sat down for a good meal, some wine, and some well-deserved relaxation."

As soon as the chief gave the word, we rushed around getting things ready. I went into the kitchen and set up the big round table that was leaning against the wall, then I laid out bowls and chopsticks for seven. Little Jade put water on to boil for the noodles. Wu Min heated up the wine. It took us until about eight o'clock before we were finally ready to eat. Papa Fu took the seat of honor, the chief sat across from him, between Wu Min and Little Jade, and A-xiong and I sat next to Papa Fu; Mousey's place was between Wu Min and me. The swelling in his face had gone down quite a bit, but the bruises were still angry-looking. His face looked like he had plasters stuck all over it. Little Jade got up from the table to get the heated wine. After pouring a cup for Papa Fu, he filled the rest of the cups. The chief stood up and we followed his lead, raising our cups to toast Papa Fu:

"Papa..." The chief was holding his cup in both hands and was about to propose his toast when he was stopped by Papa Fu:

"Yang Jinhai, none of that nonsense. Sit down and eat."

"Papa," Chief Yang went on anyway, "no nonsense. I only have one thing to say. We owe our good fortune at the Cozy Nest to you. So this cup of wine serves two purposes: first, to wish you a long and happy life, and second, to celebrate the success of the Cozy Nest."

The chief tipped back his head and drained his cup. We did the same. Papa Fu picked up his cup and slowly drank down the wine. It was the first time I'd seen him drink, so I laughed and said:

"Papa can really put it away!"

He smiled and said:

"I used to drink a little. Back on the Mainland I drank my share of sorghum spirits. I gave it up after I got sick. But tonight, just seeing how excited you all are, I might as well join in."

Little Jade quickly invited Papa Fu to start eating. There were ten separate dishes on the table, all colorfully prepared. Little Jade's fish, with the head tucked underneath, the back arched, and the tail stretching out behind it, really did look like a squirrel. Using his chopsticks, he put some on Papa's plate.

"Papa, I cooked this myself. Tell me how you like it."

"I didn't know you were so talented," Papa Fu smiled as he tasted the fish and nodded his approval. He turned to Chief Yang.

"I frequently ask A-qing how things are going at the Cozy Nest. He tells me it's full nine nights out of ten. At this rate you shouldn't have any trouble staying in business, and that makes me very happy."

"I'll tell you the truth," Chief Yang smiled. "You blessed our tavern from the very beginning by picking the perfect name. And I'll say this from the bottom of my heart. These kids have worked hard this past month, even this little fool."

The chief patted A-xiong on the back.

"Dada, bottoms up!" A-xiong held out his cup to Chief Yang, who was taken aback by the action. He laughed loudly.

"Good boy! I couldn't be more surprised if roosters laid eggs! Even this idiot knows how to show some filial respect to his daddy. All right, Dada will drink to that."

The chief drained his cup without spilling a drop and breathed a long sigh as he looked at A-xiong and nodded.

"You little fool, it's heartening to know my feelings for you haven't been wasted."

The chief stood up, broke off one of the duck drumsticks, and put it on A-xiong's plate. A-xiong picked it up with his fingers, held it up in the air, and grinned.

"Duck, Dada..."

That cracked us up. Even Papa Fu had to laugh, and his back arched even higher than usual. Little Jade quickly patted his back, then filled his bowl with piping hot chicken broth.

"Yang Jinhai, taking this one on was no mistake." He drank a couple of spoonfuls of the broth and cleared his throat.

"Ai, Papa," the chief sighed emotionally. "It's not easy being a father to him. He's probably taken ten years off my life."

Papa told us to drink as much as we liked, and not hold back on his account. Before long, we started playing the finger game across the table, Little Jade against Wu Min, Mousey against me. Papa Fu laid down his chopsticks, picked up his winecup, and watched us having a good time. Pretty soon, Little Jade and Wu Min were red in the face from their contest.

"Min," Little Jade shouted, "don't play if you're afraid to lose. When you lose you're supposed to drink your penalty."

"Two out of three," Wu Min defended himself. "I don't have to drink if I only lost one round."

"Who wants to play your sissy rules? A full cup for every round. Come on, drink up!"

Wu Min refused, so Little Jade got up and went around the table, grabbed Wu Min's collar, and threatened to pour the wine down his throat. Wu Min struggled so hard to keep from drinking that the wine splashed all over Little Jade's hand.

"Little Jade," Papa Fu spoke up, trying to make peace, "Wu Min probably can't hold his liquor. Let him go this time."

"Papa," Little Jade argued, "it's all a sham. When he's drinking with that old Scarface of his, he gleefully tosses down one drink after another."

"Who's Scarface?" Papa Fu asked.

"He's the guy Wu Min tried to kill himself over that time."

"Oh." Papa Fu gazed at Wu Min.

"Don't listen to his lies, Papa," Wu Min said anxiously.

"Lies? Then what's this?" Little Jade grabbed Wu Min's left wrist and turned it over, revealing a long dark red scar in the shape of a centipede. "If you've got the guts to slash your wrist, how come you're afraid to drink a lousy cup of wine?"

Wu Min wrenched his arm free and stuck it under the table, out of sight.

"Wu Min, let me see it." Papa Fu held out his hand.

"No, Papa, it's ugly," Wu Min pleaded, his face flushed with embarrassment.

"It's all right, let me take a look at it." Papa Fu spoke very gently.

Wu Min reluctantly pulled his arm out from beneath the table, and Papa Fu held it up to examine the scar. It seemed to radiate a red glow under the light. Without a word, Papa Fu removed the watch from his left wrist and slipped it around Wu Min's wrist.

"Papa..." Wu Min was shocked. He just held his arm up, not knowing what to do with it.

"As long as you're wearing this watch no one can see your scar," Papa Fu said as he patted Wu Min on the shoulder. The stainless steel stretch band covered it completely.

"Thank you, Papa," Wu Min said softly as he pulled his arm back. He kept touching the watch with the fingers of his right hand.

"It's an Omega, not a new one, but it runs well. I asked someone to buy it for me in Hong Kong..." Papa Fu paused. "I bought it for my son Fu Wei. He'd just been promoted to platoon leader and didn't have a decent watch to wear. After a while I started wearing it. I've only had it repaired once, because of condensation, but it's very accurate."

He stared at Wu Min for a minute longer, then shook his head and sighed:

"Such a foolish boy. How could someone so young do something like that?"

"Wu Min," the chief said from across the table, "you go kneel in front of Papa. If it hadn't been for him, you wouldn't be around today!"

"Yang Jinhai," Papa Fu cut the chief off brusquely with a wave of his hand, "this is none of your business." Then he turned to us and said, "Hurry up and eat, the food's getting cold."

We'd been so wrapped up in our drinking games we'd forgotten about the food. Now we all filled our bowls with birthday noodles and, after toasting Papa Fu again, dug in. Papa Fu put a little snowflake chicken into his bowl, took a couple of bites, and put down his chopsticks.

"Papa," I said softly, having noticed that his gray head was starting to droop and his eyes were getting glassy.

"Hm?" His head jerked up, and I could see he was sleepy.

"Are you tired?" I asked softly.

"A little." He forced a smile. "I'm getting old. I can't even handle one cup of wine anymore."

He stood up.

"I'm going in to lie down. Keep the party going, and don't worry about me."

I got up to give him a hand, but he pushed me away, turned, and hobbled into his room, his hunched back looking like a little mound.

As soon as Papa Fu was out of the room, Little Jade stuck out his bare wrist and sighed loudly.

"Wu Min sure is lucky," he said. "Papa just gave him a wristwatch for nothing. I've spent my whole life trying to get one, and so far nothing yet!"

"Didn't Manager Wu of Blue Skies promise you a Seiko?" I teased him.

"That dirty old man? Guess what he said to me the other night. 'Instead of a watch I'll give you my crotch. What do you say?'"

17

It started raining at about six o'clock Monday evening, and the lane was quickly filled with three inches of water. Cars had trouble driving into the lane. It was our slowest night since the opening. By ten o'clock only about a half dozen regulars had dropped in. Yang Sanlang wasn't there, so the organ was silent, which made the place seem even more deserted. Captain Long was the only customer at the bar, and Little Jade was keeping him company. Since I had nothing else to do, I picked up the final volume of Zhuge Jingwo's *Revenge at Great Bear Mountain*, which Yu Hao had given me, and started reading. Just as I got to the place where the Flying Roc, Ding Yunxiang, has been mortally wounded by his son, the Manchu general E Shun, someone called my name softly:

"A-qing."

"Huh?" I jerked my head up. A tall man in a white raincoat and a white rainhat pulled down low was standing in front of the bar. Water was dripping from his raincoat onto the floor, drops from the brim of his rain hat were falling onto the bar. His gaunt cheeks were pale in the amber light.

"Mr. Wang!" I shouted.

"I heard you were working here . . . I didn't know where you were," Wang Kuilong, the Dragon Prince, said. He didn't move, and the water kept dripping onto the floor. I immediately thought back to that night just before the typhoon hit. It was probably that very raincoat that had billowed up in the winds and turned him into a ghostly white figure.

"Would you like something to drink, Mr. Wang?" I stood up and asked.

"Okay . . ." He didn't sound sure. "I'll take brandy." He took off his rain hat. His uncombed black hair was soaked, all plastered on his head, looking darker and thicker than ever. I went over and poured a glass of Hennessey brandy. He was still standing.

"Do you want to sit at the bar or would you prefer a table, Mr. Wang?"

"I'll sit over there." He pointed to an empty table in the back.

I carried his drink and a pack of State Express as I followed him to his table. After he took off his raincoat he pulled out a handkerchief and wiped his wet forehead and face before sitting down.

"Join me," he said, pointing to the chair opposite him. I put the drink down in front of him and sat down.

"How've you been, A-qing?" His radiant dark eyes were fixed on me.

"I've been fine, Mr. Wang," I replied.

He picked up his drink with both of his bony hands and sipped the brandy. He smacked his lips and sighed.

"I never stopped thinking about you. I didn't know you were working here at the Cozy Nest until someone told me. I came by tonight just to see you."

"Thank you, Mr. Wang."

"This place isn't half bad. How's business?" He raised his head and took a look around.

"We've been packed every night until tonight. The rain did it."

I opened the pack of cigarettes and offered him one, then lit it for him. I lit one for myself.

"The life of a bartender isn't bad, is it?" He looked at me and smiled.

"It's a good chance to meet a lot of strange people," I laughed, exhaling a mouthful of smoke.

"I was a bartender for two years in New York, A-qing," he said. "The place was called Happy Valley. It was on 72nd Street in Manhattan, not far from Central Park. The place was well known, but it was a dive. We had black customers, Puerto Ricans, and every imaginable kind of white person. There were a few Asians, not many."

"Are there bars like ours in America?" I asked him. I knew there were a lot in Tokyo. Little Jade had told me that.

"Lots and lots of them, more than you can count," Wang Kuilong laughed and sighed. "I'll bet there are nearly a hundred in New York alone. Some are pretty fancy, where the rich and famous go. Doctors, lawyers, in their suits and ties. Some are near colleges, where students hang out. Then there are some strange bars where the customers all wear leather jackets and ride motorcycles. They're called S & M bars."

"What's S & M?"

"Sado-masochism, people who like to hurt others and people who like to be hurt."

"Oh . . ." I wanted to tell him we had them here, too. Mousey knew that first-hand, and had the cigarette burns to prove it.

"Happy Valley was kind of special. Most of the customers were drifters, and a lot of them were runaway kids. For them, Happy Valley was a place where they could stop and catch their breath, a place that offered them temporary shelter. Most of the kids were drug addicts or had V.D. I took the job as bartender both to make a little pocket money and to have a place off the beaten path where I could hide myself and hang out with the drifters . . . most of the money I made went to those kids. They couldn't afford to see a doctor, and they couldn't break their addictions . . ."

Wang Kuilong shook his head. There was a helpless smile on his pale face. He raised his glass and drank quietly.

"Mr. Wang . . ." I felt like prying. "Where's Golden Treasure?"

Flower Child, one of the hustlers from Three Rivers Street who often dropped in, said he'd seen Dragon Prince walking in Westgate a week or so before with Golden Treasure. Wang was so tall and thin, while Golden Treasure was small and gimpy. He was walking ahead of Wang, hobbling along like a bouncy little puppy. All the hustlers from Three Rivers Street said that Wang Kuilong had been keeping Golden Treasure ever since the night of the typhoon, when he'd taken the boy home with him. Flower Child said enviously, even jealously:

"The Dragon Prince has bought the little cripple all kinds of new clothes. But how's he supposed to wear them with a body like that? He can't put a shoe on that club foot of his...all he can do is hobble down the street barefoot."

"Golden Treasure? I just came from seeing him...in the hospital." His dark, sunken eyes suddenly seemed to glow.

"Is he sick?"

"He was operated on yesterday at Taiwan University Hospital by one of their best surgeons. Everything came out fine, except it's been hard on him...you knew he had a club foot, the right one, and had to walk on the side of his foot..."

I recalled how painful and exhausting it had been for Golden Treasure to climb the steps of the lotus pond in the park, so he rarely showed his face there. He'd wait until it was very late and there were only two or three night spirits left around the pond before emerging from the trees, his eyes darting left and right like a frightened deer.

"Will his foot be okay after the operation?" I asked. I'd only really seen Golden Treasure's deformed right foot once. Since he couldn't wear a shoe, the side of his foot was covered with dark, ugly calluses.

"I discussed that with the doctors, and several of them at Taiwan University say there was a sixty percent chance. When I told Golden Treasure, he said okay, so we decided to go ahead with the operation. It's been hard on the little guy, but he's got guts. After the anaesthetic wore off, the pain was so great he was bathed in sweat. But he never so much as moaned."

Wang Kuilong sighed again.

"That deformed right foot of his has caused him a lot of suffering. He told me that the hustlers from Three Rivers Street are always playing practical jokes on him, like surrounding him and making him hobble around in circles, while they laugh and clap their hands. He grew up in the dark lanes around Three Rivers Street, where his mother was a streetwalker. He told me that when he was a kid he had to stand at the entrance to the lane and be a lookout for her while she entertained a John inside. She even had a couple of regulars he used to call Daddy. So when I asked him, 'How about your real father, Golden Treasure?' he just shook his head and giggled. 'I don't remember,' he'd say."

"A-qing..." Wang Kuilong's voice was quivering. "I rubbed that deformed, calloused foot of his, and it nearly broke my heart. I wished I could do something to make it better. There's no guarantee that this operation will do the trick, but at least there's a sixty or seventy percent chance. I promised him that the first thing we'd do after he got out of the hospital was go to the Shengsheng Shoe Store and have a pair of soft-soled leather shoes made for him. The poor kid's never worn leather shoes in his life! When I saw him in the hospital today the pain wasn't quite as bad, but his whole leg was swollen, and there's probably some infection. He has to lie in bed without moving. They won't even let him go to the bathroom. Those horrible nurses at Taiwan University Hospital just ignore him. So I sat with him all day, and when I walked outside it was pouring. For some reason I couldn't get you off my mind tonight, and that's why I'm here."

"Would you like another brandy, Mr. Wang?" His glass was empty. He was clutching it in his hand.

"Okay," he said after thinking it over for a moment. "I guess I'm just tired. I had a headache a while ago, but the brandy seems to have helped."

I went back to the bar and poured him another brandy.

"A-qing," he said when I returned with his drink, "how's life been treating you lately? Do you need anything?" His eyes were fixed on me. "You know how concerned I am about you."

"Everything's fine, Mr. Wang." I looked away to avoid his eyes. For some reason, just the thought of him getting near me made me feel like running away. I remembered the night I stayed with him in the aging official residence of his father and how I was in such a hurry to get away that I cut my leg climbing the wall. "Honest, Mr. Wang, things have really settled down. By opening the Cozy Nest, the chief has given us what you would call a 'haven.' When business is good, we get plenty of tips. And I've just recently moved into Papa Fu's house. Fu Chongshan is an honest-to-goodness benefactor. He treats me great, and I live at his home for free."

"Fu Chongshan...who did you say?" He sat up abruptly, obviously agitated.

"Do you know Fu Chongshan—Papa Fu? He's from Shandong. He was an army commander back on the Mainland..."

Wang Kuilong reached out his bony hand and grabbed my wrist so hard it hurt. There was fire in his eyes. He spoke urgently and solemnly:

"A-qing, you go home and tell Fu Chongshan, your Papa Fu, that Wang Kuilong has returned from America and hopes that Papa Fu will consent to see him, no matter what. Ask him to wait for me at his home tomorrow afternoon at two o'clock."

18

I gave Papa Fu Wang Kuilong's message the following morning. He didn't seem surprised. He thought for a moment, then sighed and said:

"I heard he was back, and I figured he'd be coming to see me sooner or later."

"So you know him?" I asked out of curiosity.

"His father, Wang Shangde, and I were old friends. During the War of Resistance we were in the Fifth Military District together as fellow officers. But I left the military early, while he kept getting promoted, all the way to the top. Since we both lived on Merciful Lane in Nanking, we saw each other quite a bit, but that changed after we came to Taiwan. Kuilong...I watched him grow up."

Papa Fu had made plans to go to the Divine Light Orphanage that afternoon, but instead he changed into a casual white linen Chinese gown and sat in the living room to wait for Wang Kuilong. He told me to make some tea. Wang Kuilong arrived exactly at two o'clock. He was wearing a black business suit and a black tie that made his face looked extremely pale. He was freshly shaved and his thick black hair was neatly combed and oiled. I led him into the living room, and when he saw Papa Fu he greeted him in a shaky voice:

"Uncle Fu."

"Kuilong," Papa responded as he got shakily to his feet and stuck out his hand in greeting. He straightened up as much as he could and raised his head. Wang Kuilong rushed over and shook hands with the old man, then the two of them stood there looking at each other for a long time without saying a word. Finally, Papa Fu asked Wang Kuilong to sit down. I'd made a pot of strong oolong tea, which I carried out into the living room on a tray. I poured the tea. Papa picked up his cup and blew the floating tea leaves off to the side, then took a sip. Wang Kuilong also picked up his cup and drank it silently.

"Uncle, I've been meaning to come see you ever since I got back." Wang Kuilong broke the silence.

"I know," Papa Fu said with a nod of his head. "I've been waiting for you."

"I always wanted to come back."

"It's been tough on you out there all these years," Papa Fu sighed loudly as he gazed at Wang Kuilong.

"When Mother died four years ago I sent Father a telegram to ask if I could come home for the funeral, but he wouldn't let me."

"Kuilong," Papa Fu held up a hand to stop him. But then he didn't say anything.

"Your father . . . ," he said after a long pause, "it was very hard on him, too."

"I know," Wang Kuilong said with a tragic smile on his face. "It's the Wang family's misfortune to have had an evil son like me. Father's reputation was ruined because of it."

"You have to understand that your father was not just an ordinary person. He did a lot for his country," Papa Fu explained. "His position in society was very high, and he had to take that into account. You must try to put yourself in his place."

"Uncle Fu, I hid myself in America for ten years, drifting around under a different name, all because of one thing Father said." Resentment crept into his voice. "Just as I was leaving, he said to me, 'I forbid you to come back as long as I'm alive!' There was no room for argument. I knew that I was the great shame in his life. We have lots of relatives in New York, but I never went to see any of them, and I didn't even let them know I was there. I didn't want to add to Father's troubles. But, Uncle Fu, when he was dying he wouldn't let me come back and see him one last time. He didn't even want me to attend his funeral. My uncle told me that on Father's orders, he didn't send the telegram until after Father was buried."

"I was at the funeral," Papa Fu said, his voice having grown slightly hoarse. "It was a state funeral, and your father left quite a reputation behind. Everyone was there, including all your many relatives. There are good reasons why your being there would have been a bad idea."

"I know that," Wang Kuilong said with a bitter smile. "That's what my uncle told me. I caused Father an enormous loss of face while he was alive, and it served no purpose to make him look bad on the day of his funeral. In all this time I've been back, I stayed away from his grave until the seventh week after his funeral, when my aunt and uncle took me up to Yangmingshan. There was still a mound of earth over Father's grave, which was covered by a piece of black oilcloth. I stood there in front of his grave without shedding a single tear, and I saw the look of anger on Uncle's face. I knew he was steaming, thinking to himself, 'How can that piece of scum stand dry-eyed in front of his own father's grave!' . . ."

Wang Kuilong laughed resentfully. There was fire in his eyes and a growing redness on his pale cheeks as he abruptly lifted his head and said passionately:

"Uncle, how could he know what I was feeling in my heart? I wanted to rush forward, rip that oilcloth off the grave, and throw myself down on the mound of dirt, dig down into the hole, wrap my arms around Father's body. I could have cried for three days and nights, cried till blood ran from my eyes, to try to wash away the hatred that had filled Father's heart—oh, how he loathed me! He didn't even want me to look one last time into his face. I waited for ten long years for only one thing—his forgiveness. The last thing he said to me became a curse that I carried on my back like a banished exile, scurrying in and out of the dark shadows of New York skyscrapers for ten years. I was on the run for ten years, carrying that curse on my back as it burned more and more deeply into my flesh, and only he, only he had the power to remove it. But he didn't leave a single word behind for me before he was lowered into the ground. That was his curse, a curse that will always keep me from transcending this existence . . ."

So much pain his voice quaked.

"Kuilong," Papa Fu broke in, his protruding shoulder blades showing his own agitation. His hunched back seemed to be pressing down until he could no longer bear it. His steel gray eyebrows were knitted in a frown. "You shouldn't say things like that about your father, it isn't fair!"

"It's not? It's *not*?" Wang Kuilong shouted. "Uncle, the reason I came to see you today was to ask if you saw Father before he died. You must have."

"I went to Veteran's Hospital to see him once or twice when his health was failing fast."

"What did he say to you?"

"We talked about the past, but I didn't stay long because he was very weak."

"I know he wouldn't have mentioned my name. His feelings for me had died." Wang Kuilong shook his head spiritedly.

"Kuilong, you're taking it all out on your father, but I wonder if you've ever thought about how much he suffered on your account." He was getting angry.

"Of course I have!" Wang Kuilong said helplessly. "All I wanted was for him to give me a chance to pay him back for some of the pain I caused him."

"That's easy to say!" Papa Fu said loudly, with a quiver in his voice. "You all think you can pay your fathers back for the pain you caused them, don't you? You're right, Kuilong, your father never mentioned you to me, and besides, we didn't see each other much during those last years. But I know he suffered as much as you did. I know that a lot of bad things happened to you during your years out of the country, but do you really think you were the only one? Your father was here sharing your load. No matter how great your agony, his was greater!"

"But...Uncle..." Wang Kuilong reached out and held Papa Fu's hand in his bony fingers. "But why wouldn't he even let me see him one last time?" he asked agonizingly.

Papa Fu looked straight at Wang Kuilong. There was intense pity in his wrinkled, spotted face as he mumbled:

"He couldn't bear to see you...not even after his eyes were closed."

19

By the time Wang Kuilong left, Papa Fu was so tired he could barely stand. Exhaustion was written all over his face, his back was bent almost double, and he was experiencing pains in his chest. I quickly gave him his medication and helped him into his room to rest. Since he didn't feel like eating dinner, I just ate some leftover rice and what remained of that afternoon's beef and celery. I told him there was some ham and winter melon soup in the refrigerator that he could heat up if he felt hungry. I wanted to ask the chief for the night off to stay with him, but he wouldn't hear of it.

"You go to work," he insisted. "Don't worry about me, I'll be fine after I've had some rest."

But I couldn't get Papa Fu off my mind, and when I told the chief, he let me knock off early. I was home before ten o'clock. I was surprised to find him up, sitting alone dreamily in the living room, an overcoat thrown over his shoulders. Incense was burning on the rectangular table again, sending its heavily aromatic smoke up the wall.

"Are you feeling better, Papa? Any more chest pains?"

"I feel a lot better after getting some sleep," he smiled. But he still looked tired. "What are you doing home so early?"

"The chief wanted me to come home in case Papa needed something."

"I'm sorry if I worried you."

"Are you hungry?"

"I heated up the soup. It was just what I needed."

"I can make you some noodles."

"No," he waved me off, "but you can make a pot of tea for us. There's something I want to talk to you about."

I went into the kitchen and boiled some water. After steeping some Dragon Well tea, I carried it into the living room on a tray, poured Papa a cup, and sat down on a stool by his feet. He picked up his cup, sipped some tea, and said to me sympathetically:

"I never dreamed that Wang Kuilong would change so much. I feel I don't know him at all . . ."

"They say he used to be really handsome," I interrupted.

"Not bad. He was a noble, dignified boy, and a good student. His father, Wang Shangde, had high hopes for him, maybe a diplomatic career, a chance to really make something of his life. He was going to send him overseas for advanced studies, and had made all the preparations. But then he got himself mixed up in that terrible murder, ruining his own life and nearly killing his father in the process . . ."

"They say it was front-page news for days."

"It made things so bad for his father he wasn't sure he could go on. He dropped out of sight for a long time. So what right does Kuilong have to accuse his father of letting his feelings for him die!"

Papa Fu was staring at me, his steel gray eyebrows knitted in a straight line.

"What makes you kids think you can understand the pain in a father's heart?" He reached out and laid his hand heavily on my shoulder as he continued somberly, "A-qing, you've been with me for several days now, and I feel like you're one of the family. Your father's alive, and I'm willing to bet that he's suffering on account of you right now. I had a son once, and, just like Wang Kuilong, he broke his father's heart, too. Tonight I want to tell you a story, a father's story . . ."

20

"A-qing, do you kids know what's in your parents' hearts? Do you think you could ever know? If A-wei were alive today he'd be thirty-seven, the same age as Wang Kuilong. His birth was not a normal one. It was a caesarean section, and the surgery was too much for his mother, who was a frail woman. She died not long after A-wei was born. He was an only child, and a motherless one, so I can't be blamed for loving him too much. I was strict, because I wanted him to have a bright future.

"He was an easy child to love, bright and accomplished in just about everything, mental or physical. I taught him a military treatise by Zhuge Liang once, and he committed the whole thing to memory. He was always with me, except when I was in battle, so I could personally take care of his education. In fact, I took him with me when we were stationed at Hanzhong in Shaanxi, where I taught him how to ride and hunt. Every morning I got on my horse Moonwatcher and put him on his silver pony Snow Lion, and the two of us galloped round and round the track, me in front and him behind. The horses were thoroughbreds from Qinghai, and there's quite a story about how I got them. After the war against Japan was over, I was sent on an inspection tour to Qinghai, and I took A-wei along with me. The commanding general of the Qinghai Military District was an old classmate of mine and a close friend. Since Qinghai is famous for its horses, my friend picked out several to show me. Moonwatcher was his favorite, and he said he'd give him to me if I could break him. So I jumped up on his back and we took off like the wind. Well, he was as good as his word, and he gave me the horse, sadly, of course. A-wei, who was standing behind me, pointed to a silver pony named Snow Lion. 'Daddy,' he said, 'can I ride that one?' Naturally, I liked the idea of showing off my son, but I didn't want him to make a fool of himself in front of all those officers. So I asked him softly, 'Can you handle it?' 'Sure I can, Daddy!' He was only fifteen, but tall and athletic. He was wearing a military uniform and boots that I'd had made especially for him, and he looked pretty cocky. He grabbed the mane of the silver pony and jumped up onto its back. Well, the horse took off, and he ran that horse for all it was worth. It looked like a silver streak tearing across the grass steppe. That commanding general friend of mine gave him the ultimate compliment: 'A real chip off the old block! The horse is his, my present!' You don't know how pleased that made me. My son had brought me honor.

"A-wei always wanted to be better than others, and he was arrogant. He always had to be on top. He graduated from the military academy at the top of his class of 250, academically and militarily. His commanding officer told me he was perfectly suited to the military. Words can't express my happiness over having a son like that, and I was content in the knowledge that the twenty years I'd spent bringing him up hadn't been wasted.

"But . . . but, A-wei only lived to be twenty-five. His death was inglorious, unnecessary, and tragic. When he was made a platoon leader he was assigned as a drill instructor. I went to his training camp once as an observer. A-wei was excellent at his job, and every soldier in his platoon followed his orders to the letter. They worshipped their Platoon Leader Fu. He was impressive and extremely competent. But then something happened during his second year. He was relieved of his duties and court-martialed. One night, when the commanding officer was making his rounds, he discovered A-wei in bed with one of the reserve soldiers. They were doing something unspeakable. I collapsed when the news reached me. How could A-wei, whom I'd raised to adulthood by myself, the son I loved and revered, a young man perfectly suited to the military, do something so shameful, so despicable, and with one of his own soldiers? I immediately wrote him a long letter, condemning his actions in the strongest possible language. He called me long distance the next day. It was the eighteenth day of the ninth month on the lunar calendar, my fifty-eighth birthday. Some of my friends and relatives had planned to celebrate my birthday, but I begged off, saying I was ill. A-wei pleaded with me to let him come to Taipei and explain, since the court-martial was scheduled for the next day, but I flatly refused. I said there was no need for him to come home, that since he'd broken a military law he had to stay in camp and think things out while he awaited the court's verdict. His voice was shaky and hoarse on the other end of the phone, like he was about to cry. He didn't sound at all like the valiant young military officer I knew. My anger grew and my feelings toward him turned to revulsion and disdain. He tried to explain himself, but I screamed at him to shut up and slammed down the phone. At the time I didn't want to see anyone, especially the son who had become my great disappointment. That night some soldiers from his platoon found him dead in his own bed, still holding his revolver in his hand. The bullet had entered his mouth and passed through his brain, shattering his face. The authorities concluded that he had been cleaning his revolver when it went off by accident. But I knew that my proud, self-assured, ambitious son had taken his own life on my birthday.

"I was bothered by nightmares for a long time after A-wei's suicide, and the same face always appeared. It was a young man's face, ghostly pale, with wide, staring eyes and a mouth that kept opening and closing, as though in its extreme fright it wanted to shout, but no sound came out. Those eyes stared at me, pleading for something, but I didn't know what. The look was one of sheer anguish. I knew I'd seen the face before, but I simply couldn't remember where. Several nights in a row I dreamed of that ghostly, panic-stricken face. Then one night I woke up in a cold sweat after seeing it again, but this time it was covered with blood. That's when it hit me. It had been years ago, during the War of Resistance, when I was on the front lines in the Fifth Military District. Just before the battle broke out we executed a young soldier. We were in Xuzhou and the situation was very tense. My troops were responsible for holding the front lines. One night, when I was inspecting the positions, two soldiers who had left their posts without permission were brought to me. They'd been caught in the weeds in a compromising situation. The older one showed no fear, but the young one, who was no more than seventeen or eighteen, was shaking in his boots. All the blood had drained from his face and his eyes were as big as saucers. His mouth was open, like he wanted to beg for his life, but he was so frightened he couldn't make a sound — just like the face in my dreams. Naturally, given the situation, I ordered that they be shot immediately. At the time, my mind was at peace, and as time passed I forgot all about the incident. I never imagined that the same panic-stricken face would suddenly reappear in my dreams after so many years. I suffered a heart attack that night and was rushed to Veteran's Hospital, where I stayed for several months. I nearly died.

"After I was released from the hospital and sent home, for two solid years I locked myself up in my house and refused to see anyone, while I tried to regain my health. I just gave up after A-wei's death and vegetated. Life was meaningless.

"It continued like that until one winter night ten years ago, on the last day of the lunar year. I was having trouble with high blood pressure, which often made me light-headed, so I went to Taiwan University Hospital to see the chief of internal medicine. He was so busy I had to settle for an appointment at the night clinic. It was after nine o'clock when I left the hospital, and I still recall that a cold front had moved in, chilling the night air. It was also raining. On my way home I walked through New Park to get to the bus stop on Guanqian Road. The park was nearly deserted, probably because of the rain, and as I passed the lotus pond I heard sobs coming from the little gazebo at the head of the pond. They sounded terribly sad in the cold, wet night air. Inside I found a young man sitting alone on the bench. He was wearing a thin black shirt and holding his head in his hands, his shoulders heaving with each sob. I'd never seen anyone cry so pitifully in my life, like he was suffering the greatest injustice the world could inflict. I walked over and shook his shoulder and said to him, 'You're too young to be crying like that.' He gave me a very strange reply. He said, 'My heart's all swollen, and I have to cry to relieve the pain.' I asked him if he had a home, someplace he could go, and he said he didn't. It was so cold that night that I felt chilled even in my lined jacket. And all he had on was a thin shirt. His teeth were chattering. Suddenly I couldn't bear it any longer, and I took him home with me. He probably hadn't had a decent sleep for days, and the first thing I did when we got home was fix him some warm milk. His eyelids started to droop, so I took him into A-wei's room and put him into the same bed you're using, without even taking off his clothes. He was asleep as soon as his head touched the pillow. I took A-wei's comforter out of the closet and covered him with it. He was lying on his side with his head buried in the pillow, like he was freezing. His face was deathly pale. I studied his face closely, and he really was an unusual-looking boy. He had a triangular face with a short, pointy chin that curved slightly upward. Even when he was sleeping his eyebrows were knitted in a straight line, like a canopy over his eyes. I know a few things about physiognomy, but I'd never seen anyone with such an ill-starred look about him. He was clearly fated for tragedy. All of a sudden, why I don't know, I felt immense pity for him. I pulled the comforter up over his shoulders, so he was completely covered. That was the first time in two years, ever since A-wei's death, that I'd felt anything stirring in my heart.

"He didn't wake up until the next afternoon. It was the last day of the lunar new year. I wasn't going to celebrate New Year's, but because of him I told Auntie Wu to prepare a few year-end dishes so we could celebrate New Year's together. If only I'd known it would be his last meal on this earth. I've never seen anyone eat and drink with so much excitement and enjoyment. He finished off almost an entire pork shank all by himself, until his lips glistened with oil. He patted his bulging belly and laughed, "Papa Fu, this is the best New Year's dinner I've ever had. In the orphanage we only celebrated Christmas, never Lunar New Year's.' He started getting talkative and told me all about himself. He'd lived an unusual life, and a bleak one. You kids in the park must know the whole story. He was A-feng, the kid who ran wild in the park, the one you call Phoenix Boy. He told me all about that park of yours. He said there were lots of homeless kids like him, whose lives were just as bleak. He excitedly pointed to his heart and said, 'The wildness is in our blood — Grandpa Guo, the park gardener, tells us that, he says we have a wild streak that's as much a part of us as typhoons and earthquakes are a part of this island, and just as uncontrollable. That's why I cry, Papa, to wash the poison out of my heart.'

"Later on, at the Divine Light Orphanage, I met the Catholic brother from Henan who'd raised Phoenix Boy, and he told me he was indeed a strange child, who'd go out to the chapel in the middle of the night and cry alone, waking everybody up. A mean old Irish priest took a real disliking to him, and all you had to do was mention his name for the priest to say angrily, 'That kid's possessed by the Devil. Why, he even smashed the holy statues in the chapel!' After A-feng and I had finished our New Year's dinner, he said he had to go. 'A-feng,' I said, 'if you don't have somewhere to go you can stay here for a few nights.' But he just smiled and said, 'No, Papa, I don't want to put you out. Besides, there's someone waiting for me in the park.' He told me he was being kept by someone, and when he ran away, that other person looked everywhere for him. He smiled and said, 'Tonight I'll see him in the park, and since it's New Year's, I want to settle things with him.' The next day it was in all the papers, and that's how I knew what had been going on between him and Wang Kuilong . . .

"Ai. Strange as it sounds, even though he only spent one night in my house, I developed a special fondness and concern for him. For him to die like that came as a severe blow to me. I felt so sorry for him. My heart, which had been as good as dead ever since A-wei's death, suddenly came back to life. And all because I'd met the hapless A-feng in the park and learned of his tragic end. At that moment I promised myself that I'd extend a helping hand to you park kids who lived such uncertain lives . . ."

"A-qing." Papa Fu finished his story with one hand on my shoulder, while he wiped his rheumy eyes with the other. He heaved a long sigh. "All you kids know how to do is be resentful of your fathers, but have you ever thought about how much your fathers have suffered because of you, or how deeply? After the incident with Wang Kuilong, I went to see Wang Shangde, his father. His hair had turned completely white in less than six months, snowy white . . . A-qing, how about your father? Do you know that he's suffering on your account?"

21

I gently let down the mosquito net over Papa Fu. He lay on his side facing me, his hunched back giving his body the shape of an "S." I turned off the light and quietly closed the door behind me. Then I walked into the living room, where the heavy smoke from the incense continued to coil up the wall above the table. After pouring a glass of water to douse the last embers in the incense burner, I looked up at the photos of Papa Fu and Fu Wei in military uniform hanging side by side, and suddenly recalled Papa Fu's birthday on September 18th of the lunar year. He'd gone out early that morning and returned with a bunch of white chrysanthemums, which he put into the sky-blue porcelain vase on the table, then took his brass tripod incense burner, put it on the table beside the vase, and lit some sticks of sandalwood incense. He was sitting there so quietly and solemnly that I didn't want to disturb him. No one knew that his birthday was also the anniversary of his son's death. No wonder he'd gotten drunk on two cups of wine during dinner: he'd had something quite different on his mind. Why had Fu Wei killed himself on his father's birthday? Could he possibly have resented his father that much? I studied Fu Wei's photograph intently: he had an even, well shaped face with high cheekbones, tightly closed thin lips, and the clear, radiant eyes of someone who was self assured, even arrogant. He was standing ramrod straight in full uniform, his cap placed squarely on his head. It sure looked like someone perfectly suited to the military, and there was an unmistakable resemblance between him and his father.

When I went to bed I thought of my own father. I recalled the time he'd pinned his Order of the Precious Tripod on my lapel, so seriously, so grandly. He probably thought I looked a lot like him, too. Too bad he had to go and pin all his hopes on someone like me. I really felt that if I hadn't been expelled from school and could have passed the Army Officers Candidate School exam, I could have been an excellent military officer and made my father proud of me. I always got high marks in military training in school. I did well in basic drills, and our instructor often called me out of the ranks to demonstrate the proper moves. That always pleased me and made me feel that I was the true son of a military man. Not only that, I enjoyed target practice and had a great time when we went out on the firing range. The sound of bullets flying in the air was music to my ears. Several times at home I took the pistol Father had carried as a regiment commander back on the Mainland out of its hiding place under his mattress and played with it without his knowledge. Since he seldom cleaned it, the barrel was getting rusty. I'd stick it in my belt and march around with my head held high, back and forth like a military hero, feeling very impressive. On the day Father kicked me out of the house and chased me with that pistol, it was unloaded — since he'd been drummed out of the service he wasn't qualified to have any bullets — but he probably felt that the pistol in his hand carried the authority he needed. He'd also waved that rusting pistol in his hand on the day he went looking for Mother, the day she left home.

No, I think I knew how much Father had suffered. In the months since I'd left home, my knowledge of the terrible agony he was enduring pressed down more and more heavily on my heart. That unbearable agony was probably what I was trying to hide from. That time I'd gone back to our dark, dank home with the pervasive smell of mildew to deliver Mother's ashes, just looking at Father's shiny, empty rattan easy chair made me feel like I was suffocating and that I had to get out of there. I had to keep away from Father because I knew I couldn't bear to see the look of anguish on his devastated face.

Papa Fu coughed in his bedroom, and I couldn't help wondering whether Father was sleeping at that moment, too, or whether he was pacing back and forth in his bedroom.

22

Mr. Yu invited me to join him on Friday night for a midnight snack at the place called Sichuan Noodles on Xinyi Road. We arranged to meet at the intersection of Xinsheng South Road and Xinyi Road, near his home, after I got off work at the Cozy Nest. Just before midnight I slipped into the back, changed into my street clothes, and asked Little Jade to wash the dirty glasses for me and tell Chief Yang that I was leaving early because I had a stomach ache. Actually, my stomach was bothering me, but that's because I was famished. Anticipating a delicious midnight snack, all I'd had for dinner was a tiny bowl of rice noodles at a roadside stand. By the time I got off work, my stomach was growling and my mouth was watering. Mr. Yu was waiting for me when I arrived at the meeting place. He was wearing a loose-fitting dark-blue hooded sweatshirt and had a pair of leather sandals on his feet. He looked very handsome. Most likely he'd come straight from home. He was happy to see me.

"My Little Qing," he greeted me, "you're right on time."

"I slipped out of there before closing time." I laughed. "See, we said twelve-thirty, and that's exactly what time it is."

"Have you ever eaten at Sichuan Noodles?" he asked as we walked up Xinyi Road to the restaurant.

"Once, when I was a kid, but that was a long time ago. Back then it was nothing more than a little roadside stand."

One night three years earlier Father had taken Buddy and me to Sichuan Noodles for a midnight snack — it was the only time he ever took us out to eat. I'd passed the high-school entrance exam earlier that summer, and since it was my birthday, Father broke precedent by taking us out, probably to reward me. Since he couldn't afford a big restaurant, he took us to the Sichuan Noodles roadside stand. But for Buddy and me it was one big deal, and we were so excited we could barely contain ourselves. Father only permitted us to order one bowl of spicy wontons each, and when we asked for seconds, he frowned and said, "No, that's enough." But he gave us each one of the wontons from his bowl.

"Mr. Yu, will it be okay if I eat two bowls of spicy wontons?" I smiled. "I had a light dinner, and I'm about to pass out from hunger."

"Eat as many bowls as you want, My Little Qing. You don't have to leave till you're stuffed, okay?" He reached out and tousled my hair.

We went straight to the second floor when we got there and had to wait for about ten minutes until a table opened up in the corner. As soon as we sat down, Mr. Yu pointed to the menu under the glass surface of the table and said:

"Their steamed intestines, porkchops, and lotus leaf beef are all terrific."

"I'd still rather have spicy wontons, Mr. Yu."

"Okay, okay," he laughed. "We'll order spicy wontons *and* some appetizers."

When the food was brought over, he told the waiter to bring a bottle of sorghum wine. I finished off the wontons in short order, popping them into my mouth one after the other. They were piping hot and super-spicy, and my forehead was dotted with perspiration. When I finished the first bowl, Mr. Yu was as good as his word, because he immediately ordered me a second.

"Here's to you, Mr. Yu," I said, raising my cup of sorghum wine. It burned all the way down, and I suddenly felt hot all over. He got quite a kick out of watching me wolf down my food, and kept putting pieces of pork intestines and porkchop on my plate.

"My Little Qing," he said with a smile, "you're still a growing boy, so eat as much as you can."

"Mr. Yu, *Revenge on Great Bear Mountain* was great!" When I'd finished my spicy wontons my thoughts turned to Zhuge Jingwo's martial-arts novel. I'd already read the whole thing twice. "But why did E Shun have to die like that? Couldn't his father, the Flying Roc, have let him go?"

The final episode, where Ding Yunxiang, the Flying Roc, traps his son E Shun and kills him with his own sword, shocked me.

"It's what they call sacrificing your own kin for the sake of honor!" Mr. Yu said with a laugh. "When E Shun admitted his crimes against his father, Ding Yunxiang had no choice but to kill him. That last part, where the Flying Roc touches his son's dead body, with tears streaming down his face, is a good piece of writing, very moving. No wonder they call Zhuge Jingwo the Master Story-teller."

"Do you have any more novels like that, Mr. Yu?"

"Lots of them, a whole bookcase full."

"Any by Zheng Zhengyin?"

"I've got *The Iron Horseman's Silver Vase.*"

"Great!" I exclaimed excitedly. "Could you lend it to me, Mr. Yu? I've wanted to read that for a long time, but I can never find it."

"Sure. When we're finished here, come over to my house and I'll give it to you." We raised our cups and drained the last few drops of sorghum wine.

Mr. Yu lived in a third-story apartment on Xinsheng South Road, Lane 145. It was a small apartment, but very comfortable. He'd furnished it with a set of rattan furniture with soft, thick, bright-red cushions on the chairs and sofa. A string of three lamps, the largest of which was as big around as my arms, hung from the ceiling in a corner of the living room. The lamps cast a milky white light all over the room. Mr. Yu turned on the radio. The U.S. military station was playing late-night mood music. He signaled me to follow him into his study, where there were two bookcases, one completely filled with martial-arts novels by old masters like Wang Dulu and Wolong Sheng and more recent authors like Xiusi Maling and Dongfang Yu. He took Zheng Zhengyin's *The Iron Horseman's Silver Vase* down and handed it to me. He pointed to the bookcase and said:

"My Little Qing, you're welcome to come here any time and enjoy martial-arts novels with me."

"Long live Mr. Yu!" I exclaimed happily.

We went back into the living room and sat down. Mr. Yu poured two glasses of cold water to wash away the dryness of our mouths after all that spicy food. We were sitting together on his rattan sofa. I took off my shoes and curled my legs under me. The soft white light lit up his face. His eyelids were flushed from the wine, his arched eyebrows shone darkly.

"Mr. Yu, you look just like the Southern Hero Zhanzhao!" He reminded me of the character in the cartoon version of *Seven Heroes and Five Gallants* I'd read years earlier. He laughed loudly.

"You think I look like the Imperial Cat? Then how about you? Are you the Bright Fur Rat Bai Yutang?"

"No, no," I shook my head. "I'm not as dashing as Bai Yutang. I used to call my kid brother the Bright Fur Rat."

"Your kid brother was a martial-arts novel fan, too?"

"He got interested in them through me, but he got more hooked on them than me. If I brought one from the lending library, he'd snatch it away from me and read it first."

"It's always like that," Mr. Yu said with a sigh. "Whenever I bought one, Little Hong would grab it out of my hand before I got through the first page."

"Who's Little Hong?" I asked him.

"A kid who used to live with me...he was drafted into the army. He's on the offshore island of Matsu now. I bought most of those novels you saw in there for him."

Mr. Yu told me that Little Hong had come to Taipei from Pingdong to go to school at the Datong Technical School. He'd lived with Mr. Yu for more than two years. Since he was from a poor family, Mr. Yu had taken care of him and paid for his schooling. He'd even taught him English. Mr. Yu took a photograph out of his wallet to show me. It was a picture of the two of them, with Mr. Yu's arm around Little Hong's shoulder. They were smiling broadly.

"Now that's the Bright Fur Rat Bai Yutang," I said with a laugh as I pointed to the handsome boy in the photograph.

"Little Hong's a good-looking boy," Mr. Yu said with a sigh as he examined the picture in his hand. "I miss him a lot."

"How long does he have to serve?"

"Two more years."

"Wow, that's a long time!"

"It sure is," he said with a shake of his head. "So when I get to feeling really lonely I go over to the Cozy Nest for a drink."

The music on the radio came to an end. The announcer said it was two a.m.

"I'd better be going, Mr. Yu." I started to get up, but he put his hand on my shoulder to stop me.

"My Little Qing," he said, "you don't have to go home tonight. You can stay here with me."

"Mr. Yu," I hesitated.

"I don't often get to meet Sichuanese boys like you. I've really enjoyed talking with you like this, so don't go."

Several customers from the Cozy Nest had asked me to go out with them, but I'd always begged off. But Mr. Yu seemed like such a nice man, and besides, like he said, we were both from Sichuan, and that made our relationship special. I really liked that little apartment of his. It gave me a warm, comfortable feeling.

"We can talk some more in bed," Mr. Yu said.

"Then I'd better go take a shower first, is that all right?" After working all day and finishing off two bowls of hot, spicy wontons, I was so sweaty that even I thought I smelled bad.

"Sure," he said as he stood up. "I'll light the water heater for you."

When he returned he handed me a clean towel and led me into the bathroom, where he told me there were two bars of soap in the dish beside the tub; the white, fragrant one was a face bar, the other was regular bath soap.

"Take your time, I'll go make up the bed," he said as he closed the bathroom door behind him.

I hung the shower nozzle up on the hook and turned on the water. I took a long shower, soaping up and rinsing off twice, and even shampooed my hair. When I finished I dried my hair, then walked out of the bathroom, bare-chested, carrying my clothes in my hand, into Mr. Yu's bedroom. It was a small room, but very neat and orderly. He'd put a fresh blue sheet on top of the double bed and was changing the pillow cases when I walked in. After putting the pillows down on the bed next to each other he said: "You sleep on the inside."

I got into bed and lay down while he took off his clothes and turned off the light on the headboard. As we lay next to each other in the dark, he began asking me about my past. So I told him about the shabby house I'd lived in, about how my mother and Buddy had died, and about the tormented life of my father.

"Too bad, My Little Qing," he said sympathetically. "If your Buddy were still alive, you might not be all alone in the world."

"Mr. Yu, if Buddy were still alive he'd fall in love with all those martial-arts novels of yours. He only managed to read the first two volumes of *Revenge at Great Bear Mountain*! Once I dreamed he was fighting with me over one of those novels, and in the scuffle I hit him. Do you believe in ghosts, Mr. Yu?"

"Don't know if I do," he said with a little laugh. "I've never seen one."

"Ever since Buddy died he's been in my dreams a lot. Once I was sure I held his hand when he reached out for his harmonica."

"Harmonica?"

"It was a Butterfly harmonica. I gave it to him. A birthday present. He wanted it back."

"You probably dream of him so much because he's always on your mind."

"But I never dream of my mother . . . she never liked me when she was alive, so she probably doesn't want to see me now that she's dead."

"I doubt it, My Little Qing. Don't think thoughts like that."

We changed the subject. He told me that back in Chungking he used to go swimming in the Jialing River. He could cross it when he was sixteen. I told him I liked to swim, too, and how I used to take Buddy to the river.

"I'll take you to Egret Lake for a swim in the summer."

"Okay," I said.

"The water's cool and clean. I'm sure you'll like it."

"Okay," I said vaguely.

My eyelids were beginning to feel heavy, so I rolled over to face the wall and fell asleep. I had the feeling that he had his arm around me as I slept.

"Mr. Yu . . ."

I woke up with a start and moved closer to the wall. His hand was still on my shoulder. It was very warm.

"Mr. Yu, I'm sorry . . ."

"My Little Qing," he said gently.

"Mr. Yu, I'm really sorry . . ." My voice started to tremble.

"Then . . . you go to sleep." He hesitated for a moment, then patted me lightly on the shoulder and took his hand away.

"Mr. Yu, I . . ."

Suddenly overcome by a feeling of overpowering sadness, I began to wail. The more I cried, the harder I cried, until I felt like my entire being was turning inside out. All the grief, indignities, humiliation, and injustices that had filled my heart over the past months came flooding out in one huge rush. Of all the people I'd been associated with, Mr. Yu was the most decent, the most endearing, and the easiest to get along with. But when he'd put his arm around my shoulder a moment earlier, I felt ashamed, like my body was covered with sores that I didn't want anyone to touch. I couldn't tell him about all those dark nights in low-class hotels behind the train station, or about the filth that was left on my body by those faceless men in the foul-smelling public toilets at the China Bazaar in Westgate. I couldn't tell him about that huge, puffy man who was hungrily feasting on my rain-soaked body in the gazebo next to the lotus pond while the typhoon was raging all around us. What was tugging on my heart at that moment was the thought of that dark urn sitting on the table in our shabby, mildewed living room, filled with the sin-infested ashes of my mother. Mr. Yu never stopped patting my back to comfort me, but my crying grew more and more violent.

23

Mr. Yu was already gone by the time I woke up the next morning. He'd left a shirt on the bed. It was a Smart brand blue-checked sportshirt. There was a note on top of it:

My Little Qing:
    I have two morning classes. When I come home at noon I'll take you to Liu's Barbecue Duck House for some cured food. The shirt's brand new. It's for you.

                                                Yu Hao

I looked at the alarm clock on the headboard. It was already 11:20. I jumped out of bed and tried on the shirt he'd left me. It fit perfectly. But I quickly took it off, folded it neatly, and put it back down on the bed. I turned his note over and wrote:

Mr. Yu:
    I'm sorry for all the disturbance last night. I'll come back some other time and borrow Zheng Zhengyin's *The Iron Horseman's Silver Vase*.
    Thank you!

                                                Li Qing

Outside, the sky was a gorgeous blue, the sun's rays were radiant. A crisp autumn breeze cooled the people on the street. I bought an oil fritter at a roadside stand and ate it as I walked along aimlessly. I was feeling sort of lost, but incredibly relaxed. All that crying the night before seemed to have purged my heart of the melancholy that had accumulated over a long time, and now I was empty inside. Heading down one street after another, I discovered that I had walked all the way to the end of Chung-king South Road, where it crossed Nanhai Road. Ever since getting expelled from school, over six months earlier, I had avoided this section of town, since Yude School was on Nanhai Road, and the last thing in the world I wanted was to meet up with any of my schoolmates or teachers. But a sudden impulse had brought me here to see my school again. Since it was Saturday afternoon, there were no classes, and even if I did run into any schoolmates or teachers, they might not even recognize me. I'd let my hair grow until it covered my forehead and I was wearing blue jeans. I didn't look anything like a student. The school wall was made of brick, and very tall. Both metal gates were open, so I went in and walked past the administration building. The bulletin board was filled with notices, as always, including two lists of demerits for students who had broken rules: Huang Zhuguo, sophomore, one demerit for cheating on a math exam. Liu Jianxing, freshman, restricted to campus for theft of school property. No expulsion notices. Sand was swirling in the "Gobi Desert" behind the administration building, as always. Whenever winds swept across the school athletic field, clouds of dust filled the air, so we called it the Gobi Desert. Once our military drills were completed, we'd return to the classroom with a fine layer of dust covering our faces. The athletic field was completely deserted at this time of day, but there were some kids playing basketball on the court next to the field. Mixed in with the staccato sounds of the ball hitting the ground were shouts of "Good shot!"

I strolled over to the court. The players, all five of them, were middle-school students in Boy Scout shorts and no shoes. I stood beneath the basket and watched them for a minute before I realized there was a game going on, two boys on one team, three on the other. It was a heated contest that was clearly going against the short-handed team, who had missed several shots in a row. The taller of the two had just thrown up a wild pass that made him look terrible, and the three boys on the other team were laughing and shouting confidently.

"Quit hogging the ball! I told you to pass, but no, not *you!*" the shorter boy was complaining angrily. He was smaller than all the other kids, but he had the quickest moves. His round baby face was bright red and covered with sweat.

"I had a layup, so why shouldn't I shoot?" the taller boy defended himself, his arms outspread, a silly grin on his face. Although he was the tallest boy there, he was clumsy and slow, and loved to hog the ball.

"Go *shoot* yourself! You let them score on us!" The little one huffily tossed the ball to the other side as he kept grumbling.

The team with three players was so far ahead they'd gotten cocky. A little dark-skinned one caught the ball and dribbled

273

straight to the basket. Baby Face, sensing another disaster, rushed over and covered him like a blanket.

"Foul!" Little Darkie threw up his hands and shouted after missing the shot.

"What foul? Stop cheating!" Baby Face shot back in exasperation.

"Foul! Foul!" his teammates joined in, strengthening their claim by making a referee's foul signal.

"Bullshit!" Baby Face screamed angrily. "Ask him!"

He pointed to his clumsy teammate, who just stood there for a second, then smiled bashfully.

"I'm not sure."

The three teammates cheered. Free throw time. Baby Face ran over and punched the tall kid.

"You jackass!" he snarled.

"I'm really not sure," the big kid said honestly as he scratched his head.

Little Darkie made both free throws, the second one hitting nothing but net. The three of them really whooped it up now, clapping and shouting ecstatically, while Baby Face just stood there holding the ball, his eyes blinking a mile a minute, the veins on his forehead popping out.

"I'll play!" I shouted as I held my hand up in the air. I quickly shed my shirt and shoes. While the three teammates just stood around looking at each other, Baby Face's anger quickly turned to glee.

"Come on in," he said before anyone else could react, "glad to have you. 'Reinforcements have arrived!'"

My addition immediately turned the game around, and the first half ended in a 20 to 20 tie. Baby Face was so happy he was nearly jumping out of his skin. No more yelling at his tall teammate. The second half began. With Baby Face and me playing perfectly together, we jumped out into the lead. I passed the ball to him, he went up for the basket. Even though he was short, he had a wicked right-handed hook, and he made three or four shots in a row. I'd been the captain of the evening senior class team, playing center. When we beat the day school team, I was the one who went up at the awards ceremony and received the championship banner from the principal. We were so far ahead in the second half that the other team was in complete disarray, dispirited and fighting among themselves. I sunk the winning shot from half-court, hitting nothing but net.

274

"Great shot!" Baby Face clapped his hands and jumped into the air.

The final score was a lopsided 45 to 28. Baby Face ran over, threw his arms around me, and hopped up and down. He gave his clumsy teammate a kick in the butt.

"Ready to admit we whipped you?" Baby Face gleefully pointed at Little Darkie. "You buy the ices!"

"Up yours!" Little Darkie spat on the ground and complained breathlessly. "You had help, so it doesn't count."

"Well, it looks like someone's trying to weasel out of it," he turned and shouted to his tall teammate.

"Let's play a rematch," one of Little Darkie's teammates, a boy with protruding lips, said as he came up to add his support. "Then we'll see what you cowards are made of."

"Enough of that," Baby Face shot back as he pushed the kid aside. "You lost, right? 45 to 28, a wipe-out. We agreed that the losers pay. You're the cowards if you don't pay up."

The boy started puffing, his thick lips sticking up in the air. Baby Face looked at him and pointed to his mouth.

"Go look in a mirror, Fat Lip. You know what your mouth looks like now? A duck's ass!"

Fat Lip's face turned red as he charged Baby Face, fists flying. Baby Face tried to get away, but Little Darkie stopped him. Fat Lip grabbed hold of Baby Face's head, and the two of them started wrestling on the ground, while Little Darkie got in his shots from the side, which landed on Baby Face's head and body.

"Help me, big guy!" Baby Face screamed for his teammate.

The big, clumsy kid ran over and joined the fight, followed immediately by a pimply-faced kid from the other team. All five of them were rolling on the ground, fists and feet flying, with everyone hitting everyone else. What had started out as a game played for ices had turned into a war. The laughter that had accompanied the fighting at first died away as the punches started acquiring some force, especially between Baby Face and Fat Lip, who had already given each other black eyes. It was starting to turn ugly, so I rushed over and pulled Baby Face and Fat Lip apart, and shouted:

"Fight's over!"

All five of them froze. One after the other, they put their hands on their hips, cocked their heads, and glared at each other.

"You had a bet on the game, right?" I asked them.

275

"We all agreed before we started that the losers would treat the winners to ices," Baby Face said indignantly.

I turned to the losers. "Since you lost, are you going to treat the winners or not?"

"You helped them, so the bet's off!" Little Darkie objected.

"If you hadn't helped them, we'd have beat the pants off them!" Fat Lip piped up.

Baby Face jumped over in front of him and shouted:

"Who cares how we won! Everybody can see you guys are trying to weasel out of the deal. Anyone who does that is a bastard's grandson!"

Fat Lip and Little Darkie started grinding their fists in their palms. I quickly inserted myself between them.

"Okay, I'll mediate, I'll be the peacemaker. You kids all want ices, right? Well, since nobody's willing to treat anybody else, I recommend that everybody pays for his own, what do you say?"

The three members of the other team exchanged glances. Since it seemed to be the only way out, they said:

"Okay."

"You guys are getting off easy!" Baby Face grumbled to show his dissatisfaction.

We picked up our shirts and threw them over our shoulders. With Baby Face holding the ball up against his chest, the six of us, all sweaty and grimy, swaggered barefoot out the schoolyard gate. Old Li's pushcart, where he sold ices, was right there where it always was, across from the school gate. His pushcart was so old and rickety it creaked and groaned when it rumbled down the street; the ice shaver had turned black from rust, and the glass jars filled with several flavors of topping were so discolored you could barely see inside them. Old Li was so fat that in the summer his huge belly stuck out from under the buttons of his shirt. I never saw him when his face wasn't all sweaty, but instead of wiping the sweat from his face with a towel he just flicked it off with his hand, then went back to shaving ice. Business was brisk, and none of the other stands could compete with him. That was partly because he sold his ices cheaper and gave more than they did, and partly because he was so friendly with everyone. He was a retired soldier who had traveled all over the China Mainland and knew all kinds of folk tales. He was a favorite of the students at Yude school. On summer evenings, after school was out, if I had money in my pocket I'd line up at Old Li's with some of the other kids to buy an ice and listen to him tell the

Hunanese story of the ghost chaser. His carbide lamp, which gave off noxious fumes, cast a pale light over the pushcart as he hopped around stiffly like a ghost chaser, his huge belly sticking out, and we laughed till our sides were about to split.

"Old Li," I laughingly called out to him.

He took a long look before he recognized me. He smiled broadly.

"Well, if it isn't Li Qing. Long time no see. Did you graduate?"

"Six ices," I said. "We're dying of thirst."

Baby Face ran over and took the lid off the glass jar with the red flavoring and sniffed its contents. Old Li grabbed the lid out of his hand and put it back onto the jar.

"You're a frisky little devil. What do you think you're doing?"

"Do you guys know why Old Li's ices are so special?" Baby Face giggled. "He adds a special ingredient — his aromatic sweat."

"You damn..."

Old Li's eyes were as big as saucers, but he was speechless. He flipped the sweat from his brow with his hand, and that broke us up. He went back to shaving the ice, grumbling non-stop. After filling six bowls, he added the flavored toppings and handed the ices to us. Then he turned to Baby Face.

"What does a little twerp like you know? Old Li here's the Living Buddha, and anybody that drinks his sweat lives forever!"

"Old Li does kinda look like the Living Buddha," Baby Face laughed as he pointed to Old Li's belly. "Look, you guys, you could scrape a bowl of clay off that belly of his!"

Old Li raised his fist, but even he couldn't hold back the laughter. He pinched Baby Face's cheek and said:

"This little baby's the Ox Demon's Red Child, always raising cain!"

We slurped down our ices and handed over five yuan apiece. The ice had cooled everyone's temper, so the big, clumsy kid, Little Darkie, Fat Lip, Pimples, and Baby Face said goodbye to me and ran off.

24

Baby Face headed off by himself toward the botanical gardens, holding the ball in his hand, his shirt draped over his shoulder. I followed him in. It was the first time I'd been there in over six months. For more than five years I'd walked through it to and from school every day. For Buddy and me it was like our own private garden. Back in school we'd form gangs and come here to have our swordfights. Dabao and Erbao, the two sons of Staff Officer Qin from Lane 28 of Longjiang Street, were our enemies. I'd made a couple of bamboo swords with my Boy Scout knife, one for me and one for Buddy. Mine was called Dragon Roar and his Tiger Growl. We were the Dragon and Tiger Swordsmen of Kunlun Mountain, Dabao and Erbao were the Two Goblins of Zhongnan. Armed with Dragon Roar and Tiger Growl, Buddy and I fought the Two Goblins to the death on the steps of the artificial mountain, making the place look like it had been hit by a whirlwind. Since right always vanquishes evil, the Dragon and Tiger Swordsmen invariably drove the Two Goblins of Zhongnan out of the botanical gardens. During one swordfight, I knocked Dabao off the steps, and he banged his head on the cement, raising a bump the size of a walnut. His mother was so upset she came over and said to my father, "Those brats of yours are out of control. You'd better watch them." Dragon Roar and Tiger Growl were confiscated and burned as kindling. Neither Dabao nor Erbao passed the entrance exam at Yude, so they were sent to another high school, where they turned into juvenile delinquents.

Every blade of grass in the botanical gardens was as familiar as an old friend. In the spring we caught tadpoles, in the summer we climbed eucalyptus trees to catch cicadas, in the fall . . . in the fall we went over to the lotus pond to gather seedpods.

Summer had passed since my last visit, and the lotus flowers had already bloomed. The surface of the pond was covered with pink lotus petals, and the leaves, which stuck three or four feet out of the water, were like huge open fans, glistening green and bathed by the rains. The green seedpods were filling up with seeds, and the fragrance of the leaves and flowers filled the air like a potion that cooled you to your core.

"In another week the seedpods will be ready to pick," I said to Baby Face when I caught up with him, pointing at the seedpods waving in the wind.

"In another week those big ones over there will all be gone!" he said with a laugh. "I've been over here every morning for a week, and as soon as they're ripe I pick them."

"It's too bad we can't get to those out there, they're probably already ripe," I said as I pointed to the biggest ones in the center of the pond.

"I've got a long bamboo pole with a knife tied on the end. I'll go get it and we'll see if we can reach the big seedpods."

"They're too far. If you're not careful you'll fall in."

He just laughed and said, "Fat Lip and I came here once, and three pods weren't enough for the greedy guy, so he slipped and fell into the pond. When he climbed out he was covered with muck, like a big old turtle."

He tossed the basketball in the air, ran over and caught it.

"What class are you in?" I asked him.

"Last semester of lower middle school."

"Oh, then your homeroom teacher must be Duckbilled Platypus, right?"

"That's her, all right. How'd you know?" He laughed.

"I used to be in her class. That old dear's a real slave-driver!"

Wang Ying was acknowledged to be the strictest teacher in Yude School. She graded papers with a vengeance. Her natural science questions were always tricky and capricious. Once she had a question about the duckbilled platypus that no one could answer. That's where she got her nickname. Actually, she was a pretty woman who came to class carrying a pink parasol.

"You're probably failing natural science," I remarked.

"No way!" he protested. "Last year I was at the top of the class in botany, ninety-five percent."

"Wow, you're really something! They say Duckbilled Platypus never gives ninety percent. How come you're so good in botany?"

"I live in the botanical gardens," he said. "My daddy works in the Agriculture and Forestry Laboratory here. He's taught me all about botany ever since I was a kid."

By this time we'd crossed the stone bridge and were in the flower garden attached to the laboratory, where there were five greenhouses filled with potted plants set amid rows of flower beds with all kinds of seedlings, each segregated and labeled with signs giving their scientific names in Latin. We walked past one of the greenhouses with ferns hanging from the ceiling, their lush leaves cascading to the floor like green ribbons.

"Those are golden mosses," Baby Face said, pointing to a row of downy green plants suspended in the air.

"And those are called maidenhair ferns. They're hard to grow, since they need a damp climate. But the humidity in the greenhouse is controlled . . .

"Hey, look here, they're in bloom!"

Baby Face ran excitedly over to one of the flower beds, knelt down, and waved me over. I walked up next to him. The flower bed was filled with tiny purple and red flowers that had just blossomed.

"My daddy put these in," he said excitedly.

"What are they called?" I never could remember the names of plants and flowers. The only way I passed botany was by taking a makeup exam.

"You don't even know that?" he said smugly. "They're pansies. These colors are mutations my daddy created through cross-breeding. Look closely, what do they look like?"

"Cat's face," I said.

"Ha, ha!" He waved his hand and laughed loudly. "Wrong! Wrong! They're like people's faces. That's why they're called face flowers."

He stood up and we walked some more. He told me his father often got up in the middle of the night to check on his flower beds. We'd come to the end of the gardens and were standing in front of the Agriculture and Forestry Laboratory living quarters, a row of old Japanese-style wooden buildings surrounded by tall shade trees.

"That's where I live," he said, pointing to the second building. It was almost completely obscured from view by the lush green leaves of banana trees.

"Hey, Bud!"

A boy of seventeen or eighteen came running out of the house, screaming at Baby Face. "Where the hell have you been? I've been looking for you all afternoon!"

"I was playing basketball over at the school." He tossed the basketball to his brother, who caught it and said reproachfully:

"So, you stole my ball again."

"We played Fat Lip and the others for ices. They lost, but they tried to weasel out of it."

He turned to me, made a face, and laughed.

"All you ever do is play. Well, now you've done it. Daddy told you to go over to Uncle Liu's and borrow his encyclopedia. So where is it?"

"Oh no! Damn! Damn!" He thumped himself on the head. "I'll go get it now."

"You thought we'd wait for you? I already went over and got

it. Daddy's really steamed. You'd better get your butt inside before you get smacked!"

Baby Face's brother dragged him toward the front door by his ear. With his hair falling to one side, he hopped and stumbled along. When they reached the door, he pulled his brother's hand away, turned to me and grinned. The last thing I saw of him was a wave of his hand before his brother slammed the door behind them. *Thump thump thump.* The sounds of the basketball dribbling on the floor came through the door.

The sun was sinking in the west and the shadows of the trees were getting longer and longer, stretching out over the lawns. As my shadow got longer it threaded its way through the shadows of the trees. I climbed a grassy knoll, watching my shadow rise up to meet me, then try to escape as I headed down the other side. When I emerged from the wooded area, a gust of wind brought with it the faint, quivering strains of a harmonica. For a moment the sound seemed to be coming from far away, like from somewhere on the other side of the lotus pond, then it sounded as though it were right behind the nearby banyan tree with its beard-like streamers nearly touching the ground. The sound came and went, rose and fell. Drawn to it, I broke into a run, through the dense bamboo grove, trampling noisily on the leaves and branches strewn on the ground and covering my head with my hands to protect myself from the sharp bamboo stalks. I was thinking of that afternoon, the last time Buddy and I came to the botanical gardens together. After agreeing to meet there after school, I'd told him to wait for me beneath the tall breadfruit tree at the head of the stone bridge just beyond the bamboo grove, so I could give him a ride home on my bicycle. There was no trace of him when I got there. Buddy, I called, Buddy, where are you? All of a sudden the high-pitched strains of a harmonica burst through the dense emerald leaves of the breadfruit tree. I looked up and spotted him sitting on a branch, surrounded by lush foliage like a huge fan that completely blocked out the lower half of his body. Only his head and shoulders showed. He was playing the Butterfly harmonica I'd given him. Buddy, I shouted. Buddy, I screamed.

The music stopped abruptly. I emerged from the bamboo grove. The pond was covered by lotus plants waving gracefully in the evening breezes, sending their delicate fragrance to every corner of the garden. A strong breeze swept across the surface of the pond, bending the plants over on their sides. The heads of three or four boys in school uniforms appeared above the gravel path on the other side of the pond. A moment later, the strains of a harmonica came floating on the wind again, growing fainter with each gust, until they faded out completely.

25

WANDERING INTO A DEN OF FAIRIES

Last Saturday night your reporter entered forbidden territory quite by accident. Liu Ruan of ancient times ascended to Heaven, your reporter stumbled upon a den of fairies. Both were eye-opening experiences. In the heart of our fair city, on Lane 125 of Nanking East Road, there is a convergence of restaurants and nightclubs where the nights are witness to unusually bustling activity. And there, tucked in among the barbecues, coffee houses, and Japanese restaurants, shrouded in secrecy, is a tavern called the Cozy Nest. If the reader enters through the narrow door beside Golden Angel and descends to the basement he will find himself in an amazingly different world, a den of fairies. Don't be afraid, there are no three-headed, six-handed cannibal spirits. No, here you will find only a group of pretty-faced, scarlet-lipped, giggling "fairies." Your reporter inadvertently came upon the watering hole of our fair city's boys of the night, a dazzling discovery that sent him head over heels in wonderment, as though he had been transported to a new "Peach Blossom Spring." The Cozy Nest is decorated in opulent style, the atmosphere bright and lovely; this plus the high-pitched singing, the whispered conversations, and the titterings make it a gentle village of red lights and amber drinks. The people who gather here to taste the forbidden fruit are reputed to come from all walks of life, from the upper strata of society—businessmen and rich merchants, doctors and lawyers—to the lower strata of clerks, soldiers, and students, all sharing the same "affliction." When your reporter made discreet inquiries he learned that the Cozy Nest owes its existence to a famous movie mogul, which explains why the stars are always out there. Even an up-and-coming star of the silver screen was in attendance that night. But fairies travel different roads, and a den of fairies cannot long exist in human society. After finishing his glass of beer, your reporter made a hasty retreat to the land of mortals. This report on the "den of fairies" is offered to the reader as a sampling of this strange encounter.

Reporter Fan Ren

As soon as I walked in the door of the Cozy Nest to go to work I could hear Chief Yang in a heated discussion with Little Jade, Wu Min, and Mousey. When he saw me, he angrily thrust a copy of the *Shanghai Evening News* in front of me. There on page three, the society page, was an article by Fan Ren under the title "Wandering into a Den of Fairies" in bold type. The *Shanghai Evening News* was the Taiwan version of a sensationalizing tabloid originally published in Shanghai by the Green Gang. Just the month before, it had exposed the dancehall-girl background of Lily Luo, a popular movei star, in such a lewd and tawdry manner that she took an overdose of sleeping pills and nearly succeeded in killing herself. Tongues wagged all over town.

"Boys!" the chief called us together, waving the copy of *Shanghai Evening News* in the air. "This is what's called a 'calamity sent down from Heaven'! As though we didn't have enough problems, now this malignant star has appeared in our sky to expose us to the world. I'm afraid our peaceful days are over. Over the past couple of months we've all had a taste of the good life and have come to know what it's like to live as human beings. The future of the Cozy Nest seemed assured. I haven't totaled up the receipts for this month yet, but I'd be surprised if they weren't triple those of last month. At that rate, none of us would have to worry about our livelihood anymore. One of the major reasons I worked so hard to open this tavern was to make a nest for you to keep you off the streets. I've done everything I could, and it's not my fault things have turned out like this. No, it looks like you were born to bounce from pillar to post. A stable life isn't in the cards. Those bastards at the *Shanghai Evening News* are no one to mess around with. You remember the Lily Luo incident, don't you? Her life was ruined, her death botched. As soon as this news makes the rounds, we're going to be the number one attraction in town. Compared to us, Lily Luo is nothing. Lord Sheng probably hasn't read today's *Shanghai Evening News*. He'd have a stroke if he had, and the last thing he'd do would be to come over to the Cozy Nest to show his support. That rotten reporter Fan Ren, do any of you recall seeing a suspicious-looking character like him hanging around last Saturday night?"

We exchanged glances for a moment before Little Jade blurted out:

"I remember! There was a stranger that night asking all kinds of questions. He wanted to know whose place it was. A sneaky-looking guy in a black business suit. I knew right off he wasn't one of us. But an assassin for the *Shanghai Evening News*?"

"Oh," the chief said with a knowing nod. He was thoughtful for a moment, then he told us what to do: "Now that the story's broken we can expect all kinds of curiosity seekers to drop by. Now listen up. Tonight I want you all to keep a low profile and take things as they come. Talk only when you have to and no flying off the handle. We're in for some stormy times, and anyone who screws up and finds himself heading to Fire Island will take the rest of us with him."

The chief had barely finished his little speech when the automatic doors opened with a whoosh and a bunch of people we'd never seen crowded into the bar. They sat down at the tables without being too conspicuous. The chief told us to act normally and serve them. After eight o'clock, however, things started to change, as more and more people from the outside flocked to the Cozy Nest, and in the space of fifteen minutes our little basement was overflowing with first-time customers. The flock of birds that made their nightly journey to the Cozy Nest must have known what was in the wind, since they all stayed away, except for one or two who came flying blithely in the front door, only to find that their nest was occupied by a new breed of birds they'd never seen before; instinctively knowing that something was wrong, they slipped away at the first opportunity. Most of the new customers were young, including some of the flippant young men who hung around the Barbarian basement coffee shop. I'd seen them there before. A few of them had even brought their girl-friends along to check out the scene. The minute they stepped through the door their eyes darted back and forth as they took in every inch of the surroundings. Then the whispering and pointing began, followed by peals of laughter. The shrillest, most grating laughter came from a girl in a ponytail, wearing high boots and heavy blue eye shadow.

Where?

Where?

Which one?

Those two over there?

Didn't the article say there were lots . . .

The ponytail was standing near the bar firing off one question after another to the young man in a fiery red T-shirt standing next to her. In the midst of the raucous laughter a constant refrain echoed throughout the misty amber-colored basement, from one corner to the other, and back again.

Fairies
　Fairies
Fairies
　Fairies
Fairies

As Little Jade and I worked behind the bar, our every move was followed by pairs of laughing eyes. We were scrutinized from head to toe and back up, inch by inch, until they rested on our faces. The gazes came from every direction; we couldn't escape them, there was nowhere to hide. I thought back to the year Mother left, when I was only eight. I'd taken Buddy swimming over by Shulan Street. There, hanging from a branch of a willow tree on the riverbank, was a big hornets' nest. Too dumb to know what I was doing, I picked up a dirt clod and threw it playfully at the nest. Well, I hit it, and out came a swarm of angry hornets, flying straight at me. I screamed and ran, but they caught up and stung me all over my face. No matter how frantically I swatted at the angry attacking insects, it was impossible to drive them away. By the time I got home my face was puffy and discolored, and both eyes were nearly swollen shut. The pain was so excruciating I didn't sleep a wink that night. That's what those eyes reminded me of, a swarm of angry hornets boring into every exposed part of my face and head with ferocious tenacity. My hands began to tremble slightly as I served up the glasses of beer, spilling foam all over my pants and shoes. Little Jade must have been under the same visual attack, for he dropped a glass; it shattered on the floor. No one seemed to pay any attention to Mousey as he threaded his way through the crowd carrying drinks to the tables. All the abuse appeared to be directed at Wu Min, who was suffering one indignity after another at the hands of the flippant young men. One of them blocked his way. "Crystal boy," he shouted. "Little queer," another one said as he rubbed Wu Min's head. He was ducking and swerving so much he looked like a frightened rabbit trying to escape a hunter. The chief had told A-xiong to stay in the kitchen and not come out, no matter what. He was afraid he might be goaded into fighting back.

Off in his corner of the bar, Yang Sanlang sat at the organ, unaffected by what was going on, his dark glasses in place, as always, head slightly raised, a vague smile on his face. He was playing his own composition, "Taipei Bridge Blues," at his usual unhurried pace.

<h1 style="text-align:center">26</h1>

By closing time that night we were beat. Every minute of the few hours we'd been open was an ordeal. The chief actually praised us for managing to keep a low profile and avoiding an incident. After totaling up the receipts he gave each of us a hundred yuan, accompanied by an emotional comment:

"Boys, tonight you saw just how bad our predicament is. Most of the time you're too busy grumbling about how strict I am to see what the outside world thinks of us. I ask you, is it a friendly world? If that jumbled mix of outsiders comes back to the Cozy Nest tomorrow night, and the night after that, to cause mischief and make things tough for us, well, boys, I don't see how we're going to make a go of this thing."

It was very late when I got back to Papa Fu's home. Even though it was a chilly night, I was wearing one of Fu Wei's army jackets. The lights were out, so I had to feel my way through the darkness up to the vestibule. Papa Fu normally went to bed early, but he always left a small light burning in the vestibule for me. I was feeling uneasy about not coming home the night before. I walked inside and tiptoed over to his bedroom door, where I listened very carefully. Were those moans I heard inside?

"Papa," I called out softly. No response, just more moans. I opened the door and walked in. The room was pitch dark. The moans coming from his bed were more distinct, like he was having trouble breathing. I turned on the bedside lamp. He was lying there, an awful pallor on his sweaty face. I knew from seeing how his steel-gray eyebrows were knitted in a frown and hearing the hoarse moans coming from deep down in his throat that he was in bad shape.

I knelt down beside him. "Papa, what's wrong?"

"A-qing..." He could barely speak. "Bring some water."

I ran into the kitchen and poured a glass of lukewarm water from the thermos, then took it into Papa Fu's bedroom.

"That bottle of medicine..." He raised his arm and pointed to a plastic bottle on his dresser. In it were some green capsules, not the liquid medicine he normally took. I remembered hearing him say that he only took those capsules when he was experiencing severe chest pains. The dosage given on the label was one capsule every six hours. I took out one and helped him sit up. After putting it on his tongue, I raised the glass to his lips. He sipped nearly half the glass of water, then I laid his head back down on the pillow. His hair was soaked with sweat, cold sweat. I took out my handkerchief and wiped the sweat from his face and forehead.

"Papa, would you like me to take you to the hospital?" It looked like he was in a bad way this time, and I was a little flustered. But he waved me off and said, without opening his eyes:

"Now that I've taken the medication there's nothing to worry about for the time being. I'll go see Doctor Ding at Veterans' Hospital tomorrow."

Doctor Ding, Ding Zhongqiang, was the the cardiologist at Veterans' Hospital who always took care of Papa Fu's heart condition.

"I'll take you there first thing tomorrow, Papa," I said.

He nodded, and after a moment opened his eyes. He explained what had happened. He'd gone to Zhonghe that morning, to the Divine Light Orphanage, to pick up the armless boy, Heavensent Fu, and take him to see a doctor at Taiwan University Hospital. Heavensent had been running a fever for a week. The doctor who made visits to the orphanage had written out a prescription, but it hadn't done any good. Since Papa Fu couldn't bear to see the boy suffer, he decided to take him to Taiwan University Hospital. As luck would have it, the hospital elevator was broken, and the department of internal medicine was on the third floor. Heavensent didn't walk very well under the best of conditions, and frequently fell; now, of course, he was sick. So Papa Fu half-carried, half-dragged him up to the third floor, and when he got there he collapsed, complaining of chest pains. He nearly passed out. He stopped at that point and took a long look at me. He smiled weakly and mumbled:

"A-wei's clothes fit you just fine, A-qing."

I looked down at the dark green jacket I was wearing.

"It's chilly out tonight."

I slept in Papa Fu's room that night, on a rattan reclining chair. Neither of us got much sleep. He still wasn't feeling well, and every so often he'd groan, waking me up right away. That's how it went all night long, until dawn finally broke, when I got up and heated some water to make a glass of Ovaltine. He said he didn't feel like any, but I coaxed him into drinking it all. Then I took out a jacket and helped him put it on. At eight o'clock, after I'd hurriedly washed up and combed my hair, I went out into the the lane and hailed a taxi. Then I went back inside and helped Papa Fu out of bed. We slowly made our way over to the vestibule, with his right arm around my neck as he leaned against me, and my left arm around his back for support.

We drove up to the Veterans' Hospital just before nine o'clock and registered for urgent care. Papa Fu was scheduled to be Doctor Ding's first appointment. A nurse came out with a wheelchair and wheeled him into the doctor's office. After I'd been sitting in the waiting room for nearly forty minutes, Doctor Ding came out to talk to me. He was a tall, distinguished man with gray hair, dressed in a hospital smock. Very dignified. He took me aside and said in a low voice:

"Your papa's a very sick man. He has to be admitted right away."

"Today?" I muttered.

"Today," he said decisively.

He described Papa Fu's condition to me in lay terms. Bothered by a weak heart to begin with, there was always the danger of a myocardial infarction. If it happened, and he lost consciousness, he could fall and be in real bad shape. He handed me a signed admission slip.

"Go downstairs and get him admitted. We're giving him an EKG now."

I went downstairs to the admitting desk and took care of the paperwork. Since he was a veteran, no deposit was required. By the time I got back upstairs, the EKG had been completed and Papa Fu, who had changed into a green hospital gown, was sitting there hunched over in the wheelchair, waiting for the nurse to push him into the consulting room. When he saw me he signaled me to come over and said weakly:

"Go home and get me a couple of sets of clothes. Oh, and my toothbrush and face cloth . . . anything else I need you can bring later. I'm afraid you're going to be busy running back and forth for a few days."

"That doesn't matter, Papa," I assured him. "Do you want me to bring your medicine from home?"

"No," he said with a weak wave of his hand, "Doctor Ding is going to give me a new prescription."

"I'm going now, Papa. I'll be back as quick as I can. I'm not going to work tonight."

His lips quivered momentarily, as though he wanted to say something, but he just nodded and made a slight sound. As I turned to leave I heard his hoarse voice behind me:

"Do you have money on you?"

"Sure do!" I said with a smile as I patted my pants pocket.

27

I rushed back to Papa Fu's home. It was deathly still inside. The house seemed empty now that he was in the hospital. I went into his room to get a couple of changes of underwear from his dresser, then put his toothbrush, a tube of toothpaste, and his face cloth into a plastic bag, found a green canvas knapsack in the closet, and stuffed everything inside. On my way out I picked up a can of Ovaltine.

On my way back to the hospital I made a stop at the Cozy Nest. I wanted to let the chief know about Papa Fu's condition, but he wasn't in. Little Jade, Mousey, and Wu Min were sitting around the table eating and arguing about something. The sight of the food reminded me that I was hungry. Might as well eat something before going to the hospital. When Little Jade saw me he pointed and laughed:

"Here comes another one! What'll we call him? How about a carp fairy!"

Mousey and Wu Min laughed.

"What the hell is that supposed to mean?" I sat down and slid Little Jade's bowl and chopsticks over. I quickly shoveled some rice into my mouth. "I think *you're* a fox fairy!"

Mousey jumped up and pointed at Little Jade.

"See there, Wu Min and I said you were a fox fairy, but you didn't believe us. Now it's unanimous!"

"Okay, okay, then I'm a fox fairy," Little Jade said as he thumped his chest. "You're a rat fairy. And you," he pointed at Wu Min, "you're a rabbit fairy." Then he turned to me. "You're a carp fairy, the chief's an old tortoise fairy, and A-xiong's a gorilla fairy...so our 'den of fairies' has one of every kind. Tonight if people come over to gawk at the fairies, we'll sell tickets at a hundred yuan apiece. If they look too long it'll be another hundred. That way we won't have to sell booze to stay

289

in business." Little Jade snatched Mousey's chopsticks out of his hand, banged them against the side of his bowl, and sang the children's song "Two Little Tigers" with new words:
Four little fairies
Four little fairies
All the same height
All the same height
This one has no pecker
That one has no nuts
Isn't that weird
Isn't that weird
We laughed like crazy and joined in the next chorus of our "Fairy Song."

"Where'd the chief go?" I asked Little Jade after I caught my breath.

"Lord Sheng summoned him. He saw the *Shanghai Evening News*, and was fit to be tied. He called an emergency meeting. It doesn't look good for the Cozy Nest. I don't know what your plans are, but as for me, Captain Long's *Cuihua* is setting sail next month, and I'm going to be on it. I've already gotten my chef's license, so I'll sign on as galley helper. I'm having my appendix out next week. How about you, Mousey? What are you going to do now that you can't go back to Raven's? Back to picking pockets..."

Mousey showed his nicotine-stained teeth in a foolish grin.

"And you, Wu Min, are you determined to go back to live with Scarface as his little mistress? You've got the best deal, A-qing. With Papa Fu as your protector, you don't have to worry about anything. Why don't you take these two along and get Papa to show a little pity by taking them under his wing, too..."

"Papa Fu's in bad shape. He's in the hospital," I said.

"Oh..." They were shocked and speechless.

I told them what had happened the night before and how I'd taken him to Veterans' Hospital that morning. They anxiously asked what the doctor had said.

"Doctor Ding said a shock could come at any time!"

"A shock?" Mousey asked uncomprehendingly.

"He could lose consciousness, understand? Hick!" Little Jade grumbled under his breath.

After talking it over, we decided not to wait for Chief Yang to return, but to go to Veterans' Hospital instead to visit Papa Fu. At the end of the lane we passed a fruit stand, where Little Jade suggested that we buy some Japanese apples for Papa Fu. They were fifty yuan apiece, so we all kicked in fifty and bought four shiny red Japanese apples, hailed a taxi, and drove to the hospital.

Papa Fu was in room 305, which he shared with another patient, separated by a white curtain. Papa Fu occupied the bed farthest from the door. Little Jade, Wu Min, Mousey, and I tiptoed over to his bed. He was sleeping on his side, covered by a white sheet, so that only his face and mussed-up gray hair showed. The light was too dim for us to get a good look at his face from where we stood at the foot of the bed, but we could hear his labored, uneven breathing. We stood there, me holding the army knapsack in my hand and Wu Min holding the plastic bag with the four apples. Wu Min and Mousey stood quietly behind us, breathing softly so as not to disturb Papa Fu. After about fifteen minutes, he rolled over and woke up.

"Is that you, A-qing?"

I moved quickly to the head of the bed and bent down.

"I'm back, Papa." I held up the knapsack so he could see it. "I brought your clothes and face cloth. Little Jade, Wu Min, and Mousey are here to see you," I said, pointing to them.

They walked gingerly up to the head of the bed.

"Aren't you kids supposed to be working?" he asked weakly.

"It's still early, Papa," Little Jade said. "A-qing told us you weren't feeling well."

Little Jade handed me the bag with the apples. I took it from him and showed Papa Fu.

"Little Jade and the others bought some apples for you."

I took one of the bright red apples out of the bag. A faint smile appeared on Papa Fu's face when he saw it.

"Ai, why waste your money on things like that?"

He had me put his pillow up against the headboard so he could sit up. After catching his breath, he looked at each of us and signaled Mousey to come closer.

"After the way your brother treated you, I'm afraid things are going to be pretty tough for you from now on. I told A-qing to look after you."

Mousey grinned foolishly and sneaked a glance at me.

"Wu Min, you've been given a second chance at life. That's something you must cherish," he said as he looked at Wu Min.

"Yes, sir," Wu Min replied softly.

"I hear your heart is set on going to Japan," Papa Fu said as he turned to Little Jade.

"I want to see a little of the world, if I get the chance," Little Jade explained.

Papa gazed at him for a moment, then nodded and said:

"Wanting to look for your father is a good thing. I hope Heaven shows its mercy and lets your dream come true."

Little Jade lowered his head. We all grew silent. Clearly, sitting up was taking its toll on Papa Fu, so I said:

"Papa, you should be resting. Besides, they have to go to work."

"The chief didn't come along because he doesn't know you're sick," Little Jade explained as he was leaving. Papa Fu moaned for a moment, then said:

"Tell Yang Jinhai to come by to see me tomorrow, alone. I have some things to say to him."

After Little Jade, Wu Min, and Mousey were gone, a steady parade of nurses came into the room to take Papa Fu's blood pressure and temperature, or to give him medication or an injection. He'd no sooner dozed off than one of them came in with a bedpan and told me she needed a stool specimen. She handed me a plastic specimen bottle and a sliver of bamboo, telling me to take a specimen after he'd finished and give it to her. Papa Fu said he'd been constipated for a couple of days and hadn't had a bowel movement. I went out and borrowed a paring knife from a nurse, then came back and sliced one of the apples, which I fed him after pouring him a glass of water. After an hour or so, he felt some rumblings in his bowels, so I tried to slip the porcelain bedpan under him, but his hunched back made it impossible while he was lying down. I lifted him up so he could sit on it with his arm around my neck for support. It was hard work, and his forehead was beaded with perspiration, as I strained to keep him propped up.

"Sorry to put you to all this trouble, A-qing," he apologized.

"It's okay, Papa. Keep trying."

It took a long time, but he finally managed. We laughed like we'd been relieved of a heavy burden. I handed him some toilet paper to wipe himself, then he lay back down with a sigh of relief. The bedpan was filled with a dark stool. His condition over the past couple of days had affected his digestion, producing a dark, smelly stool. I carried the bedpan into the toilet, put a specimen into the plastic bottle, and gave it to the nurse.

I stayed with Papa Fu until eight o'clock that night, when visiting hours were over. Just as I was leaving, he stopped me.

"Tomorrow morning I want you to go over to the Divine Light Orphanage in Zhonghe and look in on Heavensent. I told him I'd come by to see him tomorrow. I don't know if the doctor's found out what's wrong with him yet."

"Okay."

"No need to tell the people at the orphanage that I'm in the hospital," he added. "Just tell the boy I'll come see him in a couple of days. Give him these apples."

I took two with me when I left, leaving one behind.

28

The Divine Light Orphanage was located on the outskirts of Zhonghe County. After crossing Firefly Bridge, address in hand, I continued on ahead for several blocks before turning into Nanshan Road, where I spotted a compound with several brick buildings behind a high wall. It was standing off by itself, like a country school. A weather-beaten sign with the faded words Divine Light Orphanage hung above the gate, the words Society of Jesus in the corner. I walked in. Off to the right was a playground with a seesaw, a set of swings, and some hobby horses. At the time there were seven or eight children playing there, all in white aprons with the words "Little Angel" embroidered in red. An elderly man and woman were watching over them. Two chubby little boys were riding up and down on the seesaw, squealing with laughter. The two brick buildings on the left were classrooms. Through the window I could see several children of varying heights and ages sitting in class. A priest in a black cassock was talking behind a lectern. A music lesson was in session in the other building, where a chorus of boys were doing their best to sing along with an organ, their off-key rendering of a hymn making it sound almost funereal. Behind the two brick classrooms stood a little chapel, so old that the bricks were covered with moss. The wooden signboard above the door declared that it was the Divine Light Chapel. All of a sudden I thought back to what Grandpa Guo had told us about Phoenix Boy's strange behavior as a child at Divine Light Orphanage, and how, one Christmas night, after being scolded by the director, he'd gone on a rampage and smashed the statues of Mary and

Jesus. Often, in the middle of the night, he'd gone to the chapel to cry alone. This was the place, all right.

"Who are you looking for?" The chapel door opened and an unusually tall Catholic brother in a black cassock and black velvet square cap walked out. His dark, wrinkled face looked like a tortoise shell.

"Papa Fu, Fu Chongshan, sent me here," I quickly replied. "He can't make it today and wanted me to see how Heavensent Fu was doing. I brought some apples for him." I lifted up the plastic bag to show him.

"Oh . . ." the brother's dark face softened into a smile. "Heavensent Fu is much better today. His fever went away after taking the medicine the doctor prescribed."

The elderly brother led me around the chapel toward another brick building in the back.

"Are you Brother Sun?" I ventured. It sounded to me like he had a heavy northern accent.

He looked down at me with a curious look on his face.

"How do you know who I am, son?"

Grandpa Guo had told us about a brother from Henan in the Divine Light Orphanage who was the only one who'd treated Phoenix Boy with tenderness. Papa Fu also mentioned a kindly northern brother who showered affection on the disabled children. It was he who took special care of the armless Heavensent Fu.

"Papa Fu told me about you," I said.

"Old Mr. Fu is a wonderful man," Brother Sun said approvingly. "He's so generous with the children. Over the past few years he's taken full responsibility for Heavensent."

"Do you remember someone called Phoenix Boy, Brother Sun?" I asked, glancing at him out of the corner of my eye. Grandpa Guo had told us about how Brother Sun had regularly knelt alongside Phoenix Boy and recited the rosary in an attempt to win him over.

Hearing the name Phoenix Boy stopped him in his tracks. He looked at me without saying a word for the longest time.

"Phoenix Boy? Ai . . ." He heaved a long sigh, as a look of deep disappointment spread across his dark, wrinkled face. "I raised that child by myself, how could I forget him? He was such a strange boy that no one else could understand him. I helped him as best I could, but all for nothing. I hear he sank very low after leaving the orphanage. And to meet such a tragic end, well, it's just heart-breaking. But he wasn't a bad boy at heart . . ."

Brother Sun spoke of Phoenix Boy with excitement. As we stood on the steps behind the chapel he told me all about Phoenix Boy's strange behavior at the Divine Light Orphanage years earlier. Even in his infancy there'd been a number of unusual signs. When he was just beginning to learn how to talk, the very mention of "papa" or "mama" had produced tears and sobs. Never before, Brother Sun said, had he seen a child so given to crying. The more anyone tried to cheer him up, the louder he wailed, until he cried himself hoarse. Once, when Phoenix Boy wasn't even a year old, Brother Sun carried him in his arms while he cried for two solid hours, until he was blue in the face and went into spasms. The doctor had to give him a tranquilizer to save him from what could have been a very serious situation. It was as though he was born with a bellyful of grievances, and all the tears in the world were insufficient to wash them away. Actually, Phoenix Boy was an exceptionally gifted child with extraordinary powers of comprehension. Whatever the subject, if he put his mind to it, not only did he master it before all the other children, but with far greater results. He memorized the Catechism perfectly and could flawlessly recite any number of Bible stories. Brother Sun taught him the classical piece "Peach Blossom Spring" as part of his Chinese language studies, which he committed to memory, word for word.

"But . . . but . . ." Brother Sun hesitated, a perplexed look in his eyes. "Inexplicably, some of the things he did were bizarre beyond belief, totally unreasonable. Like the director said, sometimes the child seemed possessed by the Devil. Whenever I think about how he came to such a tragic end, it depresses me. I often pray for him, pray that he's with the Lord and at peace . . ."

The elderly brother had grown very sad. He shook his head and sighed.

"Old Mr. Fu told me he saw Phoenix Boy the day before it happened. It goes beyond understanding."

Brother Sun led me over to the doorway of a dormitory. He stopped and looked at me, then asked with a gentle smile:

"And you, son, what's your name?"

"A-qing."

"Oh, A-qing," he said with a nod. He pointed to the apples in my hand. "Heavensent is going to be thrilled when he sees such big apples."

The children in the dormitory room, five of them, were all handicapped. One, who had no legs, was sitting blankly in a high-backed chair, with nothing to hang over the edge of the seat. Two of the children appeared to be mentally retarded. They were sitting across from each other on the floor playing with blocks and making a series of mysterious grunts. An older boy, probably in his early teens, was doing something very strange: he was bending his head down until it nearly touched his left shoulder, then snapping it straight up again, over and over, like there was a spring attached to his neck, over which he had no control. A look of agonizing helplessness showed on his face. Three elderly women were looking after the handicapped children. Papa Fu had told me about the elderly people who donated their time to help out. Some were Catholics, some weren't, but they shared a common loneliness, now that their own children were grown and out on their own.

Heavensent, a frail child of six or seven, was lying in bed, dressed in an old blue short-sleeved shirt. The sleeves, with nothing to fill them, hung limply at his sides. Weak from the effects of his prolonged fever, he had absolutely no color in his face. When Papa Fu talked about Heavensent at home he explained that the child had always been anemic, and that no matter how well he was fed, he was always getting sick. But while physically weak, he was a bright child who was particularly sensitive to his own frailties, and that compounded his suffering.

"Papa Fu sent me over to see you, Heavensent," I said as I stood at the head of his bed. "Feeling better?"

He opened his sunken eyes and stared at me out of curiosity. His lips were pressed tightly together.

"The fever's gone," Brother Sun said as he put his hand on the boy's forehead.

"He just finished a bowl of cereal," one of the elderly women said. "He's got his appetite back."

"Where's Grandpa Fu?" the boy blurted out.

"He couldn't make it today, but he asked me to bring you these apples. Look." I took the two bright red apples out of the plastic bag. Having gotten even riper since last night, they smelled sweet and delicious. I put them down next to his pillow. He shifted his body and turned his head to sniff them.

"Don't they smell sweet?" Brother Sun bent down and asked him.

He nodded and smiled.

"Don't look so greedy," the elderly woman said good-naturedly. "You just finished breakfast. Grannie will peel them for you at lunch."

"When's Grandpa Fu coming?" he asked me.

"He'll be over in a couple of days," I said.

"Oh . . ." He breathed a sigh of relief, then closed his mouth and said nothing more.

Anxious about Papa Fu's condition, and eager to get back to Veterans' Hospital, I told Brother Sun I had to be going. After saying goodbye to Heavensent, I walked with Brother Sun out to the main gate. As we passed by the classroom building, the orphans inside were still singing their mournful hymns, still loud, still off-key.

"You really boosted Heavensent's spirits today," Brother Sun said to me with a smile when we reached the main gate.

"I'll tell Papa Fu when I get home," I said.

29

Papa Fu wasn't in his room when I arrived at the hospital, but Chief Yang was sitting in a chair waiting to talk to me. A nurse had just taken Papa Fu out for some tests.

"He's very, very sick," the chief said when I walked into the room. "I talked to Doctor Ding this morning. He said Papa's systolic pressure has shot up to 125, and for a man of his age, that sort of wild fluctuation is very dangerous. I want you to stay here. Don't let him out of your sight. I talked to the nurse, and she said you can sleep on the floor next to him. It's going to be tough on you for the next few nights, but it's important for you to stay awake. I'll get Little Jade and the others to relieve you during the day."

He took 2,000 yuan out of his pocket and handed it to me.

"I have to go now to take care of some things for Papa Fu. It's sheer chaos at the Cozy Nest, and there's no end in sight, so I have to be there. If anything happens here, call me at the tavern immediately."

After he left, I rushed down to the cafeteria and ordered a plate of egg-fried rice. The nurse had wheeled Papa Fu back into room 305 by the time I'd finished and gone back upstairs. With the curtain drawn, the room was as dark as night. An oxygen tank had been placed by the head of his bed. Since he was lying quietly with his eyes closed, I sat in the chair at the foot of his bed so as not to wake him. The patient in the adjoining bed was also a retired general. Evidently he'd had a cerebral hemmorhage and had been in a coma for days. Members of his family took turns staying with him. The room was filled with flowers sent to him by friends and relatives, and the fragrance of the flowers mixed with the smells of medicine and human excrement to make the air in the room very stale.

At about six in the evening the nurse came in and woke Papa Fu for dinner. His meal consisted of beef broth with stewed carrots, two slices of preserved chicken, and some green beans, plus a small helping of steamed rice. His hand was shaking too much to hold his chopsticks, so I propped him up, laid the napkin on his chest under his chin, and fed him the broth, one spoonful at a time. When he'd finished about half, I shredded the chicken and fed it to him with the chopsticks. He could only manage a couple of bites. After the nurse had taken away the dinner tray, a young intern came in to feel Papa Fu's pulse and take his blood pressure. After checking to see that the oxygen was flowing properly, he asked him a few routine medical questions before going over and taking the pulse of the comatose general in the next bed. Then he left the room. As I was adjusting Papa Fu's sheet I gave him a brief rundown on my visit to the Divine Light Orphanage to see Heavensent.

"He asked when Grandpa Fu was going to come see him," I said with a smile.

"Ai, that child is my greatest concern," he sighed. "What little I have I'm leaving to him and the other children at Divine Light."

He looked over at me and added:

"A-qing, I'm sorry to say I don't have anything to leave to you..."

"Papa, what kind of talk is that?" I cut him off.

"Bring your chair up closer," he said.

"You should be resting. We can talk tomorrow."

"No, there are some things I want to say to you while I'm still able," he insisted.

He seemed a little more spirited than he'd been, his voice was stronger. So I dragged my chair up to the head of the bed and sat down.

"I hear some people are causing trouble for the Cozy Nest, is that right?" he asked.

"Some rotten reporter for the *Shanghai Evening News* wrote

a stupid article, and a lot of curiosity seekers have been coming over to see what's going on...I think it'll blow over in a few days."

"I'm afraid that the Cozy Nest, your new little home, won't be around much longer!" he said sadly. "It looks like you kids are going to be cut loose to drift again. I've helped a lot of kids like you over the past ten years or so. Some of them worked hard at making something of themselves, but others just sank lower and lower, while I could only stand and watch. You and your friends are going to have to trust to luck this time. A-qing..."

He pulled a trembling hand out from under the sheet and reached out to me. I held it in both my hands.

"I know I haven't got long. This morning I told Yang Jinhai that after I'm gone, I don't want to put anyone out. Make it as simple as possible. But there'll be some loose ends that someone's going to have to tie up for me. In the time you've been with me you've had a chance to get to know me, so you take care of things the way you think I'd want them taken care of. Like Heavensent. I'd be pleased if you could find the time to go over to Divine Light and look in on him from time to time."

"Of course, Papa, I'll do that," I assured him.

"A-qing," he said, clasping my hand tightly, "I've been very troubled the past couple of nights. The minute I close my eyes I see Fu Wei. I see such suffering in his face..."

As I looked into his wrinkled, mottled face by the dim light of the lamp on his headboard, I noticed lines of teardrops rolling down his gaunt cheeks.

"Papa, you get a good night's sleep." I gently put his hand back under the cover. "I'm going to stay here with you tonight."

After turning off the light on his headboard, I moved my chair back to the foot of his bed. I took off the jacket that had belonged to Fu Wei and draped it across my chest to keep me warm as I kept my vigil in the darkness. Nights pass slowly in a hospital; every minute, every second, seems like an eternity. And there is such a pervasive stillness; even the footsteps of the nurses who occasionally walk the halls are muffled. I forced myself to stay awake so I could listen to Papa Fu's labored breathing. At some time late at night, there was a sudden change in his breathing—he seemed to be panting. That was soon followed by a strange rattling sound from deep down in his throat. I jumped up and turned on the light. His mouth was open and saliva was running down his chin. He was staring wide-eyed at me, but the only sound he uttered was a throaty grunt. His face turned deathly pale. I pushed the emergency call button and rushed out into the hall to find the nurse on duty, who came running into the room, immediately turned on the oxygen, and put the mask over Papa Fu's nose and mouth. Just then, the intern on duty rushed in, accompanied by two nurses, and quickly gave Papa Fu an injection. He ordered the nurses to wheel the bed and oxygen stand into the intensive care ward.

I waited outside the intensive care ward for two hours before the doctor came out, his smock soaked with sweat. He told me that Papa Fu's condition had stabilized, although he'd slipped into a coma.

Papa Fu stayed like that, without regaining consciousness. It was terrible. With the oxygen mask over his face and tubes dangling from his arms, and with all the trouble he was having breathing, he lay there more hunched over than ever.

In the morning, the chief brought Little Jade, Wu Min, and Mousey over; even A-xiong came along. Everyone just stood quietly around the sickbed, not saying a word. A-xiong was so frightened by the scene that his mouth hung slack. In a very soft voice I told the chief what had happened during the night, how at the most critical stage, Papa Fu's diastolic pressure had dropped to 70 and that his systolic pressure was nearly down to zero. Doctor Ding examined him as soon as he arrived in the morning. He told us candidly that he had three or four days at most. The chief gave us our assignments: Little Jade was to spell me so I could go home and get some sleep before coming back for the night shift. The chief and A-xiong would arrange for a casket, the mourning clothes, and the graveclothes. It was time to make funeral arrangements. Wu Min and Mousey were sent back to the Cozy Nest.

Just as Doctor Ding predicted, on the fifth day, at ten o'clock in the morning, Papa Fu passed away without regaining consciousness. Chief Yang led A-xiong and the rest of us into the hospital room, where we stood on either side of the sickbed. After Doctor Ding pronounced Papa Fu dead, a nurse shut off the oxygen tank and removed the mask. His face had darkened and his eyebrows were firmly knitted, evidence of how hard his last moments had been. With his mouth twisted and the rest of his face contorted, it looked like he was still struggling. The nurse pulled the sheet up over his head. The curved outline of his body showed beneath the sheet.

We took Papa Fu's body back home that same day. During those final days, the chief had made all the necessary arrangements. The casket, which had been bought and delivered the day before, was lying in the living room, supported by two benches. The chief told us that Papa Fu had instructed him to keep everything simple. No announcements were to be sent, no funeral parlor was to be involved, no religious ceremony, and, most importantly, a simple, inexpensive casket. He'd bought a China fir casket of rough design, unpolished and uneven. The paint, which had just dried, was dark and flat. It was standard size, long and thin, with raised edges at the head and foot. As soon as we got home, the chief told us to bathe and dress Papa Fu's body, so I went into the kitchen to boil the water, which I poured into the tub, added some cold water, and swished it around until it was lukewarm. We laid Papa Fu out on his bed. He was already cold and beginning to stiffen. We easily removed the hospital gown, but the T-shirt underneath was stuck to his body, and his arms were so stiff we would have had to force them to take it off. So I got a pair of scissors and cut the shirt up the front and back, then Little Jade helped me slowly remove the two halves. Last we took off his underpants, which were soiled, since I hadn't been able to change them the last two days. I told Wu Min to wrap the soiled underwear in the hospital gown and take it away. Then Little Jade and I picked up Papa Fu, with me holding his upper body and Little Jade his legs, and carried him into the bathroom. We rolled up our sleeves and bathed him with bath soap. Papa Fu had nearly wasted away in his final days, accentuating the hunch in his back. Since the lower half of his body was covered with dried excrement, we had to draw a second tub of water to clean it all off. Mousey brought in four towels, and we all pitched in to dry off Papa Fu. After Little Jade combed his mussed-up gray hair, we carried him back into the bedroom. By that time, the chief had come back with the graveclothes, as well as some candles and fresh flowers. He'd chosen a white silk Chinese jacket and trousers. We got him dressed, then lifted him up and placed him in the crude Chinese fir casket.

We turned the living room into a simple mourning hall. From the kitchen we brought out a pair of earthenware bowls to use as candle holders; after putting a layer of uncooked rice on the bottoms we stuck a candle into each bowl, then placed them on the offerings table against the wall beneath the photo of Papa Fu in uniform, and lit them. Chief Yang had bought some joss sticks, but since Papa Fu had always used sandalwood incense, I dug up a few sticks, stuck them into his incense holder, and lit them. The flowers were ginger blossoms. I changed the water in the vase, put in the flowers, and placed the vase on the table between the candles. With the candles burning on the table, we all gathered around Papa Fu's bier and sat down to begin the wake.

The chief sat in Papa Fu's favorite chair at the head of the casket and, in a low voice, explained the funeral arrangements.

"According to custom, we should go to a temple and chant prayers to release Papa Fu's soul before we take him to the cemetery. But he was insistent that there be no ceremonies and that we bury him at once instead of keeping the body in the house for the customary length of time. He picked out his gravesite long ago, on a hilltop at the Eternal Repose Cemetery at Six Plows. I went over to look at it yesterday, and it's all ready. We don't have to do anything. So we'll take him there tomorrow."

The chief also told us that more and more people had been wandering in to the Cozy Nest, and that sooner or later the police would get involved. With the death of Master Fu, we'd lost his protection. "Starting tonight," he announced gravely, "the Cozy Nest is temporarily closed."

We took the news silently. The chief then gave out our next assignments:

"A-xiong and I will take the first watch over the body tonight. Little Jade will be second, A-qing third, Wu Min fourth, and Mousey fifth and last. There are candles burning, so be careful. Don't fall asleep."

Those who weren't on watch were to get some sleep in Papa Fu's and my rooms. I went into the kitchen to make a pot of rice porridge for anyone who got hungry during his watch. I ate a bowlful in the kitchen, since I didn't plan on sleeping until my watch was over.

When Little Jade's watch was finished, he came into the kitchen, ate some rice porridge, then went into my bedroom. It was my turn. As I sat alone in the living room in the flickering light of the candles, I gazed up at the framed photos on the wall. Papa Fu, in his general's uniform with the leather strap diagonally across his chest, looked very impressive. Fu Wei, in the photo next to him, was a spitting image of his father as a young man. He had the same even features, the same resolute mouth with the corners turned slightly upwards. But he was in the uniform of a junior officer, with a different insignia on his collar. And there was a strange radiance in his eyes, a look of unrestrained arrogance, that was missing in Papa Fu's eyes. I recalled that night when Papa Fu told me how, after the War of Resistance, he'd taken Fu Wei with him on an inspection tour in Qinghai. Father and son had acquired a pair of horses on that trip, Moonwatcher and Snow Lion. After climbing onto Snow Lion, Fu Wei had taken off like the wind across the green fields, earning him the praise of all the officers present; his joy and arrogance had probably reached their apex at that moment. The candles on the offerings table were burning down, while the aroma of incense was getting heavier. The exhaustion I'd been forcing back for several days suddenly hit me. My eyelids began to droop, the photos on the wall grew hazy. I dimly spotted two figures sitting in the living room. One was Papa Fu, who was in his favorite chair. The other was Wang Kuilong. They were sitting across from each other, just like they had that day. Papa Fu was dressed all in white, his hunched back sticking up like the peak of a mountain; Wang Kuilong was all in black, and there was fire in his eyes as he urgently tried to pour out his heart to Papa Fu. His mouth opened and closed, but no sound emerged. He was waving his bony hands in front of Papa Fu to get his point across. Sadness filled Papa Fu's face as he looked into Wang Kuilong's face, but said nothing in reply. The two of them confronted each other without saying a word. As I walked over, Wang Kuilong gradually disappeared, but Papa Fu rose slowly and turned his face to me. But no, it wasn't Papa Fu, it was Father! His short gray hair was standing straight up, and he was staring at me with his bloodshot eyes. Sparks of anger flew from them. I turned to run away, but my legs were too rubbery to do my bidding. Aiya! I woke myself up with a shout. I sat there wide-eyed, drenched in a cold sweat that flowed in rivulets down my back. A black casket stretched out in front of my eyes.

30

When morning came, we went off separately to take care of things. The chief went to a funeral home to arrange for a hearse, while I went over to a tailor shop on Changchun Road to pick up our mourning clothes. When I got there, the woman who ran the place said she was putting the finishing touches on the last two sets. I told her the funeral was today, and that they must be ready by noon, no matter what. After promising they'd be ready in an hour, she sat down at a sewing machine to help out. The shop, which specialized in mourning clothes, was filled with bolts of white linen. The sound of the tailors cutting the cloth grated on the ears, their quick movements sent white thread flying all around, clogging the air of the shop. Sleep had been a very elusive thing for me over the past few days, and I suddenly felt parched and thirsty; my head seemed weighted down, I was feeling strangely edgy. The nightmare was still on my mind, and I could see Wang Kuilong's bony hands waving urgently in the air.

After telling the woman I'd be back in an hour, I walked out and headed down Changchun Road, all the way to Nanking East Road. I was looking for the aging official residence of Wang Kuilong's father. All I remembered from the night Wang Kuilong had brought me home was that it was down a lane not far from Songjiang Road. I wandered in and out of several lanes before turning down one on Section Three of Nanking Road, where I spotted the familiar dark metal gate with spikes rising above it. An elderly caretaker came out when I rang the bell.

"Is Mr. Wang Kuilong home?"

The caretaker looked me over carefully.

"It's urgent business," I said.

"The young master went out early this morning."

"When will he be home?"

The caretaker shook his head. "I don't know."

When he saw I was reluctant to leave he added, "He went to see a friend at Taiwan University Hospital. He's been going there every day recently. Sometimes he comes home for lunch, sometimes he doesn't. I can't keep track of his comings and goings."

"Would it be all right to leave him a note?" I asked.

He looked at me without saying yes or no. So I squatted down and tore a page out of my address book. Then, using my knee as support, I wrote a note to Wang Kuilong, telling him that Papa Fu had passed away and would be buried today in the Eternal Repose Cemetery at Six Plows, on top of the highest hill. I handed the note to the caretaker, then turned and walked out of the compound, pulling the metal gate closed behind me.

When I returned to the tailor shop, the last two sets of mourning clothes were finished. The woman wrapped all six sets up into a bundle, tied it with a white strap, and handed it to me. The chief hadn't returned home by the time I got there, but Little Jade had heated up some steamed buns to go with a plate of cured meat

304

he'd bought and a bowl of egg-drop soup. We helped him set the table and get ready for lunch. None of us had slept well, and it showed on our faces. Mousey, who had caught a cold, was wheezing and had a runny nose; but instead of using his napkin, he just wiped his nose with the back of his hand. The chief showed up right at noon. He told us that today was an auspicious day, so the hearses at most of the funeral homes were already booked. But he found one place that promised to send one over that afternoon. We sat down and ate lunch; after the table was cleared off, we changed into our mourning clothes. Since they were all the same size, mine fit perfectly, while Mousey's were too big; they hung down to the tops of his shoes, and when he put on the hempen head cover, all we could see was the bottom half of his face. His robe dragged on the ground when he walked. On A-xiong's frame the mourning robe was both too short and too small. The sleeves barely covered his elbows, the hem stopped at his knees. Once we'd put on our robes and head coverings we gathered around Papa Fu's bier and sat down to wait quietly until around three in the afternoon, when the hearse arrived. We hoisted the casket onto our shoulders and carried Papa Fu out the door.

Cars could only drive half way up the hill at the Eternal Repose Cemetery. From there to the top you had to walk up a path that snaked up to the crest of the hill. There were thousands of graves on the hill, old and new, row upon row of them, one right next to the other. The valley beneath the hill was covered with stone markers, big and small, a stone forest amid a smattering of green pines. It was an immense, vastly overpopulated cemetery. It was nearly dusk. Those who had come to bury or visit their dead had left, leaving behind a stillness in the bleak graveyard.

We carried the casket up the hill, three on either side. The left-hand column was headed by the chief, followed by Wu Min and A-xiong. Little Jade took the lead on the right, ahead of Mousey and me. All of us, in our white mourning robes, were bent over by the weight of Papa Fu's heavy, dark casket resting on our shoulders. The path up the hill was steep, the footing treacherous, so we were careful to stay in step to control the shifting weight. Step by careful step, we carried Papa Fu's casket up the hill. The higher we climbed, the steeper the hill, and the heavier our burden became, particularly for A-xiong and me, who were at the rear. The coarse wood bore down painfully on my cheek. Sweat streamed down my face and back. By the time we'd struggled halfway to the top our strength was nearly sapped. But we kept at it, silently moving upward to the accompaniment of our own heavy breathing. Suddenly my right foot slipped as I stepped on a loose rock. I stumbled, my leg buckled; the casket shifted on my shoulder and dug in painfully. My eyes clouded and filled with tears of pain. I started to fall, I didn't think I was going to make it. Panic set in. But I knew I had to endure the pain. I threw my shoulder into the shifting casket. Fortunately, A-xiong was strong enough to keep the rear of the casket from crashing to the ground. The others strained to hold on, and we managed to keep the casket steady. I forced myself to straighten up but my left shoulder had grown numb from the excruciating pain. After standing there for a moment to catch our breath, we started up again, step by slow, tortuous step, until we reached the top of the hill, where we carefully lowered Papa Fu's casket to the ground. Then we stood there wiping our sweaty faces. I reached under my shirt to check my left shoulder. It felt sticky. It was blood, as I discovered when I pulled my hand out. My shoulder had been rubbed raw by the shifting casket. I began to feel a sharp, pulsating pain.

The crest wasn't nearly as crowded as the rest of the cemetery; a sort of wasteland with a few grave markers here and there, and clumps of high weeds tipped with white fuzz. Papa Fu's grave was ready and waiting, a tomb covered with a dark gray polished stone, half of it aboveground. Next to it was an older, occupied grave, whose stone was dark and discolored. The grass above it had been neatly trimmed. I walked over to read the marker. It said:

Army Lieutenant Fu Wei
1932 – 1958.

The December sun was setting in the west and would soon disappear behind the hill; it was staining the countryside with its blood-red rays. The gravestones, the pine trees were all enveloped in a pale red mist. Weeds on the crest hill looked like they'd been immersed in a vat of red dye, even our white mourning robes were tinged with the color of the setting sun. A stiff breeze whipped the hems of our robes up into the air. After a brief rest, we removed the stone from the grave, then strained to carefully lower Papa Fu's casket into the hole. Just as we were about to put the stone cover back in place we heard footsteps coming up the path behind us. A man appeared on the crest. It was Wang Kuilong, the Dragon Prince. He'd gotten there just in time. Dressed in a black business suit and tie, he was carrying two dozen large white chrysanthemums. We knew he'd run up the hill by the way he was breathing so heavily. His dark eyes, set deeply in his pale face, were dancing like they were on fire. When he saw Papa Fu's casket he stepped forward, bent down, and gently laid the white flowers at the foot of the grave. Then he straightened up and stood there with his arms at his sides, his head lowered as he gazed down upon Papa Fu's casket for a full ten minutes. Suddenly, he fell to his knees at the foot of the grave. He bent over until his head touched the ground and began to wail. His sharp, bony shoulders heaved violently as the wails grew louder and more hysterical. The sound of his crying, increasing in volume and mournfulness, barely seemed human. He was a wounded animal, his agonizing death cry shattering the night calm as it rose to heaven from a deep, dark cave. The bright red setting sun was sinking behind the hill, bathing Wang Kuilong in its blood-red waves. His agonizing cries were swept down by the bloody waves into the valley below, where they surged back and forth. The rest of us, following the chief's lead, fell to our knees on the ground, wisps of white, washed by the blood-red rays of the setting sun.

BOOK FOUR

YOUNG BIRDS
ON THE WING

I

December 30th

Dear A-qing:

Well, I finally made it to Tokyo! It's already my tenth day in Japan, but sometimes I can't believe I'm really here, that it's just a dream. Sometimes I wake up in the middle of the night and think I'm back in Taipei on Jinzhou Street in that little room we rented from Moon Beauty. But when I stick my head out the window and see all the neon signs of Shinjuku I breathe a sigh of relief. I really am in Tokyo! You can't believe how easy it was to jump ship, and all because of Captain Long. I told him the whole story (of course I made it sound a little worse than it really was), and when he realized I wanted to go to Japan to find my father it really got to him. So he let me go, and even helped me get a job at a Chinese restaurant called the Three Cardinals run by the third mate on the *Cuihua* who jumped ship just like me. He looks after me. Who said there aren't any good people in the world? The Old Dragon King is a living Buddha, and after I make it here I'm going to set up a memorial tablet to his goodness. Now don't worry, those rotten sailors on the *Cuihua* didn't lay a finger on me. One Cantonese wanted me to be his "bosom buddy" and offered me a Hong Kong–made cashmere sweater vest. That son of a bitch thought I'd jump at the chance, but I told him, "I've got the clap." Well, he just stared at me and took back his sweater vest.

Tokyo can really get you excited, and confuse you, and scare the wits out of you! I walked around the Ginza yesterday, and there were so many cars and people and tall buildings I felt like jumping in the air and shouting. The Ginza's like our Westgate, but it's a hundred times bigger, and as far as style is concerned there's no comparison. The Japanese are all rich! They dress great and everybody has a car. Talk about luxury, I love it! There are huge department stores all over the place, and even if I can't afford anything it's great to walk around in them. No wonder that damned old man of mine went to work for Shiseido. I went into the biggest department store in Ginza, a place called Matsuzakaya, and the whole seventh floor was nothing but Shiseido cosmetics! Little dear, you'd die if you saw how many different things they sell. Who knows, maybe someday I'll get a job with

Shiseido and wind up doing better than my old man. That way my mother won't have to worry about rouge and powder ever again. But that's thinking too far ahead. My biggest problem now is I can't speak Japanese and don't understand any of the gibberish all around me. I might as well be deaf and dumb, so I pretend I know what I'm doing by bowing all the time. But I started Japanese lessons. My teacher works at the Three Cardinals. He also jumped ship, and he's been in Japan for years, a real Tokyoite. The first thing he taught me how to say was get laid. It's "saigusu, saigusu." I catch on pretty quick, and he says I'll do fine. A good beginning is fifty percent of success, at least that's what the principal of my elementary school told us.

My job in the restaurant is as helper, stuff like plucking chickens, peeling shrimp, scrubbing pots and pans, and cleaning the stove. All the things I learned at the culinary academy in Taipei, like crystal chicken and squirrel croaker, are all wasted here. The head chef is mean as hell, and even the owner's afraid of him. I was a little slow peeling the shrimp, and he raised the roof. Of course I didn't talk back to him. A gentleman has to know when to speak and when to keep quiet. Since my feathers haven't all grown out yet, for the time being I just grin and bear it. But when he wasn't looking, I swiped the two biggest shrimp in the dish he was preparing and gobbled them up. I sleep in a storeroom above the restaurant, only four tatamis. It's filled with dried shrimp, dried abalone, beans, salted fish, cured eggs, and other stuff, and in my ten days here I've just about lost my sense of smell. But rents in Tokyo are so high you wouldn't believe it, at least ten times as high as Taipei, so I'm happy to have a little four-tatami room where I can get some sleep. It's just that sometimes I wake up in the middle of the night and get to missing Taipei and you guys. How are you doing, A-qing? How about Wu Min? And of course that little thief Mousey. If you see the chief say hello for me, and tell him I'll write. If anyone in that old crystal crowd, like Death Angel Zhao, asks about me, don't tell them I'm a kitchen helper in a Chinese restaurant. Tell them Little Jade Wang is setting Tokyo on fire!

Happy New Year,
Little Jade

P.S. Remember how you used to kid me about my cherry blossom dream? Well, now I do dream about cherry blossoms. When the cherry blossoms bloom in the spring, I'll have my picture taken in a kimono under a cherry tree and send it to you.

A LETTER TO LITTLE JADE

January 17th

Dear Little Jade:

We were all relieved to get your letter. The past few days Wu Min and I have been wondering if you jumped ship and if you got picked up by the Japanese authorities. I showed him your letter and he was so thrilled he ran out and bought a bottle of beer and we drank toasts to your good luck. We agreed that Little Jade is a nine-tailed fox who found a way to make it to Japan! In your letter you made Tokyo sound like a world of delights. You must be like a fish in water, happy as can be. Hurry up and try some of Tokyo's "sashimi," then write and tell us how it tastes. Guess who I ran into in Westgate? Old Zhou! The jealous old tub heard you'd gone to Japan, and you know what he said? "I hear the little tart's trying to sell his ass in Tokyo. I doubt he'll get much for it there!" I just casually answered him, "His overseas Chinese sugar daddy sent for him. He wrote to tell me his sugar daddy took him to the hot springs at Hakone." Well, Old Zhou just sneered, but I could see he didn't know whether to believe me or not.

Since you left, lots has happened in our crowd, and there have been big changes. The Cozy Nest closed its doors for good. That guy Fan Ren wrote a couple more pieces for the *Shanghai Evening News* and kept revealing more and more details. He stopped just short of mentioning Lord Sheng by name. Our Chairman of the Board of Eternal Youth Film Studio was really bummed out, and we heard he had to bribe the rotten reporter to keep his mouth shut. Of course, that sealed the fate of the Cozy Nest. It hit the chief hardest. The day we went out of business, he got roaring drunk with the rest of us. He said, "Boys, you'll have to fly on your own now. Your chief can't take care of you anymore." There were tears in his eyes, and A-xiong was so scared he grabbed the chief's hand and kept saying Dada. I went by the Cozy Nest last week, but now it's called the Courtesan by its new owners. It's a bar that caters to Japanese tourists, and I hear there are bar girls.

I'm working as a bartender at the Round Table on Sun Yat-sen North Road. It's a high-class bar with lots of atmosphere. A great place for society men to come and meet their mistresses. They sit there and nurse one drink all night long. But the pay's good, 3,000 a month, and the tips are great, since they all want to impress their girlfriends. The work's easy. When I'm not mixing drinks I just sit there and listen to the Blue Danube on the tape deck. I moved out of Papa's house. He told me he wanted to leave it to the Divine Light Orphanage, so the director came and took possession. Papa took full responsibility for the raising of a handicapped boy he called Heavensent Fu, who was born without any arms. I go over to see him a lot, and I'm teaching him how to write with his mouth. I visited Moon Beauty the other day. She's rented out our room. If not, I'd have moved back to Jinzhou Street. I used to like Obasan's fried squid and pickles. Moon Beauty told me that when your mother found out you jumped ship she grinned from ear to ear. She said she's waiting for you to send for her. I'm living at Dragon Cave, and even though it's a little expensive, the room is large and airy, and I don't have to put up with the smell of dried fish!

Wu Min found a job. He's a busboy at the Catherine Western-style restaurant. But he's really been in a funk lately. That Mr. Zhang of his, old Scarface, got drunk last Christmas and fell in the bathtub. He had a stroke, and now he's in Mackay Hospital, the whole left side of his body paralyzed. Wu Min has to go take care of him after work every day. I went with him one day. It's not the Mr. Zhang we knew. All that handsome charm is gone, and he's like a deflated ball lying there like a blob with a droopy eye and a twisted mouth. And his temper's worse than ever. All he ever does is yell at Wu Min. Nothing pleases the guy. When we left I said to Wu Min, "How can you put up with it? Now's your chance to leave the guy." Well, Wu Min got on his high horse and said, "How can you talk like that? Now's when he really needs me. It wouldn't be right to leave him now!" I guess it's not in the cards for Wu Min to have a good life. As if he didn't have enough trouble with Mr. Zhang, he's also got his gambler father to worry about. He came to Taipei after a big blow-up between him and Wu Min's uncle, and now Wu Min has to take care of him. So Wu Min's got both a sick man and his father on his hands. The good news is he's holding up pretty well.

As for Mousey, well, we all knew what would happen to him. He's in a reform school in Taoyuan, where they're trying to turn him around. A couple of weeks ago he was up to his old tricks at the Ambassador Hotel. He lifted a tourist's fountain pen, but this time he was caught by the manager. Wu Min and I are going to Taoyuan to visit him next week. We'll take along some fruit and see if we can't make our problem child feel a little better. Who knows, maybe being put away will help him see the light.

Little Jade, now that your cherry blossom dream has come true, I'd say a little dried fish is worth putting up with.

All the best in the new year,
A-qing

A LETTER FROM MOUSEY

January 21st

Dear A-qing:

Great friends you and Wu Min are! I've been in here for over two weeks, and you haven't visited me once. It's sure no picnic getting "reformed" in here. What they mean by reform is teaching us to be good people. We have to study every day, then write a report on what we learned. I never read a single book after leaving elementary school, so how do I know what I learn from these books? Every day we have classes in Chinese, history, and national spirit. Talk about boring, I can barely keep my eyes open. But since I don't want the teacher to yell at me, I keep pinching my leg to stay awake. This morning during the national spirit class the teacher told us the story of Yue Fei, the Song general who fought the soldiers of the Jin. You know who I mean? The teacher told us that Yue Fei's mother tattooed some words on his back — she must have been some kind of mother. The teacher wrote the words "Serve Your Country Loyally" on the blackboard. One stupid kid asked him what "loyally" meant. Talk about dumb! He'd never seen the slogan "Serve Your Country Loyally," can you believe that? They always put it up at the railway stations, don't they? The teacher said that at home it's important to be taught by your mother. He said Yue Fei became a national hero because he had such a righteous mother. He told us how important it was for us to listen to our mothers from now on. Well, the stupid kid wanted to goof off again, so he said, "Teacher, my mother's a prostitute in Baodouli, so how righteous is she?" The teacher's face got all red and he didn't say a word. The rest of us just looked at each other and laughed under our breath. The afternoon vocational training is better. I chose cloth dyeing. My teacher's from the Great China Dye Plant in Zhongli.

Today we learned how to mix colors, that was lots of fun. You can mix any color you want. He told me my colors were perfect, so I asked about my chances of finding work in a dye plant after I got out. He said no problem, as long as I worked hard at perfecting my skills.

A-qing, this place is a den of thieves. All I did was pick someone's pocket in a tourist hotel, and that's nothing. The things the guys here have done put me to shame. Some of them broke into houses with guns. A leader of the Bamboo Gang is here because he almost killed a member of the Heaven and Earth Gang in Sanchong City during a gang fight. This guy's the devil in human form, and everybody calls him Big Boss. He's got a bunch of guys who hang around him like bigshots and pick on everybody else. He's one mean guy. Sometimes for no reason at all he points at you and says, I'm going to get you! I'll tell you, old pal, I've got my heart in my mouth all the time with this bunch of gangsters around me. I made up my mind I wasn't going to suffer any more than I had to. Yesterday the gang leader hit me so hard I saw stars. So I just fell to the ground and stayed there like a dead dog. What else could I do without you guys around to help me? One stupid kid didn't know what was good for him and talked back, so that night they dragged him out, and guess what they did to him. They poured piss down his throat!

The thing that bothers me the most around here is they've got me classified as a "kleptomaniac." How does that sound? Every Wednesday a graduate student in sociology at Taiwan Normal comes over to talk with me. He says he's doing research on the problem of kleptomaniacs among the youth of Taipei. He asks a million questions — gathering data, he says. He asked me why I liked to steal, so I said that when I see things other people have I take them and play around with them. So he says taking people's things is stealing. But I said I don't take money, only things I like, so that didn't make me a kleptomaniac. I guess I stumped him, because he just mumbled. I told him about the time I lifted a man's wallet that had a lot of U.S. dollars in it, but nothing else, and since the wallet didn't interest me, I slipped it back into his pocket. He wrote down everything I said. He told me I was an interesting, exceptional case study. He said I had psychological problems and he was going to recommend that the reform school give me psychological counseling. Fuck him, there's nothing wrong with my "psyche."

A-qing, how about my treasure box? Make sure you keep it

hidden, and don't let anybody steal all my treasures. Bring one of my fountain pens when you visit me. Not one of the good ones. Bring the blue Sheaffer. Nothing's safe around the creeps in here. Just when are you coming, old pal? If you don't hurry, I'll suffocate in here.

Have a happy new year,
Mousey

P.S. Chef Lu from the Cornucopia came to visit me today. He brought along a smoked chicken as a treat. His heart's in the right place. I asked him to mail this letter for me, because they say all outgoing mail is checked here, and you have to be careful not to say anything bad about the place. A couple of the kids tried to run away the day before yesterday, but they were caught and brought back in shackles. They walked like crabs.

A LETTER FROM LITTLE JADE

February 1st

Dear A-qing:

I haven't written in a long time because I've been so busy I don't even have time to fart. Business has really been good at the restaurant this month. The place is full every night. These Japanese are really weird. Instead of going out for sashimi they bring the whole family over for Chinese food. The owner's so happy he can't wipe the grin off his face. Of course, it's hard on the kitchen help. We're at it every night till one or two o'clock, then we drag ourselves off to bed. Who's got the energy to write letters? Besides, I spend the little free time I've got taking care of important business. I've started trying to track down my father. The first thing I did was start calling Shiseido dealerships to see if they have an employee named Nakajima Masao, a Taiwanese who became a Japanese citizen. In Tokyo alone there are dozens of Shiseido dealerships, and I called every one of them. There was a Nakajima Masao in the Asakusa dealership, but he's in his twenties, and there's no way he could be my father. Besides, he's from Osaka. Then I went to the Tokyo Overseas Chinese Lin Clan Society, and they had a Lin Wuxiong, a Lin Shengxiong, and a Lin Jinxiong, but damn it, no Lin Zhengxiong. So I got a phone book and started with the Shinjuku district, copying down the addresses of all the people named Nakajima Masao. There were twenty-seven in Shinjuku alone. I couldn't just call them up and ask if they had a bastard son in Taiwan. Things sure are complicated. Even if I got them on the phone, how was I going to talk to them after only a month of Japanese lessons? Even if I could, nobody's going to admit over the phone that they left a love-child behind. So for the last month, whenever I've got time I go looking for Nakajima Masao at the addresses I wrote down. Streets and addresses in Tokyo are impossible to find, so I just wander around Shinjuku like I was in a maze. By yesterday I'd only checked out ten, and they're a real mixed bag. One's a plastic surgeon, one sells wigs and falsies, one's the manager of an appliance store, one had pockmarks all over his face and was blind in one eye, and I was so scared I turned and ran. If my father looked like that, I'd just as soon not have one!

Yesterday was a national holiday, so I spent all day looking. It's snowed a lot in Tokyo this year, and there's a foot of slush on the streets. That makes it hard to walk, because the snow gets into my shoes and freezes my feet. I went to the homes of three Nakajima Masaos, but they were all Japanese. Then just before nightfall I found one who was Chinese! My heart almost flew out of my chest. When I started asking questions, I found out he was a Manchu named Jin from Tianjin. He was about sixty and very dignified looking. His house was beautifully decorated. He was so happy when I told him I was from Taiwan he invited me in for a cup of tea and a chat. It was snowing by the time I left, and the neon signs of Shinjuku were flashing like crazy in the snow. I stood there in the street feeling lost and very, very small. That night I went to a place in the Kabuki-cho called Paulownia Chamber, Shinjuku's most famous gay bar.

They say there are hundreds of "Cozy Nests" in Tokyo. Twelve in Shinjuku's Kabuki-cho alone. Tokyo's birds of youth are really something. They flit up and down the streets without worrying about the police. In the bars they dance with each other and kiss, anything they feel like. There's a New Park in Shinjuku, too, called Gyoen. It's at least ten times bigger than New Park, and the birds of youth that hang out there play a lot wilder game of hide-and-seek than we do. A-qing, compared to these Japanese birds, we're real goodie-goodies. Paulownia Chamber is two or three times as big as the Cozy Nest, and the lighting is all avant-garde. It's packed on the weekends, when they have dancing. But yesterday was Monday, and it was snowing hard, so there were only about ten people in the bar, and they didn't stay long. I ordered a bottle of hot sake and spent most of the night there. They've got a jukebox, and all they played were songs by Mori Shinichi. He's the hottest male singer in Japan right now, and the gay bars can't play enough of his songs. Always sad songs. By midnight I was pretty drunk, and a middle-aged Japanese guy in a gray business suit came over and struck up a conversation. He rattled on and on, but I couldn't understand a word he said. When he realized I was a "Chinaman" he took out some paper and started writing some Chinese characters. He wondered why I looked so forlorn. I said "Sabishi! Sabishi!" The third cook at the restaurant taught me that. It means "I'm lonely!" So he took me home with him to Ueno, which is a long way from there. We had to change subway trains twice.

A-qing, I'm going to keep looking. After I've checked out all the Nakajima Masaos in Shinjuku, I'll start looking in Asakusa, Shibuya, Ueno, all the way down the line. When I work my way through Tokyo, I'll save up some money and start looking in Yokohama, Osaka, and Nagoya. I'm going to search through every inch of Japan, and if Papa Fu was right when he said that Heaven will have mercy on me, one day I'll track down my father. You know the first thing I'm going to do when I find him? I'm going to take a bite out of that bastard's dick and ask him why he had to bring a bastard like me into the world to suffer like this.

I wasn't surprised to hear that Mousey was sent to a reform school. Maybe getting locked up will do him good. Don't feel sorry for Wu Min. He asked for it. I haven't looked up my overseas Chinese sugar daddy, Lin Maoxiong. I hear he's pretty influential among overseas Chinese in Japan and well respected. He was good to me in Taiwan and didn't look down on me. He said I was a hundred times more savvy and considerate than his own son. If I looked him up now, it'd make things difficult for him, and I don't want to do that. I want him to always have good feelings for me. I was only with Lin *san* for a short time, A-qing, but those were the happiest few days of my life.

Wishing you well,
Little Jade

 PS. I just remembered, Lunar New Year's is only ten days away. I need a favor. Please go to Liu's Duck House on Xinyi Road and buy a couple of duck cakes (I'll pay you back later), then take them to Sanchong City on New Year's day and give them to my mother. She loves those things. She likes to heat them up with some wine on New Year's. She drinks Wujiapi.

2

A cold front moved in on New Year's Eve, and as night fell the thermometer dropped quickly, as a blanket of cold air settled over the city. Even without the wind it was freezing outside. I stood at the Guanqian Road main entrance to New Park, and off in the distance I saw someone on the steps of the museum. His hair and beard were completely white, and he was wearing a dark Chinese gown. He was waving at me.

"Little Hawk . . ." Guo, the park gardener, was shouting to me.

"Grandpa Guo, how are you?" I greeted him as I rushed over.

"Long time no see, A-qing," he said with a sigh. "So you finally flew back."

"Yeah," I replied with a smile. "Since it's New Year's Eve, I came back to our old nest to see the new year in with the others."

"Ai . . ." He stroked his long white beard. "I figured you young birds would all come flying back. I hear a bunch of you opened another tavern. What was it called?"

"The Cozy Nest."

"Oh, the Cozy Nest. I hear you had to close it down."

"Business was pretty good," I said, "but some people made trouble."

"That's how it always is." He shook his head. "Chubby Yang just wouldn't give up. When he opened the Taoyuan Spring ten years ago, it got off to a great start, and then before you knew it he closed it down. Over the past few years there've been others. Like Champagne, White Nights, Six Happinesses, this one opens, that one closes, round and round it goes. They're all gone without a trace. But this old nest of ours is still here, just waiting for the tired birds to come home to roost, to rest. Risks are hard to avoid, curfews and things like that, but all you have to do is put up with the rain until the blue skies return. Go on in, Little Hawk, they're all there around the lotus pond." There was a kindly smile on his face as he waved me in.

I walked in through the gate. There they were, on the steps of the lotus pond, and even from where I stood I could hear their raucous laughter. Our leader, the chief of New Park, Yang Jinhai, was holding forth to the fledglings gathered around him. He had on a dark brown satin Chinese jacket with a floral pattern, a dark purple kidskin cap, and a long sapphire blue scarf around his neck, one end lying across his chest, the other draped down his back. The outline of his paunch under the jacket seemed bigger than ever. He was pacing back and forth on the steps truculently, cursing non-stop, the ends of his scarf flapping in the air. There was a youngster in front of him and another behind him. Most likely the newest fledglings to arrive in the park, and the chief had their heads swimming with his directions. The primitive A-xiong was to the left of him, matching him step for step. He was wearing a short wool jacket of alternating red and black and a red stocking cap with a purple button on the top. He seemed to have gotten even bigger since I'd last seen him. He was holding his head high and throwing out his chest as he followed the chief complacently back and forth on the steps, the purple button of his cap bobbing joyfully at the back of his head.

"Chief," I said to Yang Jinhai, the chief of New Park, with a bow as I walked up the steps. He stopped pacing and looked me over without acknowledging my greeting.

"Chief," I repeated, clearing my throat, "A-qing's come to pay his respects to the chief."

"Are you talking to me?" he sneered, giving me a hard look. "I thought you guys had washed your hands of your chief!"

"What kind of talk is that, Chief?" I replied quickly with a smile. "I've got a job at the Round Table on Sun Yat-sen North Road now, and I don't get off till one or two in the morning. I haven't been by to see you because I've been so damned busy. I'm off tonight, so I came over especially to wish you a happy new year." I folded my hands in front of me and bowed.

"Oh, no wonder. You've flown up to a higher branch," he snorted. "I've got nothing to say about the others, but that Wu Min, I wasted my time caring for him."

"Don't blame him," I tried to explain. "His Mr. Zhang's back in the hospital, and this time it's serious. He's paralyzed, so Wu Min has to help him with everything. He asked me to beg the chief's forgiveness. He won't even be able to come tomorrow, New Year's Day, to wish you a happy new year." I reached into my jacket pocket and took out a box wrapped in red paper. Inside was a silver-plated tieclasp inlaid with costume sapphires. Wu Min had asked me to buy it. "He told me to give you this."

"Um." Chief Yang took the gift box from me. His expression

began to soften as he said in a gentler tone, "Well, maybe he has a conscience after all."

As he held the box in his hand there was the trace of a smile on his pudgy round face.

"A-qing," A-xiong called out as he walked up and threw his huge arms around me.

"Aiya." Talk about a bearhug! "Take it easy, you're going to crush me!" I kept smiling.

A-xiong released his grip and laughed. He put his hands all over my head and face. I punched him in the chest and laughed.

"Say, A-xiong, that's some beautiful cap you're wearing!"

He reached behind his head and held up the purple button.

"Dada bought this for me!" he said proudly.

I reached into my other jacket pocket and took out a plastic bag of candy kisses wrapped in gold and silver foil. I waved it in front of A-xiong's face.

"Call me elder brother," I teased him, "and I'll give you this chocolate."

"Elder brother, elder brother," he shouted as he snatched the candy out of my hand.

"Dada, candy, candy . . ." He held the brightly wrapped chocolates in his hand and shouted gleefully.

"You raunchy thing," Chief Yang snarled at him. "How can you run around showing off your goodies like that!"

I walked beside Chief Yang as he made a couple of turns around the pond, filling him in on what the others had been up to lately.

"How about that fox fairy, Little Jade? How's he getting along in Tokyo?" he asked.

"He's hot stuff around the gay bars in Shinjuku!" I laughed. "He gets to eat sashimi every night."

"That little cunt-brat!" he cursed good-naturedly. "It looks like our little fox fairy made it after all."

I told him I'd gone to see Mousey at the reform school in Taoyuan, and how he'd complained that the little gangsters there took advantage of him. But when he talked about his vocational training in dyeing, his tears turned to smiles, and he told me all the things he'd learned. He said the dyeing teacher had nothing but praise for him and used his work as models in class.

"Mousey stuck his hands out to show me how his fingers were stained by the different colors. It won't wash off."

"That little thief," Chief Yang snorted. "I should have chopped off those thieving claws long ago!"

New Year's Eve. Everyone had returned to the old nest at New Park to exchange holiday greetings. It was so cold they huddled together on the steps of the pond to keep warm. We could see our breath, white puffs of mist coming from our mouths and noses. Streetlamps had been added on all four sides of the pond, which made the bright red and purple nylon jackets of the hustlers from Three Rivers Street fairly shine. As always, they were standing around in tight little groups of three or four, prancing back and forth on the steps. Flower Child wasn't singing "Three Sighs" any longer. Now he was singing "Waiting for the Spring Winds" with all the enthusiasm he could muster. Death Angel Zhao was in real decline. He was standing wretchedly all by himself, an old black windbreaker thrown over his shoulders. He'd told those hoary stories of his so many times even he couldn't get excited about them, and his listeners had lost interest. Old Dick-Head's raunchy behavior had earned for him the anger and scorn of everyone, and since he didn't have the nerve to go up onto the steps, he was reduced to standing far off in the darkness and looking on. Fatty Lu, the chef at the Cornucopia, still laughed like the Happy Buddha as he picked out a nice lean porkchop to gnaw on. Once the curfew was lifted, the Master Artist had gone back to work on his masterpiece, "A Gallery of Youth." His latest model was another wild kid from Sanchong City. Everyone said he was a real primitive, a perfect replacement for Iron Ox, who was still serving time on Fire Island. A few timid college students who'd been afraid to come near finally couldn't stand it any longer and screwed up enough courage to walk up the steps around the pond; even some reserve soldiers showed up. So finally, on that cold, moonless New Year's Eve, under clear, starry skies, all the differences among the old, the middle-aged, and the young, the high-class and the low, the affectionate and the heartless, the suffering and the contented, simply vanished on the steps of the lotus pond of our secret kingdom that was so removed from the outside world. We stood there as equals; then, like cutout figures in the revolving lanterns of the spring Lantern Festival, we began to move, stepping on each other's shadows. It made no difference whether we were innocent or evil, experienced or degenerate, for all our footsteps in that kingdom of ours wrote a page of history on the steps of the lotus pond.

Then in the midst of our orderly parade around the pond,

there was a sudden stirring in the ranks. News began to spread of a New Year's Eve party at the Eight Virtues Road home of Lord Sheng, the aging Chairman of the Board of the Eternal Youth Film Studio, our most venerable citizen. The party, planned to welcome in the new year, would begin at ten o'clock. The ranks were buzzing with excited whispers as the anticipation rose. The first to walk down the steps were the young hustlers from Three Rivers Street in their flashy nylon jackets. Before long, the students slipped away; then others began to walk down the steps and out of the park, alone or in groups, where they climbed onto their motorbikes, jumped into taxis, or started up their private cars, and headed for the same place, like bats in the night, flying straight to Lord Sheng's home on Eight Virtues Road.

"Little Wan, Little Zhao, Jin Wangxi, Lai Wenxiong." Chief Yang was like a drill instructor calling out the names of his troops.

"We're here, Chief," they replied in their young voices.

Our chief, Yang Jinhai, was the last to walk down the steps, surrounded by an honor guard of noisy, crowding teenagers, with A-xiong bringing up the rear. The newest troops of General Yang marched proudly out of New Park.

In an instant, the area around the lotus pond grew silent, and there was a sudden emptiness about the concrete steps and stone railings. I walked alone around the deserted pond a couple of times, the crisp sound of my solitary footsteps on the steps floating unimpeded in the air. In the months since the last time I'd been there, the lotus leaves had all withered and disappeared, leaving an unbroken expanse of water in which the stars that filled the sky were reflected in all their brilliance. I was suddenly startled. Only nine months had passed since that sunny May afternoon the year before when my father had kicked me out of the house to roam the streets of Taipei; it had been less than a year since that first night I'd set foot in this kingdom in New Park. But it seemed as far away and as hazy as if it had happened in a previous life. I remembered the fear, the trepidation, the nervousness, even the sense of adventure that filled my heart as I walked into the park under a bright red moon. I was so hungry my stomach was growling; growing light-headed, I was shivering as I walked up the steps and hid in the octagonal pavilion in the center of the pond.

Suddenly the footsteps of another lone person resounded on

the steps on the other side of the pond. A tall, thin figure was walking toward me. The hem of his dark overcoat rose and fell as he approached me.

"A-qing." It was Wang Kuilong. His sunken eyes were flashing like blazing wildfires in the surrounding darkness.

"Mr. Wang!" I shouted, pleasantly surprised.

"I thought I'd find you here tonight, A-qing." I detected excitement in his voice.

"Mr. Wang, I was waiting for you, too. Honest." Just a moment before, when everyone else was leaving to go to Lord Sheng's party, several people had urged me to come along, but I begged off. At the time I didn't know why I'd chosen to stay behind, but deep down I had the vague notion I wanted to wait for someone. Now I knew, I was waiting for Wang Kuilong, the legendary Dragon Prince of our dark kingdom.

"That's wonderful," he said. "We should be together on New Year's Eve. There were so many people here I decided to wait."

"Yeah, the place was really hopping. Everybody was here. They've all gone to a New Year's party at Lord Sheng's."

"How about Golden Treasure, Mr. Wang?" I asked him. I'd heard that Golden Treasure was up and around these days, and even though he still limped, at least he could finally wear shoes. Several people had seen the two of them in restaurants.

"I took him to Taoyuan this afternoon," he said with a smile. "He has an elderly aunt there, his only living relative. She wanted him to have New Year's dinner with her."

Wang Kuilong and I were walking side by side around the pond. Our footsteps blanketed the cement steps.

"I planted some trees and flowers near Uncle Fu's grave," he said.

"So that's it!" I blurted out. "I went there last week and saw all the azaleas and cypress seedlings, but I didn't know you'd planted them."

"The azaleas will be bright red when they bloom in a couple of months. But it'll be years before the cypresses are tall and sturdy."

When we reached the center of the steps, he stopped and looked up at the sky, his black uncombed hair falling around his ears.

"It was just like tonight," he mumbled, "the sky was filled with stars that night, too ..." A note of excitement crept into his voice. "Ten years ago, New Year's Eve ten years ago, at this very hour, midnight, millions of stars in the sky ...

"On this very spot." He pointed to the cement step at his feet. "He was standing right where you are." He pointed to the spot beneath my feet. "'Phoenix Boy,' I said to him, 'come home with me. I've come to take you home to celebrate New Year's.' I coaxed him, I begged him, I threatened him, but he just shook his head and smiled, and such a strange smile. Finally, he said sorrowfully, 'I can't go with you, Dragon Prince. I'm going with him...' He pointed to a drunken slob standing beside him. 'He's going to give me fifty yuan, a fifty-yuan New Year's present!' Then he pointed to his own chest and said with a strange laugh, 'Do you want this?' He stuck his chest up next to me and laughed. 'Do you want this?' I stuck my knife squarely into his chest, buried it in his heart..."

Wang Kuilong got down on his hands and knees and felt the cement with his bony hands.

"Phoenix Boy's warm blood gushed out and covered the ground, right here. I took him in my arms, and he looked up at me with his almost lifeless eyes. No resentment, just a look of apology and helplessness. Those great big, pain-filled eyes of his were darting back and forth in their sockets. Those eyes will haunt me as long as I live, no matter where I am. That night, I remember, I sat on the steps and screamed hysterically, Fire! Fire! Fire! The stars were dropping out of the sky, one after the other, right into the lotus pond, where they burned brightly..."

I joined him down on the ground and looked into his face. His voice kept changing, from high-pitched excitement to heavy sadness, from frenzied joy to desperate grief. He began to cry. Once again, on a New Year's Eve ten years later, that ancient legend of the Dragon Prince and Phoenix Boy, the wild phoenix, the bird that would never die, was reenacted from start to finish on the steps of the lotus pond at New Park.

This time I was hearing it from Dragon Prince himself, and I felt different than I had before. At first I'd been afraid and puzzled, but not now. I listened without saying a word, and when he'd finished and calmed down, the two of us just looked into each other's eyes. I reached out and shook his bony hand, shook it hard.

"Goodbye, A-qing," Wang Kuilong said as he got to his feet.

"Goodbye, Mr. Wang," I said with a smile and a wave of my hand.

Before leaving, I walked into the octagonal pavilion in the center of the pond. Someone quickly sat up on the bench beneath the window and uttered a cry of alarm. I walked toward him and, in the light from the window, saw that it was a boy of fourteen or fifteen. He'd probably been sleeping on the bench when I walked into the pavilion and woke him. Quaking with fear, he quickly huddled up against the corner. It was the same bench I'd slept on during my first night in New Park.

"Don't be afraid, little brother," I tried to put him at ease him as I sat down beside him. "I hope I didn't scare you."

Dressed only in a thin blue cotton jacket, he was so cold his face was turning blue. His hair was closely cropped, he had a pointed chin, and his eyes were clouded with fear.

"What's your name, little brother?" I asked as I patted him on the shoulder. He jumped like he'd been electrocuted.

"Luo . . . Ping . . ." Such a thin voice I could barely hear him. His teeth were chattering.

"You can't sleep here tonight in the cold. You'll freeze," I said. "Do you have somewhere to go?" I asked him.

He shook his head.

"Then you come home with me," I said. "You can stay at my place tonight."

He looked at me apprehensively, not knowing what to do.

"Don't be afraid," I comforted him. "I live at Dragon Cave, alone. It's a nice place, certainly better than staying here. Come on."

I stood up, and he followed me, hesitantly. We walked out of the pavilion, down the steps of the lotus pond, and headed toward the main gate, where we were met by a gust of icy, bone-chilling wind. Luo Ping walked alongside me, his hands thrust into his pants pockets, his neck tucked down under his collar. I stopped and removed the scarf from around my neck, a heavy woolen scarf that had been Fu Wei's, and wrapped it around his neck.

"Where do you live?" I asked him when we had reached Guanqian Road.

"Yingge," he replied, in a slightly louder voice. His teeth had stopped chattering.

"It's New Year's Eve, so why aren't you home instead of being out here?"

He lowered his head and didn't answer.

"There's some leftover chicken soup at my place. I'll heat it up for you when we get there." I rested my hand on his shoulder. "You must be starved, right?"

He turned to look at me and nodded. There was a smile on his face. We headed down Loyalty West Road. Lights were on in the houses we passed. People were in their warm houses on this cold New Year's Eve, enjoying their family gatherings. No one was out on the streets, just a few taxis and buses rushing their passengers along. Bursts of firecracker explosions erupted and died out off in the distance and nearby. Luo Ping and I headed toward the bus stop to catch the last bus of the night. The night was getting colder.

"Let's run, Luo Ping," I suggested.

"Okay," he said. With a laugh he flipped the front end of the scarf over his shoulder.

Luo Ping and I ran side by side down deserted Loyalty West Road. I was reminded of my school days, when I was a platoon leader during military drills, responsible for calling the cadence as we ran laps around the athletic field. Luo Ping and I, accompanied by the sound of exploding firecrackers and met by a chilling headwind, ran down Loyalty West Road, with me calling out the cadence:

> Left right
> Left right
> Left right
> Left right

Biographical Note

Pai Hsien-yung was born in Kweilin, Kwangsi, China, in 1937, the son of Pai Ch'ung-hsi, a prominent Kuomintang general. After World War II he accompanied his family to Shanghai, Nanking, and Hong Kong before settling in 1952 in Taipei, where he completed high school and studied Western literature at National Taiwan University. Upon graduation from the university in 1961, he came to the United States and studied at the University of Iowa, where he earned an M.F.A. from the Writers' Workshop. He now teaches Chinese language and literature on the Santa Barbara campus of the University of California.

A recent critic states that "there can be little doubt that Pai Hsien-yung is the most important Chinese short-story writer since Eileen Chang. His best stories have a supple, limpid style capable at times of sheer magnificence; a strong note of compassion rendered all the more poignant by the deliberate use of irony, and a comprehensive awareness of China...." His first stories were published in Taiwan in the *Literary Review*. Before graduation in 1961 Pai Hsien-yung founded the literary magazine *Modern Literature*, which over the years has featured his own stories as well as those of such writers as Wang Wen-hsing and Miss Hung Chih-hui. His published books include *A Celestian in Mundane Exile* (Taipei, 1967), and *Taipei Jen* (1971), translated into English as *Wandering in the Garden Waking from a Dream: Tales of Taipei Characters* (Indiana University Press, 1982). In a review of the latter book published in the *San Francisco Chronicle Book Review* critic Tom Gold calls Pai Hsien-yung "possibly the top stylist writing in Chinese today. His stories make liberal use of classical Chinese and are replete with allusions to Chinese literature and history." A reviewer of the same book in *World Literature Today* (Winter 1983 issue) writes that Pai Hsien-yung is "arguably the most accomplished contemporary writer of fiction in Chinese." Henry Miller called him "a master of portraiture."

The novel *Nieh-Tzu* (*Crystal Boys*) is translated here for the first time into English. It was first published by Horizon Publishing Company in Taipei, Republic of China. The second, revised edition of 1984 is the one used for the present English edition. Two editions of the novel have appeared in Mainland China: one by Bei Fang Publishing, Harbin, 1987; the second by Peoples' Literature, Beijing, 1987. There has also been an edition in Hong Kong published by Wah Hon Publishing Company, 1988. A film of the novel, entitled *Outcasts* and directed by Yu Kan-Ping, appeared in Taiwan in 1986. It is currently available in the United States on video cassette, subtitled in English, from Award Films, Los Angeles.

Translator Howard Goldblatt teaches Chinese literature at the University of Colorado at Boulder, where he also edits the scholarly journal *Modern Chinese Literature*. His recent translations include *The Butcher's Wife* by Li Ang, Xiao Hong's *Market Street*, and *Heavy Wings* by Zhang Jie.